MW01503591

To my dear wife, Jan, my typing timekeeper, who persuaded me to remove the A4 sheets and send for publishing. And thanks to Austin Maccauley Publishers for the opportunity.

The author lives with his wife, Janet, in South East Kent. A retired Chartered Architectural Technologist. He and his wife have two sons and six grandchildren. Writing is a "New Toy" undertaken during the Covid Pandemic Lockdown simply for something to do.

At retirement he returned to the piano and enjoys writing short stories (for fun) along with drawing, painting as an occasional sideline and reading. He has written a sequel to this story but as yet remains unpublished.

Eric Hooles

SWEET DREAMS… OR NOT SO SWEET?

AUSTIN MACAULEY PUBLISHERS

LONDON * CAMBRIDGE * NEW YORK * SHARJAH

A CIP catalogue record for this title is available from the British Library.

ISBN 9781035809776 (Paperback)
ISBN 9781035809783 (ePub e-book)

www.austinmacauley.com

First Published 2024
Austin Macauley Publishers Ltd®
1 Canada Square
Canary Wharf
London
E14 5AA

In a strange way, I acknowledge the pandemic Corona virus lockdown! I wanted something to do, so tried to write a book – which actually became three. I only wrote this story for my wife to read, then I packed the A4 sheets away to collect dust. If it hadn't been for my wife's encouragement, they would still be there!

Works by this author:

New Cross to London Bridge
Sweet Dreams… or Not So Sweet
Assassin

Chapter 1

A warning to anyone who considers promotion a good move… it was not for me! My job at the Ministry was really as a paper-pusher at the Secret Service office, but to my regret, I was too good at my job! So when I was offered a better job which included travelling and more pay, I jumped at the chance. This new role made me a sort of an agent… a 'soft spy' some would call it.

My next overseas job was in Moscow; challenging! Not as a James Bond job assassinating enemy agents! No. It was a role of observation and reporting. That is usually what my new job entailed. No guns, bombs or beautiful blond double agents for me. That nonsense was for other departments.

I go, I observe, I stay for a few days, a week or so, I return home and report… easy!

The bone-shaking Lada taxi at Moscow airport took me to my 'digs' and I settled in to my mediocre accommodation. This wasn't 'James Bond-ish' either! I was told to visit the Glavny Magazine department store. Our UK agents had determined reasons to believe English nationals, unknown to us, were conveying some sort of information, to 'someone, somewhere' within this department store. My brief was quite simple, easy, straightforward; find out and get out!

My first full day. I visited 'the' department store to browse, walk around and observe as a casual shopper would do. I decided to buy some cigarettes. I inquired in my 'fractured' Russian which brand are not too strong. The assistant informed me of a brand that young girls smoke. They are quite mild and it makes them feel grown up. That would do for me; I like to feel grown up! Whilst purchasing a packet of cigs called 'Sweet Dreams' (honestly!) a nearby woman bent over the counter, grabbed some cigarette packs, put them into her bag and rapidly turned to leave without paying. This was seen by a shop assistant.

The thief brushed past myself and a nearby lady shopper nearly knocking her over. That *very* moment a loud siren went off. A burly man appeared from a back-room and grabbed the wrong lady, violently pushing her against the counter, which must have hurt her back considerably.

I shouted *"Net. Eto byla ne ona. Net."* (No, it was not her.) *"Drugaya zhenshchina."* (It was the other woman.) I pushed the man sideways as the lady was suffering from his vice-like grip and the violent push against the counter. He released her and turned on me. A scuffle commenced. It seemed unlikely I would get the better of this great two metre high muscled thick-set hulk.

Within minutes, uniformed secret police arrived. This was rapidly getting out of control and out of proportion. I was held by these two policemen who searched me and took my passport.

They conferred in Russian. My Russian, learnt after leaving school, was fairly basic and could be described, compared, as one might say, a bit like 'schoolboy French.'

The police asked numerous questions in both broken English and Russian and stated I was spying! That was a word I picked up on. I protested very vocally in English. I gently tried to wriggle free of their painful grasp but was immediately struck in the chest, in the abdomen, and then on the side of my face. I dropped to the floor unconscious.

In a daze I started to revive, I imagine to be a few minutes later. I was flat on a stretcher, and looking up, I could only see a blurred vision of the ceiling. I ached! A female face appeared, also very blurred. She stooped and whispered directly into my ear before she was fiercely grabbed and thrown aside. I did 'catch' some spoken words, known to me.

"Ne bespokosya." The first part was comparable to "Do not worry," but the last part something like, *"Leena, Gleena, doskipushkin,"* or similar.

I did not understand at all. They were not words I had heard before. I will try to remember them when I get my translation book.

I was whisked away into a van and travelled a short distance. Upon arrival, I was roughly dragged out of the van. Between the two police officers, manhandled into a lift, up to the top floor and pushed into a large office. The violent push sent me to my knees. Two men sitting at a desk. One invited me, in broken English, to stand up, come forward and sit.

I was then told to empty my pockets, which I did, and to place the items on the table. One man remained seated. The other stood and fingered the contents from my pockets that I had placed on the table. The seated man spoke in broken, but quite good English. The other man who resembled the actor Peter Lorre remained standing immediately beside me.

"Do you know where you are Mr Hartland?"

"No," I replied. (Actually and regrettably, I suspected where I was.)

"You are at 2 Bolshaya Lubyanka Street. Does that mean anything to you? Tell me why you here."

"Tell me why you attack my officers. Why you come Moscow; *Stroit?*" (To plot.) *Peter Lorre* stared at me and yelled something in Russian. A course dialect. I understood none.

"A tourist," I replied. "I like to visit countries I have not visited before, so I thought I would come to Moscow. I am staying at an hotel in Tverskoy Passage near the football ground."

"Ah yes, the landlady, Monika, who needs a new broom. Krull here once broke her garden broom over her back when she was... how you say... not cooperating. You English agents like to use this, eh? You call it hotel and you agents know it as safe house, yes, good for your agents?"

"How do you know where I am staying?" (I need to inform HQ when I return, about this hotel.)

"I am investigating officer Petrov and this is my friend Krull. He has less patience than do I. We understand each other we do Mr Hartland. That is not real name, no?"

I told him it is my real name.

"I was visiting the store; I bought some cigarettes and a woman thief stole some cigarettes. Your police thugs accused the wrong lady of the theft and then beat me up."

"Not a very nice welcome for a peaceful tourist Mr Petrov, and as you no doubt know, I came by Aeroflot which, from memory, is about as luxurious as my soap box when I was ten years old." Krull then shouted at me. My ear drum was ringing.

"It will get you not anywhere by giving insult to our airline. Would you like a cigarette?"

I nodded. He took one from my packet and handed it to me.

"A light?" I said.

"You only asked for a cigarette Mr Hartland and I give you," he laughed.

I could see there were games here to play. One speaks calmly in English and the other shouts in Russian. The cat and mouse... Mr nice and Mr nasty routine... a cigarette without a light... pathetic!

"You speak Russian Mr Hartland. You were overheard speaking to the shop girl. English tourists do not speak Russian. You are *ty shpion,* Mr Hartland, a spy. You are here to spy for your government. You are *ty anglishysky* agent... you know very well what that means, Mr Hartland, as I do. You are English agent but what I want to know and will be told is why you here today?"

"I told you; I am on holiday. I went to buy some cigarettes and..." I was interrupted by the yelling of Krull in my ear followed by a further stupid question from Petrov.

"Your cigarettes, Mr Hartland, they are the brand that Russian girly like. Why not Sobranie?"

"The girly cigarettes, as you put it, I was told by the sales assistant are very mild. That is why I bought them. I imagine they will taste of mild cow dung, but preferable to 'strong' cow dung! What did you do with that unfortunate lady who was wrongly accused of stealing cigarettes?" Petrov casually looked at his wristwatch.

"So, now, he also insults our cigarettes! I think we now have little rest and will have accommodation for you in this night. We talk again tomorrow. I'm sure you agree?" My protests were discounted. I was roughly escorted to my 'accommodation' which was a windowless basement cell. A hard bed, a mattress, a metal clock with numerous dents, a hard pillow, a bucket and a thin blanket were all the luxuries provided.

I was informed the recessed ceiling electric light would be left on and the alarm clock would be set each hour. This I did not understand at that moment. It soon became very apparent.

The metal door clanged, was locked shut and all was quiet. Upon every hour throughout the night, the guards came, threw me against the wall, tipped the bed over, tossed the pillow, mattress and cover across the room and kicked the bucket over. The rear of the clock was removed by a special tool and replaced after resetting. It was a large box type covered with scratches and dents.

There had obviously been many failed attempts to stop it ticking and had sustained many missile impersonations but it was well-designed to be prisoner-proof! The internal part had a mechanical winding mechanism. The clock alarm was reset by the guard for the next hour and all was repeated, throughout the night. It was impossible to sleep even between hours because my brain would not relax. I could not help watching each hour pass and the guards repeated their hourly task with precision. This is soft torture; obviously, one of Lubyanka's more gentle specialties!

The following day I was dragged up to Petrov and Krull. Further repetitive questioning continued throughout the day with a barrage of questions about being an agent, plotting and spying for the English government. Of course, they *were* correct, but I could not let myself down and demonstrate any sign of a confession. It was imperative I stick to my "I'm only a tourist" story but I was increasingly concerned how long this was going on for and how long I would be deprived of proper sleep. This, combined with little food and drink, was also making me very depressed.

The next night time was repeated with the hourly disturbances by the robotic guards, but early in the morning, which I observed to be four o'clock; thankfully, I did drop off to sleep. I did feel quite sick. The cheap drink of coffee provided during the last interrogation surely had something in it other than ground Arabica beans.

I awoke and in doing so, felt myself scratching. Scratching my soft fleshy inner elbow.

I observed a red soreness and puncture mark. I had been injected with a dirty needle and it could have only been by my Lubyanka 'friends' after drinking drugged coffee. The dirty needle had caused an irritation. Their cleanliness was, needless to say, not A1!

I was being prodded by two people shouting at me in Russian which I did not comprehend.

"Ya turist," I said. "Ya turist." (A tourist.) After a lot of head shaking by my 'prodders', I sat up and left the bench seat which faced a bus stop. The passengers required and deserved their seat!

A nearby road sign indicated Pokrova Street which meant nothing to me. I checked my pockets and found wallet and money – everything but my passport. Petrov must have it! I inquired to those waiting at the bus stop for directions: "Bolshaya Lubyanka Street?" They shrank away and grouped together gabbling to each other before nervously replying. I did not comprehend everything, but they pointed down the street. I did understand the distance stated.

It was a bright sunny day and good for a stroll… even in Moscow. *I'm still scratching!*

Reaching Lubyanka, I passed an official looking guard at the front entrance who continually eyed me suspiciously. The only thing I could think of saying was "passport" and "Engleeesh". He pointed inwards and I walked casually to the reception desk. It seemed every eye that was about was on me in this lobby area… all watched me suspiciously. Everyone is suspicious in this country!

"Mr Petrov, please. Can I speak with Mr Petrov?" I smiled.

The receptionist who only just qualified as a female of the species replied in fairly good English: "Name… your name pleees!"

"Hartland, Mr Ric Hartland."

She fingered her book along a list of names.

"No Meester Petrov is here. You now go. Thank you."

This was utterly absurd. To believe there was no one named Petrov in the building. It was like me walking into any large office building in London and being told there was no Mr Smith here!

Dropping her eyes, ignoring me, she commenced writing in her book.

"Mr Krull?" I ventured to add. "What about Mr Krull?"

She looked up and with pained expression slowly replied, "No Meester Krull. No Meester Petrov. You now pleees to go. Thank you."

A silence ensued.

Again, dropping her eyes, ignoring me, she re-commenced writing in her book.

"I think he has my passport?"

She slowly lifted her head, heavily breathed and simply stared at me saying nothing more.

Her green eyes were very pleasant, nothing else. Nothing else seemed feminine or friendly.

She continued to stare.

"My passport. Mr Petrov has my passport, madam." (Being very polite.)

She continued to stare and then glanced sideways at the security guard.

No point in arguing with her any further. They had my passport and would retain it. Obviously, she had been well-briefed not to let me into the building and to deny the existence of Messrs Petrov and Krull. She is not one to negotiate with.

I now wonder how I can retrieve my passport. I spoke to the front guard: "Tverskoy Passage?"

Similar to the folk at the bus queue, he gabbled away in Russian but, fortunately, once again, I did catch the distance stated. I thanked him and gave a courteous smile and nod.

He grinned at me, lips in a straight line as if to say… "I could have you on toast, comrade."

No doubt he could!

Chapter 2

It was a long walk back to the hotel, but still being a pleasant day, it mattered not. I did feel very sick and my arm was fiery red and itched like fury but the fresh air will do me some good enabling me to make some sense of all this.

Arriving at my hotel, or safe house as Petrov had called it, I was met by a different lady in the main entrance lobby.

"Hello. Monika please," I said in English. I hoped she would understand. I want to avoid using the limited Russian I have where possible. Instantly recognizing me as a non-national she said: "Moya sastra... she is sister mine. In bed now. I Irina. Two men come. They very bad men. Your name please, you will stay here?"

"Yes. Mr Hartland. I am staying here but I have been away for a couple of days but back again. Room seven. The room at the back facing the garden." She verified this in her desk book.

"You know Monika. You visit her. She in room nine same floors. OK you will like to?"

I said I would be happy to see her. It was a strange request for a complete stranger to visit her sister but I have already found out, these people do have strange customs! One such custom already experienced is to be beaten to a pulp simply for buying cigarettes!

Irina escorted me to room nine which was just a few doors from my room. She knocked and instantly went in. Monika was sitting propped up in bed reading a book. She 'sported' two magnificent black eyes and what looked like a recent cuts to her upper and lower lip.

Recognizing me, she spoke to me in Russian 'over' her sister. Then gestured me to sit on a chair near the bedside. It appeared Irina had more English than Monika so I asked her to be interpreter. Monika pointed to my eye which on the cheek edge was also beginning to blacken.

The two sisters chatted away using my blackening eye as the principle subject.

"So what happened to your sister Irina?" I inquired.

"Two men come. I not here but table turn over and I come home, Monika has eyes black, a nose that bleeds and she holds her ribs like so." Irina held her side to demonstrate. I bent towards Monika and said something like "oooo!" and did a "tut tut" which must be universal in all languages.

"Ya Upal s Lestnitsky," declared Monika. Irina interpreted that as, "I fell down stairs."

Irina launched into a tirade admonishing her sister for the stupid story but she only repeated: *"Upal s Lestnitsky."* (I fell down stairs.) Irina continued with the 'telling off' shaking her head and waving of the finger.

"She tell lies, comrade Mr Hartland sir. She not tell the true. It bad men that beat her for nothing, and you it be too that you have black eye from same men, yes?" (*Why did she think that?*) Not wishing to divulge too much I said, "I walked into a door."

Irina was quite cute saying, "Door with probably, gun, big hands and boots, yes?"

I said to Monika I hoped she would soon be better and to Irina to let me know if there was anything I could do to help, "If so, please ask me." Irina thanked me.

Monika half smiled with her swollen lips, waved and nodded as I left the room.

Back in my room I sank onto the bed and settled into my English/Russian dictionary.

Those words issued into my ear at the department store were puzzling me. Try as I may the last part made little sense. I could find nothing that sounded similar to those few words. The first part about "Not to worry,"… or was it "do not worry". I heard clearly but the last part is not to be recovered.

A luke warm shower in a microscopic cubicle was essential. I was beginning to smell like last week's fish and chip wrapper, with considerable vinegar!

Have the Russians discovered hot water yet?

Smelling sweet… clean and changed into fresh clothes I did some more reading and at the appointed time I went down to the small dining room for dinner. It seemed good Russian food was a bit like their hot water… it was waiting to be discovered! Each plateful looked different, but to be fair, there was a similarity… each course tasted like tepid tissue paper.

However, I was grateful and after being deprived of food and drink over the last thirty-six hours it tasted better than I deserved after such criticism!

I finished my meal, leaving some beetroot soup stains on the already "whiteish" beetroot-stained table cloth and returned to my room. A thought… back to reception area to talk to Irina.

I inquired about Monika who was recovering as well as could be expected. My sympathies were with her particularly as my chest and sides still ached as did the side of my jaw. The black eye was also worsening by the minute. Surprisingly, Irina told me Monika would be back at the reception desk later today. The hotel won't run itself!

I liked Irina, she was about my age (30ish) and despite many pre-conceptions, all Russian women do not look like twenty-five stone 'Shot-putters'. She was a very pleasant trim, well dressed and attractive lady and obviously the younger of the two sisters by at least ten years or so.

I felt I could tell Irina about my trials of the recent past in view of the treatment her sister had received so, I "spilt the proverbial beans". She did not seem to be too surprised as such treatment towards non-nationals was apparently not unusual, particularly if they think you are a spy… and everyone is a spy to the Russian government! It is a sickness with them!

I tried to explain the words whispered in my ear during the department store fiasco.

Irina agreed with the first line. "Do not worry." The second part she literally stopped me in my tracks… almost yelling…

"Galina, the first is Galina. It is female name. She sing at I Brodsky, Pushkin. I know her." It was not a code as such, but a message… "Do not worry. Galina, Brodsky, Pushkin."

"She well known, she good singer at Cafe Brodsky all day, she mean you go there. You go see her at Brodsky. You know Galina lady?" I assured Irina I did not.

The message identified the person and the place, the only thing outstanding was "the reason?"

"Comrade Mr Hartland sir, you go to Brodsky, it good place in Pushkin. I take with you next tonight if like with you. You want to go. You will like if I come take you to find Cafe Brodsky?" I almost kissed her with enthusiasm, not really a good idea… just a thought! We agreed to visit Cafe Brodsky but I felt more comfortable to go for lunch at daytime. Irina agreed for a departure at noon

18

tomorrow. A visit during daytime was, I considered, sensible considering… "everything".

I had an early night, well, earlyish and slept like a dead person. The following morning I enjoyed some good boiled eggs, fresh bread, butter and jam with very good coffee. It made up for the unappetizing meal of the previous evening. I took a stroll down to the Moskva River and feeling relaxed I tried to breath in the air and pretend nothing else mattered. Unfortunately, it did!

Returning to the Hotel I asked Irina if I could pay for a phone call. I needed to telephone home. A white lie… I needed to contact my office.

"This phone on desk bad for that. You go into office behind. To protect you know all cupboards locked in office so no one accuse you. Do you understand?"

I think I knew what she meant?

Irina took me through into the back office and I was able to speak to the head of my department and pleasingly, call charges were reversed. I told them chapter and verse and "softly" suggested I might be allowed home, but they wanted me to find out about the activities at Glavny Magazine and I was reminded that is what I am here for. The lack of a passport, I was also curtly reminded, prevented returning, so I should immediately go to the English Consul to report the matter.

I was instructed it was imperative to maintain the story that I was a tourist. The Consul must not know the reasons as to why I was there nor who I worked for.

"Tell them anything you like but not the truth. Inform them; in the UK you work as road sweeper, a window cleaner, a footballer… anything other than the real reasons as to why you in Moscow. It is essential they must not get a whiff of anything unusual. Do you understand?"

"Blimey." Yes. That was very clear!

I "cleared" the matter of "expenses". The Hotel stay and return plane ticket was "open ended" but other numerous costs would be incurred… food… buses… taxis, etc. All agreed without question.

I was also informed I would need to telephone the Embassy to arrange a consultation.

They gave me the phone number and spelt the address… it needed to be spelt; British Embassy, Smolenskaya, Naberzhnaya, 10 Moscow 121099. I wrote it down in caps!

I telephoned the Embassy and was surprised to receive a rapid answer and similarly, an appointment made. A good time… noon, tomorrow.

Irina was pleased my London call had been paid for by my office but I had also made a local Russian call. She refused to accept money for it saying, at the most it would only be a Ruble but I insisted, as I may wish to use the phone again (if permitted) and would feel unable to ask.

So I paid a Ruble for the call, (approx. equal to one UK pound per one Ruble value). Irina and I agreed upon a time to depart for Cafe Brodsky. She indicated only one bus would take us. Not a long journey and quite cheap. Readily, I consented and returned to my room to rest for a short while. We then met at reception area and took the trip to the bus stop, then on the bus to I Brodsky. I paid the fare for both of us and indeed it was cheap by the London prices I was accustomed to. The Socialist idea was working here! The "rip off" prices worked well in the UK!

The bus came, called a Marshrutka. It was a type of minibus to UK standards, and apparently, they came in all different sizes. They were slightly more expensive that the municipal buses but met the demand required. The Marshrutka pushed out copious white exhaust fumes as it left each stop. This one was an older model! Irina said they were not all as antiquated as this one. It got us there!

A hundred metres or so from the bus stop, we were soon at the Cafe Brodsky. Irina wanted to know how I was going to approach this situation. I advised I could do little more than observe and ascertain if I could recognize the "ear whispering lady!"

We were seated at a pleasant table near the window and within easy sight of a small stage. Irina studied the menu, and after hearing from me I eat anything legal, she ordered for us both. The window "grinned" through posters of artists that sang at the cafe, mostly women. Through the light I could see the pictured visage of each. None familiar to me. Irina thought I would be drinking Vodka but coffee was my tipple this time of day. She had a half bottle of Russian red wine. I wondered what it would be like. She gave me a "sip" It was very palatable. I suppose it should be… after all… it was "red!"

The food came. Commencing with a very pleasant vegetable soup, superb bread rolls with butter followed by a dish called "Pelmeni" Irina described it to be a type of minced dumpling with sour cream and butter. It was really nice but made me feel wonderfully slightly sick!

"It is what we Russians like it is national dish here," she educated me. Various green vegetables were served and all was well cooked and equally, the quality was good. Ice cream and coffee topped the meal just as music started to introduce today's singing artist: "Galina."

Lights were spotted on to Galina as she came on to the small stage which followed her around the room as she sang a selection of very nice folk-ish type songs. Nice voice.

Spotlights were not really needed as it was daylight in the Cafe but it did help to clearly see... what I was supposed to see!

Galina wandered around with a portable microphone singing songs unknown to me, but appreciated by those dining. I thought she was a very attractive lady, similar age to ourselves and a very competent singer. She was very smart. A little overdressed for a lunch time session, but nice.

"What are you think now, Comrade Mr Hartland? Do you see this lady?"

Irina whispered, "Oh please call me Ric Irina. I don't like the Comrade Mr Hartland bit."

"Bit?"

"Oh, just an English term Irina. I really do not recognize her. I was flat on my back on the shop floor at the time. Having been soundly beaten by the police, and at that moment I was just coming back to my senses. I don't think I would have recognized my own mother at that particular time."

"You do not recognize your mother?" I can see I need to be frugal with my puns!

After approximately half an hour, Galina disappeared into a backroom, changed her clothes into something more casual and came to our table.

"Do you mind if I sit down?" I pulled out the spare chair for her to sit. I was nervous. Why?

"I will introduce myself... although you know me as Galina." Piped music was playing in the cafe at that time and speaking was easy, so no whispering or shouting necessary.

"I am Galina Fedorova and you already know Irina Karashenko." This was moving on too fast! "Yes, well no, I mean I only know you both by your Christian names, no more."

"There is no reason for bush beating... beating about the bush. (Her English was perfect although her pun a little mixed!) Irina and I... and Monika work for the British government here in Moscow, not your department. You appear to have got mixed up in something beyond your remit issued by London. I whispered into your ear at Glavny's in Russian because if those pigs that beat you had got a sniff of me speaking in English, there would have been plenty trouble. I thought it best to give you a coded message so you could find me.

"Irina at that time, in fact only up until now, has not been given official instructions to let you know her involvement, neither to give you hint that she knows who you be... who you are."

I was struck dumb. Speechless... unusual for me! So I just listened.

I looked at Irina, she was smiling... just a half smile.

"We talk now, just look normal talk, not too serious you understand and a laugh every now and then helps but not as in theatre... not theatrical I think... you comprehend me?"

"Yes, of course," Irina added.

"Galina will tell you why you are here doing and what you do."

"Your investigation at Glavny Magazine is for to find which English may be involving in something that may have espionage. You find and go back to England yes. Correct?" I replied.

"That is correct, but I have only had one visit to the shop and have not had time to establish anything. In fact, most of my time I have spent as a guest at Hotel Lubyanka. I don't recommend the room service. Difficult to sleep!" Irina looked puzzled. (Another pointless pun.)

"Your role in Moscow has overlapped with ours. I will explain. We are investigating the illegal storage of approximately one metric tonne of cigarettes which we believe to be in the back room of the store. Your role will no doubt establish an English organisation that are swapping secrets with the Russian Mafia whilst dealing with those cigarettes. You follow?"

"Well, yes, but I didn't know the details about cigarettes or the Mafia. I only know someone is doing something? It seems a lot of fuss about a few thousand cigarettes. I mean, it's not exactly a fortune in money is it, a few hundred thousand Rubles at the most, eh?"

Galina continued: "Yes, if it were tobacco. Today the load is at least one metric tonne, probably much more, of top quality heroin manufactured and concealed in cigarette form. Serious, yes?"

"It is worth a fortune to the Mafia and the street sellers. Add to that, someone is change classified information between English and Russian Agents killing two birds with one stone." (Her puns are improving.)

"Are you with me Ric?" (She even knows my name?)

"I am with you. Blimey, that is, as you say, worth a fortune."

"It may be necessary to… are you alright? You seem to having trouble with arm. You keep rubbing and scratch it, have you been bitten by insect?" Galina observed.

"No, not an insect, although an insect of sorts! Our friends at Lubyanka, who drugged my coffee and afterwards left me on that bus stop bench had jabbed me with something. That is why I was out cold for so long. I think their needles are not as clean as they might be. It seems to have set up a localised infection. It is very angry. I even woke myself up last night scratching, which of course only makes it worse, but it is driving me mad. I will have to buy some antiseptic cream."

"You angry with your arm?" Irina added. "Let me see arm please."

I turned sideways so as not to be observed by those on other tables. It would not be a good ploy for people to get the wrong idea. They might think I am showing my arm as a drug user.

Galina and Irina studied my red patch. It was quite sore for them to touch. They commented that it was very hot to touch. They both talked very quickly and in hushed tones so as not to be overheard by adjacent table diners. And finally stated, "Obnaruzheniya ustroistvo slezeniya." (What is that?) "You wait with Irina. I be back."

Galina left us at the table and disappeared once again into the back room. Whilst she was gone I selected some Ruble notes from my wallet. I told Irina I will be paying for our three meals today. "It is what we English call "a treat" I would like to do that… treat." She understood that one!

A few minutes elapsed and Galina returned.

"A car come soon. You will come with us, with Irina too. We go for your red wound on arm. It needs to doctor seen now… what is the money for?"

I told Galina I wished to pay for the meals but she would not agree, saying it is on the house, or something of a similar meaning.

"I would not hear of it. I don't want the cafe to be out of pocket." Galina then replied: "It now. I part own it, shared with the State… not problem for me, also have Borodino's!" She partially owns it! In Russia? I'm learning all the time! and Borodino's?

A burly male entered the Cafe Brodsky, stood at the door and nodded in the direction of our table. We all stood to leave. Galina also nodded to someone at the far side of the cafe who waved in return. We were soon out into the fresh air and then into the car, a very large and highly polished Lada, not quite like the boneshaker taxi previously experienced.

Galina sat in the front and I in the rear seat with Irina. The car drove to the river, a short trip and parked. The driver handed a package to Galina. She unwrapped it and handed it to me.

"You put this band on arm. You wrap tightly around arm more times."

I was amazed how heavy the bandage was and inquired why so much trouble about this wound. It was beginning apparent that it must be infectious! I pondered, *What if it is a bio-hazard of some kind intended to spread.*

"I tell you again now, Ric. This band is lead lined. It breaks signals. River is a safe place for last signal send to Lubyanka. You were injected with drug serum but also, how you would say 'detecting tracking device'? You have been injected with a miniature device. They know where you go. They know you at hotel, Cafe Brodsky and at river at this time now." Irina and Galina asked in unison as to where else I have been.

I had not much opportunity to go anywhere thanks to my Lubyanka sojourn, but, other than staying at the hotel, a stroll by the river, and being at Cafe Brodsky today, is about as far as I have travelled. All harmless travels of a tourist! (I wish I was!) There is nowhere that could be considered suspicious or "anti-State" but it is alarming they should find it necessary to track my movements. No wonder I am scratching!

My arm was duly wrapped and I felt comforted that Petrov & Co no longer know my whereabouts. The wrap was inspected and deemed satisfactory. Galina handed me a mask to wear. I was informed it was not necessary for me to see where I was being taken, it would be a security breach. For twenty minutes I sat blindfolded only hearing the whir of the Lada engine and fluid conversations in Russian between the three in the car with me. Upon arrival I heard what I assumed was a security guard who checked us in. A book was signed (on my behalf) and a hanging ID tag was placed around my neck. I was led, again still blindfolded into a building and a lift. The mask was removed and I blinked myself back into the sighted world. Galina apologized for the methods, but all was deemed necessary.

The lift doors opened and straight to a room immediately opposite. The door had numerous keypad locks, a hazard warning sign and a notice in yellow and black declaring;

"Biologicheskaya opasnost." It doesn't take a rocket scientist to realize this is a bio hazard area. Galina telephoned someone utilizing a telephone on the adjacent wall. A few seconds later there was a mechanical electrical hum as the door slowly opened by itself. A huge thick door.

Galina and Irina ushered me in. The room smelt like a hospital. No windows. Everything white. The door was closed by a man in a white coat who gestured the two ladies into chairs and me on to a hospital type flatbed couch. Galina stated I could now remove the arm band (as she called it) as this room was also lead lined. Signals from the device within me was not possible.

I did as instructed.

Galina advised me the man was a medical scientist and would remove the offending device as painlessly as possible. She also stated (and this had not been suggested before) that hopefully it is only a tracking device and nothing more sinister. "Oh great!"

An inspection ensued with much poking, chatting and nodding. A swab cleansing wipe with cotton wool followed with a local anaesthetic by syringe. Not at all painful.

The doctor gently and politely pushed my face sideways… away from the job in hand and all I felt was a lot of pricking and prodding. Despite the original entry of this device via a small syringe needle it had been necessary to do a small incision. This left me with two neat stitches.

The doctor beamed as he held the tiny object aloft with minute tweezers and said something to Galina. Her translation was: It was out, antiseptic cream had been applied, I must take two tablets three times a day for two days (provided) to clear up the infection and best of all… it was only deemed to be a detection tracking device and I was now a "free man".

The device was so tiny. How can they make such amazing things?

We all three walked to the lift. I was again instructed… place the mask on and be guided down to the ground floor. The reverse of the checking in process was undertaken and my ID tag removed.

I was led to the car and we took our seats as before. We were soon back at the I Brodsky whereby my mask was again removed. I posed no further security risk. We all three went into the cafe and coffee was ordered… most welcome! Our previous table was free next to the window. Galina invited us to have dinner together enabling us to "chat" more extensively.

I agreed, providing I pay.

"That is very kind of you, although not necessary. You lucky too, I not have to sing again today!" Who said Russians don't have a sense of humour?

Irina requested use of the telephone. She needed to let Monika know, two meals less tonight. That carried out, we studied the menu but again, I left it to the experts to decide.

"What are you plans now, Ric. You still have a job to do. How do you start from now?"

"I have to say I am a little worried because of our duties. I am very mindful that we are investigating the same thing and we must not clash, otherwise things will obviously get difficult, and back at Vauxhall, questions will be asked."

"You will not talk of where your office is, Ric. We do not speak such information. If we were under interrogations, we now know information that was not wanted to know. You understand me?" It was clear that the two ladies, although similar in age, have more experience under their belts than my meagre years in the job. I understood her soft, but quite correct reprimand.

"Tomorrow, I have an appointment with the British consul. A man with a double-barrelled name, I can't quite remember at the moment, but I hope to get help concerning my passport."

"His name is double-barrelled?" Irina asked, puzzled.

"His name is hyphenated, Irina… S perensom."

"Oh!"

"We only need to remember our task are in same place but yours is for to see who English is to be doing exchanges of information with Russians. That is where it ends. Ours is to the heroin trade. Although in the store Glavny Magazine our job need remain separate and as long as we stay on for that we will be right course. We not know you, and *you* not know us. Agreed?"

"Yes, I can see the logic and as long *Krull*… that is *Krull*… *he* just walked past. In a green military uniform, black boots. That's him!"

"Who is Krull?" Irina asked.

"Petrov and Krull. the two who held me at Lubyanka… they have my passport."

Galina, tipping over her chair, ran out to see if she could recognize Krull. She saw the short stocky bald man disappearing along the footpath, but had no recognition. Half the men in Moscow look like him she said, and from the rear there is not much chance.

The food arrived. The usual superb bread rolls with butter and a soup called Solyanka which was meal in itself. It had everything in it except a whole pig... and I'm not so sure about that!

An intermediate taster was next. Ikra, which is caviar on a small crepe. Next, beef Stroganoff and terminating in Morozhenoe. In our language is a type of ice cream summer pudding. Fabulous meal, delightful company and certainly a lot to talk about. And we certainly did.

My expenses were now entering my thoughts! Galina asked for a cigarette.

"Oh. I'm Sorry," I said, "yes of course." I went for my packet of cigs.

"I don't permit to smoke in my cafe. Fire dangerous. I want to see the cigarette you have."

I pulled from my pocket the packet of cigs purchased from the Glavny store and laid them on the table. Irina and Galina looked at each other, then at me. What was strange about these cigarettes? "I know what you are going to say." (I wrongly thought.) "These are the brand that girlies smoke and men usually smoke Sobranie?"

"Not so," was Galina's sharp response.

"Sweete Dreams are the name used for the heroin. There are two brands sold which appear to be same, but not. One sold... under the counter you say. In shop. They are made containing heroin and are Sweete Dreams the other brand contain mild tobacco are the legal brand Sweet Dreams. Do you understand difference. Packs look same. At the counter ask for Sweete Dreams with 'e' on end and you will buy high quality heroin at a very high price. The proper brand is cheap and is mild tobacco, you are follow me now Ric. You purchased Sweet Dreams tobacco cigarettes?"

"Oh yes. I do. Now I understand that woman in the shop. When the assistant turned her back, she leaned over the counter and stole packets of cigarettes. She obviously knew she was stealing pure heroin cigarettes and thought she could get away with it. Actually she did!"

"This method Ric, to sell heroin is of course only very small way of to distribute but it brings in many Rubles each day for dealer is to sell packets to those who know, and those who ask!"

Chapter 3

A return to the hotel with Irina after a fabulous meal at Brodsky's left me feeling rather "fat" and left her looking the same smart elegant lady she always seems to be. There is no doubt her English is better than I originally thought. Perhaps my English is "rubbing off" on her.

I wish her Russian language would rub off on me!

I spent the remaining time on my bed reading a novel but also dedicating some moments in learning more Russian pronunciations. Laying on my upright pillow, I could see my reflection in the mirror on the opposite wall. This gave me the opportunity of watching my contorted mouth and lips twist and turn as I negotiated some of the more difficult words. If I looked like that, I pondered... any person listening to me on the highway might consider sending for an ambulance for, clearly, I may appear to have departed an "institution" before my time! However, I did make some headway and those important vocabulary and words (such as; can I have a beer etc.) already learnt before coming to Moscow did so increase and improve.

I slept well, and up early for breakfast which was once again not always "top notch" at this hotel... but I liked the people and would never complain. If coffee is tepid... it is tepid!

Sufficient time was allowed, after consultation with Irina for the journey to the British consul. A car taxi was to bring me back when all was completed, hopefully satisfactorily. A small Marshrutka followed by a secondary larger type ferried me without too much difficulty. Satisfactory, even though bus journeys I find tiresome.

However I arrived at 11:45 am in time to verify details with Reception. The building was huge and quite magnificent. There are apparently several Consular offices scattered around Moscow but this one is noted to assist with passport difficulties such as mine.

The "heavy mob" (two security guards) were at the front steps. They took details and "frisked" me for weapons, drugs etc. One guard stayed out front, the other walked aside me into the building and stood attentively whilst I addressed the receptionist. She also took details from my wallet, closely noting bank card, credit cards and studying a small family photo.

Impressive; if I was an aggressor there would not be much I could do other than "fisticuffs" and I would not fancy my chances with either of the two out front Their black leather zip jackets and the holsters made them look like a Marlon Brando, and smiling came as an extra!

When she was happy, the receptionist telephoned the man I was to see. A lady secretary came down and escorted me to the office of Sir Grantham Hargreaves-Sykes. It makes the name of Ric Hartland sound quite insignificant, which actually, I was feeling at the time.

I added Mr to it to extend my lack of importance!

A tall upright impeccably dressed military looking man of approx. forty. Immaculate English double-breasted suit all buttoned up which looked as if he had been born in it. It fitted so perfectly.

A chair was proffered. I sat nervously, I don't know why, I just felt out-classed!

"Sorry about the long name old boy, there is also a *Captain* at the front but I don't use that part. The Grantham bit was also a bit tough, even at my private school (still feeling out-classed) they called me Granny Grantham. That wasn't so bad, but now, if I was in a shop with the 'ol memsaab and someone shouts out... Hello Granny, well, she does not take too kindly, if you follow my drift... yuk, yuk, yuk." His laugh sounded like a chicken.

"Still, Granny is short for Grantham to my friends, how about you... is Ric short for Richard?"

"No. Its long for Ric!" (In some ways I wish I hadn't said that.) "Yuk, yuk, yuk."

The internal phone rang. Granny answered it and whilst looking at me said: "Yes, he's here now, no I'm sure that's OK. Only got passport details to clear up."

Phone down. "Colleague James. Wants to ask a few questions. I'm sure you are OK with that?" I nodded.

Captain Sir Grantham then pulled out a file and we got on with the details of the day.

"Got a right shiner there, Ric. How did you come by that, not the proverbial door?"

I told him "chapter and verse" about the store Glavny and the ensuing saga with Petrov and Krull. He said he had never heard of those two characters... but there are thousands like them apparently.

Whilst passport details and reasons for the loss were being entered into his paperwork, the door opened and in walked another stereo type Embassy officer. They must have a generous clothes allowance. He briefly introduced himself as "James" and sat behind me saying: "When you've finished Sykes?" (That makes him sound senior?) Paperwork completed.

Captain Sir Grantham etc. stamped a duplicate copy and advised me an official formal document would be sent to my hotel within a few days. This would then allow me safe passage home and would be acceptable to all custom officials both here and in the UK.

"In the meantime, sir, we will place an official complaint about your treatment at Lubyanka and endeavour to retrieve your passport from the Ruskies, but if we don't succeed then all well and good eh? Use the substitute document." James moved his chair.

"All right if I take over now?" He did not wait for an answer.

"Mr Hartland. You are staying at the Moskovkaya Zvezda... sorry, The Moscow Star. You claim to be on holiday, *(claim to be?)* Why are you staying at this hotel?"

"It's as good as any I suppose."

"I will be candid with you, Mr Hartland. We have been keeping an eye on this hotel. By coincidence a lot of English, so called tourists stay there. It's not the best on the planet and if it were me I would find better. Why did you choose it?"

"Well, I suppose it's cheap and good value."

"What is the cost to stay there?"

"Oh... I don't know."

"You don't know the price of the hotel you are staying in? Am I being interrogated?"

"No," (A quick lie to answer.) "A birthday present from my mother." He examines his paperwork.

"Your birthday is in six months' time it states here." (more lies to come!)

"Oh, yes… at the time of my birthday my mother said she had not saved up quite enough so would I mind if it were delayed. Of course *I* did not mind. That is the reason for the time delay, also there is the season (I am gaining ground now) the season has to be right and that did not correspond with my birthday date. Anyway, why are you so interested in this. You are beginning to sound like Petrov and Co?"

"Oh no. (Big smile.) Please don't think that. Can I be personal? It is important I am afraid. If you do not wish to answer it will be necessary to pass you on to another department and they… how shall I put it, do not have such a kindly tone with their questioning." (This IS an interrogation!)

"Go ahead."

James then asked me if I lived with my mother. If I was married. If I liked women and worst of all, as he so politely put it, do I pay for my enjoyment with unknown women.

I kept my cool and answered as calmly as possible. What on earth is he coming to?

I answered in that order. No. No. Yes and No!

"To be candid with you now, we have to ascertain why many English males stay at this hotel and whether it is being used for prostitution? A sort of arranged go-between… between England and Moscow. I am sure you follow me?"

I inwardly heaved a sigh of relief but I could only state that it was a nice establishment and not a "house of sin" and the owners are very pleasant.

I know that the reason why so many English males visit is they are likely to be from "Department Blue 17" stationed at Vauxhall. I could not divulge that, but it would easily clear up everything.

I have already sworn secrecy, so what could I do other than act innocently surprised.

"Well, I can assure you I do not use women and pay for." Sir Granny etc. interrupted.

"For a bit of the old any punky eh. Ric… yuk, yuk, yuk!"

"Yes," replied James, "Quite so. What do you know about Irina and Monika Karashenko?" I stated, from my very brief experience, I knew them to be very decent ladies who ran the hotel. They were about thirty and forty years of age and I did not believe for one minute they were involved in prostitution. I suspected nothing of that nature and any suggestions, in my view, were quite wrong and unfounded. Although, of course, I'm only a staying tourist. "How long am I to be kept here? I have a taxi calling for me at 1:30 pm."

"Cigarette? You are not being kept here, Mr Hartland. Just answering a few questions. You will not miss your taxi and if you did, we would chauffeur you back to your hotel. This is not Lubyanka!"

A silver cigarette case came from his inside pocket followed by a silver Dunhill lighter. I took one as did Sir Grantham etc. who removed a chained key ring cluster from his pocket, unlocked and opened the window slightly. I wondered who would want to break in here at this level, although one might wish to break out! Sir Grantham etc. poked his cigarette into a gold coloured holder and kept it in between his teeth as he spoke, saying; "Could do with a gasper, but I will have it in a few minutes James. Don't want to cloud the room eh? Yuk, yuk, yuk."

He did look like a big girls blouse with it protruding from his teeth. James lit my cigarette and inquired which brand I smoked. My reply was, "same as this one." (I saw the name) Sobranie. Was this just a matter of interest or a probing question to ascertain if I smoked "Sweet Dreams… with or without an extra 'e'," I wondered… *Do they know about the heroin business with those cigarettes?*

"So, that is all you know about the two sisters Karashenko," I nodded. "So why did you escort this lady to the Cafe Brodsky and in doing so meet another female during the afternoon. I'm not suggesting prostitution is, or you, are in any way involved, but it does appear strange to us. Hotel under some suspicion, and you lunching with Russian women you hardly know. Mr Hartland.

"You must see our point of view. Prostitution leads to drugs, or can do… and money, murder and pimps and all sorts of undesirables who associate and control these types of women. This is normally a police matter but we have been requested by our London Embassy to keep a close eye due to the number of English males who happen to be tourists on holiday staying at The Moscow Star."

"Following us ol' boy?" exclaimed Sir Grantham etc. "Seems a trifle dodgy Eh? Yuk, yuk, yuk."

"Miss Fedorova took me to the cafe. I did not know where to eat. She met her friend there and we had lunch. There was and is, no soliciting and nothing sinister or suspicious at all, so I would respectfully suggest you drop the subject as far as I am concerned. They are just pleasant ladies." James looked at his watch. I stubbed out my cigarette which was quite a strong blend.

"Well, time to move on, Mr Hartland. You have been most helpful You will soon have the final document for your travel, and meanwhile, as stated, we will seek out more information with our friends at the Russian Embassy. We will detain you no longer, sorry wrong word, you have not been detained as such. Always free to leave eh? Be in touch."

I shook hands with both. A secretary was summoned and I was escorted down the Reception area where all signing out details were finalized.

Chapter 4

I was "escorted" once again to the main highway area by one of the guards. No complaints, they are doing their job properly, but one would think being English, they could at least force a smile!

1:25 pm. Just right for the taxi. I stood with arms folded, with hands in pockets, with hands on hips, with hands scratching head, in fact hands in every conceivable position but there was no sign of my car and at two o'clock it was obvious there would be no taxi.

The observing guards were no doubt curious as to why I was spending so much time waiting... Waiting for Godot as they say in the play! Of course, Godot never comes!

Bus was the only alternative left apart from a hailed taxi. I knew the route. It is the way I arrived so it should present no difficulty. A Marshrutka came within a few minutes and I selected a seat half way down the bus. I was told not to sit near the back as with older buses a smell of diesel was customary. A male passenger at the front looked back at me and gave a "half smile"; I did not know him. He stood and came to my seat and sat in the seat in front and half turned to speak.

"English. I hear you speak You smoke, no?" Assuming he was offering a cigarette I politely refused stupidly stating: "I don't smoke." I should have simply declined.

"You smoke, I smell breathing. You smoke!" Of course, he could smell it on my breath. I had recently finished a Sobranie at the Embassy. From the dreadful odour of alcohol on his breath I was surprised he could smell mine or anything at all!

"You smoke? You like snort? Like inject or you like swallowing drugs. Can sell you now too." Oh great a drug dealer to harass me on a bus of all places.

Today is transpiring to be another one most forgettable.

He kept persisting and this was observed by the driver. The next bus stop came and the burly driver left his seat with engine running and came to our position on the bus. He touched the man on the shoulder. He brushed it off. He grabbed the man more severely by his coat and uttered a stream of Russian at him whilst dragging him from his seat, literally throwing him off the bus. In our stupid country (the UK) the driver would probably have been arrested for verbal abuse, physical assault and a stream of other nonsensical human rights accusations, but here in Russia… you misbehave and you're "out" mush! I'm in favour of that, in this specific situation!

The driver spoke to me in Russian, waving his arms about and thumping his closed fist into his other hand. I picked up a word here and there and got the general idea… the man needed a good thumping! He returned to his driving seat and we were off again.

The ejected male banged on the side of the bus swearing (I imagine) as we drove away.

My first experience of a drunken drug dealer did offer a lesson worth remembering and that was to sit nearer the driver, especially if he resembled Arnold Schwarzenegger!

The second and final Marshrutka journey was serene compared to the first and I was soon pleased to be on the short walk back to The Moscow Star Hotel.

Encountering Monika as I walked into the Reception area I was conscious she was inspecting my black eye and I could not but help to look at hers. Both eyes still blackened. She stated she was feeling better in her broken English, but she did still appear quite poorly.

"I get Irina," she said disappearing into the back room. Irina came and asked about my visit.

"A most strange interview. They gave me a duplicate copy. An original document will be sent by post to act as a substitute passport, but the remaining time was spent being grilled."

"Grilled?"

"Oh yes, sorry, interviewed, about possible involvement in prostitution."

"Prostitutsiya!" exclaimed Monika who had obviously understood the word. Monika and Irina then rapidly gabbled away in Russian. Too fast for me.

Finishing their fierce Russian dialogue, they both eyed me suspiciously. I felt embarrassed as if I was actually guilty of something, which of course, I was not.

I asked if we could go into the quiet dining room lounge. Irina and I found a soft comfortable seat and I told her in detail what the embassy officer was suggesting and there was an accusation against The Moscow Star. Irina was a little shocked but not as much as expected.

Apparently there had been similar accusations levelled at them before. The parents of Monika and Irina had run the hotel for all their working lives. When they died the two sisters took over.

A few years previously, a male guest, an Englishman, had brought a "hooker" as Irina called her, into the hotel one night and wild rumours had spread about that singular happening.

"People get the wrong idea and mick (she meant muck!) sticks."

Irina was saddened this had not died a death, so to speak, and was regrettable the English Embassy still harboured wrong impressions. Not uncommon for them!

I assured Irina that I stated the hotel was a good one and there was no reason to suspect anything bad about The Moscow Star nor the two sisters.

Irina was very gratified that I had been "in their comer". I saw no reason not to be. It was true.

We drank coffee, "on the house" and the conversation softened. I told Irina I now need to concentrate on finding out about the activities of the Glavny Magazine. That is what I was sent here for. Irina indicated she would help if necessary but I must remember that she and Galina were also on their trail, but principally for the heroin side of things, and as previously agreed... investigations must not clash or overlap. We understood each other perfectly.

I went for a walk down to the river again. It is a good place to contemplate and get one's thoughts in order and to try to place matters in perspective. I would go to Glavny Magazine tomorrow. It would not be easy but I must try to be "the tourist" again and not let those last events with Petrov and Company cloud things.

I returned to the hotel and had what was a pleasing dinner late evening. Then, a read on my bed and once more, further torture of the language whilst viewing myself in the distant mirror.

The following morning I had breakfast fairly late, changed into "tourist-ish" looking clothes and took a slow walk to Glavny Magazine. On entering the shop I tried to appear "not too inquisitive". I saw the cigarette counter from a distance and for the time being, distant is what it remained.

I wandered all around the shop to generally get my bearings. If there are any "problems" I may need to get out PDQ! The shoppers all seemed quite normal, just like in any other large general store, but from my information there is something going on underneath this charade cover of normal-ness!

I hatched a plan. Return half an hour before closing time and hide. So, I exit the store and visit The Pushkin Bakery to buy lunch on my way down to the river. Sourdough sandwiches. Borodinsky bread with Russian sausage displaying and unpronounceable name and some Vatrushka cream cheese buns, a real treat, with a ring pull can of Coke to wash it all down. (Where can you not buy a can of Coke?) Down at the river I found a nice bench seat with a view, weather good, so I spent the afternoon day – dreaming after eating my very pleasant snack lunch. It may be snack lunch but very filling. A lot of garlic in the sausage… "yuk" I hate it I must have smelt like a drain!

The store closing time was early today, 5:30 pm so I made my way back so as to enter the store at five o'clock. There was a type of commissionaire at the door who I had not seen before. This was not good for me. I did not wish to be observed going in and perhaps not be seen going out later. That worried me considerably, but I decided to press on with my plan.

The first floor had the toilet and wash room areas for males and females. It was not too busy on the first floor. That was a good sign.

A lady friend, five years ago in the UK had made her way into the ladies toilet in a well-known large department store in London, half an hour before closing time.

She regrettably had a severe stroke and fell to the floor unable to move or speak. Closing time came and the staff obviously did not do their job properly because the store was locked shut. No one had properly checked the toilet cubicles. If they had simply called out, my friend could not have replied. They did not undertake a visual inspection of the cubicles. Negligence!

On that floor she was later found… too late to save her.

I am going to try this as a ploy to remain in the store after closing time. If I can hide in the toilet cubicle and they, like the UK staff, do not check thoroughly, then I'm in. If they do their job properly, I will simply be a person using the toilet and there should not be any suspicion.

There were ten separate cubicles. Toilet users came and went. There was a male still remaining in one of the cubicles when the Tannoy system announced the pending closure of the store. Most of the message passed me by, but I did grasp "my zakryvayem" which in English is; "we are closing etc., etc." The male user in the end cubicle departed as instructed.

I stood on the toilet pan as best I could and pulled the door in towards me and waited. Thirty minutes passed. The main toilet entry door opened and a person walked in some of the way. I hoped it was not a cleaner. I'm done for if it is… it wasn't! The store piped music stopped.

The person shouted; "privet… yeast zedes kto-nibud," and a host of other Russian words not understood. The words I did understand were: "Hello… is there anyone there?" I stood on the pan, hushed, and with cramp coming on rapidly.

The person left, the main entry door closed, and I was down nursing my creeping leg cramp, soon mended after a massage. I sat on the pan lid for anther thirty minutes when the lights went out. There were no windows, so it really was very dark. I leaned back onto the rear wall with the flush handle gentle probing my spine and rested for a further thirty minutes. Long enough I thought for everyone to have departed. No one wants to waste time when "the bell goes". The only other possibility to consider was patrolling security night time guards, if there were any.

That is a worrying unknown factor of risk.

I quietly crept out through the main door. It creaked! Don't remember it creaking before!

The store was in darkness apart from some fire escape lights which must be the non-maintained version. That means they stay on all of the time, an advantage for me. There were also perimeter windows and being summer time there was plenty of natural light across the main shop floor. I quietly tiptoed across the floor and elected to use one of the narrow fire escape stairs rather than the large and rather grand staircase in the centre of the shop floor. Sedately I trod each step down to the ground floor level and at the bottom of the stair, listened, waited and panted!

There were no sounds to be heard. I delicately pushed the double doors inwards toward the ground floor department and let each door leaf swing back slowly and quietly. They did not creak! I could see no signs of life, so I made my way over to the tobacco counter where I had purchased the packet of "Sweet Dreams" cigarettes and got a good thrashing for my trouble! Bobbing down behind the counter I selected various packets of cigs. I could not see very much, so it was time for my key ring torch to get some exercise. Laying packets on the counter I could see two types of "Sweet Dreams" and, as I had been informed… both appeared identical, but one type was spelt with and "e" at the end of the word "Sweete". A carefully and skilfully manufactured packet signified the contents contained heroin and the other only tobacco. I was not aware of the potential value but I suppose if twenty king sized heroin cigarettes when emptied, the resale value would no doubt be quite high, and for some hoods… worth killing for! What would a metric ton be worth? I shudder to think! I placed the packets back into their original position and at that moment heard an audible "bang" from what seemed below.

I walked to another dedicated fire escape that went from the ground floor to the basement level car park and as before, gently tiptoed down the concrete stairs, gingerly holding on to the handrail so as not to trip. There were noises and they became louder as I approached a large steel roller shutter at the end of the basement zone.

This I assumed to be an incoming point acting as a loading bay… a goods delivery zone. It was not necessary to lean my ear against the shutter for I could hear quite clearly there was a lot of activity. Both Russian and English was spoken, sometimes calmly other times shouted as an order. I sat on a box deemed as female cosmetics and listened intently as the various orders were given. Vehicle doors opened and closed, goods and boxes were dropped and, or placed on top of each other. It seems a strange hour for the delivery of genuine goods, but not totally unknown. I sat for at least twenty minutes hoping to hear something to my advantage then it happened… an English voice shouted out orders for Sweet Dreams cigarettes to be stacked "somewhere" and when finished to contact… what sounded like ray, may or jay… it was too quick to be certain. A Russian male then gabbled away in strong dialect and another mentioned words that sounded like – documents and Lubyanka and obtaining something else later tonight. There was a lot of patchy verbal information passing from one to the other which remained rather undecipherable but clearly this was not a legal delivery of King Edwards spuds!

I listened considerably longer. I needed to gain as much information not only for myself but for Irina and Galina. This I considered must be a late heroin delivery of Sweete Dreams… cigs (with and "e") and references to "documents and Lubyanka" required verification as a matter of importance to my own assignment.

A torch light beam suddenly shone at my back throwing my silhouetted profile on to the steel shutter door. I then felt a sharp thud on the back of my head and I was "out!"

I awoke seated in a chair. A male was bellowing a stream of Russian at me at great speed. Gathering my thoughts I knew this was a time to present a plausible story. The male shouting at me gave me a minute to concoct my reasons for being there.

"Sorry," I said, "I'm English. I do not understand what you are saying." He ceased shouting. "OK, Dima, Ill deal with him. Who are you and what are you doing here… in a locked department store, this time of the evening? This had better be good!"

"Well, firstly, I'm an English tourist in Moscow, just come to see the sights on my tod. Last night I met some old pals who were here and I had no idea they were here (I'm beginning to gabble now!) Well, we got absolutely splatted last night and I didn't get back to the hotel, well, I did, but it was shut at that time… four o'clock. (I'm still gabbling but it's going well!) I did a bit of shopping in the Glavny this afternoon and when I got back into my car, just at the end down there, (this is chancy) I began to doze. It's not well ventilated down here and it's not very…"

"Get on with it idiot!"

"Yes, I put my goods into the boot and as I said I fell asleep. I found out to my cost they lock the garage car park gates at six o'clock so I had no choice. I wandered about and heard voices. I was the other side of that roller shutter (pointing) knocking on it. Did you not hear me?"

"No."

"Well, I did, and sat on a box and your hooligan banged me on the head. Rather impolite, eh?"

"Got any papers. Passport?"

"I've lost my passport I'm sorry to say, or it was stolen last night, I will make an appointment to go to the British Embassy tomorrow, so I don't want to be late for that."

"So, where was this drink-up then?" (I had all the answers)

"Oh, a place called café Brodsky. Do you know café it's a great place, a bistro type of…"

"Shut up!" The Englishman and his two Russian "hoppos" rabbited away for a full two minutes. I imagine they were determining my fate. Has my story held up?

"What did you hear when you were the other side of the roller shutter?"

"Only voices, nothing for me to understand, I don't speak Russian. Other than that, just the sound of you delivering the goods to the store. That's all, I meant no harm, only to find a way out of here which would be without my car, till tomorrow when the store opens. I would have to walk."

"Shut up! You can go through this way, out the back to the side street. You'll have to find your own way back to where ever your hotel is. Get your car tomorrow and be careful what you do in future, especially in locked department stores at night time. The Ruskkies don't take kindly to burglars in big departments stores. You don't seem to be one, but they have ways of changing your mind, if you get my drift?"

"Yes. I do. I think I do. Thank you. I'll be off then." I walked out of the rear delivery goods entrance with my heart leaving my chest. I casually strolled along the roadway, down the hill and turned the corner. I stopped and leaned against the wall panting and swallowing hard.

I had just confronted the heroin mob and survived! but my head hurt!

I wandered back to my hotel. Took the key from Monika. She was looking a little better after her ordeal. Too late to order dinner, but she ordered sandwiches and coffee to eat in the lounge part of the dining room. Russian sandwiches bear no resemblance to our sandwiches but they went down well. I played cards with myself, had a read of an English newspaper three days old, and retired to bed. This evening… no lessons of Russian in the mirror. The lump on my head was increasing by the minute but I thought best to clean it and get some antiseptic cream from Monika tomorrow.

Late breakfast and Irina was serving this morning. I arranged with her for a "little chat" after the initial panic was over. She sat with me when all other guests had gone and we shared a new pot of tea. Straight into discussion, I told her about my latest ordeal.

"We pass this to Galina as soon as possible. It difficult not to lap our task with this people but we do what we should eh Mr Hartland… sorry… Ric. I telephone now."

Irina left me for about five minutes and returned bulging with instructions.

"Galina say we go together now Ric. We find out some. They do this we know each Friday. Other time they is for normal deliver goods to the Glavny Magazine. So we go Friday again and you. We do, it the same time as you have. It a good way to be into Glavny store. Galina likes idea. I think most queuing plan... is that right?"

"No... I think you mean cunning?"

"Yes, cunning, that mean very diver, yes. So you now wait for paper passport to come but you not go to England now. Too many things, and you need find more as for who is passing secrets, yes? And we find more for the heroin trade." I nodded in agreement.

"If we find we catch them. Then police can prison them, but we must see this first. Do nothing for us now. We talk about this again Ric for Thursday and make plan for time to go on Friday, Yes. Galina say she may come also to us all together, the three. Galina has authorized gun but I do not have authority for gun and gun is use fill no?" I laughed...

"Oh yes, a gun... bloody useful!... by the way, have you got any antiseptic cream?"

The rest of the week I spent keeping my nose clean so to speak. I did all the things normal tourists do and see all the things normal tourists see. No matter how hard I tried I could not think of myside as a normal tourist. I will be pleased when this is all over. Hopefully, I can find out who is passing "what and to whom"... sign out from the hotel, and back to... as the song goes... back to dear old Blighty, although the UK is nowhere as dear as it used to be due to all the political clap trap. In some ways I can understand why people come to a decision... and just bugger off! Here in Moscow everyone knows and understands the clap trap. Ridiculous as it is, it is there, but they don't invent it daily! The only difference is, you get hauled off to Lubyanka even for sneezing when the President (or whatever he is called) passes by! Knowing that, one resists sneezing!

Irina made a date with Galina. Thursday late afternoon for an early dinner for three, and a "get together" briefing at Cafe Brodsky. Galina, who I realized was the senior "spy" of the two, had decided she would accompany me without Irina. Galina had the gun and it was mutually agreed that for three people it would be a difficult and dangerous operation to undertake within the close confines of a department store.

Irina and I journeyed to Cafe Brodsky by Marshrutka, it is easy and relatively fast.

Galina was obviously ready for our arrival. She held the door and kissed Irina as we stepped inside. Galina whispered into my ear…

"Kiss me like we are old friends and talk cheerful greetings in English."

Quite puzzled, she grabbed me and we kissed each other on our cheeks occasionally colliding! "Hello etc., etc.… nice to see you etc." Kiss, kiss, kiss, with gentle hug and handshakes too. She whispered again quickly, "Best to look like old friends today."

We went to the, well tried and tested table by the window. Galina softly said: "Some strange men near the stage, sitting, do not look now, best to look like old friends, spies do not kiss each other, only friends. Do you understand?" (She was deadly serious.) "Yes, I do," feeling a little embarrassed, "all very theatrical eh Irina?" Irina frowned.

Greetings concluded we settled down to dinner.

"Avoid the Stroganoff," was Galina's advice. "Today it not good."

"Strogen. Offs. Off," was my less than witty reply, (I must stop doing that) "What do you recommend Galina?"

"I order. I know what you like and you not afraid of eating meat like some delicacy, eh?"

"No, indeed I will eat anything as long as they remove the hooves." (Oh dear, I've done it again!) "We not eat hooves Ric," was Irina's comment. (I resolved to stop now!)

The meal was, once again really good, as was the wine and coffee. The whole of the afternoon and early evening spent with two delightful ladies could not have been better. I was very concerned with the amount of wine Galina was pouring down our throats but she confirmed it was "a drivers wine"… only 2%. low alc but very good.

There was a singing duo starting, a woman singer, folk music and with a male on accordion. I was sorry to miss the folk music.

Galina stated: "We now go to my flat and discuss details for Friday. My flat upstairs. We all go together and talk happily as we go to the stairs, and avoid looking or to stare at anyone at the tables. OK?" Politely shuffling dirty plates in some type of order I nodded and we ascended to Galina's flat above the cafe. Surprisingly, for Russian socialist ideals, it was very stylish.

Galina I considered was a little more right wing than many Muscovites are supposed to be. She made some coffee in a perc. and we sat comfortably with a low table fronting a leather sofa.

"I have to tell you now a matter serious. This work by our department has been interfered by your department. It is unfortunate, but your trivial investigation has compromised ours…"

"Trivial… that's a bit harsh!" was my response.

"Our task to eradicate this heroin trade is more important and I have to tell you words by my department, that it is too important to mess up due to some imbecile from London."

"Imbecile! Look, it's not my…"

"It is words from department," added Irina, "not Galina, you understand?" Galina continued: "Our work is planned for many weeks now and you come along – don't interrupt!" (I didn't!)

"It is unfortunate that our works do clash but there is a compromise…" Irina interrupted, Galina gabbled in Russian to explain the word compromise.

"You have a choice. You help us as a team of three and you may find information you need to get… and you help us also. You do, or you do not. Do you understand?"

"Yes," was my reply, "but I don't suppose I have a choice really?" Irina then continued: "You have choice Ric, but choice is you do help or you do not and if you do not, the department come to talk you and then they see you have holiday in Russia longer that you did want!"

"Are you saying I would be politically removed… removed… and by people on my own side?"

"Irina gives you facts, Ric. She can do no more. We all are responsible to the department of our making whether it in England or in Russia. You say, make bed, so lie in it eh?" Once again Irina was lost with this cliche and she explained it. Irina nodded.

"I am happy to help." *Do the two departments know what the other is doing?* I thought to myself.

"Good. That is good for us all. I must go more to say that you are in a most dangerous position. We deal with the Russia Mafia. They very nasty people, I'm sure you know. Are you married, Ric?"

"No. The department forbid it."

"Good… and how shall I say politely… you like women?" my quick reply.

"I think I know what you are suggesting, and yes, I do like women and I thought I liked you two up until now! Actually yes, I still do, sorry, that just came out!"

Irina put me in the picture...

"People who are married or people who are a little. (She asked Galina for a word)... oh yes. People who are a little *weird* are weakness that can be black manned... blackmailed. You understand that?"

"Yes. I adore women and I am not married... not yet... I hope to live long enough to be."

"So," added Galina, "you wish to be with us?"

"I am happy to help," Galina added some final words for my forthcoming, "recruitment."

"It is good for you to be with us Ric. Better than the alternative suggested by the department, but once again I say it most dangerous and they have guns and very nasty men who have fun to torture people and do unspeakable things not only to get information but for pleasure. I expect you have heard the expression *concrete boots* and connection with deep river? A favourite of theirs."

"Yes, but no more details please, I think I know what is involved and the dangers attributed. Do I inform my department in London?"

"You inform nobody yet!" A sharp reply from the two ladies in unison. (I almost jumped!)

"Good. Irina." A request came from Galina.

"Yes," Irina took out a document from her bag and unfolded it on to the table.

"We now go. This is a plan of the store." This surprised me. "We have made searching in store a lot over many weeks and is now all known to us. Map... I mean plan, is good for us to move freely. There is a large room store on top floor and only using by cleaners in mornings at five o'clock. It's not locked. We know no one go to store but cleaner people. There is place you will hide on Friday."

"I am sure it is more sanitary than my toilet hiding methods but are you certain if we hide in there, no one will discover us?"

"Ummm, yes, as much as can be sure. It may be hot as no window, but it big storage room and if people do open door when you hide, it possible to stand behind many diner boxes at end of store. Galina," the plan was then handed back...

"This is the plan we have made. It is easy but must follow it closely. We will dress normally like any shopping people. I will carry the Magazine paper carrier bag. It will be folded under my arm. When in the store I will unfold it when not seen and carry it big as if I am shopping with the bag. It looks normal. I will have two thin strong steel bars... I know you call them Jimmy's, yes... which will be concealed in my bra (Blimey! What is coming next?) is specially made, at bottom has... as you English say... below and between the boobs (I'm sure I'm going pink!) is special compartment for small ladies Beretta. They are a small, can sit in the palm of your hand, very small but capable. I expect you have seen them? the guns I mean!" (Oh, they do have a sense of humour!)

"If people search me by casual tapping body they not feel it. They only feel it, if they feel me!"

"You understand, Ric? It is specially designed by our scientific small arms department." I smiled and nodded. Nothing surprises me anymore. This is surely a different league for me. Look calm! I don't think I would know a ladies Beretta if I fell on one, but the other things... (Stop there!)

"A car," Irina continued with the plan, "will be driven by my friend, will collect you and then Galina four o'clock on Friday. We go to store and you leave car two streets away from Glavny. You walk to store. When finished in store you telephone me at hotel and I come with friend in car to collect same place. It expects to be eight o'clock in evening. If you not telephone, no car will come. You understand?" Again I nodded.

What am I getting myself into? I'm not James Bond. But I have to face up to it... these ladies are from a higher division than my "Department Blue 17" Licensed to kill... yes... they are!

We don't carry guns for a 'kick off' but the two ladies have a job to do and so do I. My London department totals twenty-one in all. They start at a lowly number one for very safe simple tasks, and rise according to their difficulty and danger level. Even being in Blue 17, guns are not prescribed, that is only for those in Department Blue 21. They are the real James Bonds.

I think I now know enough to realize I never want to rise to that level... this is bad enough!

I had hoped my task in Moscow was to be a little less potentially dangerous... but here I am, and I must do the best I can. Not exactly 007 but perhaps a bit more like double 0 four and a quarter! Galina proceeded describing the plan in more detail.

"We go into store at five o'clock. It close at five thirty. We have insider information that they arrive to deliver cargo of heroin at seven, we must be quick at what we do. We go around shop as shopping but, five fifteen o'clock we go to store on upper floor. When no one seeing, we go in store to hide and wait. The store will tell all people to leave store on loud speak as it closing... we do not, we hide. It very unlikely anyone look in store. It only for cleaners and fire door unlocked.

"Six o'clock we go to the fire escape stair at the side of the shop floor. It very narrow stair and go down all floors to basement car parking. There are two doors, double doors that open into car park and never locked. Fire escape doors swing away from shop. We must be quick.

"We have one hour, if our information is true, so must be very quick. There is single door beside large roller shutter door to goods area at far end. The single door is fire escape from shop so is unlocked... this is door we go through. We hope no one in there.

"There should be many boxes of all store goods. All types, many to look. We need to find the boxes with Sweete Dreams cigarettes and as you know there are two types. We must find the heroin cigarettes and I will examine them and take samples with me too.

"If all go to plan we after go to ground floor up same stair and at the side of store there is another toilet room for the ladies. It has high long window that opens. It may be locked but if is, then I will open with Jemmy. We slide through and drop to ground in side road. It is eight feet, so no broken ankles please."

Irina continued with the plan: "You telephone me and I come same place to collect as before in car. I drive to hotel. If no call I not come, you understand? Monika will give dinner when you back and she will do between nine and ten o'clock. Galina will be sleeping in hotel that night. It easy to do, she go to Brodsky Saturday. Any question you make?"

"I think you have covered it all but what if we do get caught by either the store security guard or even worse, the Mafia mob delivering the heroin?"

"If the store detective should catch us. I hold him at gunpoint and force to open store front door for us to escape. If not able to do that we have no choice, we both fight him or them if more than one guard. If the bad people catch us, there is no plan. We do the best we can. We are where we should not be and they will not like it, so things... as you English say... will get a little rough!

"If you find any evidence for your investigation when we in store then that will be good for you. If not, it may be end of your work in Moscow. It possible you will not be able continue as it will affect our work here, and as said to you, our work is vitally important too. You may need to change your original plans to find out who is passing important documents from English to Russians. It very difficult for you... time then for more thinking, or may be necessary to talk to your London office. They tell you more."

"This is all a bit hairy." I remarked... "Sorry... a little... dangerous. Can I be nosey and ask how do they operate and distribute the heroin?" Galina described the way they do things.

"We know they have many shops in Moscow in their pay. Small shops and large stores. They organize heroin cigarettes to be sold... the term you know *is*... *under the counter*... and this does take a lot of money in Moscow. If small shop owners do not like, they find shop badly broken one night or themselves badly broken also, so most do not disobey. The other side of the distribution is also from this store, go to countries all over the world in solid KG packs. This is the main distribution point. That is why there are such many heroin cigarettes here, is the information. That is why there are tonnes that come in and tonnes go out on regular journeys.

"This is big business for these nasty Mafia people and with very big money, life is cheap. This is *the place*... the big place... the main distribution for heroin in Moscow and this is why we have been planning this for several weeks... then you come along... we won't go into that again! It not your fault Irina and I have been chosen to investigate this. We women usually have more persuasion over men when necessary if need arises, but be assured, Ric, there are tough people from my department not far behind me, watching. You will not see them but they are there!"

It passed my thoughts that these two attractive ladies are licensed to thrill, and licensed to kill!

"I think I know all there is to know now. I'm glad to be part of the team. Let's do it!"

We were all agreed. One more cup of coffee. More of a sociable "chit chat" and Galina arranged for one of her waiters to drive myself and Irina back to The Moscow Star.

A reasonably early night followed, but it was far from relaxed. Continual wakening throughout the night disturbed my slumbers, and when I did sleep my head was full of "demons of the night". Dreams which did not make sense, and full of frustrations. Being in the wrong place at the wrong time... missing train connections... falling off a cliff... and worst of all, attending a funeral service to someone I did know, but I did not know. We have all had them! Was that last one an omen?

When I did gain decent continuous sleep, I overslept and missed breakfast time. Little consequence, I was still fairly "topped up" from last evenings meal. We all shifted quite a lot of good grub! Some further reading in bed and a pleasant shower pulled my senses rapidly back together. I stood under the warm water, ran through all the instructions, and analysed the numerous "what ifs" that could occur! There are many, but the foreseeable one's have been fully discussed.

Making a point not to miss lunch I was five minutes early and stopped at the reception desk. I passed some idle moments with Monika. She was looking very much better although those bruises will linger a long while yet. She pointed at mine and said: "Look good now Mr Hartland."

"You too," was my reply. I wondered how the ribs were feeling after her – "fall down stairs!" Into the dining room. I was served by a new waitress and elected to have a well-chosen, safe, large omelette with a type of potato chips as a main course. I did select wisely and made a point of not drinking too much coffee both now, and for the rest of the afternoon. Visits to the toilet or an uncomfortable "turn" would not gel well with the task in hand. I need to be fighting fit. Two diners on the adjacent table had steaks. When they left I glared at the used serrated edged steak knives. Should I take one? It could be concealed and "You never know?" Sensible risk assessment should discount the idea… what if we are caught tonight and they find a steak knife "stuffed down my trousers". Suspicious to say the least… but?

Chapter 5

I decided to take (borrow!) the steak knife. Concealing it, I and left the dining room.

It was good to relax, sipping my coffee which I took into the hotel rear garden. The paperback I had brought with me to Moscow accompanied me. The first volume of "War and Peace". Perhaps a bond novel "You Only Live Twice" might have been more appropriate! If the title was correct, I have already used up one life during this assignment with Messrs Petrov and Krull!

This quiet period was, the "lull before the storm"; I could only think of it in that way. A plan such as this, even well organized as it was, left me troubled. We might be successful, and what a triumph that would be not only for Galina's department but for mine in London. The reverse side of the coin was, and is… we are "spies" and the opposition are deadly. Back-up from our departments may be there as Galina had intimated, but from my experience over the few years in this business is… you mess it. And "we" don't know you chum! The other alternative is, we could get caught by the store security and then if arrested, we face the Russian police, and who knows… perhaps a return visit to my "pals" at Lubyanka. The ultimate alternative is, and I don't want to dwell too strongly is, we could both be killed… oh brother… or tortured and then killed! All daunting prospects!

A magpie squawked as it hopped past me breaking my morose concentration. How lucky you are, my little fellow! You only have to fly to escape your aggressors, although a shotgun would easily dispel that theory. I flicked open the novel to page fifty, but my thoughts again wandered, this time back to my training days. Finger in page… book down.

A period of intense training preceded any real duties for those in Department Blue 17 and one such day was a course named "Methods of concealment". The class of twenty, both male and female enjoyed a day of sheer inventiveness. We were constantly reminded of our roles – solely for the passing of information…

and information gathering, but none the less fraught with danger. Some of the ideas were most interesting. The microfilm transportation was particularly inventive, one I recall. One method with a small plastic cover, would be adhered to a small portion of the shaved head, approx. 5mm square, and hair then interwoven back with special glue. This was particularly effective with males and females who had a good crop (not me!) Another was a contact lens. The eye colour matched the other eye but vision was impaired on one side, but again, very clever for transporting microfilm. False finger nails was another. This was suited to both men and ladies. We were informed one female agent transported ten separate micro films within each false finger nail covering. However, she had been discovered and the "enemy" removed all false nails, discovering the films... and for fun, removed the real ones too! A loud sigh came from us all.

Methods of concealment also included those natural apertures within the body. The instructor pulled no punches, and discounted any embarrassment by indicating in graphic detail how various methods were employed by both males and females for concealment. He also added how some vicious sadists kill... "And remember ladies and gentlemen, even in these civilized times." The instructor emphasised: "Methods of death employed by vicious aggressors are not purely confined to the history books. It is most regrettable to recall occurrences such as that for our treasured Jesus Christ. Also, Guy Fawkes and the demise of King Edward the Second! Recent events report such atrocities are not uncommon. They have no rules, no consciences, they don't just shoot you!" There was a lot of hushing and nudging by all attendees. Those with a sound history knowledge whispered the facts of those deaths to those adjacent who were less knowledgeable... and again a lot of gasping and grunting. The instructor continued;

"So my friends, remember, this is not a game of beer and skittles; it's bloody dangerous and you do not have the benefits of firearms such as that for Department Blue 21"

"However, you do have the freedom to carry knives, but that can be a considerable hazard. Airport x-ray machines will reveal them and you will have them confiscated. Should you wish to conceal a knife, obviously not at airports, there is one fairly assured way that a body frisking might leave your weapon undiscovered; did say, might!

"For this you will need good quality sticky tape. Wash your back clear of natural body oils and place strips of sticky tape vertically. This is to restrict the possibility of cuts to yourself. Place the knife in a vertical position over the tape high between the shoulder blades with the point upwards. Bind the sticky tape around your body several times. This should secure the knife for a few hours. It does of course depend upon your movements, but for a short period of time, let us say a couple of hours the knife should stay in place. If you need it quickly, you will be able to grab the handle that protrudes downwards, which needless to say, must be left un-taped.

"This is a crude rather un-subtle DIY method but it might save your life, and you do not require any specialists to organise it for you. Your concealment is completed in a matter of minutes. The only consequence we have found thus far is a skin rash due to the adhesive... the choice is yours." There were so many other ideas the instructor had identified on that day that the scientific wizards had come up with. We all left the lecture on that training day both enlightened and disturbed.

My immediate thoughts were now with the knife concealment. I need to shop for some good quality tape... but an immediate thought came to me! The waitress came out clearing and cleaning the tables. I ripped the cover from my paperback and went into the dining room. I held the torn book in front of the waitress and said in English;

"My book is torn; do you have any sticky tape?"

"Ahh... kleykaya lenta," she replied and disappeared, returning with a roll of brown Gaffer tape... perfect! I thanked her; "Spasibo," and gestured that I would go upstairs to repair the book. She smiled and nodded and went back to her table cleaning.

Returning to my bedroom I was most careful not to drop the knife en-route, that would be more than embarrassing! I washed and cleaned the knife blade and addressing the sticky tape, it appeared very satisfactory for the task in hand. Nearing the appointed hour for collection by Irina, I scrubbed myself bodily and stuck tape vertically "as trained". I then wrapped the tape around myself a few times (not easy by one's self) and secured the steak knife in a vertical position directly, high between the shoulder blades. The handle protruding downwards was left free of tape and I practiced grabbing it. It was a crude method of concealment but was feasible as indicated by our training instructor. It was far from comfortable but could be a "lifesaver" if such a time presented itself... and I will not hesitate to use it if necessary. I would like to have laid on the bed to rest waiting for Irina's knock but that was far from practical, so I sat at the dressing table examining my sticky taped chest in the mirror. When that comes off, many hairs will come with it! Shirt on, buttoned up, then with tight fitting waistcoat to keep knife secure, I'm ready! The departure time arrived and Irina firmly tapped on my door. The door was locked; we went down to the car parked at the front. Galina was already in the back seat, smiling as if we were going to the zoo! Perhaps we are!

I was walking a little stiffly, and sitting in the car presented difficulties. So be it!

Irina drove carefully and both she and Galina sang to the tunes on the car radio. Some kind of Russian folk songs. Galina was clearly the singer of the two. How relaxed they both were! We arrived at the side street… two streets away from the store. We left Irina with a parting comment: "Hope see you again soon."

Galina held her folded corporate paper carrier bag under her arm and we casually walked into the store, with plenty of time for browsing. She opened the carrier bag and it certainly looked as if we were genuinely shopping. Taking careful watch on the time we sauntered to the upper floor and wandered around, falsely looking at goods for sale. The cleaners store was easily located and we entered when "the time was right" and no shoppers were visible. There was a light switch inside the door but to turn it on might have sent a shaft of light below the door so, we quickly gained a mental image of the items within the store and closed the door.

The trick now was to negotiate the floor area without clattering the brooms, vacuum cleaners and numerous metal buckets. Such a collision could have jeopardised our plan and discovery then inevitable.

We listened, and waited for the Tannoy.

There was little sound noticeable apart from our breathing. We leaned against the safety of a wall without buckets etc. below. We did not even whisper. The Tannoy was heard audibly announcing the store was to close and all shoppers must now leave. My luminous dialled watch was a benefit and at six o'clock precisely I held the watch to Galina. She whispered… "We go now." Gingerly we opened the door and peered through a narrow slot. The store lights had been dimmed. The fire escape signs were thankfully glowing and natural daylight was coming via the high level windows to one side of the store. We could see plenty, but heard nothing. The store door quietly closed, we walked across the shop floor to the fire escape staircase, directed by Galina. I had seen the shop plan but in some respects had lost my bearings. The top of the escape stair had narrow double doors opening to the direction of escape. They squeaked!

Slowly down the concrete stairs we tip-toed passing each floor, momentarily stopping to listen. No sounds heard at each floor level. Proceeding down the ultimate flight we arrived at the last set of narrow double doors, which again opened to the direction of travel for fire escape. Predictably they squeaked also. We manually shut them avoiding the clatter of the self-closing hinges. Crossing a short distance we arrived at one more escape door and this would be the one leading through to the goods storage area. This flush fire door was adjacent the huge metal roller shutter that I had seen before. This is an electrically operated shutter and not of any use to ourselves. We placed our ears to the escape door, and each in turn, acknowledged there were no sounds to be heard beyond. We both nodded in agreement and slowly pushed the door outwards into the main goods storage depot. It was vast and dimly lit, fortunately scattered with illuminated fire escape signs everywhere. These signs were certainly a blessing in disguise for us and it offered the opportunity to find the bank of light switches. When located I turned them all on, illuminating the whole of the goods store.

It was now 6:10 pm. We must be out by 6:50 pm at the latest. This is going to be really tight! Galina and I ran about like demented souls searching for the containers of cigarettes. We located numerous large boxes in scattered positions, all fairly neatly stacked, some up to the roof level, and all appeared to have manufacturing labels on two or more sides.

We located a vast mass of boxes stacked against a wall near the rear roller shutter at the extreme end of the goods store. There must have been a hundred large boxes sporting the name; "Sweet Dreams". I took one of Galina's jemmy's and we both commenced prising open the boxes which were a little like tea chests but more robust. Galina found many genuine articles which she discovered by simply breaking open a quantity of cigarettes, thus revealing tobacco, but no heroin thus far. Dismayed and frustrated we both stood with hands on hips, looking, panting.

"Up top," I said pointing upwards, "They may be the high boxes piled up top near the roof away from prying eyes. I will climb up." Using the boxes as steps I cautiously went from one to the next. *Must be like climbing the Egyptian pyramids,* I thought to myself. At the top, several metres above the floor I reached a plateau where numerous containers resided like a sea of woodwork. I commenced prising open a box. The "Sweete Dreams" inside were annotated with an "e" at the end of the title. I knew this to be "It". Breaking open a packet and tearing at the cigs, they revealed white powder. I did "thumbs up" and threw a packet down to Galina. I opened two more large container boxes repeating the exercise and behold, all white powder… "Eureka!" I threw two more packets down to her hitting her on the head, she grinned!

There was a loud metallic clunk as the roller shutter responded to electric power and slowly unfolded upwards. I looked at my watch. It was 6:40 pm. We had not overstayed… but?

Two men came in followed by a third. Galina was instantly seen. One shouted at her in Russian. Before awaiting her reply they commenced manhandling her and violently pushing her about.

I had not been seen by them at that stage but very soon they did. I rapidly descended the "pyramid". One man pointed and shouted "Maxim!" Floor level reached, Maxim pulled out a retractable knife and "came at me" with a horizontal lunge. Galina shouted something in Russian. Time for the unarmed combat training, page one, to come into play! The jemmy that I held partially concealed behind my back was the first part of my defence. I quickly thrashed at his knife blade and the weapon was dropped. I grabbed his wrist and violently pulled him towards me whist simultaneously kicked out at his chest. This pushes the arm forward and the body backwards. He didn't like that as his shoulder becomes dislocated and pain immediately ensues. It seemed to work well! This was then followed by a kick to the knee. He went down rolling and groaning just as the text book accurately describes. Everything done in a matter of seconds.

Another training course well worth its salt!

The world explodes at that moment. I can only recall a massive striking force upon my shoulder. The goods store and I parted company! I awoke seated in a chair. My shoulder and neck was in torment. I lifted my head and my eyes began to focus. I was tied to a chair as was Galina next to me. One male was standing like a sentry nursing his musket vertically, however, this musket was a baseball bat. I realised what had struck me and obviously why it was so effective. Another male was sorting some paperwork whilst a third stood right in front of me glaring at the pages of a passport. It appeared to be an English passport?

"So," said the passport reader, "you are Mr Ric Hartland and you are English, living in England and I suppose you are going to tell me you are on holiday?" He continued flicking through the pages of the passport. "What precisely are you doing here? Don't mess, the truth please unless you would like him (nodding sideways) to take some more baseball bat exercise on your lady friend here?"

"No, I don't, and I am a tourist here in Moscow on holiday." That answer of course, bearing in mind where we were was utterly ridiculous. His English was very good. "You speak good English?"

"That is because, idiot, I am English. You put my friend Maxim in hospital two hours ago. (Was I out that long?) Normal English tourists on holiday do not, so effectively I may say, dispense with a six foot three brute like Maxim with such skill and ease. You are not a tourist."

"I'm one of those old fashioned men who don't like to see hooligans knocking ladies about and as far as your Maxwell, Maxim or whatever he is called, he came at me with a knife... another thing I'm not too fond of. I'm not going to stand there and be stabbed, now am I? What are you doing with my passport, how did you obtain that so quickly. You did not know who I was until recently. How did you get it?"

He did not answer my questions.

"You madam are that Fedorova woman that sings at Brodsky's. What are you doing in here with this man Hartland. A Russian native, who sings in a cafe, is with an English tourist who is obviously trained in the killing trade, says he is on holiday... and decides to spend some holiday time with you looting a department store. I wasn't born yesterday." He turns his questioning back to me.

"My friend Dima who is currently on a mission, will soon return. He tells me he has seen you before Mr Hartland, when he was with my other English friend. You have been here before with a stupid story about being shut in after closing time. Remember that? Do you like honey? My friend Dima has a garden not far from here, where he keeps bees, he will bring you some honey soon."

"Yes, I was shut in the car park once, recently. What are you talking about... liking Honey?"

They all walked away and held a discussion far from our ears. I spoke to Galina. She was, up to that point unharmed apart from being pushed about. I asked if they had frisked me.

Fortunately, she did understand the term, "frisked".

Galina replied: "The other thug that hit you with the baseball bat He frisk you when you were on floor."

"You were flat on your back for long time. I thinking you are dead. They search your pockets and not find. Just key ring and keys. I tied with rope before

56

you then they tie you also to chair. That is all. I pleased to see you not dead, but still unconscious in chair with head down. You are a dark pony Ric, yes… dark horse I mean. That thug Maxim won't walk about for some time soon. I can see you are a good man to be with at these times. They did frisk me but my bra is still unmoved but how to get Berretta tied like this is not good. A time will come, and they shall see." The group returned.

"We will decide what to do with you later. Our top man is coming and will decide your fate.

"He won't be too pleased when he knows how you have treated Maxim, for sure.

"By the way, we tied you with a special type of synthetic rope, not the Manila hemp type. Our Russian friends developed this and is well favoured at Lubyanka. With this thin cord rope firstly well soaked, as they dry, they go tighter and cannot easily get loose. The knots are also impossible to undo, so wriggle as you may my friends, you will not undo them or slide from them. This is why it is so well liked by the Lubyanka morons. They enjoy tying people up and the cords cut into the skin as they dry out. Pigs eh? but … we like it too.

"I trust you don't think we are morons, Mr Hartland?" He laughed. "We not get out of these ropes, Ric, they cut in," whispered Galina.

One of the other members of this group came through the shutter holding some white clothing and a flat box… he was greeted as Dima. They all chatted at what was to be next.

"It best to tell me what you both know and precisely what you are doing here. You madam, were holding packets of cigarettes when we arrived. Why? and you Mr Hartland, English tourist, were on top of the boxes… sightseeing, I assume?

"My good friend Dima has a way of getting information. So easy, we just stand and watch. None of the brutal head bashing, too painful on the knuckles… so, I ask you once again and for the last time… what are you two up to?"

"We were just being nosey," Galina said. "Ric, Mr Hartland, is boyfriend, he is on holiday come to Moscow to see me, we soon to be engaged. The roller shutter was open when we pass in street so we come in. People are nosey yes? So we just walk in and see lots of boxes. I smoke cigarettes and like – Sweet Dreams, so Ric, he climb up to get some. That all. We not terrorist or bad people. We just stupid really. No more is true." I added on to Galina's amazing fable;

"That's about it, Mr?"

"English Joe."

"That's about it, Mr English Joe, we've been daft and nothing more. It's just unfortunate that I have been here before, but again, that was a case most unfortunate, being locked in when the store closed, that's all, as she says, we are not bad people. Can't you let us go now, these ropes hurt?"

"Well, that's a good one, Read a lot of Agatha Christie do you or perhaps Mickey Mouse? It is more like Disney than anything else. OK. You've had your chance."

He nodded to Dima who commenced putting on a white overall, a bee keepers hat and gloves.

I could also see a smoking can, typical of a bee keepers equipment for calming bees… but I imagined calming them was not on the agenda at this moment English Joe and his other "hoppo" retired into an office near the roller shutter door and peered through the glass observation window. Dima took the box which had small mesh sides and unclipped the lid. He brought the box over to us and demonstrated its contents. We did not need to look, although we did. Hundreds of bees scurrying around minding their own business until… now! Dima ripped open my shirt sleeves and pulled them up. He then pushed Galina's jersey up high below her shoulder level. The wet cord ropes maintained their grip. Hands tied at the back Dima sprinkled the bees over Galina's arm and then mine The bees happily settled, untroubled. I could see faces peering at the window of the office, waving and laughing as they tapped the glass. The bees scurried about and buzzed busily. Dima proceeded to poke them.

"Rasserit ich," declared Dima smiling. Galina interpreted; "He is going to make them angry." Angry they were! Dima fingered them with his gloved hand and the bees did what they do when angered. I felt intense pain as the first one stung. I heard Galina yelp also. She was experiencing the same treatment. Between stings I asked Galina if she had an allergy. She responded by saying she had never been stung by a bee only a wasp and that was equally painful. Dima continued annoying the bees by going in turn from Galina to myself. The first few stings were bad and it seemed as if further stings could not make things worse than they already were. It was excruciating, so was the grin on the face of the moronic Dima. I wished to knock that smirk off his face!

I looked across at my good lady friend and saw her rocking with the pain of the stings. Some bees began to fall off after they had done their work, many taking their bodies with them, but many leaving their stings behind.

Do not believe the myth that bees only sting once and die. I saw some sting more than once. Satisfied with his task and still enjoying his own mirth, Dima swept off the bees into the box and puffed the smoke to calm them down... too late for us.

I looked down at my arm which was decorated with fiery lumps and numerous projecting stings left by the terminal members of the hive.

Asking Galina... she replied she felt severe pain and very sick. Likewise, I agreed.

Dima covered his box and disrobed.

Now safe, English Joe and what transpired to be his "hoppo" Leonidas left the safety of their office and came over to us and gloating inquired as to our health.

"Svoloch," was Galina's comment winch I knew was a Russian word meaning fatherless child! "That's a good word for you," I said "The English version is also from me. I don't know what you intend to get from two innocent people by doing this. It only demonstrates what low pond life you and your cronies are." English Joe continued. "You had the opportunity to speak the truth. You did not. A little persuasion often helps, but never mind, this time we failed. Nothing you can do will affect our work." The roller shutter was raised and a male figure entered. The shutter was lowered again.

"Oh here is 'J'."

"These are the two causing trouble. What do you want us to do with them?" Whilst conferring, English Joe gave 'J' a large buff envelope which he was nurturing under his arm. The envelope was opened and numerous papers were withdrawn. They looked official, not the type of papers Mafia heroin importers would entertain, and it certainly wasn't money. 'J' glanced at the papers and replaced them into a briefcase he was carrying and locked it.

I remembered hearing the words... pay, may, ray, jay or something like that when I was last here listening on the other side of the inner basement roller shutter. So this is 'J' presumably the head of operations. Otherwise known to me a "James" from the British consul.

The immaculately dressed "James" was noticeably uninterested at our ordeal other than casually saying he was sorry for their "little peccadilloes"... but they will have their fun, and if you upset them... well, who knows!

"You are a charmer Mr... James, 'J' or whatever you call yourself. A British ambassador involved in the heroin trade and doubtless part of a spy network passing restricted documents. (I wished, at that moment, I hadn't said that!) How do you sleep at night, eh? people like you are an example of everything that is wrong in our country... and for Russian's too, for what it's worth... ordinary Russian law abiding people don't need your type either."

"A bold speech, Mr Hartland, and to some extent worryingly accurate, however, anything you may know or have ascertained will go no further, so it matters not, precisely what you *do* know."

"I imagine that is goodbye to my passport also? What a fraud you are," I said.

"Well, actually ol' boy, you are quite wrong there. You see, we must keep everything on a corporate plateau. The paperwork concerning your passport has all been rubber stamped, so to speak."

"All matters must appear to be taking their normal course otherwise suspicions will arise.

"No... your passport will be delivered to your hotel direct from the Embassy this very night by special courier. This will be received by the Moscow Star hotel personnel and a receipt acknowledgement processed on the door step. All very tidy. It will be met with great sadness tomorrow by the management that you will not be able to collect it. Such a shame, you will agree. You comprehend Mr Hartland, all well planned and tickety-boo, eh?

"Joseph, this gentleman and his lady friend are both official agents of their respective governments and know far too much already, so they must disappear from view. I leave you to make the necessary arrangements." English Joe nodded.

"You will stay here tonight The secure cords will see to that! Tomorrow, early Saturday morning, other friends of Joseph here will arrive and take you to your final resting place.

"These Russian brutes once favoured the Moskva river for their disposal methods, but being total thickos didn't realize it was only three metres deep, so your appointment with the almighty will be a different venue, but none the less... permanent. They never fail to please!" My comment to Galina: "This is the type of English ambassador we have these days Galina. Worthless!"

"A pity, with such a delightful lady companion of yours Mr Hartland but there we are. So be it. Oh that's a good one eh Joseph my friend... 'so be it'." They both laughed at their sadistic humour. "Honey trick next Joseph?"

"Yes, J, the honey next. Everyone likes honey and after their stinging time a little honey should go down well, don't you think?"

"J" came up to Galina and six inches from her nose said: "Don't be tempted to shout for help madam. The roller shutter is doubly insulated and so are the walls because of the storage requirements. So be assured, you are really here for the night dear lady. More of their fun. You'll like this next one... better than the last and less painful."

English Joe then handed my passport to James who pocketed it. With his briefcase, he walked to the shutter that was being raised, shouting "Au revoir, but not in this world!" Laughter was heard as he walked away with the shutter being lowered once again. We were then manhandled and dragged far away from the roller shutter to be concealed by the pyramid of stored cigarette boxes. Dima who had disappeared for a few minutes returned with two glass pots.

"He must have his fun," exclaimed English Joe. Dima unscrewed a jar of honey and held it on Galina's head draining it completely. Finally rotating the empty jar on top, where it firmly stuck; "Koroleva," he gleefully declared. He then did the same to me stating: "Korol."

The idiot, nearly suffered a hernia hysterically laughing whilst declaring; "Queen and King".

He then strolled over to the office with Leonidas, leaving English Joe to offer his farewells: "James has stated some Russians will come tomorrow, who will escort you.

"So goodbye, and enjoy your last night together... you won't untie those cords, believe me."

The shutter raised. They all left. It lowered again. Darkness; apart from the fire escape lighting and pain... and that most severe, along with saturating sticky honey. I could do nothing for my new friend Galina other than offer words of comfort and assure her that if we now proceed very methodically, we will get out of this mess.

"How will we get free, Ric? These cords are tight They cut into my flesh, I have honey in my eyes and my arm is covered in bee stings. This is no good Ric."

"Galina. I have a knife. The difficult part is how to get it and then how to cut these tight cords. A steak knife is secured to my shoulder blade with sticky tape. With the knife, we will be out of here pronto."

"I cannot possibly reach your shoulder blade, Ric. It is too high. My hands at back."

"Listen Galina. Roll on to the floor and face away from me. I will do the same. When we are back to back we are at the same level. Agreed?"

Galina could see the plan I had in mind and twisted her chair till she was on the floor. I did the same. We were then sideways back to back. Our hands almost touching.

"Slide yourself if you can, and move your hands up to the position of my shoulders."

With a lot of twisting, grunting and shuffling Galina managed to get into that position.

"Right, now your hands, although tied are just inches away from the knife, so you must wriggle into a position whereby you can grab the handle of the knife. Try it now. It is stuck to my back facing downwards. You have got to get under my shirt and grab the handle… then pull it down. It won't be easy but it is the only chance we have, so you have to do it!"

With a lot more shuffling, and considerable grunting I could feel Galina's fingers slowly creeping under my shirt and up my back. Several attempts… this took a good thirty minutes.

"I've got it!" I could feel her fingers around the knife handle on my back.

"I've got it," she said again, "but 11 don't know how I can pull it. These cords are so tight and they cut into me."

I told Galina to hold the handle as tight as she possibly can and I will move away, shuffling the chair with my feet. "You stay put."

"Hold on to it and let me pull away from you, and it should come away, eventually!"

This took another fifteen minutes and with the sticky tape "crackling" the knife surrendered its hold and I felt it become free. Bloody sticky tape… quality, far too good!

"Hold on to it, Galina, and I will nudge myself away from you, and with luck, you still holding the knife. OK, do you think it is possible?"

"It's possible Ric but painful. I do it. You move more and it is coming away from you now!" Galina lay still… panting as if she had run the hundred metres. I asked if she was OK.

"I have it. It is wet, I think one of us is bleeding!"

"Not to worry, whatever you do, don't drop the bloody thing. It's up to you now. See if you can find a piece of cord that it securing me to the chair first.

Then cut that before you attempt to cut some of the cord around my wrist... OK?"

Galina made a hold and successful attempt which took several more minutes, my hand became loose, then free, then at last, she was able to cut more cords and I parted from the chair.

Rolling away I took the knife, now bloody! And freed my legs and the remaining cords around my other wrist. It was difficult to stand. I stood with a bent back like a ninety-year-old.

My body was protesting at the position it had been in for... far too long.

I bent down to look at the poor honey bedraggled form of Galina lying flat sideways on the floor tied to the chair. I carefully cut her cords.

She stretched out flat on the floor gasping, rubbing her wrists and clearing honey from her eyes. What a pitiful sight! Filthy from rolling on the floor, numerous areas of spilt blood, covered in sticky honey, bee stings along our arms resembling a mis-coloured map of the moon, and deep red cord indentation marks around our wrists. I could never declare I was a tourist now!

When she was ready, I helped Galina to her feet.

She grabbed me and we hugged... a sort of affectionate freedom hug between spies!

"Get this tape off me please," I opened my waistcoat and shirt to reveal the adhesive tape banding. Galina removed it with ease. My torso was a deep red and itched. Jointly, we picked bee stings still remaining in our arms, the pain reducing marginally. I had five stings but Galina had fared far worse than I with a notable count of seventeen, poor lady!

"Oh... you have syp... a rash I think. You look like Red Indian, good to believe you a Huron!" We both struggled to laugh but she was quite right. I was now a honeyed Huron!

"Time to go Galina. My watch says nearing eleven o'clock. Telephone Irina. If she can collect us, tell her it is vital she covers her car seats with a good protective covering. Irina may not object to a honeyed Huron but she won't thank us for honey flavoured car seats! I will mount the pile of boxes again to get more cigarette packets for evidence."

I accompanied Galina to the office and turned on the bank of electric lighting.

With the place illuminated once more, I left her to the telephone call and climbed the "pyramid" of boxes. Taking two packets as before, I opened one to verify the contents. One cigarette stripped, white powder then observed, I descended to the ground finding her waiting.

"Irina is on way in car. We will soon be back at hotel thankfulness Ric," I handed her the packets and she broke several cigarettes open and finger touch tasted each one.

All high-quality heroin on packets with "Sweete Dreams." I take two more packets also from the other box of "Sweet Dreams" with normal tobacco.

"If the young girls who smoke the cigarettes buy the wrong by mistake, they fly to moon without wings, no doubt." We chuckled at that one!

I located Galina's two jemmy's. We did not need to escape via the ladies toilet window on the upper level as previously planned as we now have the rear shutter. Standing by the shutter and control switch, I pressed the green button. The door made its usual clunk as the roller shutter door creaked upwards. I eased Galina outside into the warm night air. When the shutter had reached the top I pressed the red button. It slowly descended; its slow pace allowed me to step out easily also. We were free and able to casually wander down the street, just as I had done so fairly recently. Turning the comer, all was quiet and only a lady walking her dog was seen. She passed us and Galina gave a greeting in Russian. She smiled in acknowledgment and gave a polite reply. How nice to be normal again. Was she too polite to remark: *You two filthy looking characters stink of honey!*

We arrived at the meeting place precisely where Irina had dropped us a few hours earlier. A lot has happened since then! Safely in the car, we were driven back to The Moscow Star, too late for the pre-arranged dinner. Upon arrival, now clearly seen under the electric light of the hotel lobby, we were obviously met with some amazement by both Irina and Monika. There were considerable verbal exchanges in Russian most of which went "over my head" but the parts I did pick out were: "Chto oni nadelali,"… and… "Moy bog,"… and… "Chto eto?" which roughly translates to: "What have they done,"… and… "My God,"… and… "What is it?" to which we calmly replied: "Honey!" and we will tell you the whole story later. I held out my arm.

A Russian equivalent, provided by Monika of Calamine soothed cooled our bee stung arms. Whilst Galina and myself had a quick but thoroughly deserved shower in our rooms, and change of clothes – all quite necessary, Monika and another waitress, still up and about, made sandwiches, baguettes, cold meat and cheese and gallons of coffee. Just passed midnight, but human again! Now quite fatigued we agreed to meet at breakfast time, 9:00 am. Soon into our respective rooms, I imagine Galina "dropped off" as quickly as I did. No "demons of the night" to contend with, I slept through to 8 am, sufficient time to get sorted for breakfast. My personal appearance no longer an embarrassment to other guests!

Monika and one other waitress buzzed about serving whilst Galina, Irina and myself enjoyed a hearty hot breakfast and considerable dialogue relating to the recent events.

"You be in trouble now they look for you more as your escape not welcome by those men," stating the somewhat obvious by Irina, she continued: "Your passport was arrive at 3 pm in night. I don't know why so early but Monika have it now." We spent a good two hours chatting about the ordeal and what would be our next plan of action when Monika came into the dining room. She said Galina was wanted on the telephone, and she seemed to be in tears. Galina left us and returned a few minutes later and she was in tears.

"I have to go home very quick now. They have fire bombed my cafe. The police say one dead."

"Oh bloody hell! are you serious Galina… we will come with you… lets go straight away." Irina quickly brought the car round to the front of the hotel and she drove like a "bat out of hell" in order to get to Cafe Brodsky as soon as possible… or rather what was left of Cafe Brodsky!

Upon arrival there was an element of carnage!

An array of vehicles, stationary, crisscrossed locations, coloured flashing and rotating lights on the top of numerous vehicles and some flood lights which have since been extinguished.

A barrier was positioned across the road with a few armed police (or military?) officious looking personnel, fire engines and ambulances still in attendance. We did a "u turn" and parked a hundred metres from the scene and walked back.

Galina and Irina was confronted by a guard. A lot of talk ensued. ID was shown and the guard called to what I assumed to be a superior officer… more talk! All four turned to look at myself standing alone and nodding, followed by the superior officer beckoning me to come forward. We three were then allowed through as the guard lifted the security tape crossing the highway. Smoke was still rising from the building that once was Cafe Brodsky.

The buildings to either side were also badly damaged. People were sweeping charred debris and glass from the footpath and highway into containers.

Ironically the only window I could determine to be intact was the one where we sat when last dining at Brodsky's. This was held in place by the many affixed advertising posters. In war time they did this with sticky tape.

Several press (I assumed them to be) were talking to residents and making written notes.

We three, then seen by some as new arrivals and possibly better stories, pounced on us rattling off questions after telling us which paper they represented. My two lady friends would have nothing to do with them so, they started on me. That was a waste of time.

"He is deaf," shouted Galina. That of course stopped them in their tracks, a perfect conversation killer, I must remember that one! We three wandered back and forth viewing the sad demise of the buildings with still some bedraggled people seated on the footpath being attended by medics. These were presumably not too badly affected and not requiring hospitalization. There was a dead dog laying in the road, badly burnt and blackened by the smoke. Won't someone cover him up were my thoughts? And a smashed flattened birdcage, a parrot or budgie had met their maker.

A lot of furniture also decorated the footpath and highway in an attempt to save some of the unfortunate resident's property... some blackened, some charred, some salvageable. Firemen were still dashing about, in and out of each of the premises especially as smoke was still in evidence and various "hot spots" would require to be controlled and eliminated.

We walked right up to the front door of Cafe Brodsky and looked in... "devastation!" Tables and chairs were the only things recognizable and they were scattered, blackened and burnt laying tipped in various attitudes. The furniture was only recognizable because we knew them. An officer who looked quite senior was standing nearby ensuring no one entered any of the three properties. Galina took the opportunity of asking the question about injuries.

She translated for me: "We know little about the extent of injuries," commented the officer. "There are some here you can see being attended to, not serious, but for others who mainly suffered smoke inhalation and minor burns, all but one were taken to hospital. It seems there was a bomb blast and one lady was instantly killed. We know very little other than she was sleeping and that is where she was found, on the top floor bedroom in Cafe Brodsky. I am not empowered to give any further details, name etc. at present, until she is positively identified and named, but she definitely has been killed by the blast." Galina sank to the floor staring outwards, her eyes fixed on nothingness.

Her words were slow, quiet and laboured.

"It's Svet... Svetlana, my housemaid. She stay when I go out for the night. She stay for security reason. To look after the cafe. She asleep, I know it, they put bomb to kill, not Svet but me! They think it me asleep last night and they try to kill me! They think they kill me but they have killed Svet... a lovely lady... Svetlana." She then broke down and sobbed. Irina and I dropped to the floor placing our arms across her shoulders. Irina cried too and I came close to it!

The officer asked if she knew the dead lady. Obtaining a positive reply gave the name and location of the hospital mortuary where the deceased Svetlana, or assumed to be Svetlana, had been taken. Irina jotted the information down on a note pad.

Galina became more relaxed after a rest and we decided to venture to the mortuary. Irina knew of its location.

Apparently a Medical Centre with a small mortuary attached. Its main use was for accidents in the locality. We easily parked and without parking fees (unlike the UK!) Leaving the car we entered a smart reception area.

Galina took control here and in Russian gave all the information that was requested by the receptionist and filled in copious forms. (A bit like the UK!)

It was quite acceptable that we were not relatives, only acquaintances, and that Galina was her permanent employer.

If this was Svetlana, Galina informed the lady that she had no known living close relatives. Examining the data in a book the receptionist was surprised to see another visitor (us) so soon to identify the body. Only a few hours ago two others came?

We were informed official representatives from Lubyanka had already been saying very little, other than stating the body was; "not her" and then left.

Questions were not asked of the officials. One does not ask too many questions of those from Lubyanka... as the famous phrase says: "We ask the questions!" (and that is not in jest) The two officials were very business-like and rudely indifferent as far as the corpse was concerned. One plain clothes male and one in a military uniform with holster. Both "stony faced" was the receptionists' comment.

Forms all completed, we were then accompanied along a corridor up to a large door with a keypad control. We were told to knock and wait. We did, and in seconds a white coated female opened the door. We handed her the paperwork and shown into a rather cold formidable clinical room. We stood and silently waited. The room was cold.

The lady mortician checked the number on the form and selected the corresponding number on the front of a hatch like door. There were approximately twenty doors, all supporting long numbers. Galina translated for me, as stated by the lady mortuary attendant: "To be prepared."

"It is not a pretty sight. The body has been burnt and disfigured by what seemed to be a blast." The mortician pulled out a door attached to a sliding trolley which when fully extended, stopped. The body was covered in a fawn-coloured sheet. We stood aside the trolley and the lady gently pulled the sheet from the face of the corpse.

We all gasped and Galina lost her speech as she swallowed, choked air and gulped simultaneously. No words came… Galina slowly nodded.

"It's her, it's Svetlana. Its Svetlana Morasova. My housemaid. She worked for me at Cafe Brodsky." The mortician asked how sure she was, because the state of the body could lead to confusion.

"I know it's her. Although the hair has been burnt I still recognise her, and do you see the half of her finger is missing. I was with her when that accident happened five years ago. It's her. Its Svetlana."

The body was re-covered with the sheet and the trolley then slid back into its slotted compartment. The assistant told us to return to the reception area and complete a form. We slowly wandered down the corridor supporting Galina who was understandably visibly shaken. We all were.

It was a terrible sight to see a body like that, so burnt and contorted in death.

The reception area reached, Galina then confirmed the name of the deceased person and undertook various s personal signatures declaring her statement that it was Svetlana Morasova, home address to be forwarded by Galina when she is able to retrieve her employee staff documents.

We sat in the car for many minutes discussing what we had seen and the possible reasons why Svet had been killed. Galina now certain she was the intended victim and suspected "the State" to be the responsible. They now know they have removed the wrong person and this demonstrates how ruthless they can be.

"We have many enemies, not only of Russia, the English Embassy, James, but mafia running the heroin trade also." Irina added.

"We be now vigilant as to what we do, where we go and who we talk Ric. I need to consult my department and get cigarettes to them now and you will telephone your London office people? Maybe London and our department talk about it together too?"

"Yes, certainly," came my response. "Let's get back and we will meet again later."

"Galina, What can we do to help you? What about your cafe, what are you going to do now?"

"Do you want come back and stay with us, Galina at hotel?" inquired Irina.

"I will get back to look at the cafe. When I can get in I go to find things. I stay tonight now at Borodinos. I have flat there also. I need to find more what happened."

Irina concluded: "We drive now and meet tomorrow at Moscow Star at noon yes, after telephone?"

Irina drove Galina in the first instance back to Brodsky's and after dropping her off, returned to the Moscow Star. Monika was in a distressed state waiting for information. She was particularly horrified at events as relayed by her sister. Difficult to "put it gently".

The following day I went for a walk, once again, down to the River Moskva to clear my thoughts. I needed to be quite concise and defined as to how matters should now proceed, if indeed my opinion counted? I once was a person simply looking for information. Now I surely am wanted by the Russian secret service, the Mafia drug smugglers and even my own British Embassy!

There is no hiding place. I do need positive direction from the department.

After a good long break, looking at the craft passing by on the river, I wandered back to the hotel. Irina was at the desk I asked if I could make the phone call now. Charges will be reversed.

Monika was in the back office at that time finishing a phone call herself, so Irina and I chatted for a while about possible future danger for us all. There were many! And how we could assist Galina after the fire. That was yet to be determined. Monika then came out and I went in.

Seated comfortably at a desk in the back office I telephoned my department, reversing charges. I was soon connected to the bureau "top dog" known as Blue. It is "Department Blue 17" – don't blame me, I don't choose the titles! I gave "Blue" all the latest information and full descriptions of all events, summarizing by requesting;

"Can I now return to the UK?"

"No. Not yet."

"I have completed my mission as far as I can. This character English Joe receives documents from someone… from whom I do not know… but it is obvious he then passes the information on to a man "James" at the British consul in Moscow. He must be the one who is doing his bit with the Russians. This handover, takes place at the Glavny Magazine. So, that is it, mission accomplished. Why can I not return to the UK?"

"You can't."

"I now have my passport, so why not sir?" I continued to be polite.

I can imagine "Blue" seated at his desk calmly munching a doughnut in one hand, sipping tea with the other whilst holding the phone a considerable distance from his ear, whilst his eyes roll upwards… and that is difficult unless you've got three hands! Of course, he has a desk receiver. "Why not?"

"From what you have told me, you will be blocked at the airport. The Embassy will have liaised with the Russian authorities and reporting you as an undesirable. You cannot fly from there. They would block your homeward passage, no doubt."

Its bloody infuriating. Blue always seems to put his finger firmly on the problem. Perhaps that is why he is there and I am here?

"This is far from amusing sir. I am still suffering from painful ribs where I was thumped. My blackened eye still shows signs of that event also. Added to that my jaw now clicks when I eat, that's a new one after the thumping at Glavny's.

"I was locked in a cell at Lubyanka and deprived of food and sleep, a thug called Maxim tried to stab me. I was struck on the back with a baseball bat. Numerous painful bee stings I received with a dressing of honey and most of all… I am now seemingly friendless and wanted even by the English Consul officials. The Russian's at Lubyanka placed an electronic tracking device in me resulting in two stitches subject to its removal and last of all, the Mafia drug smugglers would no doubt like to have words with me! I need to get out of Moscow and it is only fair because I have completed my task here. Don't you think I've had my share… sir?"

"When you leave you will not be able to depart Russia by plane. When the time is right, you will hire a car, drive to Belarus. We will organise new flight arrangements from Minsk to the UK.

"It is unlikely any border control at Belarus will know anything of you. There is little control going from Russia to Belarus only coming the other way, so you should have no difficulty."

"Oh bloody hell. Sorry sir, but I'm stack here then? Looking behind my back at every comer wondering when the fast car will pull up and then be shoved in the back seat by male gorillas, never to be seen again. Hardly reasonable when I've done my bit?" My reasoning met no sympathy. "You will check into the Moscow Marriott Hotel in three days' time. It is in Tverskoy, so not too far. All will be arranged today and paid for. Open ended, so you don't know how long your stay as a tourist will last, visiting friends and relatives… got it? Avoid too much contact at the Moscow Star Hotel after you move to the Marriott. Too dangerous.

"Do not leave the hotel now. I will telephone you at one o'clock with new instructions."

"Thank you Hartland. Goodbye." The phone went down and so did any hopeful thoughts of returning to the UK. Drive to Belarus! That must be four to five hundred miles easily? Ooohhh!

With that rather devastating news I wandered into the garden for a "slump" into a soft garden chair waiting for noon. Galina arrived a little late (forgivable under the circumstances) and we were then joined by Irina in the dining room. We ordered our favourites from the menu and I was careful not to mumble any dissatisfaction that may occur. Actually they didn't!

Galina told of the dreadful conditions of her once loved café and also the heartache of those who lived in other properties, not to mention the shop immediately next to Cafe Brodsky that was now "dead" as far as the future business livelihood was concerned.

Many injuries reported, none too serious thus far and one deceased. It could have been worse was Galina's comment two of Brodsky's waiters had disappeared and that was mysterious? They had not been part of the group of casualties sent to hospital, and no sign of them at their residences.

Is the net of intrigue spreading wider?

We were about to go into future plans when, prior to the arrival of our food. A waitress came to the table;

"It is phone for you so sir calling you now Mr Hartland. In office."

I looked at my watch. Crack on the hour of one, as predicted. I took my now well acquainted position in the back office. The receiver laying on the desk... "Hello?"

"Hartland?"

"Yes."

"Who am I?"

"Sir?"

"Who am I?"

"Blue sir... Blue."

"OK. To business. We have checked this line and it is not tapped but we must always be careful. The Marriott Hotel is all booked as stated previously. We have investigated your man at the British Embassy. He is James Macilroy, ex captain, retired of the marines, aged forty five. We will now try to embarrass him to such an extent that he will either surrender and admit his nefarious activities or alternately scoot... or if not, he must be permanently removed. Understood?"

"He must... be... what?"

"I'm sure you understand my instructions Hartland. Don't waste telephone time."

"Removed! You are suggesting that. I... eliminate him?" (I gulped my reply) "Don't be as ass man. If the time comes for that course of action we will send out a colleague from Blue 21. You don't have that type of authorisation. Now do you understand? Firstly we go for the gentle approach. We are not animals?"

"Yes, of course... but... I thought you meant..." He interrupted.

"Let me tell you what you must do. Macilroy's estranged wife is the first line of our attack. Pay her a visit and dig some dirt on her husband. She hates him but with her elaborate lifestyle she needs the money he brings in. She is not satisfied with the Embassy pay, all be it absurdly high, she needs a lot more in her allowance to satisfy her insatiable need for jewels, cars, furs etc. and possibly drugs, that part we do not know. We need to find his Achilles heel and then strike and blackmail if necessary. If that doesn't work then it is a job for Department Blue 21."

"You can't do that surely? The women Fedorova and Karashenko are investigating him also and they would not want him ... removed... as you put it They need to ascertain who is involved in the heroin trade and they would not want him out of it... not just yet. He might be the top dog? Why are the two departments not coordinating this?"

"The two women, actually its three, her sister Monika Karashenko is also part of the set up in Moscow but in a lesser way. They work for the Russian side which is also directed from London, but that is in Whitehall, not us at Vauxhall. If those buffoons at the Whitehall Foreign Office choose not to let us in on things then, so be it So, if you want to be of assistance to them whilst doing your best for our department then it is important that you do not fail. I don't want to authorise a Blue 21 operation but I will if there is no alternative. Macilroy must be stopped in some way, so it is up to you Hartland isn't it… my ol' chum? let me add… succeed, and you might be good material for an upgrade to Department Blue 18."

"I would sooner go down to Blue 16 if it's all the same to you, sir?" He laughed, but it was fact.

"Let me tell you about Capt. J Macilroy, so you are aware of his capabilities. Ex-marine, as you know. Third, Dan in Marshall arts and a regular trainer. Considerable experience in jungle warfare so he is no pushover. Don't get phased by the smart arse suits, he is potentially dangerous and he won't take it kindly to losing his source of income from the heroin trade. It's very big money and so is the passing of secret documents. He must also be highly paid from that also. So, watch him carefully and as said, find his Achilles heel. Take two weeks to undertake this then I will arrange for your plane ticket to be transferred, and heigh he. Back to the UK with due adoration."

"Two weeks… but…"

"Good, then if that's all, I'll just fill you in with Madam Macilroy's address. Got a pen and paper? Her name is Pavvla Ilyana Vassilieva Macilroy, quite a mouthful. (I then also wrote down the address as dictated.) It's a smart pad and I think she has a housekeeper which might make things awkward. Her town house is in the Tverskaya neighbourhood, a tall mewsey type of house with integrated parking.

"Very cosy and well situated for the city nightlife. Her main residence where she lives during the week is in the Ostozhena otherwise known as – The Golden Mile. These properties are multimillion dollar houses. I wouldn't recommend you go there. Big gates and big roaming dogs to match. I won't give you that address, no point, you can find her at her Moscow town house address.

"She is Russian by birth but grew up in London, that is where she met her husband. She is a retired actress. Acted under the name of Blossom Pavvla… yes honestly!

"Only in her thirties but with her big fat allowance, no longer needs to work. Her role in life is totally dedicated to hedonistic self-centred, selfish fun."

"A pretty lady but not a particularly nice one by my standards, but you might think otherwise? A lot of money is needed to have a town house in Tverskaya and a mansion in Ostozhena. The type of income I imagine one would get from drug dealing on a large scale and we know who that is!"

"Is it in order, if I hire a car?" A tame request from me!

"Yes. I have already agreed with you that all sensible expenses will be accepted. Just keep all invoices. Now, you have all I know. Keep in touch. Bye Hartland, and good luck." Phone down. He always does that! The bugger dishes out the dirt then "plunk" down goes the receiver!

I returned to the dining room and sat, facing my cooling Solvanka dish. The puzzled expression on my face betrayed my thoughts and obviously intrigued the two ladies.

"Trouble is for you now?" asked Irina.

"Amongst other things I am required to "dig the dirt" on James Macilroy the Embassy official, blackmail him if necessary (I carefully avoided the execution idea) and also meet his ex-wife to see if I can ascertain anything from her. Just like that! He makes it all sound so easy; he always does! Do you know where I can hire a car?" Irina paused and inquired…

"Dig the dirt?" Galina explained in Russian.

"Let us not worry much about anything now. We like our food today and leave other for tomorrow. Come to Borodinos tomorrow for lunch us three and then we make plan. You talked to your office; I talk to mine then we know more. First come to Brodsky and I show you bad damage by fire. Then Borodinos, and I take you to Hertz for car hire. You happy with plan, yes? Come to Brodsky tomorrow at noon. We eat at one."

We all agreed and enjoyed our meal without the encumbrances yet to be planned.

We parted and I grabbed my book for a quiet read in the garden. It was difficult however to concentrate as "again" my troubled thoughts went over and over what I must undertake.

I just could not fathom what to do. I must make a plan, but what plan? it will come! I don't really want to be part of a team that executes Embassy officials! It's down to me to resolve this.

One hour later I found myself waking after an unplanned doze with closed book on the grass.

I had been rather remiss and forgot to repair the torn cover. It was fortunate the waitress that loaned the sticky tape was not serving today… oh that sticky tape! I am still showing the red rash around my torso. The concealed knife idea worked and probably saved the lives of two people, me being one of them! Thank you scientific whiz kids! Eternally grateful!

Nothing else to report for the remainder of the day. Early dinner and later I watched Russian television in the TV room aside the lounge… weird!… but I suppose it's different from what I am used to. The torn cover of "War and Peace" repaired with the infamous sticky tape and returned to the waitress who was seen at dinner time, with a promise… she said in her very broken English, but principally Russian that "I could have it again if needed." I hope not!

The following morning I "caught" Monika and Irina at Reception desk. Whilst Monika was checking a couple out, I asked if Irina would come to the front In a quiet comer, inquired if I could have a place in the car park for a hired car. She readily agreed. Boldly I added a probing question about Monika's injuries and her attackers. We all knew she had not tumbled down stairs, I had been informed of the attack previously during "my stay" at Lubyanka.

"Ahh, yes, the men, they from Lubyanka. They visit to all hotels. They want know who stays and who people are and what they do and many questions also. My sister angry, they ask too many and she say; *You ask too much. It is for hotel to know guests unless criminal.* They take broom from my sister and beat her and punch and kick. They not nice men. No go to tell police, they no notice of it so not to do it. They no help. So that is it Ric. Is OK?"

"Yes. Thank you. I thought that is what had happened. See you later for travel to Brodsky's?"

Chapter 6

I still pondered as to what I can achieve regarding the two Macilroys, but it will come. There will be something that triggers an idea… but inspiration has not yet arrived. It will, it has too!

I confirmed departure time with Irina and went in to breakfast. I thought about returning the steak knife but erring on the cautious side, or was it the pessimistic side, decided to retain it. A good hiding place was found in my bedroom. It would not look good if the maid found it whilst carrying out room service.

We will travel by Marshrutka to Cafe Brodsky at eleven s clock (or what is left of it) to meet Galina at noon as arranged. I'm hoping her advisers at the Russky department has found on easier resolution to offer, different from mine. The assassination idea worries me, but it might be the only way if I cannot come up with something. A scheme is out there waiting, but I just haven't found it yet!

Eleven o'clock; I with Irina wander down to catch the Marshrutka. The Bus arrived after ten minutes and we sat "near the bus driver". I told Irina why I preferred that particular seat!

Moments of silence were interrupted by us both speaking simultaneously. An indication that a lot of personal thinking was taking place. It certainly was for me! She stated there was a lot of difficult times ahead for me but probably not for her or Galina. It did appear that they had fulfilled their task in establishing the storage of heroin at the Glavny store and the actual capture of the Mafia gang would surely be for the State police to intervene, but I do not know how their department operates. I wonder if they do? I don't really know how my Department Blue organisation operates. I, along with numerous others just do as we are instructed… "Follow instructions," we are told. After depositing a few tonne of diesel fumes generously, the bus arrives at our stop. Irina thanks the driver in Russian. He "grunts" a reply in everyman's language. He could be a London bus driver!

We were not too distant from Cafe Brodsky and near enough to smell the charred remains of the fire in the air. The street and footpath was now clear although few signs a streaked black marks still evident from the harsh sweeping that had been necessary. Glad to see the dog had gone.

There had been a lot of boarding up to all three properties but the Brodsky front door was propped open and inside we met Galina along with some remaining staff who were doing a clean-up on a major scale. Galina somewhat resembled a character from a Dickens novel... the ones that went up chimneys. She stripped off her once white overalls as she greeted us both.

"Stair OK and safe. I take you round if you like yes?"

We followed her up to the top floor where her bedroom was (is). The charred timbers became worse as we ascended the staircase. One boarded up window at the top level had been altered to allow it to open, no glass. She opened it and the smell of burnt wood lessened. We entered the bedroom. The ceiling was gone as was most of the wall plaster. The bed, what was left of it, was a charred and twisted mess. Pieces of metal scattered around the room; metal shards were also embedded in the wall like vicious shrapnel that one sees in war films. The result of the blast was clear to see. The shards in themselves would have easily killed. It required little explanation as to why Svetlana was in such a pitiable condition. The blast from the bomb must have finished the poor lady instantly. They were stains, scrubbed stains, fortunately impossible to determine their originality. The whole building was saturated from the fire hoses. I felt tearful, no apologies, enough to make the strongest cry! Irina did. We comforted her. Galina stated she has had many sessions such as that herself. We stood staring in disbelief... disbelief that anyone could do this, but regrettably we know they do. It is frightening to consider "they" whoever "they" are may try this again because their intended victim, happily, is still with us. We had seen enough of this damage so gingerly descended the stairs holding on to handrails where they had survived.

We three went straight out into the open air at the front of Cafe Brodsky and inhaled deeply. There are times when words are not necessary, this was one of those times. This was an unpleasant experience. Visiting a burnt property was certainly not enviable but to be in the room where a lady had been killed was beyond words... it left an impression, a feeling, a deep sadness.

Irina was the first to speak and it almost made me jump.

"That horror Galina. We come back and help another day yes. We go now for lunch?"

Galina nodded in agreement. She had already removed her overall's but still had the signs of the chimney sweep on her hands and face. She examined herself.

"Yes, we go now to Borodinos. Hope you don't mind walk Ric? It is two kilometres from here and a good walk now, but not so good in rain times, but today is nice for that. I will wash when we get there. The water at my Cafe has been turned off. They think it breaks in water pipeline and they come tomorrow to mend fracture."

"Fracture?" Irina's question. Galina gave explanation in Russian.

"Fracture… is a break, yes. I am learning new English words many times now."

The pleasant stroll along the high road and then on to "B roads" was certainly quite pleasant as Galina had stated. The two kilometres passed quickly. I spent a lot of time looking at the different buildings and the way some of them were spaced and others crammed in. The two ladies chatted principally in Russian to each other as we walked. I did not feel excluded, they are not those type of people. There were occasional words that I knew and very often the conversation was about the food selection that was on the menu today. Fifteen minutes or so later we arrived at Borodinos. Quite a surprise. It was set facing the road but detached with an entrance to a small car park leading to the rear. A two storey building and newish in design. Galina later informed me it had been a garage for car repairs originally but with State intervention all was changed for the better.

The possibility of "rich pickings" foreseeable by the State was obviously on their agenda; "You work hard, and we take a lot." A bit like our tax system in the UK!

Through what was an impressive and inviting front door, we ventured through a lobby and into the reception area. Galina was obviously instantly recognized and a waitress greeted us all and took us to a table. Galina then gave her apologies and disappeared to make her way to a back room for a welcome scrub to remove all the sooty black marks. She returned fifteen minutes later, clean, made up nicely and hair brushed. It was the Galina that we have come to know.

We all wanted coffee and that was quickly served. Freshly ground in a large cafetiere. Cream and sugar placed aside. We were handed menus and the waitress disappeared leaving us to choose. It was all written in Russian.

"Don't say it Ric! I know… you will eat anything as long as they remove the hooves! I remember that well." We three laughed. I however continued to peruse the menu appearing more conversant than I really was. A long discussion ensued and all agreed on what we wanted. Three courses will set us up for some considerable time. Rolls and butter kept us going whilst we waited for the first course. We soon led on to "business".

"I have instructions from my department. We are to do nothing more for this time. There will be another team of armed men who go to Glavny some Friday. They hope to catch them. They may go in early in morning to hide first to surprise, but that I do not know the plan, but they now take charge of this raid. It will be quiet for us for a next week." Irina then added: "It is like you say, Commando raid. Some may shoot, some may not live. Dangerous." This troubled me to some extent. It is excellent that the Mafia drug dealers will be caught "with their trousers down" and doubtless dragged off unceremoniously, but the man I want is James Macilroy and I don't want him 'removed' not quite yet, before I have the chance to carry out my investigations. I need to find out who his contacts are regarding the passing of UK government documents. I explained this in detail and it was clearly understood by both ladies.

"It gives you time to find out more Ric before our team go in. They, I sorry say but, they not interested in your office. We all on same side but we operate very different in Russia."

Whilst chatting and waiting for the food I took the opportunity to peruse the room. All was carefully undertaken displaying taste, and possibly with a strong feminine influence. Perimeter plaster swag and drop plaster cornices were evident and pleasant chandelier (but modest) lights scattered over the ceiling. Rectangular plaster moulding displays systematically placed on the walls showing pictures centrally placed in the centre, both black and white and coloured.

Asking Galina, she replied they were all pictures showing various scenes depicted by different artists, "just Prints" she disclosed, of the battle of Borodino (what else!) The furniture was attractive and comfortable, suitable for its purpose. Tables placed with low dividing screens to offer some degree of privacy for the diners. A lot of money spent and the result was very pleasant. "I love your restaurant Galina, the decoration, design and layout is fabulous. The pictures of Borodino most appropriate. I recall from my poor education days the battle was approx. two hundred years ago and unfortunately lost by Russia. There was some dispute about it… the battle won by the French but not decisively for some other reason?"

"That's correct Ric, but we got our own back later." I did not go further on that subject!

Our first course arrived. It was served by a young lad. He looked about 12! Galina could easily determine I was a little phased at being served by one so young. Would those requiring hot soup regret their choice? Irina commented when he left our table;

"I not like him. He is big trouble. He play jokes on me and I not think it funny." Galina laughed; "He know I don't like Lyagushka… what are they in English Galina?"

"Frogs!"

"That is it. He put rubber frogs on my chair when I go to the toilet. I not think it funny."

"Oh, yes. The other time we came, he did that to Irina. He is a joking lad but good at job and his father work here too, many years. Both good at their works and can be trusted."

"He is so young; he looks about twelve. He would be too young to serve in a dining room in England, even though he might be good at what he does, he is still very young."

"You are mistaking Ric It is a pass on from his father and grandfather. The Denisovitch's, they are very small people. His mother too. She is 1300 mm and his father is 1500 mm tall. That is why he is so small. Ivan the boy is eighteen years of age Ric, not twelve.

"Everyone call him Peren Denisovitch… that mean Boy Denisovitch… his proper name is Ivan but I do not think anyone know his name. That why they call him Paren… Boy in English. You understand the measuring of the people, Ric?"

"Oh, yes, I do."

"I still do not like him." Irina obviously very perturbed about the frog trick, "and the other time, he do thing with soup but not for me." Galina filled me in, so to speak.

"Oh yes, that with my permission. He want to do trick on old Uncle. Uncle who plays tricks on him too. He order Gazpacho soup; you know it, Ric? cold soup. Ivan make soup with a coloured gelatine. It look like soup but when you put spoon, it bounce. You follow? (I did)… oh and the roll. He had joke bread roll made of poly… What is it?"

"Polystyrene?"

"Yes, that is it polystyrene and with weight so it is just like a bread roll." He uncle-laughed so much he knock soup bowl on to floor, but it did not spill, it just wobbled! Then he try to cut roll. Everyone laughed. Galina and I were laughing too, but Irina expressed a long sour face.

"It funny for some but I not like him," Galina nudged her;

"Oh, Irina, smile he is only a happy lad who likes to play fun. No one hurt. Best to laugh eh? You know it only for fun. His father is same, just as much he likes to play tricks but not bad ones." Irina was never going to laugh in a million years. I watched the joking lad… Ivan the boy paren, and for me it was one of those "bubble moments" – a bubble almost appeared above my head!

A bubble of inspiration. I verbally whispered out loud: "I've got it!" They both looked me puzzled. (Not for the first time!) We ate and talked.

I was in the embryonic stages of hatching a plan. It had arrived at last! The oldest and perhaps the corniest method of all time. To get someone in a compromising position and photograph them. Contrived photos will always be examined and subsequently found to be fraudulent but not genuine ones; they always tell the truth.

"I will not go into this idea at the moment, it is only just forming in my mind, but I need to place the Captain… James Macilroy in a photo so he can be blackmailed. I will work this out over the next twenty four hours and we can discuss the possibility fully. What I will need are the players. A male who looks like a young boy, much younger than he really is, and likes to play jokes on people. Is player number one sounding familiar?"

Both, in unison, said: "Yes… Paren Denisovitch!"

"Two others would also be needed willing and taken into our confidence. It's a tall order but…"

"What is tall order?" (I've lost Irina again.) Galina explained tall order.

"One male any age, and another person male or female, any age to take a photo… the difficulty of course is to ensure they are willing to play this trick… this joke." Irina added: "I have camera, I take pictures that are good many times."

"My idea would really need someone who does not live in this neighbourhood and would not mind doing this to an Englishman."

"Oh, easy for this Ric. My cousin Kristina she is better than, she take photos for hobby, sometimes get into magazines she really good and she hate the English... sorry Ric! Her brother, Viktor, other cousin is not same. He loves English and goes to England many times for holiday. I think he just to do it to make her angry. They always talk bad things to each other, all times. All the times they fight like cat and donkey..."

"Dog."

"Oh yes fight like cat and dog. Sometimes they not seem really peopled from some place... but for Kristina I think she will do photos of Englishman to get him trouble and..."

Galina interrupted: "Who else, Ric?"

"That's about it, as I said I will work out the plan in detail later. One to take photos, one small lad and one other male who can play a good part as a drug dealer, I think, yes, that is it, a dealer."

"Paren's father is joker also as said, he is sometime in a dramatic group near his home. He does acting sometimes. He once win competition and was in a Chekov play and they made film. He was waiter, so he should be good eh? In big screen film... he come into room in film carrying a tray with drinks and say: *Your coffee madam.* We heard about that film for many years later!"

"Will he take this part in my idea?"

"Yes, he do what I tell him or no more job." (Galina's tough side appearing.) "So why this plan?"

"Your team will be going in to arrest the drug dealers at the department store. If they catch everyone, then that is good for your organisation but if Macilroy does not turn up on the night, then he gets away with it... so I have this idea to compromise him and possibly get a confession about the passing of documents. This is what one might call a *fall back plan* if he does not show. If we miss him, we get him another way. It's a bit low but effective. So let me have some time then we can meet again to detail the play and the full cast. Agreed?"

"Agreed, yes, agreed."

We took a considerable time to finish our meal. I could not resist the usual ice cream dish called Morozhende and more coffee at the end. I spent a lot of time casually watching Paren and considered him to be perfect for the confidence trick.

A small boy, photographed in a compromising position with a British Embassy official... already the idea is stacking up nicely!

I paid the bill… they reluctantly agreed.

A visit to the men's room to dispose of the gallons of coffee and a viewing of more pictures of the battle of Borodino to inspect, accompanied by piped music. Just like home. Nice loo… could be in a first class hotel… people who come here obviously respect it and keep it vandal free.

I did my customary plate tidy shuffle. (I can't seem to throw that off!)

We said our farewells to the staff. Doors were politely held and out we went, most satisfied at what we had devoured!

Next, a visit to the car rental people. We three wandered down to the Moskva river direction and the Hertz shop easily located. A nice bright reception area almost similar to a showroom. I was guided by Irina who seemed to have a great knowledge of cars. So, a GAZ was chosen (a new one on me) reputed to be fairly reliable, not thirsty and erring on the good side of "cheap and cheerful" for one week's rental.

The usual form filling was encountered and credit card details taken with a financial pledge to include all matters under a comprehensive insurance cover for a week's driving, extendable if required. My driving licence was examined and notes made. I was informed a full tank of fuel was provided and the car should be returned likewise. Keys were handed over and the lady assistant took we three to the rear of the shop where everything was explained, filler cap etc., etc.

A brief walk around the car as an inspection, and a couple of small dents noted. These were added to a document. The lady and myself signed an endorsement defining the defects. We three jumped in and fortunately I drove away without the embarrassment of kangaroo leaps, customary when driving a new vehicle. I drove back to Cafe Brodsky at the request of Galina.

We mutually agreed to meet again in two days. This time down by the river if the weather permits, at twelve noon. I then drove Irina and myself back to the Moscow Star. Don't think having a car was a means to arrive anywhere quickly! It was very busy, plenty of traffic.

Driving in to the hotel car park, I positioned the car away from other parked vehicles, in a comer and away from a rather menacing hanging branch of an oak tree. Manual key door locking… not a problem! It ran well.

We entered the hotel and agreed the time once again for our next rendezvous. I nipped up to my room for a change of clothes and returned to the garden with book for my next chapter of "War and Peace". Perhaps I might stay awake this time? I didn't!

I awoke and dinner time approaches. I don't know if I can! A slump on the bed to take in some details of what should be next. Perhaps tomorrow morning I might tackle madam Macilroy It is Sunday and I was informed she is at her town address at weekends. So be it.

A light dinner set me up for a finish to the day, again viewing Russian TV. Another spectator had put on a channel showing cartoons. Purile, but at least the visual activity was universal.

An oversized mouse being hit on the head by an even larger oversized bear wielding an oversized broom is the same in any country, and quite amusing! The mouse split in two as the broom struck!

I do hope no animals were injured in the making of this cartoon!

Predictably, I nodded in the chair in front of the TV... so up to bed; it's the right place.

Sunday morning, the day for the encounter with – Pavvla Ilyina Vassilieva Macilroy.

I spent a lot of time over breakfast considering what Madam Pavvla; actress Blossom Pavvla, would be like. Fat, thin, tall, short, beautiful or not. Whatever she is... bound to be a shrewd woman and I must be on my guard. I was well aware a lot might rest on the outcome of today's meeting and I must get things right What I am asking of her could lead to an explosion of accusations, insinuations and perceived insults against both her husband and herself. I have to do this and do it well. If there is anything to find out about James Macilroy this might be the only way. I am playing an important part in a play... a play I don't really want to be in! One more coffee and I will be on my way. Leaving early I thought a visit to The Golden Mile first. I don't know her address but it is a sound idea to see the area... just to ascertain "what she is made of" financially.

A change of clothes, fairly respectable and business like. The car, pleasingly started straight away and I was out into the traffic. Not too busy, today being Sunday.

On reaching "Ostozhena" district I was confused. It was fantastic, in some ways like Las Vegas but not brash. The area oozed wealth and rich upper... very rich upper class, if that is possible in Moscow. A millionaire and Billionaires paradise. I received many an odd look from people as I drove past various double gated mansions. I could almost hear; "He must be a vagrant diving a car like that." Actually, I could excuse them for thinking so!

The whole area made me feel excessively poor.

I "u-turned" and journeyed to Madam Blossom Pavvla's address and found various side street parking places. Some payable, some free. I located a free place, locked and wandered over to the front door. Her house was vast, six floors high and occupying a comer position. Partly overlooking the side street and partly the frontal main high road of Tverskaya Street. All very salubrious!

I rang the doorbell. I heard nothing. Did it work? I rang again. A female answered dressed like a waitress from the Lyons comer house restaurant days… very smart. All in black and white.

"Sir?" (she spoke in English?)

"Good morning. My name is…" (Do I look English?)

"Your card, sir?" I scrambled in my wallet and brought out my ID card (number two, of the three) This false card demonstrated me to be; Mr Richard Hargreaves of the English Government. Foreign Office. London, (all lies) She held out a tray. I placed it on the tray. She glanced at it.

"You wish to see madam?" (She *is* English.) She did not wait for a reply.

"Madam is at church but will be back in a short time, half an hour or so. If you would care to wait. Would you like to come in sir?" I did.

I imagine "Blue" would assume she was at church as an atonement for the previous night's excesses! "Stairs or lift?"

"Stairs will be fine thank you." I followed her up two flights of elegant stairs. She still had my card. "This room, sir." She pointed.

I was shown through elegant double doors into the drawing room. To the uninitiated, that is a room specifically for receiving guests, but it appeared this was her living room or lounge as it may be called. The doors were closed whilst the housemaid simultaneously stated;

"Please ring if you require anything, sir." I wish she wouldn't call me sir!

I sat on a sofa facing the front window. What a sofa! If my bum could speak it would have said, "Quality!" A huge window overlooked the main highway, well soundproofed, very little traffic noise. I sat perched forward and looked around what was a most elegantly decorated and furnished room. The furniture was obviously of the "Louis the something" period. Beautiful huge plaster cornices surrounded an expensively plastered highly patterned ceiling, to a style of a past period. Three glass chandeliers dropping from the high ceiling, again, very elegant.

The walls were papered, strange to see these days. The wall papering travelled across the doors. That is similar to that of French eighteen century chateau's. An odd style today but that was the thing in those days. Numerous tasteful paintings surrounded all walls. Large print by Toulouse... "Divan Japonaise" one of La Goulue and another of "The Troupe de Eglantine" – a wonderful depiction of the Moulin Rouge dancers. A few more small original oils were hanging. Prior to close inspection I did not recognise their master's hand. This lady was clearly fond of the French period. The room appeared to be straight from those elegant houses constructed during the Parisian street reconstruction by Baron Haussmann. This room would easily fit nicely within a high class Paris high street, if "street" is the correct word.

I remained seated for a while. If the housemaid was correct I still had twenty minutes before her Mistress's arrival, so I surrendered to temptation and casually wandered around the room.

Not however surrendering to temptation when viewing china ornaments. I have seen enough films when someone does the inspection and drops the article on the floor. Whatever the manufacturer's name underneath was, it remained a secret.

Along with the numerous paintings there were many photographs of a whole host of people.

Some showing awards won, some family "sit ups" and many more of, hands being shaken and shoulders being hugged by celebs of various categories. Possibly film stars, titled people and politicians. All visual name droppers duly recorded.

All in all, this lady has taste. If I moved in, nothing would change... well, perhaps the personal photographs, but taste, yes, she had it! This is a classy, wealthy, lady.

It is amazing how one could build a picture before an actual encounter. Of the numerous photos displayed, one particular lady, the ages varied, but it seemed natural that it must be Pavvla Macilroy, with the importance of her past defined in black and white for the future posterity.

Whatever this lady is really like? I like her style, as our America cousins might say.

In a comer was an elegant carved metal cane stand. Beautifully crafted and finished in gilt.

Two old walking canes, a large coloured golf umbrella and a golf club. (The only two incongruous articles in the room.) Turning my head I listened. No sign of anyone.

I pulled the club from the stand and read the affixed silver plate indicating an award to Blossom Pavvla, for some kind of celebrity golf day, dated fifteen years ago. My own personal golf lessons had been interrupted by this assignment to Moscow. I was not happy about that!... Only five golf lessons completed and then I was sent here.

I still cannot quite grasp (that's a good word) this strange little finger and thumb technique, the way one has to wrap it into the hand. I don't think I will ever get it? I lowered the club to the floor at suitable angle and endeavoured to hold the club handle with my left hand and then intertwine my right had little finger... thus... yes. That's it ... I think I have it? Slowly lift the club high and swing down, Straight arm... that's good... another go... slowly lift high and... "Clang." Not quite what I planned!

The club had struck the chandelier and was swinging wildly in the air. No shattered glass fortunately but the chandelier drops seemed to be experiencing perpetual motion! Holding the offending weapon, the club, I poked and prodded the glass drops in turn, in order to arrest the movements as the doors opened and in came the maid.

"Sir?" Time for me to be quick witted here!

"Oh... sorry... I saw a large spider and I hate spiders, so... I thought I might dislodge it and..."

"I thought I heard a bang sir. I dusted that this morning. I'm surprised there are any spiders, but if you will allow me?" She gently took the golf club and placed it back into the stand and "I will get my feather duster now if that is acceptable, sir?"

She left the room closing the doors. A few minutes later reappeared with the feather duster on a long pole and proceeded to tackle the glass chandelier. I stood looking up with hands on hips.

"Can't see anything sir, but if you see any more I would be very obliged if you will kindly ring the bell sir. It's on the wall behind you. Thank you sir, will there be anything else?"

I shook my head and sat.

"Madam should not be long now." She left the room. I felt like a naughty schoolboy.

The housemaid was something out of the nineteen twenties and overdosed on "sir" with every opportunity. It was certain that Madam Pavvla was happy to live in the eighteenth or nineteenth century France, whilst using the etiquette of England, but from what has been described by "Blue" enjoying the excesses of twentieth century hedonistic nightlife!

I am building a picture of this lady. I liked her style as previously thought, but will I like her? Does it matter... No! I decided to remain glued to the sofa.

I heard a door bang. I heard voices. The double doors opened and the housemaid entered... holding the doors... in came Madam Pavvla Macilroy. Her expensive perfume invaded the room – fabulous! The housemaid had a silver salva whereby rested my identity card.

PM (sounds like the Prime Minister!) picked up the card and handed to me. She had obviously already "digested it".

"Mr ... Hargreaves. Pleased to meet you, although I am somewhat surprised that someone from the Foreign Office in London should want to see me?"

She approached and proffered two stiff fingers of her right hand. I shook the decorated nails of two fingers delicately. She gestured me to sit. She did also.

PM was wearing a type of fascinator hat. (I think that is what they are called?) For church, very "over the top" I bet the maiden aunts at the service pointed and chatted when she arrived?

She wore a very elegant blue and white thin summer dress that had front splits, carefully designed not to open whilst walking, white tights or would it be stockings? Yes, she is a stockings type of "girl". Pale blue shoes that blended with the pale blue colour of her dress. She looked like a cross between Cleopatra and Madam Arcarti, but both stunning and elegant.

My girlfriend would be proud of my detailed description! The housemaid went to remove the hat but PM held her hand vertically, stationary, next to her ear. The housemaid knew this to be a sign... don't!

PM gradually removed it herself and placed it deftly on to the coffee table next to her. The housemaid left, as she did PM called out: "Maitland, bring some tea and some of your tartlets for Mr Hargreaves and myself would you?"

"Yes madam."

PM chuckled: "I always call them tartlets, to call them tarts sounds like a lady of the night!" (Uumm – she has a sense of humour!) Do I like her? Visually, yes.

"What can I do for you?" PM sat crossed legged with "the split" carefully opened displaying rather attractive knees. Her cat who had been concealed dozing behind the sofa appeared and jumped on to her lap obscuring those elegant knees. She lifted the cat off and repositioned her dress back to the exposed knee position. A style adopted by many a seated provocative female!

I have a facetious saying; when meeting people who have cats... "They have a cat, can't be all bad," but then I found out Lenin liked cats, uumm, probably with chips! She brushed off some imaginary cat hairs and inquired once again;

"What can I do for you Mr Hargreaves. What does Whitehall want with me?"

This was difficult. I have mentally wrestled various ideas, and especially this technique I was about to employ. How does one ask what skeletons are in the cupboard as far as your husband is concerned... and tell them all to me! That is what I needed to know and that is what I cannot state in direct terms but it had to be done.

"This is quite difficult Madam..."

"Pavvla, you may call me Pavvla if you wish?"

"Thank you. I am merely the conveyor of information, so please don't shoot the messenger!"

"The Foreign Office department have been undertaking covert operations to try to bring to justice a violent gang of criminals, currently in Moscow. This has been going on for some considerable time. This tribe of ne'er-do-wells travel from country to country focussing on British Embassy's and specifically diplomats within. Their modus operandi is to find those of importance and preferably with considerable wealth, to find a weakness, or Achilles heel to put it another way. They then blackmail those unfortunates and very often obtain very large sums of money to keep quiet."

"Such persons have no conscience, Mr Hargreaves."

"Quite so. Madam... Pavvla... the extraction of money is regrettably occasionally followed by murder or simply the disappearance of diplomatic officials without trace."

"It has to stop, and I can see you are the man to do it."

"Well, very comforting to know you have such confidence in me, but it is the information that I am assigned to correlate, nothing more. Direct contact with

Embassy officials has proved to be pointless in the past. They, when questioned, just clam up. I think you understand?"

"I do and what do you require of me Mr Har... do you have a Christian name I can't keep calling you Mr Hargreaves now, can I?" Maitland arrived at that moment with tray. Moved a low table near the sofas and daintily placed the tray inquiring: "Shall I pour for you Madam?"

PM shook her head and waved her hand... that silently indicated – "no".

PM poured the tea through a strainer into the most elegant cup on the planet and asked: "Milk, sugar. Do you fancy a tart?" There was only one answer to that;

"Thank you, no sugar, just milk. The lemon one please."

The tart... tartlet was handed to me on matching Shelly plate with cup and saucer.

Is this tart, tartlet, being provocative or just an honest choice of words? PM adjusted her skirt. Whilst doing so her short sleeved dress revealed her arms. No puncture marks noted. If she did take drugs, she appeared not to take heroin via the arm injection route. She does not look like the type of lady who does take drugs, but with her husband's activities, who knows?

"Now where were we? Oh yes, these scoundrels you were telling me about. Do go on."

"We do not involve the Embassy official themselves as I have already stated, so we endeavour to obtain information via other means, assimilate the risk and if such Achilles heels do exist then we try methods to eliminate that risk so as to leave the person no longer vulnerable..."

"In a nutshell, we find out the vulnerability, and eradicate it."

"This is sounding very complicated. Give an example of what you mean?"

"That's easy. If diplomat Mr X is a having his naughty way with Miss Y without the knowledge of his wife Mrs X, then we endeavour to remove Miss Y, then there is nothing to blackmail for."

"Do you mean she... Miss Y is killed?"

"Oh goodness, no, she is paid off handsomely and sent on her way. That is the preferred way. You see, remove the means that a person can be blackmailed."

"That sounds a most admirable achievement Mr Har... but how do I assist you. Another cup?"

"Thank you yes. This involves your husband." She stopped pouring and stiffened... "James?"

"He is an official at the Embassy and we work through all those who could be targeted."

"We are estranged. I have not seen him for two years and only spoken with him once in the last... err... nine months when he failed in his financial commitment to his wife."

"Yes, I am sorry to hear that. It is difficult for you Mada... Pavvla but should those diplomats or those targeted, become exposed in any way, the outcome could result in loss of position, loss of job and naturally loss of income and that also affect those who may rely on that income, such as wife, children etc. Financial ruin can and actually has occurred on a few diplomats. We need to stop this and we have found the most effective way thus far is with the help of family and close friends."

"Oh, yes, I see. If they found something about my ex-husband and perish the thought, he lost his job... that means for me, how shall I put it? I am also ruined financially?"

"You have it Ma... Pavvla! So can you help? I need to know everything about Mr Macilroy, so we can eliminate any likely vulnerabilities and keep him safe and out of the hands of blackmailers. We need our English diplomats to stay safe. The Foreign Office are quite determined. I don't want to alarm you unnecessarily, but there have already been two deaths, not in Russia, but another country, (playing safe here) One embassy official murdered and another committed suicide. That particular official had too many skeletons in the cupboard so to speak, and decided there was only one way out. Very sad, wife and three children."

"Oh. That's terrible! I can't believe it!"

I was very pleased with the way things were going and had to swallow hard when I presented my faith in Embassy diplomats. James Macilroy can swing as far as I am concerned but my personal feelings must not show. Stay professional!

"He is no longer friend nor husband to me, but I do not wish to lose my source of income so, I will happily help if I am able." Pavvla glanced at her elegant Cartier Tank wristwatch.

"It will soon be lunchtime. Would you like to stay to lunch?"

"Well, er, I should really be."

"Stay to lunch, then I can tell you all!"

How could I refuse? She will tell all... that's just what I require. Having just stated the biggest pile of "mumbo jumbo" I could muster, I am surely on the verge of success? It may have all been worthwhile. I wanted her to her believe my concocted story.

I needed to convince her I was on her side and draw things from her that she would not normally admit. It appears I may have succeeded, So lunch it is. I thanked Pavvla. She called in Maitland via the bell who appeared and took details for one extra to lunch. Without as much as an eye flickers she replied: "Certainly madam. I have prepared already for yourself. It will only take an extra hour to include Mr Hargreaves, will that be satisfactory?" Pavvla looked at me for a response. I nodded.

"Very well madam." Maitland left.

"You can tell me more about it and yourself. Mr Har… now look here… if I invite someone to lunch I don't keep calling them titles, unless they are Lord and Lady someone… now come on, be a good boy (good boy!) what do I call you, unless you want to keep calling me Mrs Macilroy?

"Of course, Pavvla. It's Richard." (I have to remember, today I am Richard from the Foreign Office.) We chatted for a considerable time and spent further opportunity of showing me what is a library. This House is larger than one would think. A goodly half hour discussing books, her books and books already read. The time came to wander into the dining room. Maitland brought in various wines and we sat at the places duly prepared. A huge table designed for at least a dozen diners, another splendid "Louis the something" period. Maitland removed a massive cut glass vase from the centre of the table containing an equally massive bouquet of flowers. A label hanging, still in place, from some known (or unknown?) admirer. Had she read it I wondered?

We sat next to each other.

My plan was initially to obtain information from her and to get her to talk… now she was in a mood to talk… and brother, could she talk! The whole history of the universe coupled with her acting life as Blossom Pavvla, interspersed with snippets about her husband and his dastardly deeds, (according to her!)

Lunch was expertly served by Maitland. This was in reality an "upstairs – downstairs" experience… and today, I was definitely "upstairs" Everything was excellent, more like a special evening dinner and far too much wine consumed. I had forgotten I was driving!

Pavvla was a most enticing provocative lady of about 38- 40-ish with the elegance of a titled lady and the appearance of a catwalk model (a catwalk model before the mouth was engaged!) She, as they saying goes, had it all. Even her cultured voice had class but not the marble in mouth type. It would be easy for any susceptible male to get drawn into this spider's web, but not me.

From the long diatribe, and it was both long and detailed, I only obtained some fairly insignificant information about the Captain.

He drank a bottle of vodka each day, was not a nice person when drunk and that was frequent.

His womanizing was excessive and the only real "dark side" to his past was whilst in the Marines. He left "under a cloud". He was ranked Captain at that time and he aspired to go higher but for an incident during a training session. In his regiment they had daily combat tuition and he eventually reached the Dan level, so he was "bloody good". (Pavvlas's words.) The training instructor was a sergeant who had not achieved a higher ranking and in fact, James had passed him on his way rising to Captain. the story goes (says Pavvla) they hated each other and this was obvious for a long period of time. During one such combat lesson James went too far with his techniques and the training officer died. A full inquest and inquiry ensued. James Macilroy was pardoned of any blame... but (says Pavvla) everyone knew of the animosity between the two and many thought James was biding his time and waiting for an opportunity to finish him... and finish him he did.

Pavvla concluded the tale: "So, James was given his marching orders from the Marines, but not dishonourably I think is the term is, but none the less, under a cloud. James had deliberately killed a man and his colleagues knew it, but only one person was actually certain of it – James."

When all was concluded I thanked Pavvla for the tea, tartlets and lunch, her cordiality and the information. She hoped she had been of assistance. She had. We did "get on" Maitland arrived to show me out.

The two ladies both had the last word... in their own separate way.

Madam Pavvla said: "Do come again Richard, whenever you feel the need for tea, tart included!" Maitland.

"Goodbye, sir. Thank you. I hope your golf improves!"

I sat in my car and pondered for a while. I also noted an uneasy feeling of far too much wine.

What did I gain from this meeting?

In reality, the facts; Captain James Macilroy had too many women, drank too much alcohol and he killed his training instructor. Horrific, but I don't think that is going to help me.

My other plan, still hatching, involving compromising photography will be the way, but only if he was not captured during the next Glavy store raid by Galina's departmental team.

I am not party to where "Blue" obtained his information from about Pavvla Macilroy, but I quite liked her… but was Pavvla – (Blossom) Macilroy, a lady of the night in disguise?

I wondered what she and Maitland are doing now that I have departed? Was it all a "front" and they are both nudging each other and laughing saying: "We pulled that one off, eh?" Or are they both exactly as I found them? The latter is my final decision.

It is definitely Russian born lady and English maid and where the twain shall meet.

Pavvla Macilroy was conducting a lifestyle of which she was accustomed. This house and the other mansion requires huge sums of money not only to initially purchase but to run, not to mention all the things that go with her lifestyle. She understandably did not want the hint of any scandal about her ex-husband to jeopardise this.

Clearly, my decision is, this lifestyle of hers was generously attributed to the dealing of heroin and not from an Embassy official's monthly pay-check. Of this I am certain.

I looked in my rear view mirror. A red faced, red eyed… I've drunk too much Richard Hargreaves peered back. It's time to be Mr Ric Hartland once more. Back to the Moscow Star for a rest.

I entered Tverskaya Street leaving the side road, and gingerly drove along the highway, pleasingly not too busy. A mere eight hundred metres achieved and the sound of sirens and flashing lights appeared from nowhere. A saloon car passed me, cutting me into the side. Engine turned off; a mild expletive followed. Bloody police, where did they come from? Oh deep joy!

I wound down the window (could not locate the electric window switch!) An immaculately smart police officer stood looking at me and commenced bellowing in Russian. Interrupting him I said: "Sorry. I'm English. I do not understand Russian."

"Aw. I steek Engleese a little too. I try as well now. Do you 'ave ze drive Licence pleeese?" I came with my false ID card and I never bring any others. It would look very bad if searched and found to be holding three separate identity cards, so, I must brave this out with one.

"Sorry, officer. I left it at my address, but I have an ID card?"

"ID card is good. Pleese to give now." Opening my wallet, I selected the card and handed it to him. He scrutinised it thoroughly front and rear. Will things improve when he reads – Foreign Office? "Yews is zer Engleesh officer government staying now. Why 'ere sir?"

"Holiday. I am sightseeing now."

"You smeel of ze drinking, 'ave you been drinking, sir?"

"Yes, just a couple of glasses of wine at lunchtime with friends and family officer. The wine was low alcohol. Why did you stop me. Have I done something wrong?"

The officer and I "chatted" for some considerable time! He was determined to test his English.

It was certainly better than my Russian, but his words were very slow in coming, seemingly travelling a great distance from his lower abdomen! He stated he also spoke French, fluently. "Would I prefer to discuss in French?" Definitely not... now upstaged by a Russian policeman! I refused the invitation. My schoolboy French was about as pathetic as my schoolboy Russian.

I therefore elected to listen to his fragmented "Englissshe" as pronounced by the officer. He proceeded to inform me I had been seen in the Ostozhena district. Residents had seen me. Driving in that locality is just not the one thing in a car like mine. People drive in Ferraris and Rolls Royces and not in a three year old GAZ! Therefore it was assumed I was likely to be up to no good and reported to the constabulary (or whatever it is called) The details of the vehicle were then circulated and when spotted, as I was, duly apprehended.

"Why you go in Ostozhena Golden Mile, sir?"

"Oh yes, that is correct. I am staying there with my friends and family." This fabrication of a story has to be a good one!

"The ambassador advised me not to hire a good quality car. Sometimes people who see nice cars vandalise them so, as I did not wish to be recognized I chose an ordinary car."

I think I must be related to Hans Christian Anderson!... it was such a good "fairy tale".

"Aw... You stay there with ambassador in Ostozhena?"

"Yes officer that is correct. On holiday. With friends and family."

He began to soften a little. Perhaps arresting an English diplomat did not gel on his agenda?

"You stay all time at Ostozhena with ambassador. Oh good. You not do bad things. You stay there?" He took a red book from his pocket and wrote something down. He then handed back my ID, then returning his note book to his shirt pocket. He buttoned it down.

"I say you OK, sir. I like the Englissshe Mizder Eargrives sir and we Russian now buy and like Englissshe football yes. I like Vest 'am ooneeted sir. Do you like?"

"My credit rating took a steep dive when I informed him I did not follow football, but, it did rise a notch when I stated that being a Foreign Office diplomat. (I'm really going for it now!) I did not have much spare time for sports."

He understood that and smiled graciously. "I only take name and car in book, sir. No more."

I thought he would have liked to get into the car to discuss football, the universe etc. but did eventually conclude by politely stating that it was not a good idea to drive even with low alcohol wine. Drink and driving is severely punishable in Moscow.

"You tell Englissshe friends and work job that we good and like Englissshe, we not bad and lock people in prison like nuus pippers they say." I understood what he meant.

"You go home and say me. Remember zis my name, sir." He pointed to his ID badge affixed to his shirt. I'm surprised a longer card was not available. There was just enough room for the full title, Stephan V. Tulorisovski… remember it? I couldn't even say it. It sounded like a Latin name for an important exotic hot house plant.

We said our farewells. He stepped out and stopped the traffic (there wasn't much) whilst he eased me out into the inside lane.

"Guutbye sir and guut luck."

I could see him in my rear view mirror still standing in the middle of the road, arm erect. Clearly he did take a shine to me or was it the ID card? We all know the answer to that! The police obviously must use 'kid gloves' when dealing with Foreign diplomats (even though I wasn't one!) and probably, like our own police force… hate the associated paperwork. Driving back my heart rate started to increase. My brain knew I had just escaped a very difficult situation with the Russian police but my heart had only just realised it! If I had been booked and prosecuted it would have been 'curtains' for me. They would have eventually found out I had a false ID card and it might have been the end of the road for my job. They lock you up for considerable period of time for such misdemeanours in Russia. There are stories circulating, that according to the cliche… They occasionally throw away the key!

I sauntered into the Hotel car park and found my favourite spot at the end comer away from other vehicles. I sat there for a few moments still breathing heavily and smugly smiling.

"I have just fooled the Russian police… quite an achievement!"

Chapter 7

Time for reflection. Time to consider what evidence I have and how to proceed. Not a lot can be achieved currently before Galina's team get involved. Time to go to my favourite thinking place, down by the river.

Monika was at the reception desk. I asked for the English newspaper. She offered both tabloid and broadsheet papers. If I wanted a comic I would chose tabloid, so I didn't! I asked if I could take the paper down to the river with a promise to return it. She did not understand my request.

"I get Irina," Monika fetched Irina from the back room. She understood clearly what I required and readily agreed.

With newspaper tucked under arm I sauntered off down to find "my" bench at the waterside. There are very few seats along the highway side. Perhaps the Russians don't like their citizens sitting and consider they should be working? Last night the weather did break and there was a thunderstorm due to the continuing heat but today it had cleared and the sun shone down once again relentlessly on those mortals below.

Finding the bench, I sit and spread the newspaper viewing snippets hither and thither... French fishermen causing mayhem again in the channel... FTSE maintaining its course, good level there... politicians being idiotic... film stars being equally idiotic, and some "hero worshipping" at a tennis player who had won a tournament. "You should try some of my tournaments chum!" (These are my moments of reflection!)

I consider myself fairly well off but it makes my blood boil seeing these "so called" sports heroes being paid ridiculous sums of money, hundreds of pounds each minute, when some poor sod is in a supermarket pondering whether spending £3 on a meat pie to feed the family can be afforded! It's not that I'm jealous, nor am I in favour of the equal distribution of wealth... perish the thought. The communist idea is NOT one I agree with but there does appear to be a sorrowful imbalance in the world about numerous issues. This is the time and place I become thoughtful and philosophical and today is no exception. Where does it get us?

Spreading out my paper I glanced at the top right side, and over the paper I saw a figure I recognised. Distinct by his immaculate attire and upper class deportment. It was Sir Granny Grantham etc., carrying a briefcase? On a Sunday? Curious and curiouser. I did not really wish to get involved with him so I quickly folded my newspaper. To be seen with an English paper is a cert giveaway. It was folded and sat upon. The question; how not to be see? I took off my shoe and shook it upside down rigorously in the air then stooped down to methodically tie the lace. Just prior to that I could see the briefcase being held stiffly downwards. In my stooped posture I watched Grantham's hand-made brown shoes clip clop past. He only witnessed the rear of my head.

To recognize the back of my neck would have even challenged my mother!

Sat upright, I watched him walk up to a man and stopped a few feet from him. He imitated the man by leaning on the wall looking at the river. A lady approached dutifully carrying a plastic bag. She was harmlessly doggie walking. When the lady had passed, Grantham sidled up to the man. They both looked suspiciously to the left and right about themselves. They both then stood facing each other, spoke and shook hands. They were approximately twenty metres from me but a large waste bin fortunately positioned in between gave me some cover. I slid down the bench seat slightly enabling me to peer over the bin top to observe.

Grantham shook his left arm and the briefcase dropped down swinging by a chain. He was handcuffed to the handle via his wrist. This cannot be work related? With his right hand he pulled out a chain and key ring from his pocket, selected a key and unlocked the case. The man pulled out what appeared to be an A4 manilla envelope from his inside jacket pocket and handed it to Grantham who dropped it into his briefcase.

In doing so he pulled out a smaller envelope and handed it to the man. He placed it into his pocket since vacated by the A4 envelope.

Grantham locked the briefcase, slid the key and chain back into his trouser pocket and pulled the security chain up his arm and grasped the handle of the case. They spoke very little, then leaned over the wall and artificially watched the passing river craft for thirty seconds or so. They then both furtively looked to the left and right. They shook hands once again and Grantham walked off in the direction of Tverksoy distinct. Another thirty seconds elapsed and the man

(The contact!) did likewise and followed Grantham. A strange thing for two people to do, who knew each other?

I felt inclined to follow one or the other but as they were going in similar directions I followed both at a discrete distance. I tailed them both in this way when "the contact" broke the trend, crossed the highway and got into his car. He fiddled with his newly acquired envelope which gave me the opportunity of staring at him for a good look. Would I recognize him again? Yes, I surely would. Whilst following Grantham I considered; what are my plans to be? Time to analyse.

What precisely are the plusses and the negatives?

On the plus side, I know (I feel fairly confident) that this unknown male, along with Grantham and Macilroy are involved in the transfer of documents. In all probability, from English sources to Russian. That really makes my job complete, although I would like to find more detail.

Unrelated to Department Blue 17, the heroin drugs situation is soon to be resolved by Galina's department hit team squad.

The minus negatives however are regrettably greater in number.

Petrov and Krull, the Lubyanka lot know me, the Russian police force know me as diplomat Richard Hargreaves, English Joe and his Mafia mobsters know both Galina and myself, James Macilroy has knowledge of me, I now have my passport which should be a plus but "Blue" thinks I would be "named" at the airport and prevented from leaving, thus necessitating a 450-mile trip to Belarus... and I don't fancy that! The rather charming seductive Mrs Macilroy also knows me as Richard Hargreaves, Foreign Office official.

It is complex... so, it is stay, and find out more. This has no reflection upon the possible suggestion by "Blue" that promotion might be in the offing! Don't want that!

Sir... Captain Grantham or whatever he calls himself proceeded to walk towards the Tverskoy direction and eventually reaching Tverskaya Street, casually wandered along the high road till he reached a night club. He crossed over. I observed him from the other side of the street. He entered "Night Fright" and disappeared from view. I gave a few minutes so as to ensure he was well into the building and likewise crossed the street. It was just after six. It might have seemed odd strolling into a nightclub with a morning paper under my arm, but of course, they would not know that... but generally, one does not visit night clubs to read the news!

Through elegant glass doors, I was confronted by three ladies who were behind what was similar to a hotel reception desk. One lady addressed me, understandably in Russian.

"I'm… English… Can you help?" She instantly changed to perfect English.

"Yes sir. How can I help?"

I needed to see where Grantham had disappeared to. Was he here somewhere or was there some secret hideaway meeting place below or above stairs?

"I don't know the area very well. I arranged to meet a lady friend here… outside… she doesn't seem to have arrived… I wondered if she has come inside to wait… perhaps I can look?"

"You are welcome, but no point The only customers are three men. They have just arrived. We have only just opened, its only six fifteen. We open at six."

I shot myself in the foot there, by saying it was a lady I was to meet. Bad play there!

"Well, if you have arranged to meet her, she might be late, ladies do that sometimes, or perhaps she will not show, or if early, taken herself to the ladies shoe shop a few doors along. You need to get there quick; you might save some yourself money." She tittered. She likes her own jokes!

"Yes," my reply, but I still need to look who Grantham is with. Time for another try!

"I'll go along to the shoe shop then… do you think, before I do, I could use the men's toilet?"

Her large eyes changed to slits, as did her rounded lips. Her audible "huff" could have moved the branches of a tree. Even her eyebrows moved downwards!

"It is not our policy to allow people to come in off the street just to use our facilities… sir!" The sir part was with considerable emphasis. Time for me to do a "bit of crawling".

"It would be kind of you, and I will be coming later… when I found my friend, possibly now or sometime later this evening… to the club… it just that at the moment I…"

"Yes… yes… spare me the details… go through to the far end. It's just past the dining restaurant area." She gesticulated to her right. I Nodded and thanked her. Thinking I had better add some clarity to my story… I added…

"If you see a lady hanging around outside, whilst I am there… perhaps you…"

"Yes… sir… I… will!"

I wandered off like a poor little lost boy troubled with incontinence. Past the restaurant dining area, and... there sure enough, sat the early diners, three men around a table deep in conversation. My objective had been achieved. It was Grantham. Whoever the others were, it was clear not to be a social date.

I did my time in the men's room. When I returned a waitress was standing by the three, taking their order. It seemed they would be there for some time yet. Perhaps a genuine return to the club later would be beneficial. Possibly Irina would come with me? It's worth a try. At the desk... "Thank you, very kind of you. I will be back later with my friend. I assume the club is not a members club only and I need to fill in any forms?" She found that really funny.

"Oh no... not a *members club!*" She replied, labouring the word members. What's funny about that?

I hurried back down Tverskaya Street and soon reached The Moscow Star. Monika was again at the desk. I returned the newspaper which was well flattened by that time. I asked for Irina.

"She sleep now. I call."

"No, don't disturb her. I will see if I can catch her later." One can always tell when someone does not understand what is being said... it is the way they look blank, politely smile and nod. I returned to my room, I had a face lick and changed clothes. Down to the lounge dining area for a further read. I will find Irina eventually.

Deep into my book, I was disturbed by a gentle tap on my shoulder.

"Did you want see me?" Monika obviously did understand. I informed Irina details of my recent discovery down at the waterfront. Her suspicions correlated with my own. After presenting my next plan, that is to return to the night club, Irina asked if I wanted her to come with me? It was in mind, but I did not want to make the suggestion, after all, this investigation is really nothing to do with her role. I happily agreed although hotel commitments might create a problem for her?

"No problem," was her reply. (She is picking up the language!) Irina was only responsible for paperwork – doing the books this evening and that can wait!

I waited for Irina whilst she busied herself and appeared shortly looking suitably "night club-ish" but not overdone. We elected to walk. That presents no problems regarding the drink and drive scenario... only inclement weather, but that was not likely. A pleasant clear warm evening allowed us to stroll along to club "Night Fright". (I hope it won't be!)

Entering the club… the receptionist girl, young lady, was still there…

"Ah, you find your lady friend at last… shoe shop was it?" Irina looked at me puzzled? My reply: "No, just a little late that's all." Looking directly into Irina's eyes she said: "That's the idea eh… keep 'em waiting. They think better of you for it eh?" She tittered.

"Er, um, yes, is true, they will do, yes," What more could Irina say?

It's getting quite noisy now, but you can go down to the front if you like noise, or nearer the back where it is further from the stage speaker. It is for you to decide sir.

"When you are there, a waitress will come. Is that OK for your lady friend?" She addressed Irina directly, who then replied: "Thank you." She then blurted out a flow of Russian to the lady/girl… who then stood back stiffly and permitted her painted smile to drop from her lips.

I pulled Irina away and we strolled down to the areas described. I asked: "What was that all about?"

"… and what was that you say… she say about shoes shopping and me are being late?"

"Don't ask why, it doesn't matter… what did you say to her? The girl looked shocked!"

"I say same to you Ric. Not to ask!"

We found a table for two and sat. I suddenly remembered; I meant to ask Irina to telephone Galina to cancel our meeting tomorrow.

Apparently, the meeting had already been cancelled. Tomorrow was to be the funeral of Svetlana Morasova, the housemaid who had been killed by the bomb.

The staff at The Moscow Star hotel would be in charge tomorrow, allowing Irina and Monika to attend. The remaining staff from Cafe Brodsky would be at the funeral. Borodinos was to be closed for the day for all employees to attend.

"Would you like come too Ric?"

I stated… I would if it was agreeable. Irina would telephone Galina to ensure there was a place on the bus for me. Svetlana had no known immediate family, so no blood relatives will attend, or even be aware of the death. Sad! The more that come, the better. A crowd is good at a funeral.

A bus or coach would convey everyone to the funeral, courtesy of Galina's generosity. Monika and Irina would be accompanied by Galina and all staff employees… Paren Denisovitch and his father amongst others. It might be a good opportunity for me to become acquainted with Paren (Ivan) and his father before I formalise my plan in an effort to compromise James Macilroy.

A waitress arrived at our table and took our order. Russian beer for me and a Vodka cocktail for Irina. She advised me this was a strong brew and in so many words, it would appear strong enough to knock one's socks off (the Russian version) We also ordered a meal and everything was provided with some degree of style… surprisingly, as it was a night club, not a top class diner.

The club was huge. Walls were decorated with numerous photographs of so called celebs. Large pictures of cars, motorcycles, "shots" of buildings around the world also adorned the walls. Numerous strange decorative "hanging items" were suspended from the ceiling mixed in with well-designed acoustic material. Spotlights of differing designs and sizes were everywhere pointing in varying directions, some rotated and changed colour continuously. There was enough power amperage here to illuminate the Eiffel Tower on New Year's Eve. I imagine they might hear the music in Paris also. The volume was a friend to any ENT surgeon. Work would be surely be guaranteed, and for many who attend this club regularly or specifically the employees, mid-life deafness assured.

There were many youngish people dancing, if that is what it is called and many bimbo types bobbing seductively to the music allowing various large exposed wobbly parts not fall further than the skimpy dresses would allow!

This club would have suited me many years ago, as a teenager, before common sense crept up on me. Actually, I'm pleased it did!

Irina and I discussed the people both seated and dancing, and it was difficult to see if Grantham was still here but, separating rare quiet moments between musical pieces, the plaintive cry of the demented Embassy diplomat was heard… "yuk, yuk, yuk." I would know that laugh anywhere!

I heard him before I saw him. Who didn't? After about half an hour I saw him making a complete fool of himself dancing with a barely clad blond bimbo, again, many parts vibrating. I nudged Irina and we watched carefully to see where he went after the "dance". To the far end of the dance floor area he deposited himself along with blond bimbo. Two other males sat at the table with two other bimbo lookalikes, one with flowing red haired and the other dark haired.

Over the top of some of the heads of those dining we could see a lot of drinking, laughing and rollicking at their table. Yuk, yuk, yuk!

Clearly they were having a good time and were in for the night. It was useful they were far enough away to be seen but, they could not see us. Grantham would recognise me but not Irina, so she was safe. This was a social evening for Grantham. No document passing, if there had been, it was now in the past.

We had spent approximately two hours there and little more than laughing, drinking and joking had taken place at the Grantham table. The only other movement was the embarrassment of his dancing prowess... his attempt at being eighteen again. Although he had removed his jacket he still looked a bit of a "div" and dress wise was well out of place.

The shiny handmade brown shoes were also a slight giveaway that he was not entirely "hip!"

I had consumed numerous beers and also tried some of Irina's Vodka cocktails. Strong yes!!! Designed not only to take the skin of one's teeth but to lighten the load of one's wallet. But who cares!

I excused myself and toddled off to the "gents" I wonder if Irina was secretly related to a camel, she did not go... and ladies always go... although usually in twos!

A male was at the far end doing what comes naturally and I waited politely, even though there was plenty of room. The man went to the basin to wash. The door opened, a male entered, and a voice from being said: "Mr Hartfield." (nearly correct) "It is time for you to stop your meddle. Yes. You interfere where you not wanted and time for you no more, to stop this. Understand?"

I looked in the side mirror and recognized not only the voice but the person. Petrov!

Before I could reply he struck me violently in the rear side, kidney vicinity. The man washing his hands knew this not to be a good place to be, and quickly went for the door. At that very moment my elbow came into play, designed what it was intended to do at times like this... I thrust backwards into the nose of Petrov sending him sprawling. A lot of blood ensued from his nose. I jumped on him and held his generously sized shirt collar in a neck strangle hold. His shirt collar buttons popped port side and starboard. His eyes also popped and he grew pink. He was clearly surprised by my response to his attack.

He struggled whilst I restrained him and tried to ask questions but this was not his way at this time. His knee came violently upwards, but I was not so stupid as to leave those regions exposed for what would have been a final blow. We rolled and fought around the floor thrashing at each other.

A few minutes elapsed and the door opened clouting Petrov sharply on the head. (I liked that bit!) We rolled clear, still fighting.

A voice in Russian shouted at us, then entered another male. They must have been security bouncers. It was now a foursome battle. This went on for a few minutes more.

With one bouncer sleeping aside Petrov, the remaining security guard and I came to a rapid amicable agreement by the use of hand and body motions, that it would not be necessary for me to suffer the indignity of being slowly frog marched to the exit. I held my hands up gesturing that I would walk with him, and he understood. I think he also realized that he may soon be laying aside his colleague if he decided otherwise! We left the gents toilet peaceably.

It was almost like a rehearsal in a play. We calmly walked out from the "gents" aside each other, torn clothing, numerous blue, brown and red facial marks, with blood over our faces and decorating our shirt fronts.

Just a normal dress rehearsal for the play; Act 22 Scene 4, War and Peace! Walk casually!

All the dancers and diners quite understandably stopped at what they were doing and gazed in horror at the blood-stained twosome strolling beside the dance floor. Irina also horrified, collected her jacket and handbag and followed at a safe distance. I was escorted out into the night with Irina behind and words were heard, scornfully spoken in English from the Reception area.

"I thought you two were trouble all along."

Outside, my "lady friend" took a handkerchief from her bag and gave some dabbing assistance. I told her what had happened. I had been attacked by Petrov and two security bouncers. None of this had been my fault. I had been brutally attacked. Irina inquired;

"Where is Petrov. I didn't see him come out?"

I replied: "He's resting."

"Resting?"

"Yes, on the gents toilet floor."

"Two bouncer men, you said two bouncer men come. I did not see other?"

"No, he's resting as well!"

I was beginning to feel the pain of the onslaught. My face was pulsating, my ribs hurt as did the punch in the kidney that Petrov so expertly presented. After the dabbing of the blood from various parts of my face I suggested we get a rapid move-on back to the hotel before the police arrive. Petrov is bound to take things farther… that is, when he wakes from his sleep!

The walk to the hotel seemed an eternity. With various parts of my body protesting, now my arm aches and both knees throb, as for my face, I wonder if "mother" would recognize me now? Arriving at the Moscow Star, Irina took me into the back room, so as not to frighten guests, and brought a large first aid box.

She also brought a bowl of hot water and towels for the necessary clean up before copious quantities of antiseptic cream was applied. I had (so I was informed) a nasty cut on my brow which was closed by the application of a Russian version of sterry strip. Wonderful tape, that often substitutes the need for physical stitching.

I took to my bed immediately after my "nurse" had completed her task. I had a poor night due to tossing and turning. Finding there were not many places I could lay that didn't hurt. Time's a healer!

I was tormented somewhat during the night of how to proceed with my task. Everything had gone far beyond my original instructions of: "Find out and get out". I now know the intermediaries were Captain James Macilroy and Sir Grantham Hargreaves-Sykes. Somewhere in between those two were the mafia mob, but they were also acting as a go-between, principally being involved in the heroin drug trade. The "end user" of documents was to be found at Lubyanka (not really surprising) and that was Petrov and his immediate cohorts. Who is passing documents from the English side? In a "nutshell" who gives documents to Messrs Macilroy and Grantham? The man that met Grantham at the riverside – yes, but who gives documents to him? I need to find out who that person is, then I will be satisfied, so I can close the loop… the missing link. How I am to go about establishing this person, I do not know, but my plan to compromise Macilroy is still the best way forward so, yes, that is my way. I tried to get back to sleep but all these things kept churning over and over, but eventually I did. I awoke at nine am. I telephoned down to say I would be late for breakfast. Nine thirty was acceptable. I slung my clothes on and limped down to the dining room. There were still a couple of late breakfasting stragglers and "looks" were common place due to the ol' boat race appearing to be a replacement for a Wembley cup final football!

The newish waitress served me and refrained from stating the obvious but did frequently glance at the varying colour shades over my face, along with the sterry strip across the cut brow. Fresh coffee came with Irina who sat at my table and offered words of sympathy. She is such a nice lady.

We discussed the previous nights "entertainment" and Irina said quite casually: "I am think that it may be we not liked to go there again." I held my ribs and laughed. It was the way she said it. She could not comprehend why I chuckled at her remark. Just the English sense of humour, hearing her state the obvious. I asked her to contact Galina to excuse me from the funeral. I wanted to take things easy today. This was understood and acceptable.

After breakfast I retrieved my book and did the usual... found a comfortable chair in the garden and tried to concentrate on reading. Always – the title offered some reason to inwardly smile!

Chapter 8

The weather changed for the funeral. Some might say the Gods are expressing their sadness.

Some might be right! Rain on a summer day... it happens!

The coach had arrived at Borodinos in plenty of time. There were twenty five mourners in all comprising those from Borodinos, Cafe Brodsky, The Moscow Star and from the properties adjoining Borodinos. Various neighbours knew and liked Svetlana. Galina had placed an advertisement in a newspaper about the demise of Svetlana requesting anyone to come forward who might wish to attend the funeral or hopefully be related to her... no replies to the advertisement. The journey was without traffic problems. It was a long journey to the cemetery, located outside the main Moscow ring road. Burial places were not so easily obtained in Moscow and cemetery's near one's residence were not always available. Very often full, so mourners often had to travel considerable distances to get a good plot for their loved ones.

The Khovanskoye cemetery was located within the Leninsky District and was vast, but even such a large expanding graveyard will one day be full, and it only takes a war of some kind... and then! They arrived thirty minutes before the service was due to take place. The coach parked with ease and all mourners, dressed in black attire assembled outside the chapel. Everyone knew each other so chatting was stilted and limited. The time came to pass through into a concourse where the open coffin was displayed. It is occasionally customary to display the deceased for the mourners to offer their farewells. This had been a very difficult decision. There were no close relatives so Galina had taken it upon herself to determine whether the coffin should be open or closed. The body in its appalling condition, after the bomb blast would be a terrible shock for everyone. Galina had decided the coffin should be open because horrifying as it was, she considered it important for people to witness precisely what atrocities current, so called civilized Russians are capable of. All were warned in advance and only two people thought it best to abstain. Quite understandable because the result from one lady was she was violently sick and had to be taken to a quiet room to be consoled and given a glass of water.

The passing by of the coffin had left all those attending in more of a depression than they originally were. The undertakers had done the best they could to "tidy" the unfortunate Svetlana but there is only so much even experts can do to disguise a blown up burnt disfigured corpse. Sickening! Passing through back into the air, some murmuring, some silent and others simply leaned against the chapel wall blankly staring. The rain has stopped... that is a plus!

The service was quite extensive. Similar to funeral services world-wide, those assembled took part in muffled tones responding as they knew. When finalized the coffin was taken. Ten minutes later, all followed the minister from the chapel to the graveside. It was quite a long walk. Fortunate that the rain *had* ceased although it was heavy underfoot and dodging around unmarked graves made matters more difficult than they need be. One gets a terrible feeling when graves are accidentally trodden upon.

The mourners arrived at the graveside and they assembled around the excavation with two gravediggers standing well back behind the group. The group of which had mysteriously increased by two... one unknown male and one female... not appearing to be together.

Those closest to Svetlana were invited to stand at the front on a wooden plank immediately adjacent the hole. Galina and the unknown woman stepped forward on to the plank.

The mystery woman whispered to Galina: "I hope you do not object I am Svetlana's aunt." Galina, surprised, replied: "Yes, of course. I am pleased you are here. I did not know she had living relatives."

"We didn't get on, but I am sad to see her go like this."

A further service was carried out by the minister with some responses from the group. They all craned their necks forward to observe the coffin which had dutifully arrived before the mourners.

It was a light coloured wood with a large brass plate displaying Svetlana's name, date of birth and death. The plank that Galina and Svetlana's aunt were standing on gave way slightly, it twitched just a little, enough to give them a jolt. They re-steadied themselves and stood erect.

Reporting later to all... Galina told the story that at that stage she felt a violent push on her back and naturally, down she went, dropping on to the coffin.

The minister used a term similar to that in English; "Bloody useless gravediggers." Naturally there was a loud gasp from those looking down at Galina who was lying flat on her back on the coffin looking up at them, assessing her feelings as to whether she was injured. She paused for a moment at the faces at the top all expressing horror at what had occurred, all that is, bar one... one male was peering over the shoulders of others. He was grinning... teeth widely exposed similar to cartoons that people see of Chinese people... a mouth full of teeth grinning down at the unfortunate Galina. The minister flicked his fingers at the two gravediggers who leapt into action. They did not need to be told what to do. All mourners were firmly pushed back whilst one grave digger jumped down with a rope whilst the other handed more out from the top.

Galina was eased upwards, desperately holding the rope whilst the gravedigger at coffin level firmly, and perhaps over generously, pushed her up, utilizing firm grasps of both buttocks!

At the top Galina freed herself from the buttock holder. She and others commenced brushing the mud from her clothes. They did the best they could, but a black dress and mud never did go well together. Galina looked left and right but the culprit had vanished. Galina whispered: "He pushed me, did you see that, he pushed me," Svet's aunt replied: "I know. I felt him do it He was right next to me when he did it Who was he?"

Asked the aunt: "He is no one I know and he has disappeared... and quick!"

Everyone was naturally very concerned as to whether Galina was injured and understandably to some extent they all thought it had been a ghastly accident but it was deliberate.

Someone is trying, and succeeding in frightening Galina. They tried to kill her with the bomb that had mistakenly killed Svetlana Morasova and now they are playing the warning game.

There will surely be more "games" to follow? These people need to be removed... Galina's thoughts; the RIS team are the ones to do it... and it shall be done!

The minister admonished the gravediggers believing they had been responsible due to the loose plank, but their denials fell on deaf ears as far as the minister was concerned. He had mumbled something about them being men of the Babushka women... and what do you expect etc., etc.! What the equivalent English comparison is... I cannot even hazard a guess!

The gravediggers were then given permission to commence filling in the grave and they duly shovelled away with gusto. The minister was thanked by all mourners.

The mourners wandered back to the car park area and in doing so, everyone gave their own version of what had occurred. Only two people knew the truth.

Aunt Annika was the sister of Svetlana's father. Father and mother were deceased. Annika was the only relative she knew of although obviously there were others, but their locations were unknown to her. The family had a shady background. There had been numerous disputes about the State share system. Russia went through the stages of a transitional period. The buying and selling of shares that had been provided in lieu of salaries that had been dished out by the government and various businesses had created a whole host of problems. The poor had become rich, the rich had become poor and the rich had become richer. Many family's "fell out" and the Morasova family was no exception… and as Aunty Annika had previously stated; "We did not get on!" Galina did not probe further.

Reaching the parking area they all returned to their seats on the coach. Annika had been welcomed by Galina to attend the Pominki (equivalent of a Wake in English) at Borodinos. She thought about it… and might or might not? She would consider it when driving. Annika had a lot to tell about the family but she was uncertain if she should. They arrived at Borodinos; Annika Morasova was not there. Elsewhere.

A well-earned rest day for myself. Physically and mentally. Physically because my face and body ached, seemingly all over. My knees had also taken considerable punishment due to the frolicking over the hard tiled floor… but as the cliche says: "You think I look bad; you should see the other bloke!" Of course I was unaware how the bouncer and Petrov were faring. I hope they were suffering as I, especially Petrov who was the protagonist behind the attack. The bouncer (bouncers) were simply doing their job. In times of trouble such as that, their duty is to remove all concerned with little consideration as to "who started it" but I did not like the way the bouncers had launched into me without any thought They might think things over before tackling a situation like that again. I hope so. They need to assess the situation before they start beating people!

Amusingly, Irina had quite rightly stated we would not be welcome at "Night Fright" again but personally speaking, I would not wish for a return visit. The unfortunate episode in the night club did reveal Grantham and Petrov in a close relationship. I trust I am not adding two plus two and making five, but I am confident that Petrov is the receiver of English documents.

Whether he intended to give me a beating in the gents toilet or possibly kill me and scoot… who knows? Either alternative are possible. I need to be doubly aware that Petrov is going for me and as a member of the Lubyanka crew, I have little legal recourse in Moscow against him.

I will report to "Blue" and commence some headway into a move to the Marriott Hotel. This is a good time to change my whereabouts as Petrov and possibly Grantham and Macilroy are on my trail, I have no doubts of that.

A good rest day, some further reading… oh I wish I could do that all the time' After dinner an early night will hopefully help my weary injured bones to heal. My face injuries are however slow to show any signs of improvement Shortly after my arrival in Moscow, a black eye, now one and a half black eyes, extensive bruising, painful ribs and the sterry strip on my brow… all being a giveaway that this person "might be trouble!" (but I'm not!) The swollen cut lip doesn't help either! A shower after a very pleasant dinner and bed by ten. Bliss.

Bliss changed at what transpired to be three fifteen during the night It "was" a pleasant dream!… Swimming in a pool with my girlfriend. The pool was hot on one side and cold on the other. Similar to many strange and impractical dreams, it did not seem at all odd that the water changed temperature straight down the middle of the pool! "Stay on this side I advised my girlfriend, its cold on the other side." I don't know what Freud would have made of this dream? Probably interpret it as a desire to sleep with kangaroos! However, there we were, enjoying the warm swim when a bell and siren commenced. Very odd… it seemed to be in my dream, yet it wasn't?

I awoke… it wasn't! The bell and siren were both real. I stared at the ceiling assuring myself I was awake. I heard numerous voices and loud footsteps in the corridor. The tannoy came over loud and clear… Evacuate the fire – evakurirovat ogon (or something sounding like that?) The voice kept repeating those words. I threw on a dressing gown and was nearly knocked over by boarders rushing past. The message was clear. There was a fire and we all had to get out PDQ.

I returned to my room to grab my wallet and passport (I know that was wrong – but!) left the room and joined the throng making for the staircase. Everyone was in a state of dishevelled attire. A lady fell on the half landing. Her loose nightie revealing more than she would have wanted, but being a gentleman, I looked away from her revealed naughty bits and helped her to her feet She limped badly so I further assisted her down the next flight to ground level. There were other interesting varieties of dress; the colonel from the upper floor wore green pyjamas with pink flamingos… now that might tell a story? We all followed each other through tire main reception concourse and out of the rear fire escape doors into the garden and then to the car park assembly point, north west comer. Everyone dutifully stood there huddled. A jabbering half-dressed bunch of forlorn souls, hearing the sound of the fire engine arriving (State Fire Service) who thundered past us and turned towards the fire in the car park, north east comer.

They quickly put out the fire with foam covering the cause of the fire – the vehicle in the comer. My car… that's surely my car that was on fire? Yes, it was, it is, it's my car! It's… them!

The fire was quickly under control. Two fire officers went into the hotel. They returned thirty minutes later reporting to the chief that all was well. There was no fire within the building. The chief fire officer informed all guests that they could return to their rooms.

There was still some "sleep time" to be had. Monika assisted the guests back into the hotel. I wandered over to my car which was a lot whiter than it had previously been due to the foam covering. Monika and Irina were in full conversation with the fire chief. I assumed him to be the top man because he wore a helmet of a different colour. I was introduced to the fire chief as the unfortunate owner of the car. Irina acted as interpreter, the fire chief had no English and the speed of his Russian was too fast for me. He had been in the fire service for thirty-five years and seen many car fires. This fire fitted a "picture" of many he had attended over the years and was very suspicious. It was unlikely a car with a cold engine would suddenly ignite in the middle of the night The engine section was relatively untouched and the rear part of the car where the fuel tank was located was likewise only scorched.

The main thrust of the fire was vertically in the drivers position, and the burnt areas were emanating from the floor area upwards through the driver's seat to the roof level.

This was no accidental fire… he joked a little and chucked when he said (in Russian)

"You haven't got any one who doesn't like you have you?" If only he knew! It would be for official scientific inspectors to assess, if they were called, to give a positive ID but, he considered it to be 99% certain that an incendiary device had been the cause of the fire. It was typical of a device being placed under the car below the driver's seat Incendiary devices such as this are either detonated manually or on a timing system, but which ever... he stated... it was intended to kill the person driving the vehicle. Irina and I stared hard at each other. We were both of similar thoughts. The fire chief brought out a clipboard from the fire engine cab and took various details from me. With Irina continuing with her interpretation. I was required to sign a form; he tore off section and handed it to me. I was advised to keep it for insurance purposes etc.

The guests had all returned to their rooms and the fire crew climbed into the cabin. A three-point turn and they were gone. It was suddenly all quiet and dark once more.

Irina stood with arms folded hugging her nighty and I with hands on hips. It was a warm night! "What you think Ric. It not good to be doing this here now," My reply: "What I think Irina is, 1 am now puzzled as the whether they, whoever *they* are, had set a device, that the fire chief mentioned. I had set a device to go off in the middle of the night, thus scaring the pants off me or."

"The pants... your pants?"

"Oh, yes. Sorry... frightening me... or if it had activated too early and it should have really gone off during the daytime when I might be driving the car? That would almost certainly kill."

"I am thinking it is Petrov. He can do this thing to you. He dangerous."

"I would hate to think you are right Irina, but you probably are."

"I think we now, you and me go to bed now Ric. I mean to sleep, not together I mean not that," I laughed... "Yes, of course Irina, I know what you mean. Let's get some shut eye."

"Shut eye?"

"Sleep."

"Oh yes, sleep... shut eye. I remember that, I like shut eye. This bad business Ric, very very bad." We wandered back to our rooms... "our own rooms"... but such events do not permit one to drop off without the whole scenario going over and over in one's thoughts. They are after my blood! The following day I inspected my car before breakfast The smell of burning was still very evident. The surrounding ground of the car park was scorched as was the fence and part of the oak tree from the adjoining property that had been hanging over the fence. This had been a way of trimming the offending branches but in a rather severe way... not a text book method to be sure!

The car inspected… a very sad sight. Car park eerily quiet after the night's cabaret! This vehicle is not for the open road any more. I went into breakfast. No sign of Monika or Irina. I expect they are having a well-deserved lie in. I was served by the "sticky tape" waitress. I will miss this rather ordinary but cute hotel, but it is what the Gods from Department Blue 17 require… so be it!

Yes, I *would* miss the hotel but will the hotel miss me? They could surely do without the things that occur when I'm around! My next immediate move is to take a walk to the car hire shop. Not an enviable task. A good breakfast finished and still no sign of Monika or Irina.

A good time to test my poor Russian on the lady at the car hire shop. She had some good English. A thirty-minute walk evaporated whilst enjoying the sunshine. Is everyone enjoying that brilliant blue cloudless sky… no, of course not.

I entered the car hire shop. It was a different female behind the desk I approached her and I felt an experience, as if she had seen me before, or she didn't like the look of me… yes, that was it, I keep forgetting my facial appearance, the casualty look of a battered boxer. It is alarming to some. "Do you speak English?" I inquired.

"I am speak some but no good." (Oh dear!)

"I can speak some Russian, badly, so I think we will manage." That recognition that says… Eh? The lady then went into fluent Russian. I did pick up her mannerisms as she pointed to her face, then mine. Mine was the one that was cut, black and blue!

"Vashe litso ser?" (I recall, that is something in English like… your face, sir?)

"Ahh," I waved my fists in front of my face punching, boxing style. "Thugs golovorezy."

"Ahh… golovrezy?"

"Da. Robbery… grabezh… da."

"Ah… golvorezy… grabezh. They money take and hit face da?"

"Yes. Da," I replied. "They hit face. They take money."

It was the best lie I could muster. She lifted the servery flap and came around the counter and sympathetically examined my face with her hands without actually touching it She gabbled away in Russian, obviously with words of hatred for my assailant along with words of doctors and hospital amongst the flow. I thanked her for her kindness with some English and a few strangled phrases in

116

Russian… as always, hoping I had got the words right and hadn't actually mistakenly asked if her goat was in milk this year! She did seem to comprehend.

I placed the fire brigade paperwork and documents relating to the vehicle hire on the counter and informed her I had the car for a short while. When I originally came in I was served by a lady, her colleague, a lady with beautiful long red hair.

"Ah, ooow, Katina, da, yes." There was a definite sharp intake of breath?

I battled on with my poor Russian and she attempted her poor English. Between us the message did get through. Milking goats were never mentioned!

"In the hotel car park!… *na parkovke otelya… da? moya mashina zagorelas…* my car caught fire."

"Mashina zagorelas? Yes, she got it… the car caught fire. *Lzyinite…* sorry!"

I held my hand across my throat indicating it was dead… universal language than. She understood.

I used the German word "Kaput" and that seemed to work also.

This kind lady was full of sympathy and understanding. She selected various papers from her desk and scribbled away. Many section completed, she then signed it and rotated it my way and asked me to sign. Ummm, that was the suspicious part! What am I signing for? She stated it was disposing of any responsibility by myself and I would not be held liable due to the fact the car had caught fire. She took my credit card and indicated I would have money returned and the liability for insurance along with the full tank of fuel was no longer mine. That all was very reasonable. Furthermore she asked if I required a replacement car. I thought it best to decline… for the time being! I do not want another car for the arsonists to destroy, and probably me with it! She continued;

"My sobrayem we collect… da?"

"Da," I agreed. They knew where to collect it.

All details were on my application form. I handed her the keys. She returned my credit card.

Without provocation she added;

"They fire your car and hurt Katina. It same man da?"

"Sorry?" I couldn't think of the Russian equivalent! What did she say?

Along and torturous dialogue of broken English with even worse fractured Russian followed of the horrendous story of the unfortunate Katina. A lady who had been at her desk… the car hire desk, after opening up in the early morning at seven thirty am. "They" must have been watching and waiting for an opportunity to interrogate Katina about a matter unknown, unconnected to her normal work other than... she knew the whereabouts of a certain client, Ric Hartland.

The thugs were intent in finding my hotel address from Katina at any cost. They, somehow, knew I had hired a car from here and regrettably, she politely informed these two yobs that such matters were confidential unless requested by the police. Customers details, even hotel addresses were of a private nature.

Of course "types" such as these are very remote from the niceties of courteous behaviour and good manners. Upon two refusals, the thugs pulled down the door and window blinds and set about wrecking the place. When not finding what they required, turned to set about Katina. They savagely beat her, so badly she hardly had enough remaining breath to identify The Moscow Star as my hotel. Just prior to the assault they tried some intimidating techniques discussing between the two of them what precisely they were going to do to her and chatted, slowly, sarcastically to each other... the "soft talk before the hard attack," so to speak.

The lady Natasha, arrived at ten o'clock to find the shop a shambles, blood everywhere and her unconscious colleague on the floor, shoes off scattered, and clothing ripped to shreds in varying parts, to varying degrees.

"Natasha," started to bring tears to her eyes. Understandably, this had disturbed her considerably.

I assisted her and asked if I could take her away from the desk for a few moments to another room. She agreed. I pulled down the blinds and placed the closed sign on the front door.

I sat her down in the back room. She was getting more distressed as time went on. There was a kitchen adjacent. I made her a cup of tea. She began to settle. This lady was afraid something like this assault might also happen to her at a later date.

I didn't think it would. The thugs have got what they wanted. My hotel address.

Natasha thanked me. When she was recovered and finished her tea, she tidied her rather nice face!... and returned to the front desk. I opened the blinds but kept the closed sign in place for a little while longer.

We talked further. Natasha and I both fairly certain that once information had been obtained, the two thugs would pay a visit upon me... this they did (I felt sure) last night.

Natasha said she was visiting her colleague, still remaining in hospital, after work and I was most surprised to be asked if I would like to visit with her this evening. I understood her to say that I might find out more about the two monsters who did this to her friend.

A sound idea, but what about the police?

I agreed, and accepted the details for a visit to "The European Medical Centre" located in the mid part of Moscow, easily accessible. Visiting commences at six o'clock. Natasha offered to collect and drive me by car but I declined and stated I would meet her there at the main entrance. I'm sure there must be a large main entry point that I couldn't miss. The arrangement was agreed. Assuring me she was now feeling recovered, I left the hire shop and returned to my hotel What a distressing time. Natasha was so upset and very worried for herself… not surprisingly.

I caught the Marshrupta and was pleased it stopped approximately four hundred metres from the hospital. I was a few minutes early; Natasha was a few minutes late… only a few! We jointly walked into the hospital entrance and I instantly observed a large notice board in varying languages but the principle nomenclature stated; "We are an English and Russian speaking hospital." A bold declaration that I'm sure no singular London hospital could boast. Even spoken English in numerous parts in the UK frequently presents difficulties, especially London!

A stunning hospital, very impressive in all aspects. I hoped the medical treatment was likewise. I followed Natasha along the corridor and into a lift arriving at the first floor… Borodino Ward… now there's a coincidence! A nurse met us.

After passing information back and forth, she shepherded us to the correct bedside and spoke;

"Katina Jahrysinka… posetiteli." (Visitors)

We stood aside her bed. Katina was propped up drinking a glass of water. She looked frightful. Her face bruised her arm in a cast. She smiled at Natasha and offered a puzzled glance in my direction. Natasha commenced in Russian then changed to English: "How you Katina? This Mr Hartland. Remember, he is man of the car?"

Katina looked hard at me, then remembered, her expression softened.

"I sorry for you, I give name to men. They very bad men. I must give name and hotel. You face. Have them do this to you and me. You face is not good da?"

119

Yes, I thought to myself, *not bloody good da but not as bad as you Katina.* I spoke slowly, carefully selecting my words for her to comprehend fully.

"That is not for you to worry about It is not your fault You had to do it." At that moment a doctor strolled past and I caught his attention. He stopped and spoke in Russian.

"Oh, do you speak any English doctor?" He immediately changed to perfect English.

"Yes, of course, how can I help?"

"Oh… your English is superb."

"That's because I am English. How can I help?" I commenced asking about the unfortunate Miss Jahrysinka but before he replied he gestured to my face. He suggested, jokingly that Katina and I possibly had a family dispute… he did say it as a joke and I chuckled with him, (although not really appropriately amusing at all!) He then went on to describe Katina had a head injury and was unconscious for several hours and will remain in hospital for a while he paused.

"By the way, are you a relative?" I pretended. "Just a friend."

He continued to explain that the bang on the head was not too serious, no lasting damage, but must be observed for a while longer. Her arm and wrist bone broken. This was the arm Ulna and a bone on the same side at the wrist position called the Pisiform. This is often the result of the arm being held erect to protect the face when someone is attacking. The forearm was also peppered with circular bruises which would have been caused by a hard object like a truncheon. The two bones sustaining damage are often the result of such frontal attacks.

"We see it quite often. They soon heal. If there is anything else I will be…" (He pointed sideways.) "Thank doctor. You are most kind."

We pulled out chairs either side of the bed and Katina gave her story of the two thugs, much of it I knew from Natasha. One incriminating mistake they did make was the intimidation part. This information Katina gave to the police. One assailant occasionally spoke in English, the other was definitely Russian. They had joked with Katina in a menacing way, from one to the other using their own names… (thickos!) such as: "So Joe, what are we to do with this lady if she not give us the hotel address eh?"

Says number two thug in reply: "Well, Leonidas, I think we will have to knock her about a bit until she cooperates." This type of patter continued for a short while. Katina refused to cooperate; the violence commenced. She had to give the details of my hotel, but no more she could recall. She lost consciousness a couple of times during the assault, but they kept reviving her until she gave the information required.

That information gave me a positive answer. The assailants were English Joe and his associate Leonidas, the two Irina and I had encountered at the Glavny department store.

I will try to find them myself.

Natasha informed Katina the saga of the car fire in the middle of the night at The Moscow Star. She was very distressed to hear about the incident and pleased I had not been in the car at the time.

She told me not to worry about the car. Natasha would arrange for the car to be collected and at no cost to myself. I informed her Natasha had already organized that… think no more about it!

We spent an hour with Katina who seemed refreshed after the visit. Natasha gave Katina a kiss on each bruised cheek and I shook her hand, the one that still worked!

She smiled and did a soft wave as we departed from the ward. Down the stairs this time and back to the car park. Natasha insisted she gave me a lift back to my hotel… or wherever I wished to go? On the way back to the hotel we exchanged pleasantries. Being of similar age and unmarried, Natasha inquired if I might like to go out one evening with hem? Perhaps somewhere like a night club… she knew a good one called the "Night Fright!"

I swallowed, gulped and took in air whilst exercising a choking laugh. If I had been slurping soup one would say; "it had gone down the wrong way!"

"It some funny I said, Mr Hartland?" This is not the time to be truthful!

"No… just that at my advanced age of thirty, I am a little past night clubs and also, what would they think of me arriving with a decorated face like this?" I pointed.

"Ahh, da, yes!"

We arrived at The Moscow Star and Natasha drove into the car park. We both inspected the fire damaged vehicle in dismay. She righty stated it appeared to have been a possible attempt on the life of the driver to which I readily agreed. I thanked her heartily and nothing further was mentioned about a night out. I still inwardly laugh at the prospect of me strolling into that night club again looking like this! I imagine she considered it to be a point blank refusal on a personal basis… it wasn't. We parted shaking hands and Natasha indicated I could visit the car hire shop if I wanted anything. She also stated it would be a good idea to keep informed about Katina's progress and the results of the police investigation.

"They may come you. The police, da?" I hadn't thought of the prospect that the state police might pay a visit upon myself for a statement. I liked Natasha.

Several days elapsed, uneventfully which was a welcome experience. The weekend passed and a phone call to the Moscow Star was received by Monika. She sent Irina to locate me... as was so often the case, I was reading in the garden. The three volumes of "War and Peace" should take some shifting and unlikely I would finish it whilst in Moscow. Although on second thoughts, the way matters are proceeding, I might need a whole library before this case in Moscow is concluded! Irina held the receiver... I took the phone... she smiled, saying... "Galina".

I thanked her and sat at the desk She wanted to meet me at the usual place down by the Moskva river... at noon as usual. Irina she said, need not be troubled.

We met at noon. Galina was already there, leaning over the wall watching the craft full of passengers enjoying a day on the river. We sat on the bench. We had a lot to discuss. Firstly, she was shocked at the goings on at The Moscow Star car park Then her turn, to offer the details about her attack and surely that is what it was, during the funeral. We mutually agreed there were sinister people quite obviously "after us both!"

There was some good news, some not so good. The Russian Intelligence Service had made a swoop on the Glavny store. The heroin stash was duly seized as was the Mafia mobsters. The unfortunate news was, Macilroy, Grantham and English Joe were not amongst those arrested. The RIS hit squad had apparently "roughed up" three characters (my heart bleeds!) They were named and taken to a detention centre where they would be interrogated.

Those named were: Dima Panavitch, Maxim Vulanova, both Russian by birth and Leonidas Apollo Papatholidis, a Greek national.

"Apollo. His middle name is Apollo!" I laughed. "Perhaps Hades or Ares god of war would have been more appropriate. Clearly his parents expected greater things from him in adult life."

Galina added to the comedy: "It will not be Hades who takes him to underworld, but he will be going soon I think?"

"I am certain our friend 'Apollo' along with 'English Joe' are the two thugs that beat the car hire lady, Katina, and my suspicions are strongly in favour of them being the culprits that fired my car. Whether it was a delayed attack designed to frighten, or if the timer device had not performed we will never know but, they are dangerous characters and English Joe is still out there."

I asked about the RIS interest. Whether the department is only interested in drug dealers in Moscow. "Have you heard of 'Costa Rica?'"

"Well yes, it's a place in…"

"Not the place, the man?" I hadn't.

"What about Escobar?"

"Oh yes, a big name in the drug world. Feared by everyone and manages to stay out of prison." (I'm pleased I did at least know that part!)

"That's him Escobar, or is it Escoba? Well, he, as Americans they say is small fry to Costa Rica. The RIS are after this man. He, as Americans say (what again?) is the Mister Big. He is with the heroin and Cocaine trade, prostitution, arms dealing and he not mind some espionage too!

"He might even be involved in your government secrets document passing. He also has casinos in various parts of the world. He virtually owns police forces in some South American countries. He considers himself one of the untouchables, as the…"

I joined in: "As the Americans say." We both grinned at each other at my delayed comment.

I paused for thought.

"Don't take this the wrong way Galina, but why are you telling me this? Your department have taken three of the mafia gang and confiscated the heroin stash from the Glavny store. My concern is mainly finding out who is the person passing on Government documents from the English side. So our roles don't overlap any more… or do they?" Galina's turn to pause for thought.

"Our information is, man Costa Rica may already be in Moscow. He looks for another place for the store of heroin. It already on ships on way to Moscow. We believe Macilroy is the main contact for Costa Rica. We need information from Macilroy. I tell the RIS you have plan to embarrass him and tell who is passing documents. He must also know plenty about Costa Rica and the heroin. The RIS do not want to 'go in' and seize two British Embassy diplomats, Macilroy and Grantham. It could explode into a diplomatic incident if things went wrong, so they want you to carry out your plan, whatever it is, first. If your plan works we will hope to get all we need Ric. Your government and mine without the possible clash of two governments. I not tell my department what your plan be because, I do not know, but if you tell me about this plan I will put it to my department.

"If they like we go, da, yes?"

So it's my head on the block eh? I told Galina all about my plan, thus far, as I have come, and apart from the finite details, yet to be developed, what I will need is a Mexican Passport with a photo and false name. This person will need to be Paren Denisovitch's father.

"You said he would take part? Difficult as it may be, the passport needs to be a genuine item. You told me all your staff speak good English, that is important. Ivan's father will pose as a Mexican drug dealer. He needs to grow a moustache and look Mexican, as best he can in the time, and darken his hair and appear a little swarthy skinned for the passport photograph. A scar or two would add to the effect! That is all I will need from your RIS department, that is, if they agree with my plan. Everything else is down to my planning and to do some rehearsal with those taking part. That is, Paren, his father and Irina's English hating cousin, the one with the camera."

"I like the plan Ric. It is simple but need good actors. Photo Macilroy in position that will make him talk It may work It been done before in many blackmail cases. I think my department will think it worth a try. They will like it keeps their nose out, yes. For the passport, that it not difficult."

"Oh and yes, one more thing. I need Macilroy's home phone number. Is that possible?"

"Easy. We have it on file now."

Chapter 9

Helena Maitland looked out of the window fronting the main highway of Tverskaya Street. Vehicles whizzed past unperturbed by the current downfall. The uncharacteristic summer wind and rain drenched the previously sun baked footpaths and roads along with those unsuspecting pedestrians who, now, regretted leaving home without a coat or umbrella.

The change in the weather would however not alter the Wednesday morning meeting with Viktor. She hadn't seen him for a few weeks. She knew he was back in Russia. She looked forward to seeing him.

Helena wanted to look nice for Viktor but with such unfavourable weather, looking glamorous in a raincoat and black boots with hair blown sideways by the wind did not meet with her plans.

So be it!

Being local to the thoroughfare she only needed twenty minutes to reach the café... door to door, it was quick and easy. Many shop external blinds were pushed forward so there was a possibility of some shelter whilst negotiating the footpaths. The trouble was, many other people had similar ideas and efforts to avoid the kerb splashing from passing Marshruptas was not always achievable.

Viktor had no such advantage as far as distance was concerned. His journey would be at least fifty minutes. He did have the privilege of a car, but parking some distance from Cafe Lentskis, was likely and might offer a drenching if he was without an umbrella himself.

Helena arrived early despite the short distance. She waited with her back to the Cafe window stamping her feet, but then thought it best to walk along the parade. She had an uncomfortable feeling. Always thinking people were watching her. She glared at some passersby on the opposite side of the highway, which was vast in width, and imagined there were "watchers". In fact they were only doing what she was doing... simply going about their business and observing others, no more, no less.

She crossed the vast highway and looked at the Cafe. There was not a solitary person who was watching her. Why should there be?

"Am I getting paranoid," she asked herself. Actually muttering those words out loud. A passer-by hesitated and spoke to her... more of a grunt. Sorry, no – she was not addressing that person! The meeting hour was nigh so she carefully crossed the busy highway, taking the same position with her back to the window of the cafe. Obscure faces within strained to look through the condensation of the glass. They did not know her. She did not know them.

She shook and folded her umbrella. The temperature had dropped with the unsuspected coming of the cold rain.

"Dead on time." Viktor appeared running from the direction of the side road just off Tverskaya Street. He had no umbrella or raincoat. Helena kissed his cheek and duly admonished him for coming out so stupidly dressed.

"We tough boys don't. We not wear such things," he laughed.

"You won't have much time for laughing in hospital with pneumonia," said Helena as she gave him a firm "clip" on his ear.

"Oh that really hurt Helena!"

"It was meant to," Came the answer as she kissed him again. "Let's get in."

A waitress nodded as they entered the Cafe and pointed to a table for two, a few metres from the entrance. The waitress waved her hand again and held up five fingers. In anyone's language that meant five minutes.

Helen took off her wet coat and gave it a light shake. She folded it neatly and placed it on the floor next to the table. She brushed some of the wet rain from Viktor's shoulders. He did likewise, then wiped rain from his face with a kerchief. They inspected the menu and both settled for Cappuccino with a gigantic pastry, the size of a small dustbin lid! A specialty of Cafe Lentskis.

Helena placed her crossed hands on the table.

Viktor placed his hands affectionately over hers. Two over two.

"What have you been up to? I know you have been back to England again."

The waitress arrived. Seeing the raincoat on the floor she offered to take it to a coat stand.

Helena in her average Russian said: "Not to bother, it's OK thank you." They gave their order to the waitress.

Viktor's English was excellent and always spoke to Helena avoiding using Russian. He said he could not get enough practice and it was important that he improved his English, for his work. "What have I been doing? Oh, this and that my little one."

The cafe was quite boisterous and noisy but they were both very guarded at to what they said and to whom may be in an "overhearing" location, but no one was listening.

"I am worried Viktor. I am sure I am being watched. I don't like any of this. A man came to the house to see Madam Pavvla."

"From what I have heard, that's not so unusual," he laughed.

"No, this one was different English, and at daytime. I heard many questions as I went in and out of the room to serve tea and tartlets. I could not get everything in any order, or detail, but there is no doubt he is conducting some kind of investigation Viktor. It may be he is on to you?"

"You worry too much my little one Helena. No one is on to me as you say. It two years now and all is still good da? There is plenty money for me... for us."

"I am really frightened and want you to give it up." Her brow was screwed up in tension lines. "Give it up! What nonsense is this? (his volume dropped to a whisper) Give it up. Give up all the money they pay me. I just get on plane; they give me papers. I give papers and get plenty money. Money for us one day when we shall marry da? but not yet. It not necessary. Everything is good and no trouble Helena, no trouble. It easy work."

"This man that came, has something on her husband I am sure. You deal with Captain Macilroy, so why should this man come to see his wife, especially if they do not live together anymore?"

"My meeting recent was not with Macilroy. It was with idiot Sykes."

"Sykes?"

"Yes the one with the idiot name; Sir Grantham Hargreaves-Sykes. The one they call Granny Grantham. He smokes cigarette in a long cigarette holder. Idiot he is. I don't mind him, he takes document and give me money and that is all I care and that is all you should care too, da?"

"He works with Captain Macilroy. They are both in the same British Embassy building. One knows what the other is doing Viktor, you told me that."

"Yes, my little one. They are both taking the documents but who give some money I not care as long as I am paid, that is what I want, nothing more for me, just the money for what... nothings. And I get to see England. This coffee and pasty are lovely, shall we have another?"

He waves to the waitress. This time she raises two fingers. Helena and Viktor felt sure they knew what she meant! The waitress came and took the repeat order. Helena said she did not want another huge pastry but it was too late, the waitress had gone.

"Don't worry Helena. I will eat yours." Cream stuck to his upper lip.

Within two minutes the two giant pastries arrived with more cappuccinos. Viktor once again took Helena's hand on the flat of the table and tapping them lightly with his fingers and said, she was not to worry, as there was nothing to worry about.

She hesitated and replied; "OK," but, secretly continued to worry!

The coffees and repeat pastries arrived. They were even larger than the first! The waitress said they can have a third free but it must be consumed in the shop. Helena frowned at Viktor. Viktor thanked the waitress but said he might not get through the door if he ate another. He did manage to struggle through Helena's pastry though!

They continued their chatting, much of which was of a social and amorous nature. Both mutually agreed that they missed each other whilst Viktor was on his missions.

He has saved a considerable amount of money already. Perhaps they might buy a farm and live in the country away from the hubbub of town life. Helena listened to those comforting words. They gave her a gentle warm glow but her inner most instincts were telling her the time to "get out" was now. To delay was foolish.

"This man" (she repeated herself) who visited Madam Pavvla does know something. Helena could not shake off that feeling and those worrying disturbing thoughts.

Viktor considering himself well and truly "stuffed" with pastries called the waitress, paid the bill and according to Helena gave her a most ridiculously generous tip. Remembering when she first started work after leaving school. That was the very sum she was paid each week!

The waitress was very pleased (no surprise) with the tip and taking them to the front door said: "Please come again. You are both very welcome!" (again… no surprise!)

Viktor was giving an unnecessary boastful demonstration as to how wealthy he currently was! Good thing… it had stopped raining.

Viktor and Helena parted with a kiss and hug as lovers do. With a promise to meet soon.

Helena was very troubled about the "work" that Viktor has been undertaking for the last two years. He made light of it but passing government documents is a most dangerous activity and acting as an undercover agent is spying in anyone's language. She wondered if Viktor would ever terminate this "work". She considered, from what she reads in the newspapers, most people who do this sort of thing carry on till it's too late, so what could she do about it? Appeal to Captain Macilroy. Perhaps? She gave the matter a lot of thought as she slowly walked home. An idea came, she decided to take the two Marshrupta buses and pay a visit to the British Embassy. *He always seemed a nice man to me...* thought Helena, and he may be understanding. After all, people like Viktor are surely "two a penny" and someone else will no doubt step into Viktor's shoes? There would be a queue of people wanting to be paid handsomely for this? (clearly, Helena did not understand this business!) One hour later she arrived at the Embassy. Being well presented in attire, she thought there would be no difficulty in accessing the building. The guards at the main entrance eyed her suspiciously as she approached, addressed her in Russian, then in English.

A problem with her English passport would be her ticket entry. One guard escorted her to the reception desk. The polite receptionist lady addressed her in English.

"I have lost my Passport and a friend of mine who stupidly did the same thing last year was helped by a nice man called. Now let me think? it was James Mac. Mac something?"

"James Macilroy," interrupted the receptionist. The security guard left the lobby for the outside. "Yes. That's it James Macilroy. Do you think I could?" The receptionist rotated the day book: "Please sign in. Name address and telephone number. Do you have any positive ID madam?"

"No, I'm sorry I didn't come out with my other bag... I've got my driving licence in that one... you see my other blue handbag also has..." Helena paused and added her details into the book.

"That's OK... er," the receptionist rotated the day book Miss... er... Martin.

"Take a seat and I will ring up to Mr Macilroy's office."

Helena had opted for a non de plume, including false address and telephone number. She considered Captain Macilroy would not see her if she identified herself as Helena Maitland, his wife's housekeeper!

"Mr Macilroy will see you, Miss Martin. He said he has ten spare minutes only so that will have to do. Please go along, you go past my desk to interview room number four on the left. Wait at the door. I can see you from here to let you in. The door will open electronically. There are alarm points and bell push buttons in the room if you need to leave, but the door will remain closed other than for emergency fire exit reasons. Do you understand, Miss Martin? Are you OK being temporarily locked in so to speak? Do you need the ladies room before you go in?"

"No, I don't, thanks... Yes, of course. That's perfectly clear. Thank you."

The door to interview room buzzed, in she walked... and sat at a desk. The door closed behind her and clicked audibly as it locked shut.

A clinical room painted white. Similar to police interview rooms she had seen on TV programmers. No windows, just mechanical ventilation humming overhead distributing air.

Ten minutes elapsed before Macilroy appeared at the reception desk. They spoke briefly. The receptionist pointed to room number four. The door buzzed and he entered.

"Maitland... I don't... understand... what are you doing here? She said it was a Miss Martin... I must have misheard the name? Is there a problem with Pavvla... Madam Macilroy?"

"No, sir. I have a serious question to ask you concerning my boyfriend, well, my unofficial fiancé actually." Macilroy duly puzzled, pulled a chair and sat opposite her and tightly folded his arms. That is not a good start for Helena... the defensive, "I'm closed" body posture!

"I'm intrigued Maitland, what is it you want?"

Helen blurted out all that she knew about Viktor, and his work with the English and the passing of documents. She "leaned heavily" on... it must be a very important and worthwhile job (all lies) but if "The Service" could let him go, and get someone else they could get married. Of course, that is, if Madam Pavvla would allow, and I would see to it that he gets another job. A job that would not give me so much worry. Helena babbled "on and on" (deliberately) thinking that this was falling on sympathetic ears but, unknown to her, quite the reverse!

How gullible can a person be when in love!

Macilroy's arms slowly dropped from the folded position as Helena persevered with her sob story (eyes frequently watering) and he lightly drummed his fingers on the table before selecting his cigarette case and lighting a cigarette. (He seemed unconcerned the smoke alarm might activate.) Helena refused a cigarette and finalized her story, now exhausted. Everything that was needed to be said had been said. She could do no more than await his generosity.

Macilroy's facial expression never changed during the dialogue. He is Poker trained!

"Well Maitland. Your story is interesting. I regret there is nothing I can do for you. You see, I have no idea what you are talking about and I have never heard of this man Viktor er... whatever his name is... and as for documents being passed from England to Russia... Well, your friend must be under some illusion. This is the British Embassy and we don't go in for that sort of thing. I suggest you give a good talking to this friend of yours and tell him to forget his fantasy of being some type of James Bond, and I must add such accusations are very serious. Because I know you and believe you to be a good upstanding citizen, although a misguided one, I will take the matter no further.

"I suggest you go home and get on with your work for Madam Macilroy and let this silly business pass from your thoughts. Furthermore, I think you should consider most seriously whether your relationship with this Viktor man is sensible. He is telling you yes of a most dangerous nature and can only get himself, and obviously yourself in deep water. Do I make myself clear Maitland?" Helena was deflated.

"Yes sir, sorry sir, I only thought that if..." Macilroy held up his hand, end of discussion. He stood and buzzed the reception for the door. The door opened and Macilroy walked from the interview room behind Helena (Miss Martin). The door closed automatically.

Captain James Macilroy shouted instructions to the receptionist: "See the lady out will you?" He immediately turned and disappeared along the corridor. Fortunately Macilroy had said "the lady" and not Maitland. Helena signed herself out as Miss Martin and left the embassy. A security guard escorted her from the building. She felt as if she had just been to see the headmistress at school and been admonished for smoking in the dorm!

Helena did not realize what a stupid thing she had done, but it was for the love of Viktor and she had hoped she would be met with sympathy and understanding. Instead, Macilroy denied everything. This left Helena with a smidgen of doubt as to whom was truthful... Macilroy or Viktor? Surely Viktor would not tell such stories although?

Returning to his office James Macilroy made a phone call to Nikolai Petrov at Lubyanka HQ. Five days later the Pravda newspaper read – with small headlines on page four;

"Anglichanka Naydena Utonuvshey." Generally equating to; "English woman found drowned."

Away from the "happenings" at The British Embassy with the naive innocent Helena Maitland and the not so innocent James Macilroy, Captain James's not so innocent colleague in crime Sir Grantham Hargreaves-Sykes along with English Joe had taken themselves to a warehouse not too distant from the old docks were, close to the river.

The devious duo were having to "work even harder" now that the other thugs… Dima, Maxim and Leonidas were safely "tucked up" thanks to the skill of the RIS.

They will remain captives! Russia know how to treat criminals, unlike the UK!

Since the demise of the storage facility at the Glavny store, new premises must be located. Although the heroin was confiscated by the RIS, a new consignment is on its way on a container ship and the drugs must be quickly stored safely, ready for distribution as before.

There were derelict warehouses scattered about this area. This was due to the recent insatiable appetite by Russians for demolition and new construction.

Russia was going through the very early stages of transition… from the old to the new. The principle difficulty was, and is, the people are very unsure as to what can legally be undertaken in compliance with the State. Is Russia free or is it still "watching!"

The "old school" such as those controlling Lubyanka were also themselves unsure.

When bringing in someone… him, her or them, for questioning, do they:

A. Beat the living daylights out of them, leave them without food for a week in an underground dark cell and ask questions later when they are insensible or…

B. Ask them to come in, take a vodka and have a nice chat!

The difficulty of what to do crosses all activities. But (a) is alive and kicking!

Demolition takes place of old structures and often those with important heritage disappear regardless of their possible importance, ready for the new building. In cautious situations, an old building such as a derelict warehouses will sit in a neglected condition until some capitalistic entrepreneur (dirty words) will "take the bull by the horns" to demolish and be damned.

Our unscrupulous drug dealers have located a warehouse planned for demolition two years hence, so there it will sit, empty. The owner was delighted when the offer to take a letting for the two year period and place it in the hands of English Joe and James Macilroy. For him, as warehouse owner, he need not know for what purposes the warehouse was intended;

"You take it and whatever you do is no concern of mine comrade!"

The warehouse had a side vehicle access for unloading at the rear relatively out of sight from the main road. This suited them well. The awaited third "guest" was late. Thirty minutes late.

A large black limo arrived with matching black windows. A chauffeur leapt out of the car and opened the back door. A leg appeared followed by an immaculately dressed pin stripe suited male with dark sunglasses. Two other males also immaculately dressed got out of the car and stood either side of "Costa Rica". What his name really was no one knows but like many of "his type" the reputation proceeded him. This is the "Mister Big" of the drug world.

The three stood by the car.

Costa Rica (CR) looked somewhat ridiculous at five foot three (in old English measurement) with two giant males at six feet three in their socks. All three in dark sunglasses.

Where is Marlon Brando! He should be in this!

CR looked up at the sky. He sniffed the air. He looked to the right then to the left then at the warehouse. He strolled forward with the two "attendants" glued to his side. He spoke: "You are?"

Sykes held out his hand. CR ignoring it, looked up at the sky at a large group of starlings as they flew past They dive and dart to the right, then to the left, always as if they are talking to each other so as to stay in the group, yet also, in messy format as if they couldn't see properly… but they always did seem to coordinate and fly in similar directions. "Maravilloso," muttered CR (wonderful)

It was as if the watching of starlings was far more important than shaking hands at that moment… and it probably was…

This was "Control" with a capital "C" by CR. His body language said: I'm in control, you wait upon me! He spoke: "It good to see working together. All go same way, si? Birds, like people, si, they should." A black gloved hand (gloves, in summer?) belonging to CR slowly projected forward. Three fingers gave a limp handshake. Does he not wish to touch "rif raf?" With a – yuk… yuk… yuk. Sykes introduced himself: "Grantham Hargreaves-Sykes… Mr… Cost… Sir… plea." He was not permitted to finish.

"And dis is?" (his English was just passable) English Joe held out his hand. It was ignored.

"Joe, sir, I work with Sir Grantham, they call me English Joe because I am…"

"Aw, yes, I 'ave 'erd of you. You do a lot for me, si? So, dis be der place. It looks good I think?" He walked forward, they parted like watery waves for Moses.

English Joe tackled the three huge padlocks with some difficulty, un-securing the doors.

They entered. All five, including the "hit men" Joe secured the doors inside.

The warehouse was huge, vast, high, long and wide. Quite bright due to scattered translucent rooflights intermixed with the Chrysotile asbestos corrugated sheeting. There was some signs of water penetration due to cracked sheeting but ninety percent of the floor was dry. The walls were concrete. The ground area was of a concrete floor construction with steelwork supporting the main structure. There were some small offices and toilet areas. Whether they were operative would be established later. The floor area was generally open with hundreds of small unwanted articles of debris left by the previous occupiers. Very dirty and untidy but no bad smells.

The floor was littered; paper, boxes, pieces of broken wood and twisted metal, upturned buckets, two old doors lying flat, broken glass, pieces of a bicycle, a dismembered step ladder, a torn overcoat, hosepipe fragments… in fact just about any type of superfluous debris one could name, if it existed, it was there.

The tidiness however was not the main point… which was suitability to store the awaited heroin cargo and security of the warehouse itself. That was vitally important.

It seemed to fit the purpose. There were no murmurs of dissatisfaction from CR.

They walked around and looked in every area including through the office window at the rear yard. Following numerous grunts, CR said: "That window will have to be closed and toilets cleaned and to work, si. Clean place up, I want it spody (spotless) tidiness… See to it!"

From his comments at that stage, it appeared all was satisfactory.

CR grunted and muttered further as he conducted his inspection and added.

"Doors to front and back to geeve better security locks. Cameras will needing to be fitted in and out, and loose roof sheets if they lose, need to made mending si? Do these things and I take. See to it Sykes... si? Do now. I want done by one week."

Sykes was not often upstaged by people. Any embarrassment he felt, which he did, was covered by a yuk... yuk... yuk... and as always, this he did before saying: "Of course, Mr... Cost... Sir... We... I will see it is done in time for next week."

English Joe, unusually in control of himself retorted: "No problem mate, we'll see to it!" This tended to make Sykes cringe but CR was unaffected. Sykes and English Joe walked to the front doors with CR and the gorilla duo. Stepping out into the sunshine, Joe made safe the warehouse with the padlocks, testing each one in turn with a sharp tug to ensure all was secure.

CR did actually thank Sykes and Joe but only offered his gloved hand to English Joe, and why... all part of the "controlling technique!"

"I at Lotte hotel in Moscow. You ring me there si." They entered the car and swooped off!

Several days elapsed. Nothing heard from Galina. Honestly speaking, I quite liked the silence. A perfect opportunity to relax. Not a lot of relaxation in this job, so grab with both hands. The weather had picked up again and the sun shone brilliantly in the sky.

Time to enjoy my new position in the garden, south side, for some reading. A new place away from the sight of the car park comer. I did not even wish to see the burnt black tarmac where my car was vandalised. The less I see of it the better.

Commencing the second volume of "War and Peace" – there is certainly plenty of trouble to come in this story. I know how they felt... "tip of the iceberg!"

I was just settled into my book when the "sticky tape" waitress came running out, gesturing with her hands that I was wanted on the telephone. Thanking her, I entered the reception area and walked by Monika at the desk. She thumbed her hand rearwards to the back room and smiled, a Russian smile is as good as an English one! Irina was at the desk totally surrounded by paper.

She held the telephone receiver and whispered; "Galina."

"Hello Ric, we have got it so, all in now ready. We can..."

"Galina… hold on, you've got what and what is it and what is ready?"

"The passport, Ric. My department has approved of your plan. Actually they not prevent you from doing plan because it between an Englishman and the British Embassy, but it good to know all OK. Da, yes? We have Mexican passport in name of Manuel Martinez."

It's infuriating… sometimes Galina rambles on as if one knows precisely what she is talking about. I do now!

Our last discussions related to my idea to blackmail Macilroy. I had "the play" and the actors were apparently keen. With a passport we could set the wheels in motion, but rehearsal role play would be essential. A lot hinged upon obtaining the fake passport Paren's father Igor, was obviously ready. His son Ivan was almost hysterical with excitement and Irina's cousin, the one with the camera, had apparently said: "I ready to geet Engleesh in troouble now." (Nasty piece of work that one!)

Galina went on to say they had not "let the grass grow". Igor had grown a bit of a fuzz below his nose. His hair and skin had been darkened slightly and when he resembling a dago Mexican, the photograph was taken. Galina was impressed with the result. He looked a real gangster!

I informed her I need to move to the Hotel Marriott tomorrow and when settled we can organise matters in detail for a get together… Act one scene one! She agreed and rang off.

I asked Irina if I could telephone London. She readily agreed and volunteered to leave the room;

"Not necessary," I said, "Please stay."

"Department Blue 17" was connected, charges reversed as usual. I informed "Blue" all that had occurred and everything that was "in hand". The means to get information from Macilroy in order to establish who was transferring documents from London was well favoured. He agreed the RIS would be best kept out of the actual task itself. When concluding the phone call he said: "Excellent – good luck. Don't get shot." He put down the receiver sharply as always. Comforting! Irina smiled and took the receiver from me and replaced it on its cradle.

"It good he happy Ric, yes?"

"It good he happy Irina, yes."

I discussed tomorrow's hotel move with Irina, and as for the account everything is to be settled directly with London, so nothing to pay. All now remaining was to pack and depart after breakfast. Irina called in Monika.

They both stated (with translation to Monika) that it is essential to keep in touch… I was very aware of that!… and I could return at any time for any purpose, or to use the telephone. Anything at all. I was eternally grateful to these two ladies, but matters were still ongoing and far from complete. Leaving the Moscow Star was regrettable but that was what Department Blue 17 required. So be it!

All packed. One small and one large suitcase, both prepared. A good tidy up, fold down bedding sheets etc. (It's what good English people do!) and down for a late breakfast.

Passing the desk I handed Monika the key. She was in full flow on the telephone with an argumentative person. She half smiled and held up a sideways hand. If one thinks an English person fumed in anger is hazardous… you should hear a Russian female!

I placed my two cases near to reception area and went in for breakfast. It was relatively deserted? "Sticky tape" waitress served me. I asked as best I could why the place was deserted. She replied as best *she* could, which was difficult to comprehend, but I gathered there was some kind of "event" taking place today so guests had taken their breakfasts early.

"Oh, that's good," I said to "sticky tape". "I thought I was dead!"

"Errrghh?" I should have known better!

A terrific breakfast. Full English, all designed to ensure an early death, that is, if the Mafia doesn't finish me first! The food improved considerably during my stay. Change of cook perhaps? Afterwards, I offered my temporary farewells to Monika and Irina and awaited the Taxi. It wasn't far from The Moscow Star to the Marriott Hotel but carrying the heavier of my two cases was uncomfortable, so I opted for "lazy".

Taxi paid in the Tverskaya Street front entrance, engine ticking over. Four traffic vehicle lanes on one side and two lanes on the other did not incur any hooting from irate drivers. In England there would have been a great deal of "F" words. In America someone would probably be shot!

The friendly driver helped me with my cases into the Reception area. A few extra Roubles for a tip put a smile on his face along with numerous nods, smiles and a handshake!

(Had I made a mistake and given too much?)

The reception area was stunning. A magnificent hotel without exaggeration, yet this Marriott is not expensive either by Russian or English standards. Massive concourse, huge circular marble-est columns with matching floors, glass illuminated ceiling. This was style.

I apologized to the reception lady that I was two days late, due to business commitments… this she indicated in perfect English, not to be a problem.

"The room was booked and would stay that way."

She requested my passport (giving me some degree of concern) I asked if that was essential. "For non-nationals, passports must be lodged with us for the duration of the stay, State regulations. The only time passports are not taken is for a non-national staying for one night only, and prepaid everything in advance. In that situation it is only necessary to show the passport and the details logged. Your booking is open ended and will be paid directly by electronic transfer by your business company in London on the day of your departure. I hope that is satisfactory for you sir… Mr… (looking at my passport) … Hartland?"

"Perfectly. Thank you." She added: "Please feel free to walk around. Use the gym, bar, swimming pool. All is for you to enjoy, sir." A 'slave' (Americans call them 'Bell Boys') was beckoned and she told him in Russian where to take me, giving him the key with a giant golden ball attached, (no one will walk off with that!) We took the lift up to the first floor. He attempted some words of 'Ennglleeesh' and I adulterated some words of Rooossssian!

Again, a few Roubles lightened up what appeared to be a miserable face. Superb room. Immaculate. Overlooking the car park to the rear of the hotel. I did the perfunctory walk about viewing the bathroom, bedroom and an adjoined business room with desk and telephone. Nothing was wanting. Unpacked, then slum it on the bed reading the hotel book of instructions, fire escape, places of interest, times for the restaurant etc. Very comprehensive. The only thing missing was details for my plan to "get" Macilroy. That was down to myself. I need to familiarise myself with the layout of the hotel and specifically means of escape to the car park If I can't find a quick way out without being discovered, the plan will have to be drastically amended. After lunch I will take my walkabout to get the feel of the hotel and establish how to fit it into my "master-plan."

After a methodical reconnoitre of the hotel's layout I was left reasonably satisfied that the idea to embarrass and disgrace Captain James Macilroy was possible. There are some factors that will always be left to chance but that is the risk with every operation such as this.

"Chance" that the weather will be cold or cloudy, and that affects the way people use the car park, "chance" that the car park camera might not exclude the parking space that will be needed.

"chance" that someone might be in it... the only parking space not covered by the security cameras, "chance" that Macilroy might shout and holler "blue murder."

"chance" that upon the escape from the room that "the players" may bump into a whole host of guests meandering along the corridor, "chance" that the fire escape door is alarmed, "chance" that the hotel might decide to undertake a fire alarm evacuation at the very moment of our operation... and a million other risks that could occur... but that is the "chance" we have to take!

The evening dinner was as expected, superb. Plenty of every type of food imaginable with careful attention to the whim of each of the guests by well-presented waitresses and waiters. That is also some concern. The amount of staff is vast and they buzz about like bees within the restaurants as well as serving guest in their own rooms... another "chance" enters the equation of risks!

After dinner I took myself to the lounge with a cappuccino and with "War and Peace" second volume to resume the saga of the family involved. Like many unfortunate people, their happy elegant lifestyle is turned upside down, inside out War affects everyone, the rich and the poor. The difference is, the poor had very little to lose, little more that their lives, poor souls. For the wealthy Russian nobility their lives and possessions took a major toll. To go from rags to rags is less tolerable than from riches to rags!

Deep into my book I was aware of a presence. A voice said "Mogu ya sest?" (may I sit) I fingered the page in my book and looked up. A very elegant lady of about forty years of age stood looking at me whilst balancing a saucer and cup.

"Da... I am sorry I do not speak very good Russian."

"Ahh, you are American?"

"No, English."

"Ah. That good I hate Americans. I like English. I speak some."

I shuffled sideways and moved an ashtray on the table. She sat, smiling and placed her saucer on the immaculate glass table top. The lights above shone down in reflection. It also reflected the vision of this stunning well dressed and obviously wealthy lady.

We both held our coffee cups to our lips waiting for the other the continue which we did together, virtually stating the obvious... "Are you on holiday/Are you staying in the hotel?" I held out my hand and informed her I was on holiday and staying in the hotel for a week or so and my name is Ric Hartland… pleased to meet you etc., etc.!

"I am Countess Valina Malerviana, Mr Hartland. I am as well to please to meet you." What is a countess doing in a hotel like this? It is a fantastic hotel, no arguments about that, but certainly not the most expensive in Moscow, which is where I would expect the titled to reside. "I see it, I sorry but your book, I know it saw the cover. I read it as a teen girl myself. It good da!" I explained "I was only half way through but enjoying it very much… but extremely sad."

"It sad and but not real, but just like things happen at that day. Terrible. My ancestry also had that." I did not wish to pry because this type of history opens old wounds and seems impolite. I left it to her to relay anything she cared to state… which she did. Telling me about her background and how her story of her great grandparents succumbed with similar sorrow but in a lesser capacity because her family was not as 'high' as the family in the story.

"I am very sorry to hear that madam." She laughed at my reply.

"Oh, you do not call me madam. It not necessary Mr Hartland. I call you Ric da?"

"May I call you Countess?" again she tittered.

"Yes you do that but I know you make mistake Mr… Ric… everyone does. My parents like to play funny trick on their baby. I not a countess… my *name* is Countess. I was christened Countess Valina Malerviana. It can be good to get best seat in restaurants and theatres da, especially when I travel abroad to countries oversea, they like that name to call me where I go. Do you know what I say Ric? It like you name is Lord Ric, and then everyone think you real lord then when you telephone to." I interrupted her with a "laugh-out-loud" gesture which she also joined in.

We both laughed in unison at the very idea.

"Oh me, Lord Ric. Yes I like that. It would certainly get me a seat on the bus!"

Our laughter brought the attention of a waiter who arrived in full flight asking if "The Countess" would like anything, to which she ordered two more cappuccinos. She chuckled and said: "You see what I mean Ric. My name is better than just Valina da? Sometimes people do not a want me to pay but I always pay. I do not do that things with people. It not right. Even in Russia today, many people like the idea of a countess. Many sad to see it change da? But some do hate nobility." This woman is fascinating. What a life she must have had, and is still having, because her parents gave her a first name of countess. Many times an advantage, but not always!

Perhaps I might change Ric to Lord Ric when I get back to the UK, if I ever do?

Let me consider? Lord Ric Hartland of the Secret Service Department Blue 17? Perhaps not! Countess informed me she was a war historian, partly by work and partly as a hobby and loved the numerous historic events that occurred, especially when there are secret agents like the awful Burgess and Maclean types... just like the real James Bond men da? But nasty people those men. This was suddenly getting a little close for comfort and feeling 'hot under the collar'. Does she really know who I am or is this really just idle chatter? Is she under some instruction by a Russian or English secret service herself and playing games to extract information?

Am I assessing this situation as clearly as I should? Caution!

"What do you do Ric. Are you millionaire?"

"No. I sell shirts."

"Ah... That is sounding interesting. Does it take you around the world to sell your shirts?"

"Oh no. I'm just here on holiday. I don't travel around the world on business."

The waiter appeared with two more coffees. He simply said, "Gospozha," (madam) as he placed them from his tray on to the table. Countess lifted the cup to her lips, and when replacing it on to the saucer a loud clunk as her huge gold bracelet clattered against it knocking the spoon on to the floor. The waiter turned and dived to the floor to retrieve the spoon and again whispered: "Gospozha."

"Why you here without your lady friend? I sure you must have lady friend, yes?" *Is she probing?* I thought.

"Yes, she could not come. Her mother had a sudden accident so she had to cancel, but I came." Countess excused herself for a short time to visit "the ladies room". She disappeared across the room, observed by others. She is a most elegant lady and beautifully dressed... but why do some lady's with black hair feel the need to dye their locks blond? She was gone for ten minutes or so. I saw her approaching. She was stopped by a male. His arm was in a tight sling close to his chest It was quite a distance but I know Petrov when I see him. There was an exchange of words with various hand waving and nods. Petrov must know I am here, no doubt… blast it!

Countess returned and sat. Another sip of coffee. She complained it had got cold.

"A rather nasty man stopped me and ask question. He Russian. He want to know who I talk to. I tell him who I talk is my business and not his. He not say who he was. I think he had accident. He had arm in a sling. A nasty rude man I think I not like him at all." This is worrying!

"What are you here for, Countess?" (Do I ask more about Petrov?)

"I live in St Petersburg. I fly here to see sister. I not stay with her. I not like her husband, he nasty communist radical type, so I always stay here. It nice hotel. He not like my name!"

Time to move to think! I looked at my watch and gave an excuse… phone call home… I must do it now. Countess was sorry to see me go but: "We meet later, da?"

"Da… we meet again… later. *Izyinite* (sorry)… *do svidaniya* (goodbye)"

I returned to my room.

Chapter 10

Slumping on to my bed I gave a lot of thought to Countess along with the appearance of the fearsome Petrov. Sad to see him in a sling! Was that the result of our encounter? His attack upon me certainly deserved a souvenir to remember me by, or perhaps there are others who by similar encounter rendered him injured, if so, surely deserved! He is obviously not finished with me. I telephoned "Blue". It was necessary to inform him about Petrov and obviously the need for an important fact to be stated;

"If I disappear soon… you will know why!" Blue ended the call by stating;

"Good work, carry on. Luck be with you regarding your plan for Macilroy. It is imperative you get this information about the English document courier and, if you can, do try to avoid roughing up Lubyanka Russians if possible. Strange folk, they take great exception to it… bye!"

Next telephone call was to Galina. She was "out back" at the time but would ring back. I didn't want a return call, so I waited twenty minutes and tried again. I spoke with Galina and updated her about the Marriott Hotel and my sighting of Petrov's recent appearance.

We mutually agreed this was bad news.

I informed Galina it was now a good time for our "arrangement" (carefully chosen words) to take place. She would contact the others and we would meet at Borodinos. Once again I did not wish her to telephone me at the hotel unless absolutely necessary. I would telephone Galina this evening at six o'clock. On the dot of six I spoke with Galina.

The "others" had been contacted and we will all meet tomorrow at Borodinos at eleven am.

I wandered down to the Reception desk and found the receptionist with the best spoken English to ask about the passports. She informed me that all guests upon arrival have their passports logged and details forwarded to the State

Department Only day trippers "might" be excluded and that depends upon certain prescribed factors!

"Is this a problem, sir?" she inquired.

"No, I just wondered if my passport was safe, as I had already lost it and was a bit concerned."

"Absolutely safe sir. Never had a passport disappear in my time here for... urm... ten years." I thanked her but she obviously did not know the real purpose of my enquiry. It is clear, that is why Petrov knew I was staying here. Our next meeting will no doubt involve his other "friends". Was it a genuine encounter between Countess Valina Malerviana and Petrov or was it a defined meeting and passing of information? This currently I did not know. The future will reveal the facts!

I travelled to Borodinos by Marshrupta easily.

Arriving at ten fifty, I was met by Galina and taken upstairs.

Seated around a table in a cigarette smoke filled room was Irina, Paren (Ivan) Denisovitch... his father Igor, obviously Galina and myself and lastly, Kristina Karashenko, Irina's cousin.

I had met Kristina once before but she had taken on a transformation most bizarre since that time. She did not match with the rather nice name of Kristina... Boris would have been more suited!

Today she had close cropped spiky hair with a touch of red dye, no jewellery. A ragged shirt below what looked like a second hand pawn shop welders outfit complete with fabric braces, cluttered with metal badges. Huge black dirty army type boots with ill matching bright red laces.

(This is not going to be easy!)

She smoked a stubby cheroot, leaning on the table with grubby elbows, one hand on her camera. Only an open roof light saved us all from cannabis smoke suffocation... and I am a smoker!

I shook hands with Ivan and Igor. When it came to Kristina, she simply waved her cherooted hand sideways at me, dismissively in the air fanning her cannabis smoke.

Not wishing to be unkind, but as a female, she was pretty repulsive in my eyes.

I hope she can do the "Biz" but not dressed like a relative of Fidel Castro!

Coffee was served in a gigantic cafetiere with buckets of single cream and I took the stage as the saying goes… standing at the table end, I commenced with "the plan".

The "players" turned their seats to face me. I could see Kristina's neck had a hammer and sickle tattoo on the side of her neck. It seemed without question as to whom her allegiance was affiliated!

"The reason for today… please stop me if my English is too fast or not clear (they nod) is to tell you all my plan (I tried to use simple English where possible) to obtain a photograph of an English Diplomat who works at the British Embassy here in Moscow. We need to get him into a position of embarrassment with a compromising photograph. With such a photo in my possession I intend to shock him to such an extent that he will disclose the name of the person who is passing secret information. He then has a choice, inform or face disgrace. It is blackmail in anyone's language." This plan might work to our advantage. I just want the name of this person.

Kristina lights another cannabis cheroot The others pour out coffee.

"We have a fake Mexican passport Galina tells me." She holds it erect.

"This is for Igor to pose as a drug dealer."

Kristina then appears even more interested than before!

"We will also need a fake car number plate… anything would do, even made of cardboard, and I need Macilroy's home telephone number."

Galina states she will organize the fake car number plates. The telephone number of Macilroy's private home she already has obtained.

"Igor will check into the Marriott Hotel; I will provide him with cash. It will be for one night only bed and breakfast. The hotel reception will examine the passport but not take it… that is what I have been told. When it comes to it, Igor, otherwise known as Manuel Martinez, will ask for room on the south sunny side. Try for the first floor… pretend not to like heights or something else… you need to get a room on the first floor south side and that will hopefully be near the stair fire escape end of the corridor, that is very important.

"You will all arrive by car, with fake number plates, and park on the south side near the fire exit. I am hoping for a hot day because guests try to park away from that side as it is unsheltered. They usually try to park on the other side near the shelter of the tress away from the hot mid-day sun. At the appointed… the right time, you wait at the fire exit door and I will let you in. The door has to be opened from the inside. I am also hoping it is not alarmed, I feel fairly confident it is not."

"What if it is?" asked Kristina... quite rightly.

"I'm hoping that it isn't!"

"Kristina and Ivan follow me up to the first floor, up to the room which will be occupied by James Macilroy and Igor as his visiting Mexican drug dealer Martinez."

"I not understand now. Why am I in room then with this man?" asked Igor.

"I will come to that in a minute, Igor."

"We will tap three times on the door. Igor will be ready for this and open the door from inside the room. Ivan and Kristina will run into the room. Ivan will be wearing a long jacket or lightweight coat with only swim wear or brief short pants on, so from the waist up, he will appear naked. Igor will stand to the side of the room away from the camera... this must all happen very quickly."

"Ivan will rapidly throw off his jacket and hug Macilroy and face Kristina, looking surprised."

"So what I do?" Kristina sensibly inquires.

"You take as many photos as possible only showing Ivan and Macilroy in a seemingly embrace. It must appear in the photos that Macilroy is with a naked young boy. The shock of this happening so quickly should leave him transfixed... at least, that is what I am hoping."

"I take motorized my camera. It take photos, many in seconds. You have twenty five in ten seconds. It take many good photo clear and colour, da?"

"That sounds good Kristina. A lot of shots... photos I mean... all from the waist up with the naked Ivan holding on to Macilroy should do the trick?"

"Trick ?"

"Oh... it should be good for what we need," I elaborated for the word trick.

"Then what is next?"

"Ivan puts on his coat quickly and you all leave the room. I will be outside the room and will come with you down the fire exit staircase to the car park. If I encounter anyone whilst you are all in the room... I will have to deal with that if the situation arises, but at lunchtime, which is the time I am trying to arrange, is best because most guests are in the dining rooms."

"I am in room first you say. What I do as Manuel Martinez with this man?"

146

"Ah, yes. Firstly… is everyone else clear on what they are to do?" They nod… da! "Manuel Martinez, drug dealer otherwise known as Igor. This is where your acting skill comes in… you have acted before, yes, Igor?"

"Da. I act good for you."

"Now is your chance to be a Mexican drug dealer, but the script must be your own. You will have to work out some type of believable drug dealing patter…"

"Patter?"

"Oh… Patter… words to use like a Mexican drug dealer that wants to buy a consignment of heroin. Macilroy has the means to sell heroin and you are there to buy it. He will be very suspicious and you need to be very good at your acting skills. You must keep him interested until you hear that knock on the door. Then, as I said before, you stand aside whilst Ivan and Kristina do their bit… yes… da? When finished, you all rapidly exit the room leaving Macilroy totally phased. When everyone is safely down stairs, escape is quickly made in the car."

I then went over the whole scenario again and made each person state their particular part in the plan and the way in which they all interact After five sessions they were "action and word perfect".

"To achieve the arrangement with Macilroy I will telephone him and try my best to use a fake Mexican accent. This is to get the appointment with him and encourage him to meet at the hotel Marriott. An appointment to meet a drug dealer named Manuel Martinez wanting to purchase one hundred kilogrammes of heroin each month for the next year. Understood?"

"Yes/da!"

"Igor's voice is not identical to mine but over the telephone, and for the first time, I don't think that will matter, and I am sure Macilroy will not suspect the voice on the telephone is any different from Igor's voice when he poses as Manuel Martinez face to face in the room… all clear?"

"Yes / da."

Igor and I chatted for a while listening to each other's voice with the intended phoney Mexican accent After thirty minutes we were sounding quite effective, quite authenticity Mexican!

Igor is a short man in stature, almost square. His size and new "Mexican" colouring along with the tyre-mark moustache was really the part. He reminded me so much of a friend I once had when I played Rugby at school. A short square friend who played fly half and ran like the wind.

On mentioning this to Igor, he smiled a large ear to ear grin and said he also played Rugby in his teens and often played the position of fly half.

"Ah... me too, one hundred metres in thirteen seconds," he boasted. Impressive!

Igor looked so much like a typical Russian with his rounded, slightly ruddy face and bushy eyebrows. In Moscow one would say he was definitely Russian. In Caerphilly one would say he was certainly Welsh, and as a Russian fly half, I'll bet he was good.

"I like plan. I like to get Englishman in trouble." (guess who?) "My camera will not fail. It good." There certainly seems to be a personality problem with Kristina. It's not so much she is a man hater or an Englishman hater, but an everything in the world hater... but hopefully she will do her job.

Things were becoming a little more relaxed now. Everyone seemed to understand the "plot" and apart from a few questions "the players" were gearing themselves up for "the first night". Chatting informally to Ivan, he was totally beside himself with excitement about the whole thing. He kept repeating he liked to play jokes on people... some joke!

He threatened to take all his clothes off... I left that up to him!

He'd had a haircut which in my old days was called a short back and sides. It made him look even younger. Perfect for the part. I asked him to stick it down flat with grease.

I spoke to Galina and Irina. They were full of praise for the plan and *"knew"* it would work. I was very pleased to have their confidence and support.

I spoke quietly to Irina whilst Kristina was in full flow conversation with Igor and Ivan. "Kristina can't come dressed like that. If she is seen anywhere near the hotel I'm sure they will telephone the police. She looks alarming and not really a part of hotel life. If she comes dressed like she is today, things might get tricky, if she is spotted... do you understand?"

"I speak with her. She not come like that Ric. She wear proper clothes. I tell her."

I thanked Irina. She understood precisely what the difficulty is. I left it to her.

"Does everyone understand fully as to what they must do and are you all happy about everything?"

"If there are any difficulties we need to iron them out now."

"Iron?"

"Sorry... to smooth out any difficulties now as we can't do it on the day."

"Da/yes. Is good. We do. We win it. My photos good. It be good to do, da… etc., etc."

"Ok, I will give Igor the money now. Galina will let him have the passport. The next thing for me to do is to get this appointment agreed with Macilroy for the meeting at the hotel Marriott.

"When that is achieved… and I hope it will, Igor will check in for one night bed and breakfast at the Marriott and pay cash, but now you must all wait for me to give you the date.

"Galina will organize the false car number plates as we have agreed and so, now all there is for you to do is wait for the telephone call from me. I anticipate it will be quite soon.

"Macilroy will obviously be suspicious upon receiving an unsolicited telephone call from me to his private home telephone number. He will be on his guard being approached by myself, a drug dealer… but I believe his greed for money and success in the eyes of 'Costa Rica' will be too much to resist. So I believe he will fall for it hook, line and sinker."

"Hook, li."

"Sorry… I've done it again… he will fall for the plan completely. Let's have some more coffee." Galina ordered some fresh coffee and numerous biscuits came to accompany.

Irina had an aside with her cousin. There was a lot of quiet talk and nodding, but no raised voices. Kristina rolled another cheroot type of cigarette and also offered me one.

"Sigareta?"

I politely declined. I had no ambition to start cannabis smoking today or ever! Although; with the dense fog that Kristina puts out, I feel as if I have already been smoking it. My clothes must reek of cannabis. I feel sure there will be trouble on the Marshrupta on my return to the hotel!

Ivan was interested in Kristina's gesture to me and approached her, but his father, Igor flicked his ear in disapproval and tugged his arm, with a severe frown added.

We finished our coffee and biscuits. All gave their comments and farewells to each other and in parting stated words in Russian to match ours… "See you later, see you soon etc., etc."

Galina offered to drive me back to the hotel but although it was a fair "stretch" I elected to walk so as to hopefully disperse the odour of cannabis. I needed fresh air!

I did arrive at hotel Marriott smelling slightly "sweeter" but a shower and placing all my clothes in the hotel laundry bag was the obvious outcome in order to smell "normal again".

That woman Kristina is so unlike her pretty cousin. Perhaps that is the problem? Growing up with attractive family members often makes the "ugly duckling" go the opposite way.

For today, that was – Act One Scene One concluded... now for Act One Scene Two!

I elected to rest in my room. Hot day, but the air-con sorted that out with total efficiency. What did we do before it? Sweated profusely I suppose! I looked at the Hotel Guide again and once more perused the places to go, sights to see etc. "If only." The one worrying item in the guide was the part about evacuation in case of fire. There was a caveat referring to fire escape referring to impromptu tests. The guide indicated that at "any time" as deemed by the hotel, there may be an unannounced fire escape test. Upon the sounding of the bell all guests must immediately leave their room and evacuate the building for assembly in the car park This is of course standard procedure in most hotels. It's just a nagging thought of it happening during "our siege".

A million to one chance, but the thought remained in my mind. I need to remove it!

For the rest of today, being Saturday, apart from glossing over the hotel guide I did a bit more reading of my novel. Being set in Moscow made it even more fascinating. My mind however kept wandering about the task in hand and especially my part... next to communicate with James Macilroy... to pose as a drug dealer and get that essential appointment with him.

This will not be an "easy ride" for sure, and the success or failure depends upon this meeting. I recall a previous conversation with "Blue" who considered the possible outcome of my assignment in Moscow could lead to a promotional rise to the next department. I have already discounted that prospect. My role is supposed to be "find out and get out". That was always the maxim with every assignment but this one has gone far beyond that description. My life is not always as safe as I would like it to be.

I desperately want to succeed in Moscow and more importantly… live to tell my grandchildren!

I deliberated over "the plan" time and time again and inwardly chastised myself for thinking of it in the first place, but the actors are in the wings and we must see it thorough. It is essential we get the name of this bugger who is ferreting documents from England and passing on to Moscow.

It would possibly have been more straight forward if my task had not got mixed up with the heroin situation and the RIS. However the friendship and help formed with Irina and Galina… and of course Monika, cannot be discounted. They are pretty amazing ladies to deal with these Mafia types, regularly walking the tightrope… and just how long can they stay on that slender rope? Time for dinner. I had another cooling shower and a shave. Looking in the mirror my thoughts went back to my father. How many times I watched him shave when I was a young boy. I always thought it would be so exciting to have whiskers and shave each day. That theory soon evaporated… and the nick in my chin at that moment made it all more real! Blast it!

Blood ran down my face and neck and wouldn't stop… not an omen, I trust!

With a red slit mark on my chin I eventually made my way to the dining room, fully attired of course, and settled for the best restaurant this time. A fabulous dining room with a series of large coffered domed roof lights in the ceiling. Stunning. The light poured in, diffused by solar glazing, and at seven o'clock the sky was still a cloudless blue. In different circumstances it would be bliss!

I sat at a table for two and gave my order to a lady waitress. Whilst starring mesmerized at the wonderful ceiling, another waitress came over and whispered in my "shell like" in Russian. "Sorry," I said, "I don't follow."

"Ahh… is ok, the lady Countess Valina, she ask if she can dine with you… you not mind, da?" I turned and saw Countess waiting near a column looking like a schoolgirl outside the Head's room! "Of course." I waved her in "Hello Countess, please do, come and join me." The waitress vanished. Countess was very apologetic but I insisted it was not necessary. I would be happy to share the table with her. She looked amazing. She smelt, looked, and even moved Cartier!

We chatted as she ordered. It was a delight to share dinner time with her. She has had such an interesting life and only been married once. A car crash changed that enjoyment, leaving her husband-less and with a knee replacement due to the collision impact I never noticed her limp but she indicated she had one. It never changed her appearance at all. Who would notice a limp? She seemed to glide across the floor with total feminine style... but oh that blond hair colour! The meal that evening was fabulous, as was the company, but I do miss my girlfriend.

The meals were superb as was the wine. Two shared bottles by Countess and myself slipped down without much of a trial! The waiters and waitresses were likewise in top form, very attentive. Cutlery if inadvertently slipped from anyone's grasp was virtually caught before it hit the floor... and was not wiped down the trouser leg as in certain comedy television programmes!

Ice cream and gallons of coffee finished the meal and at ten thirty pm Countess and I offered our polite but informal "good nights" Consulting her Cartier Tank wristwatch – she was having an "early night" but I was yet to linger awhile, with the excuse of a cigarette taken outside in the warm night summer air.

A waiter pulled the chair for "the Countess" (even I am starting to call her "the Countess".) and then my chair was courteously pulled aside for my exit.

They were on the table for clearance before we were able to leave the restaurant. It was certainly a most pleasant evening. How many more to follow I wondered?

I took the lift up to the first floor and then down the fire exit staircase to the car park. The exit door stood there tantalisingly, inviting me to push the bar to escape. If it is alarmed I may throw myself into the Moskva river! I looked at the bar and the triple multi shoots to the side and pressed it firmly. The push bar dropped and the door opened with ease. Silence!

I stepped out into the night air. There was that smell that one only seems to get when on holiday... warm air... perfume and food, the smell of cooking that seizes the senses.

I pushed the door slightly, not fully dosed. Out came the Gitanes packet, a cigarette selected and lit with my lighter. I looked at the Dunhill, a birthday gift from my girlfriend. I wished she was giving it to me now. No time to be morose. Think of the future. A positive one and within my grasp. I inhaled and blew smoke in the air and watched it rise. Described by my friend as tram drivers glove... not a fair description I also thought but I can understand something about these cigarettes... they are a love or hate brand. I love them, but some consider, lighting one of these, and the room is full of flies! Even an unlit Gitanes cigarette smells fabulous... to me.

Fifteen minutes of pure smoking joy!

I wandered around the car park taking in that lovely night air… the air that says, tomorrow is also going to be a good one. I found a standing ashtray and exterminator and squashed the butt into the pan. The ashtray stank just like its name and probably I did likewise, but no one to care that I smelt like the proverbial ashtray.

The car parking bay was immediately adjacent the fire exit door and if we can get this position on "the day" it will be perfect. I stood in the parking bay and moved forward and back without being seen by the security cameras on the lamp columns. There was no doubt that this bay, the only bay that could not be seen due to the position of the escape stair tower attached to the main building. In the quiet of the night it all seemed possible. Feeling a sense of success I returned to the fire escape door, stepped back in and pulled the push bar down. The side shoot bolts slid into place.

I ascended and mounted each step with a feeling of satisfaction.

The car parking bay was just right and the fire exit door was not alarmed. That is a good feeling to go to bed on. Tomorrow is Sunday. That is the day I am hoping Macilroy will be at home, the day for my telephone call disguised as Mexican drug dealer, Manuel Martinez.

I turned the lock to my room and entered thinking, *Yes… we can do it. We will do it.*

I do have some concerns about Ivan's enthusiasm. If he takes off all of his "kit" what will be the reaction from "the lovely Kristina?" With her looks it may be the only time in her life she is likely to see a … "you know what!"

I do not think it possible that she will scream and stand on a chair like a maiden frightened by a mouse… but who knows? I just hope Ivan will curb his enthusiasm and take his part sensibly and not frighten the horses!

I slept very well. Probably assisted by the quantity of wine consumed last evening.

At breakfast time I mentally ran over my own "script" for the verbal encounter with James Macilroy. My "patter" will be as agreed with Ivan. When rehearsing at Borodinos we both slipped into an easy style, speaking slowly seemed to blend well with Mexican/English and was certainly simpler to carry out. A slow drawl left less of a chance of slipping up with the accent and the assumed confidence that a character such as this, would have. Manuel Martinez would be the type of person dealing with the most hardened of the criminal world and would not be a "delicate fellow" by any stretch of the imagination. He would be confident, knows what he wants and knows how to get it. I never considered Macilroy might speak Spanish! Oh!

"Sir?" I was unaware of the waitress standing poised next to me waiting for my order. I was miles away in thought I ordered a full breakfast with coffee. No Cava wine for me. No sign of Countess this morning. She has probably been and gone.

After a good fill I returned to my room and lounged on my bed. My "script and patter" thronging in my head. My heart starts to pound, not from fear but fear of failure. I dialled. It rang ten times. Just at the point of replacing the receiver a voice said, "Macilroy." Here I go!

"Maceelroy… James Maceelroy?"

"Yes."

"Maceelroy of ze Britisher Embassy si?"

"Yes… can I help you?"

"I given name by friend. You can sell me what I need?"

"What is it you want? who are you?" (already he is irritated)

"I wanting to meet you, not talking on ze telephone, it not safe. A friend of mine say to ring you."

"Look I don't know who you are or what you want but I have no intention of meeting you, so I think it best I put the phone down as I am sure you have the wrong number so."

"Oh no, I 'ave ze right number, it friend of Costa Rica. I want buy and you want sell si?" An incredibly long pause with his breathing was audible. He continued: "How did you get my number and who is this Costa Rica?"

"Zis not time for ze messing Meester Maceelroy. You know who I am meaning and I not talk over zis phone. You 'ave goods to sell and you sell for Costa Rica so where when we can soon meet?" Another long pause. He is giving this a lot of thought. "Costa Rica he not like it if you do not sell si?"

Another long pause. More thought, coupled with suspicion and certainly fear and apprehension. "OK, what do you suggest. No dark alleyways. I'm not agreeing to that."

"Oh zat not good. I not deal in dirty alleyways Meeester Maceelroy. It not good. A hotel?"

"That sounds reasonable but I make no promises. Just you… when and where?"

"I zink it good place to meet at my Hotel si. In Moscow. We meet on Wednesday at noon si. I give you hotel and room number tomorrow. I ring you again si, zis ok?"

"Yes that will be ok. It gives me some time also. I need to make a couple of checks myself before I agree to meet you."

"Si, zis is good. You check, I happy with that (oh bloody hell!) I ring you Monday, is ok si?"

"Yes. Telephone me here at ten in the morning. Goodbye." The phone went down sharply. Amazingly I got away without him asking my name. That was a slip up on his side. Macilroy must be doing it in his pants now! Who is he going to 'check' with? That is worrying.

Macilroy replaced the receiver and lit a cigarette. (So did I!)

'Mr Big' otherwise known as 'Costa Rica' would not want to lose a potential buyer. It is necessary to verify this with him? Does he have direct contact with him? Only James Macilroy himself could answer that question.

Macilroy realised that he had omitted to ask the name of this Latin sounding 'dago' crook!

Added to that, when telephoning 'Costa Rica' at his hotel… surely that can't be his real name? Who should he ask for? Perhaps the drug baron "Costa Rica" does not really wish to be contacted at all, and that is why he did not give his real name to Grantham and English Joe at the warehouse? That is a possibility.

Oh hell! Macilroy immediately telephoned the Lotte Hotel.

"Good morning," (he spoke in passable Russian) "I am hoping to speak to one of your guests. His name is… (he cringed before uttering the name) Mr Rica."

"One moment sir. I will check the book."

He heard pages being flicked.

"Oh yes here it is sir Mr C. Rica. Mr Carlos Rica room 777, the luxury suite. He has left a note. Unfortunately he is not here at present. He is away for a few days. He has flown to Belarus for a short business trip, he will be back, he thinks, on Thursday or Friday. Is there a message you wish to leave?"

"No, thank you. I suppose he didn't leave a forwarding telephone number or address?"

"I'm afraid not sir, perhaps you might try again on Thursday or Friday?"

"Yes. Thank you. I will do that. Goodbye."

Twenty four hours passed without event.

I telephoned Macilroy at ten am. He was quite abrupt but indicated he had discussed "it" with "his people" and agreed to meet me at an hotel. I indicated to him I need to discuss this further with "my people" (everyone is telling lies!) and I will ring again before noon. That was acceptable. Phones down again.

I telephoned Borodinos and spoke with Igor. Galina gave Igor permission to leave his current duties and go immediately to the hotel Marriott and book in as agreed, not forgetting his passport, and the fact he was Manuel Martinez. Galina drove him by car immediately.

There was no time to waste. I was to await a call from Galina or Igor.

Galina telephoned me in my room at 11:30 am. Ivan had successfully booked it for one night bed a and breakfast, paying in full. The passport was glanced at but not held (thankfully).

Everything had gone to plan apart from one fact. Ivan had not been able to obtain a room at first floor level. The only room available at that far corridor end, facing south, was on the third floor room 303. This meant a long haul up and down the fire escape staircase, but the plus was the room was immediately adjacent the fire escape stair, so this location had plusses and minuses. So be it.

I telephoned Macilroy (Meester Maceelroy) at eleven forty five am. My Mexican drawl was holding up. I think it was improving!

We mutually agreed to meet at the hotel Marriott on Wednesday at twelve noon. I told him to come via the lift to the third floor, room 303 and not bother about checking in at the reception. They would not notice a person walking boldly in to the hotel, they are usually far too busy at the reception desk to notice.

Macilroy stated he would be happier to do that as he did not 'himself' wish to be observed.

This time he remembered to ask for my name, a pity, but I knew it had to be given.

The telephone receivers were placed down at both ends and I'm sure, at both respective ends, there were deep sighs of concern and apprehension... but the scene was now firmly set.

The "Plan" would take place at the Marriott hotel on Wednesday at twelve noon, room 303.

Macilroy to knock loudly upon the door and Senor Manuel Martinez, drug dealer, would be waiting inside for his visit.

I took the Marshrupta to Borodinos and had a late lunch with Galina. She permitted Ivan and Igor to "sit in" briefly. We went over the "script" again. I was assured everyone knew his role. There was some degree of excitement in the air, but not by me. I hope Kristina is similarly confident?

It transpired the day of the "siege" was a day of mixed blessings of gargantuan proportions!

It was like an inferno. The sun was fierce at thirty degrees C. An ideal temperature as far as the car park was concerned and a bonus to commence our "activity".

Most guests who had a car whilst staying at the hotel were vying for the far shady side, under the shelter of the neighbouring Plane trees. That suited our cause well enough.

The weather was scorching but, "sods law" the hotel air conditioning had broken down during the early morning. The mechanical engineers were tending the problem but up to that time, without success. This should not affect our plans.

Every hotel room window that could open on the south side was wide open. Hardly surprising, but at thirty centigrade and windless, the guests still suffered in the heat.

One bonus however, many guests were languishing in the pool taking advantage of a swim in the cooling waters. Many others were at the poolside slurping G&Ts with copious ice cubes.

11:30 am. Galina arrived by car sporting fake number plates. She parked adjacent the hotel fire exit away from sight of the security cameras and sure enough, few cars were on the sunny side.

Galina, Ivan and Kristina chatted for a while, almost suffocating in the extreme heat of the car, running over the plan and passing some idle moments.

This had been done time and time again so as to hone to the sharpest of stiletto points!

Igor was anxiously waiting in room 303, tapping his fingers on the desk and moping his brow. The sun relentlessly streaming through the window. The hot rays seeking out every opportunity to enter the room, uninvited! Macilroy arrived at twelve noon. Manuel (Igor) nervously opened the door.

At eleven fifty am I walked down the fire exit stair and opened the escape door.

Igor, and Kristina entered, leaving Galina to suffer in the waiting car. I closed the fire exit door, pushing the bar down. The side shoots performed as before. Kristina looked almost feminine! Irina's lecture had obviously worked, as she appeared very presentable, most unlike Castro!

We slowly ascended the stair up to the third floor. Even in the shade of the hotel, the heat was intolerable and we panted by the time we reached the third.

It was twelve zero five pm. We leaned on the wall inside the stair lobby doors, gaining our breath, silently, looking blankly forward at the opposite wall. I looked at my watch as did Kristina sweeping her camera on the straps carefully to her side.

We counted the minutes, the seconds, seemed like hours.

At noon, Macilroy should have been arriving to meet Manuel Martinez in room 303. We had no way of knowing whether he had arrived on time, or even at all! Another of those "chances!"

This was cutting everything so finely… we hoped Macilroy had arrived on time and was in the room negotiating a heroin deal with Igor, aka Manual Martinez, drug dealer and "actor!"

Ten minutes past the hour of noon, we pushed through the fire exit stair doors, entered the corridor, took the short route and stood outside room 303. I knocked firmly three times. We could hear voices from within. There was certainly more than just Igor in the room. The other voice was surely Macilroy. The door was opened by a tense looking Igor. I stood aside whilst the others stormed in. Outside, I waited looking up and down the corridor. No guests appeared. A period of quiet ensued from within room 303. Then, the battle commenced. Raised voices heard, accusations followed by what sounded like furniture being turned. More voices, instructions, warnings yelled! Then silence! The door opened. Kristina came out, camera in hand, saying: "Engleeshman he no more trouble,"

I anxiously asked: "What do you mean. What has happened?"

A red faced dishevelled Ivan followed Kristina, stating: "Macilroy dead!"

Chapter 11

Viktor Karashenko looked at his Rolex Datejust. He was personally proud and a little smug, that someone like himself could own such a prestigious timepiece. This would never have been achievable had he not been fortunate enough to be involved with the British. The frequent arrangement of collecting documents from England and taking them to Moscow must be the easiest job on the planet. Carrying papers… he thought… what a joke!

There was sufficient time before his flight via British Airways. Taxi (expenses paid by "client") was not experiencing any traffic difficulties today. The flight BA419, as far as he knew, was on time, and the conditions were admirable for the journey to the UK, Heathrow, as usual… all paid by "you know who!"

Arriving at the vehicular concourse, the taxi driver attempted to open the door for Viktor but he was too quick, he was out. That will save a tip! The driver offered to carry his case into the entrance area… (he was allowed two minutes stopping time)… that was also a refusal… another reason, no tip! These types of gratuities are not claimable as expenses, therefore Comrade Karashenko was always very sure how to save money, to be more specific, how to save his own money!

The taxi driver grunted at his "tip-less" passenger as Viktor strolled into the main entry concourse of the Domodedovo Airport.

The forty or so kilometres journey south east of Moscow had been easily achieved and there was an hour and a half before the scheduled departure to Heathrow. A quick telephone call to London would be necessary to advise on his arrival at the airport and to be assured of collection at Heathrow. This, soon achieved, Viktor held a cabin baggage and joined a long queue to the fight check-in departure desk.

After twenty minutes, slow footing with the flight passengers, he found he way to the front of the queue. Documentation was rapidly dealt with and information relative to his journey exchanged in brief. He then went through to the proper departure lounge in the direction via customs, baggage search and control.

He placed his case on the conveyor whilst holding his arms up "cowboy surrender style" whilst an official lightly frisked his clothing perimeter. Being cleared of anything offensive he strolled through to collect his small case and wandered past the scores of (as was his opinion) pathetic shops selling numerous goods that nobody really wants, apart from the booze… of course!

Viktor wandered into one of the many cafe, restaurant areas and had a coffee. It wasn't as bad as he had experienced on numerous previous occasions.

Afterwards he found a seat alongside a "million" other waiting passengers and watched the departure board flicker information, showing times and flight numbers. He watched his flight number BA419 gradually creep up board number three to the bottom of board number two when there was a loud commotion occurring not too distant.

A great crowd of people had assembled with some pushing and shoving along with flashing of personal cameras. (Why?)

Having time to spare, Viktor wandered over and joined the crowd, but looking over, and in between the shoulders of others he could see nothing worthwhile. Some pop star arriving perhaps?

"What is a happening?" he asked the lady next to him;

"Poliakov." He is arriving, getting off the plane now. He's just back from England. You know him? "Oh yes, I know of him, of course. Is that what the red carpet is for. Pumped up bloody politician." Poliakov is the leader of one of the many Russian opposition parties and being very cosy… a bit too cosy… with the English, he is not liked by many true Soviets.

"I don't like the man," the lady stated.

"Not many do," replied Viktor, "not many do."

Viktor craned his neck as did many other passengers as a large delegation walked through comprising numerous males and armed "henchmen".

Then followed more security men with what must have been Poliakov in the centre of the pack.

A gun shot rang out, some ladies screamed… many people dived on to the floor.

A man was seen jumping over various prostrate people and heading for… well… who knows where he was heading for. It was difficult to comprehend how he could possibly make an escape from this part of the airport, but escaping is clearly what he intended.

There was unorganized chaos. Various members of the delegation group were over Poliakov loosening his clothing and assessing the gunshot wound.

Many of the watching passengers chose to remain, kneeling low, some lying flat, some sitting but many rapidly departing the scene. This was not welcomed by the security men. Alongside the State Police, they physically gathered people as best they could who they thought could be involved, and part of what was obviously an assassination plot.

Viktor found himself within a large bunch of young schoolgirls and their teacher, who he was addressing before the gun shot occurred. They were quickly sorting out the wheat from the chaff! Viktor, was assumed to be the chaff and forcibly pushed to one side, including a few other males. With the police pistols prodding unkindly under their noses, there was no argument.

Six males were escorted (dragged unceremoniously!) across the concourse into a secure part of the airport and all bundled into a series of rooms along with State policemen. Two officers stood outside the main door leading to the rooms, with AK47's held across their chests at forty-five degrees, fingers on triggers, eyes peeled assertively!

Viktor, was kicked in the calf muscles of his legs so as to move him on more quickly.

Don't they realize, that is a way to slow a person down not speed one up. Idiots!

The part of the story will continue with Viktor in the first person!

I was shut in a room with a scowling policeman. He stood with arms folded with his back to the door after I was forcibly thrust into a chair. I sat like this for twenty minutes. The policeman remained mute staring forward, and refused to enter into any kind of dialogue.

The door was "tapped" upon, the officer stood aside, and two plain clothes officials entered the room. They sat adjacent each other in front of me and glowered across the desk.

The policeman resumed his position with his back to the door.

One official had a file with numerous papers inside which he pulled out, along with various photographs. I entered into dialogue: "I was waiting to catch a plane. I have had nothing to do with this, whatever is going on, and in ten minutes I am supposed to be going along to the final departure lounge for my plane."

It was as if they were deaf. They did not respond to my statement at all. After a body search...

"Did you shoot Comrade Poliakov or was it an accomplice? If it was you, who did you pass the gun to... I would like an answer."

"None of this is to do with me. I was watching, along with many other people when a gun shot rang out... and I saw a man fall... I assume it was the politician Poliakov... but I don't really know, I have only seen him on television."

"You have seen him on television. Enough times to know who to shoot?"

The other official took a wipe-tissue from a box and wiped my fingers. He then placed it into a sealed plastic bag saying: "That will show signs of gun use within the last half hour. Our scientist will be here in a few minutes. If you have used a gun and fired it recently it will show. You had better own up now or it will be the worse for you." (Surely his fingers contaminated the sterile wipe cloth?)

My suitcase was tipped upside down on the table. The items were picked out as if verminous. When all was inspected the contents of my case were swept aside and on to the floor like breadcrumbs.

This action was finalized by the kicking of all my items across to the side of the room and the case was similarly discarded, violently thrown.

"Empty your pockets and put everything on the table." This I did.

"Everything. Wristwatch, all jewellery and shoes too," I duly complied.

One official looked at my passport whilst the other examined my watch with interest.

"Now, Comrade Karashenko, if that is your real name, look at these photos. Do you know any?"

"No. I don't know them. Why... am I supposed to know them?"

"They are the members of *Black Four Seven.* You are a member of Black Four Seven."

I politely pushed the photos back across the desk. He pushed them back and laid them out again.

"I have never heard of Black Four... whatever it was you said!"

"I am from the State Police Service. My name is Mikanhov this is my colleague, Comrade Pelhova. We have met many like you before and we know when people like you are telling lies... you are a member of Black Four Seven...

162

the terrorist group that singles out politicians for execution... the founder members being Four female and Seven males. Which of these do you directly work for?" Pelhova carefully laid out the photographs again on the table in front of me.

"I don't know anyone and I'm going to miss my plane!" Pelhova replied.

"You are going to miss this plane and many others Comrade."

There was a knock on the door. The guarding officer opened the door and a male entered. Mikanhov handed the plastic bag to him.

"We'll have the result back to you within the hour. I can test this here at the airport."

Mikanhov stated that was acceptable as... they were "not going anywhere!"

I realized I was in for trouble with these two. They had already made up their minds about me. "One of these men in the photos is in the next room being interviewed by our colleagues. He will know you when he is brought in to identify you. It is now a good time to tell us of your involvement."

Pelhova studies the items on the desk along with my passport;

"I see you smoke the most expensive brand of Sobranie Comrade. A nice silver and gold lighter also, I think a good English make, yes? and you visit England quite a lot. There are a couple of English stamps in your passport I see. Do you also have contacts in England who do not like Comrade Poliakov?"

"I have visited other places in Europe, France and Italy... as you know only too well, customs do not always stamp passports, so there is nothing to that, is there?"

Mikanhov casually strolls around the room and asks: "What do you do for work? and why are you going to England today?" This is a difficult one!

"Oh, I buy and sell things that people want in England from Russia and vice versa." Mikanhov is getting irritated and impatient.

"I see you have a lot of money in your wallet. You don't have a proper job, a silver and gold cigarette lighter, an expensive make. You smoke the most expensive brand of Sobranie, you make many visits to England and have a very nice Rolex watch. Do you have a lady friend in England?" Why ask this?

"No. Look... I'm just a tourist going to England, that's all."

"Why, no girlfriends... you're not bent are you?"

"Certainly not, I am between girlfriends at present so to speak, and anyway, what has my girlfriends got to do with someone... someone, not me, taking a shot at a politician?"

Mikanhov stops his casual strolling and stops behind me. He places his dinner plate sized "mits" on my shoulders grabbing them tightly and, quite painfully, he rocks me back and forth saying: "A lot… everything you say and do… we want to know… and we shall know if. Understand?" There is a knock on the door. The officer stands aside and opens the door.

A dishevelled male with a bloodstained face, secured by handcuffs appears with two guards. One holding his arm and the other by the back scruff of his shirt, also very blood stained.

The first guards asks: "Well?"

The man looks at me and slowly shakes his head. The guards start to drag him out saying: "Pity for him. He fell against the door frame." They laugh and exit.

"Honor amongst thieves I think is a well-known saying in England. Yes, friend Karashenko?" Things are not going well for me and certainly not with the "interview" in the next room.

"He recognized you eh Viktor?"

"No."

"Now," asks Pelhova, "Let's go through this again shall we."

"You are standing with others at a place where Poliakov is arriving… just by chance, you happen to be there at that precise moment… and at that very precise moment he is shot from the very direction where you are standing. You chose to stand amongst a lot of schoolgirls! must admit that is clever. You pretend to be their teacher. Who would suspect a gunshot coming from a bunch of silly kids. It's clever yes? Then you pass the gun to your Black Four Seven friend who runs away to divert attention from yourself, eh? Again, very clever. Everyone starts to chase that man, the one we have in the next room, but he has disposed of the gun, probably in a waste bin somewhere. So let's stop this nonsense about being a tourist and tell the truth. We want the whole story or if you persist in this rubbish we will hand you over to our *other* colleagues… and they are not nearly as polite as we are. Do you follow me Comrade Karashenko? Have a cigarette."

He hands me one of my Sobranie's and lights it. He takes two more from my pack, handing one to Mikanhov, lighting them both, then pocketing my lighter.

Another knock on the door. The scientist enters. He whispers to Mikanhov who nods. The scientist exits. They both sit.

"Well. Let us now wonder why the swab wipe identified the person has used a firearm recently… as recently as today. Now why do you suppose that is, eh Karashenko?"

This is no doubt a ploy to make me confess to something I haven't done!

"The test is either faulty or there has been a mix up with the swabs. Perhaps it is the man in the next room, I have his results and he has my results or perhaps the whole thing is a set up?"

I felt a sharp hard slap across my face. I didn't see it coming. My nose started to bleed.

Pelhova picks up the telephone and dials. He speaks to someone in simple medical terms and the information he receives confirms the person will be there in thirty minutes.

"We have other ways to loosen that tongue of yours Comrade. A drug that never fails to get the truth. The doctor will soon be here but you can avoid that by passing on all you know about Black Four Seven."

Another slap from Mikanhov across the face followed by a punch in the eye from Pelhova sends me off the chair and sprawling on to the floor. A kick in my ribs was quick in following. Blood trickled from my nose. There is nothing I can do other than endure this treatment from these thugs. They drag me to my feet and thrust me back into the chair. Blood runs down my shirt front. More questions followed. Time and time, again the same story was repeated by myself, making them more and more angry.

Forty five minutes or so passed and I was relieved to hear a knock on the door. A doctor complete with a recognisable leather bag entered the room. He placed the bag on the table and began to examine my battered face. He looked scornfully at Mikanhov and Pelhova saying: "Is this absolutely necessary? You knew I was coming and this brutality is uncalled for."

"Sorry doc, but he fell against the door as we were bringing him in. You have no idea how they struggle sometimes. It is in their interests to behave, but you have no idea how they wriggle and kick. We do the best we can but… well."

"This is no fall against a door frame, and why is he holding his ribs?"

"Well, you know how it is doc." The doctor shook his head and proceeded to clean and dress my facial wounds… a split over the eyebrow and a cut lip. He pressed my ribs and naturally I winced. He pulled open my shirt to examine my chest. Bruising had quickly appeared.

The doc huffed!

"Roll up your sleeve. Give me your arm, young man."

The doctor wrapped a rubber strap around my upper arm and cleansed an area of skin.

He filled *a* syringe and injected me. It was like a hospital pre-med. A warm feeling of comfort, then within ten seconds I was on Planet Zog, but still conscious. I couldn't seem to say anything to the doctor. I wanted to talk with him, he seemed to be a decent fellow… but I couldn't.

I heard him say: "This is similar to Thiopental. The difference is he will not lose consciousness and will be able to speak. In the majority of cases, patients find it almost impossible to lie when questioned… but the patient must have an antivac within thirty minutes, do you understand?"

"Yes, doc."

"I will wait in the corridor. Call me in and I will give the antivac… and brutality is not necessary." Their reply: "Of course not doc!"

The doctor packed his bag and walked to the door. The guard held the door open.

"It is essential, don't forget, he must have the second injection within thirty minutes."

"Yes, doc."

"Thirty minutes!"

"Yes, doc."

The guard shut the door and stood with one hand in pocket the other on his holster.

"Now then my fine friend Comrade, what is your name?"

"Veector Kaarasheenko."

"Good… and where are you?"

"Airport."

"Where is the gun?" Silence.

"I asked you, where is the gun?"

"Don't know."

"You shot Comrade Poliakov today didn't you?"

"No."

"You are a member of the terrorist group, Black Four Seven?"

"No."

"The man in the next room. You know him?" Silence.

"The man in the next room. He is a friend of yours, isn't he?"

"Nooo."

"Why are you going to England?"

"Tooureest! am a tourist… holiday."

Mikanhov and Pelhova swear and curse in unison.

"We are not getting anywhere here. The bloody drug doesn't work!"

"I dooon't know."

"You passed a gun to a friend at the airport didn't you? After you shot Poliakov?"

"No… no gun."

There was a knock at the door. The guard opened the door and took a message. There was a lot of nodding and head shaking. The messenger left. The guard resumed his posture.

"Sir, a report from Security. Comrade Poliakov was shot through the fleshy upper part of his shoulder. He is safe. The bullet passed straight through him and left him relatively unharmed. Unfortunately the bullet struck the security man standing behind him and it entered the upper part of his heart. He died almost instantly."

Mikanhov and Pelhova changed their strategy.

"Your gunshot caused a death Karashenko. What do you think about that?" Silence.

The question was repeated. "I dooon't know… sad."

"You shot the man didn't you. Viktor Karashenko, the assassin?"

"No."

"Have you ever fired a gun?"

"No."

"You own a firearm don't you?"

"No."

"What's the bloody point of this. We may as well call in the doctor. We're getting nowhere here." Pelhova nodded to the guard. The guard opened the door and called in the doctor. He examined the "patient" and ascertained there had been no further violence. A hypodermic needle was selected and filled with the antivac. Viktor was again injected with a serum, reviving in thirty seconds.

The doctor wiped my face again with a medical swab and packed his bag;

"No more of this nonsense please gentlemen!" (A word rarely used in Russia these days!)

"Of course not, doc. Thanks for coming. We are only talking, asking questions, and after all, we must not forget, someone took a shot at Poliakov and tried to kill him. This might be the murderer. We have a job to do doc and it's not easy dealing with these terrorists. They'll blow their bloody grandmother up for the cause!"

The doctor grunted and left the room, courtesy of the door guard.

"Have a nice sleep Comrade?" Sarcasm from Pelhova.

"I was not asleep. I know what you are up to."

"Oh. That is good, then you know you gave us a lot of incriminating evidence. Evidence that the tribunal will find against you… and be aware friend Comrade, Russian prison is not a healthy place to be these days, unless of course you are convicted of murder… oh yes… murder!" Milanhov rustled his file on the table and selected a document.

"I'll just fill in the blanks for you with date, place, the event and charge etc., then you can sign it as an admission and we can all go home! Not you of course, you will be held pending trial." Milanhov completed his part of the document and pushed it across the table for me to read.

I read the document in full. It was a standard form admitting to the crime. A total admission of a crime I never committed. All presented in a corrupt fashion so as to complete their "paperwork."

"I'm not signing that. I never did anything. This is a set up."

Pelhova came across the desk with a fist clenched… Milanhov restrained him saying: "Now then Nicolai we don't need that do we Comrade Karashenko because, like a good boy you are going to sign the nice document and we can all leave this place. To sign it will help you at the tribunal and could mean the difference between a corporate execution and a prison term. Tell him Oleg, about the evidence with the wipe test and the truth drug."

"Oh yes, of course, the hand wipe test revealed use of a gun, we know that, and the drug you were under made you tell the truth so, with the signing of the form we can leave, but if you don't sign we will have to stay here until you do and find other ways of encouragement… get it?"

I picked up a pen and signed the form. They are not going to prevent me abstaining: "I will sign under protest… under duress and I will write that on the document."

Pelhova grabbed my wrist and twisted my arm whilst sneering stating: "You don't do that; you just sign your name if you wish to walk out of here. Your choice."

I signed the form after rubbing my reddened wrist. They grinned with satisfaction that they have achieved their goal. The wrong person, but the paperwork is tidy, a formal arrest now to follow.

There was loud thump on the door. The officer with his back to the door was almost thrown across the room. Two men burst in. The guard recovering himself, went for his holster dip.

Ilynoff (his name, came to pass!) placed his hand firmly over the hand of the guard.

"I would be careful who you use that on if I were you officer Comrade." Milanhov gasped. "What the… who the hell are you? what do you think you are doing, we are."

"We know who you are, and as for us… " He took out his ID card and held it out for both to see.

The card stated Comrade Vladimir Petrov of the Lubyanka Bureau…

"And this is my Comrade Pashimov Ilynoff. What are you doing with this man. Release him immediately. Why are you here…" He addressed Viktor before Mikanhov or Pelhova had time to speak further on the question asked.

I replied, "I was waiting for my plane which I have now missed and these two…" Petrov interrupted, "What plane? Where are you going?" I   responded by stating the basic facts.

"England. British Airways, but it is gone now and…" Petrov gave instructions.

Clearly Mikanhov and Pelhova were terrified of these two men from Lubyanka. "Get him another flight. … NOW!"… The rafters almost shook!

"Yes, Comrade Petrov. Pelhova see to it." Pelhova dutifully left the room. Ilynoff stood by the door taking over from the guard and Petrov picked up the paper from the table.

"What is this?" He read it briefly stating, "Rubbish."

He screwed it into a ball, tossed it to Ilynoff who placed it into his pocket. Petrov looked at me.

"I see they have been having some fun with your face, Comrade!"

Various words and accusations ensued and Mikanhov could do no more than shiver!

Thirty minutes later Pelhova returned:

"Here is the ticket and boarding documents. Flight BA420 British Airways. Two hours from now." He handed me the documents. They looked genuine.

I took them with grateful thanks but try as I may, they would not tell me why this sudden and drastic change in my life, for the better, was happening. Petrov said: "Get out and take your flight. You will hear no more from these two."

I thanked this man Petrov whoever he was?

I collected my belongings littering the floor and placing my small suitcase on the table along with the various items on the table, I packed everything, and shut the clasps. I put on my shoes. "He has got my cigarette lighter." I pointed accusingly across the room.

"Oh sorry… an oversight!" The lighter was returned.

I strapped on my wristwatch and went for the door. Ilynoff held the door for me whilst I limped out of the "torture chamber" I limped, because my sore ribs made such demands upon me. Even carrying my small case was uncomfortable. I walked out into the normal world.

After an urgent visit to the men's room I went to the display board to check the flight. Sure enough, my original flight BA419 stated "departed" but the new flight BA420 was scheduled to be "on time".

A welcome sit down in a side cafe area left me somewhat puzzled and phased. To think all this had been going on in "that room" over there, whilst everyone else was happily going about their business. Who on earth was this Ilynoff and Petrov… from Lubyanka of all places… and why were they so interested in assisting me? and why were the two State Police men apparently terrified of them… and complied with all of their requests in an instant… without question? Oh my ribs hurt! My case on the table aside the Cappuccino. I held my head in my hands for a few seconds when a voice said: "Are you alright?" A lady stood there with a cup and saucer in one hand also a cake on a plate and a mug of milk in the other (that takes talent) "There are not any seats… can I? would you mind?"

"Of course not, please." I gestured her to sit and cleared my case for some space. She sat.

"Did you see that affair earlier? Were you here a while back with that commotion and the politician. There was some gun man who tried to shoot the man… did you see anything eh?"

"Viktor. Please call me Viktor. Yes. (I chuckled audibly.) Yes, I did."

"Oh don't laugh Mr… Viktor… it was really very…" I interrupted her: "Oh, it's not funny at all. It's just that I have only been released a few minutes ago. The State Police dragged me in for interrogation with a few other men who they suspected of the shooting."

"Oh! … and did you shoot him Viktor?" She looked naively sincere with her question.

"No, but I would have like to have shot the bloody policemen! Oh, sorry."

She then looked very concerned.

"Oh, that sounds nasty. What did they do. Were they very rude to you?"

We slurped our coffee and she munched her cake. Do I tell all?

"Well," I casually replied in a whimsical tone, "If you consider a black eye, a split lip, a kick in the ribs and a hostile interrogation… Nasty, then yes, they were quite rude! God help the ones who are guilty. Can you believe it, after they thumped me about, they tried to get me to sign a form stating I had shot the man. The Bas…" I held myself back here! She is too nice for this.

"Madielana."

"Sorry?"

"Madielana, my name is Madielana. Pleased to meet you."

Viktor's new acquaintance held out her hand across the table.

"Pleased to meet you… Madielana. I can't sit here and watch you eat what looks like a wonderful cake, I think I will try one too, do you want another?"

"No. Another coffee if you would be so kind Mr… Viktor. I will give you the money."

Madielana ferrets in her bag for the coffee money and places it on the table. Viktor returns with two more coffees and a copy of today's newspaper under his arm. He sits stating: "Oh, no need Madielana I'm sure I can afford a coffee for you." He pushes the money back.

"Go on Viktor, take it, with what I am expecting, I must make a point of being fair with money."

"Where are you going today… and what do you mean by what you are expecting?"

Viktor commences eating a huge gateau whilst Madielana explains: "I am flying to Estonia," She inspects her watch "Oh, I must be aware of the time for the flight. It's a sad story, but I will cut it short. My uncle; strange, he is my uncle but only a couple of years older than me, was killed during the erection of a small land rig. Someone hadn't done up something properly, some nuts, anyway, it was the Will you see. In the Will he left his wife, my Aunt, half of his estate and the other half to me. I don't know how much yet but it must be tank loads!"

"I'm sorry to hear that, what was it for, the rig?"

"Oil. They already have found lakes of the stuff, so it looks as if my pension is quite safe!" Viktor Karashenko, the money conscious man... became even more interested in Madielana. "Oh that is fantastic for you. How interesting! Oil exploration and all that eh?"

Madielana expresses little knowledge in the scope of oil exploration but is however, grateful of what is yet to come to her, due to the kindness of her uncle.

"Where are you off to Viktor, somewhere nice?"

"England. To see my cousin Frederick. He lives there now." Madielana smiles and asks: "...perhaps a lady friend too? Your wife?" Time for the lies to flow!...

"Oh no. No wife. I don't have time. I have had many girlfriends but with my work. I get too tired."

"Your work frightens them off?"

"Not frighten them off exactly, it's just that I commit so much time to work, and I have to be on the spot at the right time. You see I work for myself, dabbling in stocks and shares. It doesn't make me a millionaire but it pays a living wage. It comes before the ladies I'm afraid. Perhaps one day I'll have more free time when I get enough money under my belt so to speak."

Madielana leans her elbows on the table with her chin supported in each hand.

"Oh. Interesting. Do you give advice on money investments and that sort of thing?"

"Only to friends on a personal basis. Some have made quite a lot though."

This gave Madielana some thoughts about her forthcoming situation. She responded by saying: "Good prospects in the money market... ummm? I have been lucky though, but a bit like you, not time to many due to my work. My other Aunt, an elderly lady, left me quite a tidy sum five years ago. I spent it all on a business and I own a small shop just outside the centre of Moscow.

"A ladies clothes boutique. It sells quite well but not as much as if it were in the centre of town, but the rental costs... ooo, but it gives me a good living but most of any spare money goes back into the business. I am also blessed with clothes, I can always pick and choose to look my best at any occasion, as the selection is all mine."

Viktor had already observed how well dressed she is... time to be nonchalant!

Viktor opens the newspaper and flicks through it rapidly page by page, not really taking in much of the news. Madielana inquires as to what is happening in the world.

"Oh, much of the usual; Football hooligans smash up a VIP suite in a stadium after losing in a European match... errmm... the English are taking sides with the Americans... the Americans are still very cosy with Israel... errmm. (still page flicking) The Palestinians are at it again... errmmm... there seems to some problem with our wheat crops due to a beetle of some kind... obviously nothing about Poliakov yet, the news will be full of it tomorrow... oh, errnnm, all the usual claptrap. I don't know why I really buy it? Like to torment myself I 'spose, but I do like to check the markets though. You know Madielana, when it comes down to it... nobody is on any body's side really."

"Oh golly, look at the time!" At that moment the Tannoy comes over loud and clear announcing the flight to Estonia. Madielana takes the final bite of her cake and slurps down her coffee saying she had left it a bit too late, and – oh damn, she wanted to buy a newspaper, too late now!

"Have mine Madielana. I think I've seen enough of the world's rubbish at a quick glance, and I can always check on the markets when I get to look at a newspaper at my cousin Frederick's."

"Oh. Thank you. Are you sure. I can give you the money..." Viktor waves his finger! Madielana gathers her handbag and flicks her hair back where it drooped popping it behind her shapely ears. She is very pretty. She opened her bag again and gave Viktor a card.

"Look me up sometime Viktor. Next month I will be back in Moscow. Maybe we can have another coffee and some more cake eh? That is of course if you live in Moscow? I live near the centre above my shop, a nice flat on two floors."

Viktor replied, indicating he too lived in Moscow, a modest drive from the centre by car... and it would be nice to meet up again.

He liked the sound of oil rigs... that word chinked with the sound of money!

"I will telephone you. Yes that would be nice," was Viktor's eager comment. Madielana waved and laughed as she departed... saying: "I hope I will recognise you... without the black eye and the swollen lip!... and thanks for the paper, and don't forget that appointment for coffee and cake, eh?"

Single lady with her own flat and business, and an oil heiress... oh no, Viktor won't forget!

She dashed off, joining numerous others who had also left it a "bit late" to reach the final departure lounge. It's not the last call, so Viktor assumed everything would work out well for her.

Viktor considered his lost newspaper. He could always buy another, but thought better of it, full of rubbish! That aspect was a "pity" because... had he retained his newspaper he might have read it more thoroughly and discovered something personal;

On page two at the top was an item;

The inquest of a drowned English lady now named as Helena Maitland was held on Tuesday last. She had been a housemaid for the retired actress Pavvla Ilyina Macilroy, known to her adoring fans as "Blossom Pavvla". The conclusion of the coroner was, Maitland had met with foul play. She had finger marks and bruising around her throat and was deemed dead before she hit the water.

The State police are continuing with their investigations. If anyone knows... etc., etc....

Viktor was totally unaware as to the demise of his girlfriend Helena. He had not informed her he was on another trip to England, neither had he seen her for a few weeks... informing her was not his way. He did not know... he soon will!

Viktor realized he was a bit slow in his commitments as far as the collection at Heathrow was concerned. He wandered over and found a vacant telephone booth. It was surprising the connection from Moscow to England "direct" was so quick today.

The call was picked up within a few seconds.

"Margarita... it me Viktor."

"Viktor. What on earth are you doing! I waited for you at the airport and the plane arrived on time.

"I asked the people and they told me you were not on the plane but your name was on their list... that is all they could tell me, so what..." Viktor came in.

"I sorry Margarita. It not my fault. I in trouble at airport, many in trouble. I tell you when I England, yes? I on next plane it good this time I not will be late. I sorry I not help this. You come again please, I on BA420. Sorry."

"Yes. OK. I've just got home and I've got to drive back on that bloody M25 again. Oh well. Not your fault. What time are you arriving?" Viktor gave all details of his flight.

"I'll be there. See you then Viktor (she laughed) I still love you though!" The phone went down. Viktor smiled to himself. Of course she loves me, she won't get better prospects than me!

He stepped back to surrender the telephone booth to the next waiting person, a rather attractive young blond lady. He stepped out with a nod and wink. She didn't return the compliment!

More time seated in the waiting area soon passed after doing a lot of "people watching". Eventually the flight details, which seemed to crawl at a snail's pace up the notification board, displayed themselves near the top of board number one. Those magical words... BA420. Gate 21.

Things now move fairly quickly as did Viktor. Along with many others he scooted along the concourse, which seemed never ending, till he reached Gate 21. Here he sat for another thirty minutes and the call to join the queue was happily received.

All passengers then shuffled along the narrow corridor to enter the plane.

Flight attendants stood greeting the passengers as they entered the plane with the "tried and tested" words. "Hello, sir. Hope you enjoy your flight." The redhead hostess looks rather nice!

Viktor found his seat and was not overjoyed at being seated next to a great fat man smelling of Garlic. *Why me?* He thought... *Why couldn't it be someone like that red headed hostess?*

The flight was very pleasant. No hitches, no turbulence, but no in-depth discussions with the read headed hostess... as for the fat man, he also had severe bladder problems. Up every thirty minutes and Viktor being on the outside isle side did not help! He suggested to fat man they change seats but no! He had paid for window seat and he wanted to look out of the window... at clouds?

The plane arrived within a few minutes of the scheduled time. The hoards disembarked and the red headed hostess was nowhere to be seen. Pity. Must be at the rear exit of the plane?

Oh well... her loss!

It took nearly an hour to get through the usual channels, customs etc. and Viktor was through into the public area searching for Margarita. She was there sure enough, waving her hand in the air. They kissed and embraced. It wasn't embarrassing, many were doing likewise.

"What has happened to your face? Let's get to the car park as quick as possible, Viktor. The robbers at the car park are going to do well out of me. They have already had a fortune out of me today." They found the parked car and paid the robbing parking meter. Soon they were on the M25 speeding their way home.

"You have two things for me Margarita. You say important and I will like them?"

"Let's get home first and I will tell you what I have. It is big this time Viktor, biggest yet! We can get big money for what I have. Tell me about the trouble you had at the airport."

Viktor went through this "chapter and verse". Margarita was horrified at Viktor's ordeal. "Swines! Those Russian State police are animals, eh?"

"They are to be called pigs Margarita, yes. I have pain in ribs too. They kick me hard."

"Swines. How did you get away from them. What made them let you go?"

"Men come from other department, Lubyanka, and they say I go, so I go." The remaining journey was accompanied by general sociable chit-chat accompanied by selected music. The M25 became tortuous as they reached the parts of outer London and the traffic was appalling as usual. After the long haul they reached the underground car park.

Margarita had her usual place. Occasionally some interloper would illegally park in her place but not today. She switched off the engine. It was eerily quiet. The car was locked. Viktor still carrying his "sacred" case... he and Margarita both strolled up the stairs, across the park garden to the entry doors of her apartment building. They ascended the common staircase and after entering her front door, flopped down on the sofa. Viktor looked out of the window over London whilst Margarita made coffee.

They both took well deserved gulps along with several biscuits.

"I know not how you live here Margarita. It cost many!"

"It does, but as you well know that bastard of a husband of mine at least did the right thing, with the divorce settlement five years ago, leaving me the flat and with a fair monthly allowance. God knows he can afford it!"

"Da, but it still cost many?"

"True. The rates are rather crippling but I get by. The Ministry are not ungenerous. I get an extra bit in my salary as I live in London, so it works out." Viktor asks: "Now, what you have for me. It good, yes?"

"More than good. Its bloody marvellous. This will knock your socks off."

"Socks off?"

Margarita holds a very important position with the Ministry of Defence. She is privy to so many important secret documents and information as a secretary and personal assistant. Joining the Ministry two years ago she has seen and "passed on" a lot of information to her boyfriend Viktor. Her immediate boss has "the hots" for her and she keeps him dangling on a string, so to speak. He therefore discloses, after a whiskey or six, a lot more than he should. He hopes, with his ongoing kindness and attention, the barrier will break down and eventually "she will be his". He, however, has no idea as to what Margarita is really "up to" and as long as she can "milk" the situation, of unrequited love, "things" will continue. The occasional evening out at the theatre, the ballet and expensive restaurants are all part of the plan to capture Margarita, as far as her boss is concerned. She however thinks otherwise – "no chance!"

When Margarita was vetted for the job she was known by her divorced married name, "Austen" Verification checks were made into her background. They were not interested in her married name of Austen, that seemed harmless enough, but her direct male family line.

Searches revealed her maiden name to be Margarita Fostor. Her parents were Foster and her grandparents on the male side were Fostor. That was good enough to satisfy the records, so she was hired. Had they gone back one further generation they would have found the family name to have been shortened to Fostor from Fostorova. Her undisclosed Russian ancestry who came to England were very badly treated according to the family search undertaken by Margarita. She had found a copy of the Last Will and Testament. Amongst the financial details, a statement had been added that her great-great-grandfather had written; he hopes one day someone will get the better of those who maltreated them. That was enough for Margarita!

"Don't worry about your socks Viktor… Last month, and this is why you are here, the first meeting was held relative to a new design concept in weaponry. I have copies of the minutes of that first meeting for you. Macilroy and Grantham Hargreaves eyes will pop when they see this one!

"A new device called "*Turncoat*" is an undetectable mechanism that can be concealed within large weapons like missiles and such. This small device is built in, and as I said is undetectable."

"What it does?" inquired Viktor.

"It does, my dear Viktor, after installing, it remains in place until it is detonated by the British from anywhere on the planet."

"Why people buy this Margarita, I do not see this is good?"

"Governments buy weapons… just think of it… they openly buy lots of weapons, missiles, bombs. Secretly concealed, is this device. If that country falls out of favour… just think one press of the button and the whole of their own armoury blows themselves up to kingdom come. They sit on their bums thinking they have got a good build-up of weapons in their cupboards but they can be annihilated at a stroke, blow themselves up with their own bombs, it's brilliant, eh?

"Added to that, if they sell on these weapons on to other sources, they too are at risk, but they don't know it. Do you follow me, Viktor?

"Such a device devised by the British could hold the trump card, yes, are you with me?"

"I see this good, Margarita. This is good one to sell. I pass a copy of the first page to Macilroy and ask plenty money. They want to see more pages after, yes. Big money I see coming for us Margarita, da! They get more pages when they pay more money." They both laugh hysterically.

Margarita retired to her bedroom. A visit to the safe. She returned with several pieces of A4 paper and a magazine. Handing the magazine to Viktor she said: "Keep these in between the pages of this photographic journal mag and don't let them slip, whatever you do… do not let them slip! I'll put them in a sealed A4 buff envelope."

Viktor took the magazine and did a page flick. He was well satisfied that, barring doing something stupid, the buff envelope would stay put, and as is often the case, they would be easily smuggled past the officials when travelling by air. It's just a magazine with an A4 envelope.

"You 'ave one more margarita. You say two things you are having for me?" Margarita handed other pieces of paper documentation and smiled.

"What this you give me now?"

Our marriage details, for it to take place on Friday at Chelsea Registry office Viktor. All as we have planned and now it is here. Are you pleased? I know I am, and it is as we had agreed last month. It was difficult to coordinate it with your visit this time but all is agreed. Margarita grinned from ear to ear and bending over Viktor, kissed him on his head. Viktor took the documents and read through them casually replying: "I am think it quick Margarita. It surprises me to be now. Might we wait some time?"

"It's what we planned Viktor. This is no surprise. We agreed it to be this summer didn't we?" Viktor is beginning to bumble and blub with his words along with his reasoning: "Ah yes but…"

"Ah yes… but what! We both agreed and planned this and I have made the arrangement for us. I wouldn't have normally been able to get this date so quickly. Its only because of a cancellation. A couple did not like Friday the thirteenth and changed their minds, so I took it with both hands."

"Yes, the thirteenth, I think that not good date. We should change too Margarita." Margarita is suspecting he is making any excuse he can to delay the wedding. The wedding that they both agreed upon during past visits. Now it's here, and Viktor is procrastinating… why?

"I don't understand you Viktor. How you can just change things like this?"

"I not change. Just think to wait a while. You are married lady called Mrs Austen."

"I am a *divorced* lady called Mrs Austen. What difference does that make. It's all legal!"

"The man you work, Captain Jarveese…" Margarita intervenes;

"Jarvis… what of him?" Viktor continues with his excuses.

"He like you and he give many documents. He not like if you married others, da."

"Come off it, Viktor."

"You know as well as I do, one of the qualifying reasons I got the job was that I was either unmarried or divorced, that is a condition of my employment This is a bloody good job. Our marriage was to be kept secret No one was going to know about it. and one day I will leave the department when we are married, and perhaps in a year or two we can vacate to the country and have a nice house, a farmhouse or something like that We always talked about it and now you are doing this! We both agreed on this!"

"I sad too Margarita it's just that. Let us have meal in nice restaurant and not talk now, yes?" Margarita reluctantly agreed to postpone the discussion. Does this break in their conversation offer Viktor more time to think up more pathetic excuses? They ceased their discussion, now becoming progressively heated and "tarted" themselves up for the evening out at their favourite restaurant.

The evening was pleasant as was the meal and they mutually agreed not to spoil it by harsh words in a public restaurant. Such muted discussions can become louder than necessary. When the bill came Viktor paid as usual. Times in the past Margarita contributed, but as they were engaged to be married... or were supposed to be! Viktor paid. He flapped open his wallet and Margarita caught sight of a card; a very colourful card lodged in the front of his credit cards.

"That's a snazzy card Viktor. What is that one?"

"Ah, oh, it business card. Business card for garage in Moscow. Car repairs they do for me."

"Oh."

They left the restaurant and made short time back to Margarita's flat. Night time in bed witnessed... what lovers do, and everything was just as it always used to be. Mutual happiness.

The following morning ran by quite normally until Margarita raised "the subject" again, over eggs and bacon. Viktor loved the English breakfast Viktor's comment, was seemingly final.

"We wait a while to marry. Another year or two. You English have saying: things good to those waiting, da?" Margarita replies and corrects him: "All comes to he who waits."

"Yes. That it, so we wait a while."

Margarita had difficulty in hiding her sadness and reached for her handkerchief from her handbag. She was having niggling doubts as to the real reason why he is doing this. There is something about Viktor's excuses that did not ring true, but she can do no more about it currently. Perhaps she will be able to think of something to coerce him into a change of mind, but what?

After breakfast Margarita decided to do a "small shop" for food. She gave Viktor the choice, but as so often, he preferred to leave it to her. He would stay in the flat and relax.

"Shopping in supermarket places for women folk not men." Margarita accepted this piggish side! When gone, Viktor took up the telephone and consulted his "garage repair card" which was the clothes shop run by Madielana. A male answered the telephone and upon request, the receiver was passed to Madielana.

"Hello," came the voice, Viktor introduced himself hoping she would remember him;

"Oh! My brother sounded mysterious when he handed me the phone, but it is you Viktor. You obviously saw my hand written forwarding phone number on my shop card. How clever you are. How nice to hear from you. Did you get to your home without difficulty and the plane did it depart on time?"

"Yes. It was not difficult for me but Margari." He could have kicked himself. The word came gushing out before Ite had time to think. Idiot!… "Margarita, that's cousin Frederick's wife, Mrs Margarita Austen (pleased he lifted himself out of that one!) she collected me from the airport She had to come to the airport twice, but all is fine now I am here."

"Oh, that's nice for you… why did you telephone me?"

"To check if you had arrived safely and, although we have only met briefly, I was keen to know if you did mean it at the airport. Are you really wanting a meeting when you return to Moscow?"

Madielana was very forward in conveying her enthusiasm and was indeed most keen. "Good, me too. How did your meeting go. Was it with the family solicitor?" Margarita confirmed all had proceeded very well. The Will has now been finally and formally read and, as stated previously… her pension was assured.

Why is this woman being so open with Viktor after such a short meeting? She is attracted to him, but knows nothing about him, and is probably acting like a woman who feels she has been "left on the shelf" in life. She's certainly liked the look of him. He seemed polite and caring… so why not… give it a go. (Foolish woman!)

"Oh. I have to go now Viktor. A taxi is outside honking his horn. Thank you for your kind thoughts and for telephoning me. Can I say a kiss for you or is that naughty? (she laughed) We will talk again eh? Sorry, I really must go, goodbye for now."

"Good bye," replied Viktor, "and take great care of yourself Madielana." Both phones down. Madielana had a sudden thought before dashing out to the taxi to check the recorded phone number so she could ring him again *if necessary*. She wrote it down… 01… etc. Make a note of the name too… Mr and Mrs Austen… yes, that's it, Frederick and Margarita Austen.

An hour later Margarita returned with the goods from the supermarket. Being a few items and only one bag she loitered whilst crossing the garden park and took a seat to contemplate for a few minutes. Her feet ached, so a good opportunity. Day time loitering in the garden is fairly safe. There were the usual two tramp like characters swigging from beer cans and lolling back and forth whilst stumbling over their words each other. Yes, day time is OK... night time a different kettle of fish. Often, amorous males of a very different offensive nature can be observed, also drug dealing is not out of the question. What has happened to this once pleasant country of mine considered Margarita and what exactly is the problem with Viktor? Up until this visit he was madly keen on the marriage. Does he want to or not? Does he have genuine reservations or is there something else? It is often difficult to get a good sensible flow of logic from him due to his culture and the lack of good English. Do I love him? yes! Does he still love me... well, I think so? That is not a strong enough basis for marriage. Margarita needs to absolutely sure. His latest hesitation and excuses are puzzling. She will have to probe into this further and not be put off with a simple... "we will wait" statement. No, that is not good enough for Margarita! She is not going to be "mucked about" again... not after the last experience!

Margarita left her bench seat and wandered over to the apartment building and up to her flat.

"It good to see you back Margarita."

"Yes, it's good to be back. My feet are telling me as such!"

Viktor assisted with the unloading and shelf filling. He is all heart this man... is Viktor! "Anyone ring?" Margarita asked: "No phone not ring, not used Margarita."

They spent the next few days roving around London to places of enjoyment A Thames river trip was also undertaken... most enjoyable. Margarita had taken two whole weeks off work for the marriage. A waste of time that was!

"Where are the Registry Office documents Viktor? Friday the thirteenth is approaching fast? I think it best to telephone the office to cancel the service." Viktor's casual comment: "I not know where they are perhaps you have them. Cancel, why do? We wait, we may change our mind, yes?"

"WE!... *We* have not changed our mind Viktor... you have changed your mind, not me!"

"Ages too Margarita. We ages are not the same."

"Yes, I am five years younger than you, does that matter?"

Viktor is struggling to present a sound case in his argument.

"I be old for you when I am seventy?"

Margarita is rapidly and understandably becoming irritated at this stupid line of excuses.

Viktor is pulling anything he can "out of the bag" none of which makes any sense.

"Yes Viktor. I would be sixty five." Margarita is now getting red florid faced and her words increase in volume and intensity.

"Oh, yes, and when you are forty I will be thirty five, and when you are fifty and I will be forty five and when I am thirty you will be thirty five. How many more stupid bloody examples do you want… Viktor." Her words evaporate and drift off into tears. Viktor rather callously faces the window, hands behind his back, staring out over London without comforting Margarita.

"Not so long ago, you a could not find any excuses to prevent us getting married and now you search for any excuse not to. What is the matter with you Viktor?" He replies: "Just to wait some while, just to wait is all I say. I make coffee now, yes?"

They have coffee and biscuits, and "things" quieten down a little. Viktor changes into his track suit that he keeps in Margarita's wardrobe and taking a towel he decides upon some exercise in the gym. A small gym in the basement of the apartment building for the residents to use with the proviso that "they" keep it clean and tidy. Margarita readily agrees and feels it a good time for a brief separation for his exercise in order for her to have some more thoughts. Hopefully Viktor might sweat some common sense into that Moscovite brain of his whilst thrashing an exercise cycle. He, at least, thrashes the gymnasium equipment and not her. That is a positive point in his favour.

He had only been gone for half an hour when the telephone rang. Margarita answered giving her full telephone number. Not many people are so efficient these days. The voice said: "Oh… 'ello… you Engleeshe? Yes, I not good. You speak Russian or perhaps perhaps Francais? I speak good French if you like? You like talk French. It better?"

"I'm afraid you will have to make do with my English. What do you want?"

"You Mrs Austen, yes, please?" Margarita is quite phased at this telephone call.

"Yes. I am Mrs Austen. Margarita Austen speaking."

"Ah. Is good you know Viktor, yes?"

"I do. What is it you want? He is not here at the moment, he is out."

183

"I give message to you please give Viktor. If will. He lovely man, yes. I Madielana his new friend. I come back Moscow tomorrow. It early so we meet early too. Yes. You give him please and he telephone me too. I thank you for that Mrs Austen. It kind for you to do. It naughty but you say kiss for me. Thank you Madam. Goodbye."

Margarita plopped on to the sofa with the receiver in her lap. Her thoughts were a mixture of sadness, anger and realisation at what was going on… I'll give her… "thank you madam!" Viktor's wallet was staring her in the face on the table by the sofa. It did not take a lot of pressure for her to resist the temptation of a search. The first thing she saw was the edge of the colourful business card. She pulled out all the cards and looked at them each in turn. They were all the usual credit cards apart from one, the colourful card. The so called garage car for car repairs… it transpires to be a ladies clothes boutique in Moscow called… "Madielana's." It all becomes clear!

Margarita now has a full understanding of "how the land lies". He is dabbling with another woman and Maigarita is not playing "second fiddle". Not to Viktor, not to anyone. These last two years have been very enjoyable, she thought, for both!… but dearly he is with another woman in Moscow. Maigarita is simply the means to obtain secret documents from the Ministry, placing her "neck on the block" (many metaphors here!) to enable Viktor to keep his money wallet topped up. "Bloody hell," she said out loud. "What a bloody fool I've been. Well it is not going to continue." Strategy is now coming into play for Margarita. She decides she is not going to confront Viktor. She has seen this all before, and to fall for a lot of blubbing and lies is no longer in her repertoire.

No… she will carry on as if nothing has been discovered and Viktor can just bugger off back to Moscow to his Madielana woman or whatever she calls herself.

Yes, that was it… Madielana… stupid bloody name!

Settling down to a coffee on the sofa, Margarita ensures Viktor's wallet is tidy and in the identical position, as left. By chance, she searches her bag for a tissue. No tissue. Finding a tissue from the box on the book shelf she attends to her nose!… and discards the tissue into the small swing bin below the bottom shelf. In doing so, Margarita observes a crumpled piece of paper screwed very tightly into a ball. Curiosity takes hold and she unfolds the paper to find it to be the Registry office marriage document. That is the final straw for her.

"That's it," she spoke out loud "That is now confirmed. He is up to something for sure." She crumples the document and returns it to the bin. A new plan is now to be formed. The brown A4 buff envelope is located from the photographic magazine. Slitting it open she removes the "Turncoat" minutes of the meeting and places it in her own bedside drawer. The buff envelope is disposed of and an identical replacement located.

Margarita has a comprehensive map. An A4 coloured plan showing all locations of missile bases throughout the world. She quickly finds it from her bureau documents. This is placed in the new buff envelope, sealed, and positioned into the photo magazine as before. Viktor will still consider he has the "Turncoat" documents but he actually has an incriminating MOD world map page showing missile locations. If discovered, and he will be, this will not go well for Viktor.

There should not be any "come back" for Margarita because this document was distributed to "specific departments" a couple of years ago and had been prepared by a different Ministry office in an annexe building, so, Margarita should be safe from any paper trail should that occur after Viktor's arrest... and arrested he shall be!

What was it Shakespeare who said about "a woman scorned". Yes, that is her!

If Margarita is to be out front with all this, she needs to be well prepared and far away from any possible connection to Viktor and his illegal spying operations.

She has a professional well paid job to do and the "spying part" is about to cease. She is not going to be a "dogsbody" to anyone else, especially if being two timed. The more she thought about this the more heated and hurt she became.

She settled down again to finish her coffee. She must appear quite normal when Viktor returns. Leaning back on the sofa Margarita shows a small grin. She has quickly settled this matter within her own mind. Feelings of affection for Viktor are now well and truly crushed. She now has to carry her relationship role to perfection until it is time for Viktor to depart the UK and return to Russia... return to Russia with him thinking he has the "Turncoat" documents. "Ha!"

"Am I smug. Yes, I'm smug, I've a right to be!" The doorbell is heard. He is back from the gym.

Margarita opened the door and made reference to how soaking wet he was with perspiration. The gym shower had apparently broken down so he had missed that benefit. It happens a lot!

After Viktor's shower and change of clothes, they sat down to a long ice cold Coke. It appeared Viktor had somewhat knocked himself out with his over exercising. That gave Margarita an opportunity to consider him easy prey... he is worn out and will answer to anything, that was the theory, so Margarita commenced with;

"I've looked for that Registry document, but I can't find it. I really do think I ought to telephone them. I need the telephone number and reference number; it makes things difficult not having it. Are you sure you haven't seen it Viktor?"

Viktor takes a sharp intake of breath (even Russians do it!) He ponders before his reply.

"I not seen it I wonder it might be in envelope Margarita. In brown envelope with papers. I think it must be. If cannot find then it there I think."

"That is possible Viktor."... she now plays devil's advocate! "If it is not to be found anywhere it may be mixed up with those minutes. You may be right. I'll open it and see if it is there."

"No need to tear envelope. It safe if in envelope Margarita. I see if it there when I in Moscow and then throw. Easy, yes?" *Yes,* thought Margarita, *that seemed to work well!*

"Yes. That will be OK, I suppose. The Registry office will just have to wait." (In her mind, thinking – *yes... you lying bugger!*)

"I'm sure they won't shoot us for not informing them. Next time I will make up some excuse, urgent hospital visit or something." That is the final clue for Margarita. What with the Madielana woman in Moscow and this deception about the Marriage Registry document, along with Viktor's procrastination about delaying the wedding, she is sure of her facts. Her next plan of action will take place when Viktor is on the plane.

The remainder of her two weeks holiday from work with Viktor was spent amicably and if Viktor did not mention the 'double u word', – wedding's, then Margarita did not. Everything jogged along nicely and there was no sign of any disagreements. That is because "it" wasn't discussed at all. There were many times Margarita was champing at the bit to ask "who is this Madielana woman," but that would make a break in her strategy, so, silent she remained on that subject too! The day arrived for Viktor's departure and his small case was packed along with the photographic magazine and A4 buff envelope intact, not containing the minutes of the meeting about "Turncoat" but the world map of missile bases. This would be incriminating enough for an ordinary person to be carrying, but within various Ministry departments, including the MOD annexe staff, it was not of much significance. It would not draw the attention to any specific individual working at the Ministry of Defence, so Margarita remained confident of her safety. More importantly of Viktor's apprehension by the officials who "nobble" him. She has a plan and feels sure it will work, also Viktor would get the message that he is no longer welcome in the UK. Their relationship is at an end, and his transactions with the British Embassy in Moscow will also come to an end.

A sensible period of time was made to allow for the dreaded M25 motorway with its stupid speed flow restrictions. "Don't they know..." Viktor Margarita fumed!

"Don't the idiots know, that bunching up vehicles by introducing a 40 mph limit on all four lanes, they are creating the very hazard they are trying to prevent? What monkeys work there, eh?"

"Where did they get their traffic training... Billy Smart's circus!"

"Who is dis Dilly Smart Margarita?"

"Never mind... I should stop rabbiting and concentrate on this high speed of 40mph with a lorry six inches up my Khyber! Sorry Viktor, I'm off on one!"

Slightly red faced and highly tempered, Margarita arrives at Heathrow and enters the car park that should be named – gold bullion car park, with the prices they charge.

A good place is located way up on high level. A ticket machine, one that works, was found on the far side of the floor on the extreme end, miles away from the lifts. Another frustration!

The lift arrived and a thousand or so holidaying morons in black vests, wearing ridiculously oversized huge straw sombreros came out of the lift singing a Spanish song. Oh deep joy! I'll bet the Spanish are glad to see the back of them... oh lucky us! The lift went down to the correct departure level whilst Viktor and Margarita enjoyed the mixed aroma of sweaty armpits and cheap sun tan cream. Doors opened and they made their way to the check-in desk. Viktor could clearly remember doing this at the other end... the Moscow end, only two weeks ago.

"I sure I will not be kick and beaten this day Margarita?" (He did a short laugh.)

"Yes, for sure, Viktor. It is not generally the way we do things here in the UK, but, with the right approach our lot can get nasty when they have to, so I am told."

The queue filtered its usual course and the documentation was efficiently dealt with. The BA lady politely asked what was the nature of his visit to Russia. Rather abruptly Viktor replied: "You can see name. It Karashenko. I live Moscow, so, why I go!"

"Thank you sir, that is all, quite in order. Please wait for your call after you have been through the baggage control and customs section. Good day to you, sir, and enjoy your flight with us. Next." They hugged and kissed. He departed. Margarita drove home. "Good riddance you bastard!"

Chapter 12

I ushered Ivan and Kristina to the fire escape lobby and instructed them to… stay inside the door and wait for me. I along with Igor entered the room where apparent carnage had taken place. It was mayhem! Table lights were overturned, the bed was a mess. The rug was sent to the side of the room and generally, the scene was that of a battle. I scratched my head and looked at Igor. No sign of Macilroy? He surely had not run away. Ivan had said he was dead.

Igor looked as if he had been in a ten rounder with the world champion!

"He tried to…" I interrupted Igor;

"Quick, tidy yourself up, you are a mess. Get your things together into your case. I will tidy the room and make improvements to the bed linen. We must get out and fast." I closed the window but firstly looked out. More sounds of activity was occurring below. I knew not what, it was a long way down. The room was quickly put back in presentable order and we left for the fire exit. I firstly peered out of the door… no one approached; the corridor was clear. We quickly joined the others at the head of the fire escape stair and we four, shot down the stairs like no tomorrow!

The ground floor was soon reached and I opened the fire exit door.

"Get to the car and tell Galina to drive back to Borodinos. Igor, give me your key. I will drop it in to reception as if all things were normal. They won't know it's not my room key. I will linger a while in the hotel and after a short time has elapsed I will take a Marshrupta and meet you all at Borodinos. It that dear everyone?" They all nod.

They exit. I returned the push bar back into its dosed position and shut the fire exit door. I then walked up to the first floor, took the lift down and came out on the main concourse at ground floor. It was a madhouse! I came out of the lift and entered what was total panic! It was as if I had stepped back to WWII after a bomb had been dropped. People, both staff and guests, were running everywhere. Both loud and muffled voices giving orders and demands. Guests and staff were scattered, sitting, standing and laying on the floor. Several staff were coming from the dining room with containers of debris. Brooms seemed to be at a premium. Numerous people were sitting on chairs in various locations being attended to for their wounds, arms, legs and facial. Care was paramount in the dabbing of cloths along with medical dressings. One woman was sobbing as a female waitress held her hand... not normally a done thing!

I walked over to a body lying on the floor. Three people were kneeling next to him attending his "difficulty". He lay motionless.

"Is he dead?"

"No, but he not good. He may have a break in leg and might be concussion to head. He land on him you see when at table to eat."

I pressed the waitress for further information on the man and the current mayhem. She informed me a guest, a man, had apparently fallen from the upper room window. "He had crashed through the roof, the dome, do you know it?" she asked. I did know it. There were several large glass dome roof lights over the dining restaurant, the really classy restaurant. It seems there is on less now. "Do you know who the man was?"

"No."

"He dead now. He still in restaurant. The man fall and land on table after crash through roof. He land on table and man's leg. That is why it is bone break we think. State police and medical people have called but not come yet. He may have done this for suicide but possibly maybe accident. Many windows open today. Air condition break down so many windows open. It is hot, yes? Engineers now mend all soon will be work again."

It seems to be sods law. If it hadn't have been for the breakdown in the Aircon, then the hotel windows would not have been open, and if it hadn't been a scorching hot day... oh, one can go on and on like that!

Suicide? Don't think so! This must be Macilroy lying dead in the restaurant, but how and why? I don't believe he jumped out of the window. If he did, he surely meant his action to be a final one. My "master plan" has turned out to be a tragedy. I never envisaged this, who could?

I spent some considerable time helping staff and guests to attend to the walking and sitting wounded. Doing the best I could, I assisted using the first aid boxes that were available. There were quite a lot of medical items in the boxes but never enough... never enough for an occurrence such as this. Cuts, splinters, wasp stings etc. would be the norm... never a flying victim through the roof.

After I had done all I could reasonably do, I left it to those already capably attending the less fortunate and walked through the reception. There was no one attending the desk, not surprisingly… so I placed Igor's key on the desk top. The medics then arrived and scooted past me. They will have a shock when they see what has happened. No splinters or wasp stings today! The outside air was indeed a breath of fresh air. I stood for a while and heard the siren of a vehicle I took to be the approaching State police. I crossed the road to be remote from the hotel and watched the distant traffic as they scattered sideways to permit the police vehicle to thunder past. They stopped outside the main entrance. One officer stepped out and stood at the front entrance. The car then carried on to the hotel car park. *What will they make of it?* I wondered.

There were a few people waiting at the bus stop but not enough to be a problem unless it was a very small Marshrupta. Fortunately it wasn't Along with the travelling natives I entered the bus and within a relatively short and fairly pleasant time, arrived at the highway near Borodinos. A further short walk and I was entering Galina's bistro. I looked to the left and right.

There sat Galina, Irina, Ivan, Igor and Kristina. Several empty coffee cups littered the table and some tea plates with partly consumed cakes.

Galina and Irina immediately stood. Galina came over and kissed me gently on both cheeks, a pleasant and new phenomenon! She held my hand and gestured to a distant waiter. He brought over a chair and I squashed myself in. They all shuffled sideways. We all now had room to breathe. "Coffee?"

"Please, gallons of it, and some of your nice gateau?"

Galina gave instructions to the poised waiter who disappeared, but soon returned with "the goods". This was now time to tell all. They all knew what had occurred better than I, and must have been desperate to inform me of the full story of today's siege blow by blow.

"So… what on earth happened," Kristina started it off.

"He dead. He do now more now!" (That is a bloody useful start.)

Galina took up the tale and conveyed everything to me that had happened. Her English was the best so it was easy to follow. Apparently Macilroy had arrived at the crack of the hour, precisely on time. He and Igor were doing their drug dealing negotiations which was for approximately over a ten minute duration. When the knock on the door came Igor stood aside, Ivan and Kristina burst into the room. Ivan dropped his coat and did a strip (not everything fortunately) and wrapped himself around Macilroy. Kristina snapped away with her motorized camera and up to that moment, everything was going to plan. Obviously, smelling a rat and an apparent "set up" Macilroy did not stand back and gasp, as hoped, but went berserk and grabbed both Ivan and Igor swinging punches wildly. Ivan went down. Igor continued with the battle, apparently a fierce one.

It was then to be… tall martial arts expert versus short, but very strong part time rugby player. Numerous items in the room were scattered as the fight ensued and after many punches were exchanged, a wrestling type of fight took over. The two combatants lolled towards the open window. It was apparent at that stage of the fight that Macilroy was trying to throw Igor out. It seemed in his attempt to throw Igor out, he stumbled over the low stature of Igor and he himself then tumbled out. The window was a top hung type and open very wide. Easy to fall out. There was no way back for Macilroy!

"He fell the full height of building finally falling through glass dome roof light windows over dining room. Many screams and much yelling happened… and… and… I think…" said Galina, almost whispering.

"You know the rest!"

I held my head in my hands. Elbows resting on the table, fingers slicing through my thinning hair: "Bloody hell!"

"You want photos. I got lot photos?"

Not wishing to disappoint Kristina after all her efforts I agreed, telling her they obviously will not be used directly as Macilroy is dead, but they may be used, possibly in another way.

The idea of blackmailing Macilroy I still believe was a good one but now the idea… just like the unfortunate James Macilroy, has gone right out of the window. That particular bargaining power devised to ascertain who the English transporting spy of secret documents is… is now lost and void! "I do prints. I bring next time, yes?"

"Yes… please… thank you Kristina. Well done, you did a good job. In fact, well done everyone, you all played your parts well and to the book. The outcome was beyond any pre thinking."

"What," Irina asked, "do think now when police find man is English diplomat Ric?"

"I think it may take some time for the police to find out who he is, or rather who he was. It's just a guess, but if it were me, I would not have taken my wallet or any identification with me to meet an unknown drug dealer, we are talking about Igor of course, in this instance. So I imagine it will be some time before he is named in the newspapers if my thoughts are correct. Not that it makes much difference now. I don't know where I can go from here on. I will ring my office for directions later." They all sat in a pensive daze. No one had any idea of what to do next. Their pensive daze was disturbed by Galina.

"I have good news about the heroin. Very good result you will find." We listened attentively as she described the latest development. She warned me; it was a long story, but she will cut it short where possible. Galinas's intelligence department, the RIS, had intercepted a huge haul of heroin. A large container had arrived by ship at the port of Rotterdam. It had been on a long crossing from South America. The drugs cargo was destined for the Glavny store in Moscow, but that outlet for the dago Mafia drug dealers has long since closed. A sniffer dog had sniffed out (wonderful noses those dogs!) a particular container that had come from South America... this one! The customs were amazed it had got that far undiscovered but, there it was. Searching the container, they had found a tightly packed frontal section at the rear doors end. When the metal doors were opened there was a tightly fitting wall... it almost spoke saying. "You don't want to come in here do you?"

However, not to be put off, the customs boys and girls dutifully removed the wooden crates and boxes and one by one, each in turn, were opened and inspected. Mechanical vehicle parts all neatly packed and labelled, they were all clean so to speak. After the removal of the boxes, the dog entered the container and went berserk wagging his tail, dashing around in circles and barking frantically. There were hundreds of packs of two and three kilogramme bags of heroin all tightly sealed in clear plastic. The customs officers guessed there to be at least two metric tonnes of drugs that had been concealed. A discreet test of a sample taken from a back pack revealed = high quality heroin. Photographs and notes were taken including sketches of the cargo, in case the photographs became lost or damaged... a sort of secondary "back up" It was agreed at a meeting, rapidly arranged, that the cargo would all be returned into its original condition, doors sealed as before, and two specially nominated official's would follow the container to where is to be finally collected. They desperately wanted to find the receiver of these goods, the end user, even though it was assigned to be in another country. That country was Russia.

The final destination was known, as was the container port en-route. A smaller ship taking commercial vehicles and containers would take the heroin cargo from Rotterdam to the port of Muuga in Tallin. From there on it would travel to Moscow by road.

It was unknown at that time if they would cut across Estonia or stay in Russia but which ever, this is over a 1000km, not an inconsiderable distance, but nothing to long distance lorry drivers!

This was a big operation for the Dutch customs, and they would do "anything" to catch the culprits. It was assumed there had been many "handouts" along the way to allow safe passage through, but this was not going to happen in Rotterdam. This heroin trade had been an ongoing problem for a long time. Disliked; even for a drug loving country like Holland!

Air tickets were obtained for the two customs men, but there was no immediate hurry as it would take at least thirty six hours for the ship to reach Muuga. The customs officers would fly to Tallin and await their prey. When there, a hire car was easily organized. This had been pre-arranged.

In Rotterdam, the following day, the container was collected by two men and formally signed for. No questions were asked. Covert photographs were taken of the two men. The container, now on a delivery lorry left Rotterdam by ship, to make its way to Tallin.

This was clearly to be a cat and mouse game and "the mouse" must never see "the cat" always behind, always out of sight. The lorry drivers never suspected they were being monitored.

Dutch customs had formed "agreements" with the Moscow customs. Over the years it worked reasonably well, with good cooperation, despite obvious language difficulties.

With crimes such as heroin drug smuggling, the RIS would also always become involved.

The lorry with container aboard, eventually reached Moscow and made their way to their final destination. The vehicle entered the rear parking area of a warehouse near the old part of the docks. This is where "the cat" needed to be very stealthy and ensure the "strike" must take place precisely at the right time. Galina's department, The RIS were contacted and the "heavy boys" arrived. They were as discreet as a hippo entering a chicken shed! Prior to their arrival there had been a lot of toing and froing whilst the custom men watched, quietly and patiently waited.

The RIS and the two Dutch custom "cats" drove into the rear parking area to catch the mob, and they did catch them… "at it… red handed… still unloading the goods."

A lot of pushing, shoving and an-element of fist fighting ensued but it was too much for the drug dealers. The RIS had the upper hand and six men were arrested, plus the two lorry drivers who of course… "knew nothing!"

The Dutch customs men made various exchanges both verbally and with official paperwork with the RIS and then, the perpetrators of crime were not too gently, "escorted" from the warehouse premises. What happened afterwards as far as the customs men is concerned is unknown but they surely, simply, "went home" by air. They had played their part admirably and it certainly was a job well done. I asked the obvious question: "Do you know who they were and where they came from?"

"My department ask questions (Galina laughed) yes, they *ask* questions and the men, they do come from South America. This was first consignment to new warehouse which had been arranged. All but one men are Latin speak drug criminals and the leader was an English man named Joseph! I have forgotten his second name, but the others referred to him as English Joe during the interrog… ah… during the questioning."

Irina, Kristina, Ivan and Igor knew about this but of course it was news to me. I inquired: "Who is the top dog, the top man, do you know. Has your department found out?"

"We think man at top is definitely this *Costa Rica*. His real name is Carlos Rica. We try to find and trace him to Estonia and to Belarus. He is always gone. He was in Moscow recently, but we don't know him where at present. You say in England… a slippery customer!"

"He certainly gets around. It's always the man at the top that seems to get away. It is a *big kill* for your department Galina and this should shut the door for further drug imports for the foreseeable future. Amazing! What a triumph, eh?"

"Yes, but one road… no… avenue you say… one avenue to be found is the cigarettes."

"We not know who collect the heroin packs and makes the Sweete Dreams cigarettes. It only a part of the selling, but a big part as you already know. They sell in hundreds of shops, Ric."

"It's certain this business is linked to those who operate under the guise of being good honest public officials at the British Embassy in Moscow, and they are the also recipients of secret documents coming from the UK… it's just that I can't quite get that bit sorted myself… but there is a way… I will find a way. I will see what my department think." Galina added: "We will help if we can Ric but in small way. The document smuggle problem not our problem, not RIS problem as told you before, but Irina and us do what we can, if we can, OK?"

"Yes, OK, thank you, any help is most welcome."

We all had a good, but late lunch thanks to the generosity of Galina and went our separate ways. It was agreed to meet again for a coffee morning in two days' time, when Kristina has the photos. Probably not going to be of any immediate use but it will be "quite fun" to see what Kristina captured on film. Hopefully, there will not be any embarrassing shots of Ivan!

I took the Marshrupta bus after politely refusing a lift from Irina. I did not wish Irina's car to be seen anywhere near the hotel. I just had a feeling that it seemed an appropriate precaution. Arriving at the Marriott, the earlier chaos had settled. The hotel staff had done a very good job of getting the hotel back to "normal" I had retained my key so no need to consult reception. I walked into the front lounge and ordered a coffee from an attentive young waitress. When returning with the cappuccino I challenged her about the earlier events. Her English was about as good as my Russian but we muddled through. I played the innocent tourist.

"What happened. I heard there was an accident of some kind today. I was out sightseeing?"

"It bad sir. Man fall from window and die. He fall into roof and through glass. It break everywhere over people eating at tables. One man he land on also not well but not die. He take to hospital. Man who die we don't know who, but he taken to hospital where they lay people dead, yes?"

"Hospital morgue?"

"Yes, I think it that called… morg – yew, yes. It terrible day this day. We not forget Police ask lot people questions. No one know anything to say… no, no one know anything. It bad for we all. It terrible day, thank you, is there anything else you want?"

I thanked the pleasant waitress and sent her on her way. Actually she knew less than myself but I didn't let on. For the immediate future I play the innocent tourist who knows nothing! After my coffee and time spent simply observing I returned to my room. It seemed an age since I was there. A lot had happened since my last visit. A little time reading and I will telephone "Blue" either today of first thing tomorrow. Is he in for a shock!

Elsewhere, Margarita gave serious thought to what she was about to do. Viktor was not going to use her again. She had been very fond of him, fond enough to marry but she was not going to be messed around. Her plan was to "Shop" Viktor to his sister and she can do what she likes with the information. Who knows, she might even get a reward? She would like that possibility. The telephone number was in her personal book. Viktor spent a lot of time at his parents' house, especially trying to avoid it when Kristina was there. She dialled and waited. No reply. Perhaps this was "The Gods" saying, you should not do this… you don't really want to do this. She replaced the receiver and thought further, yes, she does wish to do this!

Thirty minutes was spent searching for the shop in Moscow. It was called Madielanas, she can't forget that stupid name! She dialled. A couple of misdirected calls were experienced but her patience prevailed. The telephone made an unfamiliar burbbling ringing sound. It was picked up. "Da, Madielanas magazine." There was a long pause… "Chto eto?" Boldly Margarita spoke: "Hello… can I speak to Madielana… Please," another pause.

"Engleeshe, you Engleese. I Tatiana, no speak you wait."

Margarita heard a lot of muffled Russian words as the girl, sounding like a young girl. Tatiana spoke with Madielana. After a few seconds, came the voice. The voice she had heard before: "Madielana?"

"Da, privet, Madielana's magazine. I Madielana," Margarita had not really prepared what she was actually going to say but she spoke slowly: "This is England here (*A stupid start!* she thought.) I am Margarita Austen. Mrs Austen from England. You know. Viktor." She wasn't allowed to finish.

"Ah, da, Mrs Austen. You Viktor cousin and your husband Frederick too, in England yes. I remember we speak on telephone, yes. What you say to me please now?"

Margarita should have prepared a little better for this. She was becoming tongue tied.

"I will speak slowly for you… I telephone to tell you I took Viktor to the airport. He is on the plane now coming to Moscow. He wanted you to know. Is that OK?" A puzzled reply came: "Yes. I think. That ok da." Another pause.

"Well, that is all really, although may I ask you… do you think you and Viktor might marry?" Oh! Too late! She has said it… was it the best way to have said it?

"I not think, not so Mrs Austen," (Pronounced ooostin) Madielana laughed long and loud! "I only know Viktor soon, so that not good but we meet again when he in Moscow."

Margarita breathed a sigh. Was this good news or not? She didn't really comprehend the reply.

"Well that is all. Thank you goodbye."

Both receivers down. Imitating Madielana's voice she repeated her words;

"I only know Viktor soon?" What the hell does that mean anyway? She thought about the call and considered it had been a useful exercise. They are going to secretly meet again, no doubt about it. That is not the right thing to do if you were about to get married.

On the Russian end Madielana stood facing the window of her shop mesmerised by the passing traffic and saying nothing. Tatiana spoke: "Gospoza Madielana. It everything all right. Was that an obscene phone call. You look worried?"

"No Tatiana, not an obscene phone call, but a puzzling one. I met a nice man at the airport two weeks ago. We chatted over coffee and cake whilst we waited for the plane. We got on very well and decided to meet up again for coffee when he… and I returned to Moscow. All quite nice and friendly. A week ago, I spoke to this lady, the man's cousin. The man is called Viktor, he lives in Moscow, and I do remember I said to pass a kiss to him, a stupid thing to do but I was only being polite, and my English is not good. This lady, Mrs Ooostin has asked if we might get married!" Tatiana and Madielana laugh hysterically.

"Oh Madielana, what have you done… can I come to the wedding?" They continue laughing. "I think it may be this man wants something more than friendship. You need to be careful."

"1 know that, Tatiana, but what on earth has he been telling his cousin? Marriage… eh!" The shop doorbell pinged as a customer strolled in. They had to quickly modify their laughter!

On to the next call. The telephone rang a few times and just as Margarita was about to replace the receiver a male voice answered in rapid Russian. That mattered little;

"Can I speak to Kristina?" The man replied, "Da," and rested the receiver on a table. "Privet?" It was Kristina. Here I go again thought Margarita.

"This is Margarita Austen from England."

"Ah, yes. I know, Viktor other England girlfriend. If he trouble I not help so go please."

"Who is the other girlfriend… the woman Madielana?" inquired Margarita.

"I not know Madielana. No… Helena Maitland, Engleesh lady she live here. I not know more. Viktor in trouble. I kill him. I hate him. You not tell me Viktor I shoot if I had gun. He not here. That is all." It was quite clear they did not get on, but her hatred seemed a little on the strong side.

It certainly appeared that the information Margarita was about to convey will be well received. "Kristina. This is secret information. I want you to pass it on to someone, anyone you can think of, the police, or the Embassy. Do you understand me?"

"Yes. I kill him if I can. He not nice. He rape me when I twelve!"

Bloody hell. That is a bombshell for sure! Kristina is certainly the right person for this.

"Sorry for you Kristina. Listen to me, Viktor visits England to take secret papers to Moscow. Do you understand… he is a spy. He gives them to the British Embassy for money, and they pass them on to the Russian Embassy. Understand? Today he has an envelope containing secret papers."

"You sure?"

"Yes. I'm sure. This is true. He has been doing this for two years."

"I do this. I know who talk. *I* get him in trouble, it I like to do."

"Please do not tell who told you. I don't want trouble myself."

"I no tell of you I only tell of him, da, OK?"

"Thank you, Kristina, goodbye."

"Spasibo do svidaniya."

Both receivers down. Two phone calls. Probably the strangest two telephone calls Margarita will make in her lifetime. So, it's not only Madielana is it? Another one called Helena. How many more? Hopefully Kristina can pass the information on to a worthy cause and drop him in it!

For me it is now a good time to ring Blue. No, perhaps not, a bit late. I will telephone him tomorrow when I am feeling calmer. The recent events have been rather stimulating!… is that the word?

A shower and a change of clothes.

Ric Hartland was in the shower when the telephone rang. Sods law! Typical!

It might be urgent. Stepping out of the shower and being hit by the routine cold draught he slumped on to the bed with the bath towel over his naughty parts. Why worry... no one to see!

"Ric Hartland... Hello," a voice said, "wait," Ric waited.

"Hello I talk now father go. It Kristina."

"Oh, hello Kristina, is it about the photos?"

"No I not do it... brother Viktor he mad."

The bed is getting dampened and so is Ric's patience.

"Mad, Kristina. What are you telling me?"

Kristina passed on the tale of her brother Viktor and confirmed the source to be genuine, but she could not divulge any more other than to say Viktor Karashenko was "the spy" taking documents from England to Moscow. This is the man he has been after. This is the name "Department Blue 17" want, and tomorrow "Blue" will be the recipient of this valuable information. Ric could not believe his luck... if, of course, it was true? Kristina had also stated Karashenko had an envelope containing some documents. He has just returned from the UK!

"We need those documents." Ric sat on his bed and lit a Gitanes cigarette. Viktor Karashenko, eh? Kristina's own brother. Golly, what a find! Being so transfixed with this amazing coup, Ric walked straight into the shower with the cigarette still in his mouth. Laughing to himself he thought... doing something like that... would anyone want him in Department 18? He hoped not. Perhaps he'll use that in his defence "not" to be promoted!

He now has the name... time to pass on the info and go home. Ric Hartland has done his work.

Let's not forget the Department's instructions... "Find out and get out!"

The always reliable lift took me along with others down to the dining floor level. Wandering into the smartest restaurant I could not help but observe the damaged roof light.

There was physical barrier around it. The wall and floor areas were immaculately clean with no sign of glass shards.

The uppermost part of the dome had areas of ply and plastic sheeted covering to resist any water penetration. There was a large proportion of glazed panels damaged.

James Macilroy was a "big bloke"... tall... and these were big holes to be sure!

I lingered for a while when I spied Countess Valina Malerviana, seated at a table for four by herself. Not wanting to "push" myself upon her I stood like little boy lost hoping she would spot me. She is the font of all knowledge, it would be useful to hear her side of events, if she had any. From the corner of my eye I saw she had seen me and began to wave. I did not want it to seem obvious that I wanted to join her. I responded to her waving and waved in return. She then beckoned and pointed downwards to a chair. A good result! I nodded and wandered over to her table.

"Please join me," she said.

"I will, if that is OK. Thank you." She held her shapely arm high in the air and two waiters were there in zero point five seconds! Countess had just entered so I quickly studied the menu and gave my order. A whale sized steak was awaited. We started a conversation together saying virtually identical words…

"What did you make of that man… falling from his room… terrible?" Her soup arrived. Acting a little ignorant on the subject I tackled Countess for more detail, as far as I was able. She knew as much as most The only new information she conveyed was the police had interviewed many hotel guests, and they were "getting around" them all in time, because they suspected the man may have been the victim of murder. I gulped and swallowed hard.

"Oh really, how awful, why do they think that, Countess?"

"A guest in room floor below where they think man was staying had heard fight… they could not swear to room being immediate on top, it may be side room. They hear argument, and what is more is to say the man unknown to hotel. He not stay there. So what he doing here, eh?"

"Ah, yes, very intriguing I must say. What a puzzle for them and not fun for the hotel either?" A diner a few tables away started making quite a fuss shouting "Steklo" so loud. I expect it was heard in the "White House". She wanted everyone to know a piece of glass had been found in her soup and she wanted the manager "immediately" and possibly money and a Rolls Royce as compensation. I spoke softly: "Oh get a life, woman. If they bring a deeper bowl of soup, I'll put you in it too."

Regrettably, Countess found this to be so funny she nearly choked on her newly arrived leek and potato soup. Two waiters and a waitress arrived in the routine zero point five seconds. The last thing the hotel needs is a choker as well!

"Where do you get all your information, Countess?"

"I talk to waitresses. They like gossiping. You know gossiping, yes?"

"I do. I tell you what I think Countess, from what you have told me I think he was a bit of a ne'r do well…"

"A what is that neer do…"

"Oh, a ne'r do well, a no good, a thief who was caught raiding a room. He was discovered, they had a fight and he fell out of the window."

"Why does guest in fight not tell this man and fight to the police?"

"Perhaps he should not be in the hotel. Perhaps his wife doesn't know eh?"

"I think that you tell the police about ne'r do well person. You may be true in what you say? The man die was very well dressed, not a bad look for thief."

"Of course, he would be well dressed eh? He wouldn't look like a coal man in The Marriott. He would not get about the hotel otherwise."

I did everything I could to set the theory of a burglary in Countess's mind. She talks to many and using her as a vehicle to spread this reasoning to take the idea of what really may have occurred is useful. Countess listened with interest I think I have planted the idea quite firmly in her mind.

"It surprise me that dead man did not have anything on him. No papers, no wallet, nothing to say who he was. Is that strange, Ric, yes?"

"I think he was careful, not to carry anything, in case he was caught by the police. He did not wish to be identified if he was caught stealing in the hotel rooms." Countess pondered and replied: "That sounds good idea. I think you be better than the police Ric. They just seem to push people about and not use their brains, if they have brains. I think you be better to take different job and be in police or secret service, then many crimes would be solved, eh?" She laughed. I didn't. Too close for comfort!

The remainder of the meal with Countess did not include further discussions about "the obvious". That avenue was well and truly explored and exhausted.

We consumed the usual two bottles of wine (that girl certainly can drink) and she ordered a third. At the end of the meal Countess asked if I would like a large brandy to "satisfy the digestion". I declined the large, but accepted a small glass, but not she, a large brandy was easily consumed! I hoped "Blue" would honour all my expenses as promised!

We finished with chocolates and coffee and then strolled to the lifts for bed. After consuming the majority of at least two of the three bottles, Countess walked a straight line as if she had just drunk a bottle of water. We said our "good nights" and I entered my room knowing I had drunk too much. I slept quite well that night other than the occasional wakening thoughts about how I will be able to "give it to Blue gently" about the "cock up" of the Macilroy siege. Otherwise, I slept well. Breakfasting was late the following morning. There was no sign of Countess in the breakfast room. After a full breakfast I returned to my room and dialled London.

After a period of "hold" I was put through to "Blue".

Almost holding my breath I informed him about the Macilroy saga. Fully anticipating a reprimand he simply said something to the order of, "Oh well, these things happen."

Lastly I gave him the good news about the discovery of the document spy. I could tell in his voice he was delighted at that result but, being "Blue" he did not go overboard. Must not let the Agents know they are doing a good job. They might ask for more money!

"I can return to the UK now then?"

"We will let you know when you can return. There is still the problem for you at the airport. You remember me telling you your name is probably blocked. They will be on the lookout for a Mr Ric Hartland, so let things settle down a bit before we talk about a return to England. Anyway, I have some more things for you to do."

"Blue" then informed me to wait for a return call within the hour. I waited. After fifty-five minutes "Blue" returned the call with further instructions.

"I want you to meet our man arriving in Moscow, on flight number..." I interrupted him.

"Look sir, I have done my bit, this is unreasonable to expect..." He interrupted me.

The flight number and time was given. "Blue" was not listening to any pleading. I was to meet this man tomorrow. That was a nuisance as I had planned to meet Galina and Kristina to look at the photos. That meeting will have to be changed. "Blue" continued: "Our Agent from Department Blue 24 will be wearing a black trilby hat and..."

"A trilby hat in summer?"

"He will be wearing a black trilby hat. You will approach him, offer a cigarette and he will state your name and..."

"Oh, real James Bond stuff, eh?"

"No!... real common sense stuff. He will state your name. You will then know him. You will collect him in a car, hired in your name, and drive him to The Moscow Star. Everything is arranged. You will assist him in every way possible, but he will be responsible in finding the man Karashenko and the document he carries. Understand?"

"Yes. I will find out Karashenko's location from his sister. She will know his whereabouts."

"Unless there is anything else, I will not take up any more of your time. I want that document and I want that man Karashenko. Got it?"

"Sir. Yes, what is the man's name?"

"Black."

"What is his first name?"

"Black… Well if that's all for now, I'll leave you to it. Goodbye." Typical! That is just like "Blue" Dish out the dirt then bugger off! So, now I have to play bloody dogs body to one of those in Department Blue 24. I've heard they are a nasty bunch up on floor twelve. A nasty bunch that have to deal with *very* nasty characters… so what have I been doing then? Rehearsing for an Enid Blyton play!

Better telephone Galina to change the day to look at Kristina's photos. Why I am bothering with this now… I don't know! It gets us nowhere, but in fairness to Kristina we must do it. I also need to track down her brother. This man Black needs the information on his whereabouts so he can find this Viktor Karashenko. I will do my best to assist.

I telephoned Galina and changed the day, the following day at noon.

I did little more that day, as so often in the past, I wandered down to the river for a healthy stroll and then went to the car hire company office.

Upon entering the office Natasha was dealing with a customer. She acknowledged me and beckoned her colleague. A new girl I had not seen before, why should I? The girl came over to meet me and before too much limited Russian had been exchanged, Natasha called her back to the desk and asked her to take over. Giving full instructions, she then handed the client over and came to my direction, I now comfortably seated by the window.

She sat beside me and inquired, "How things were going?"

I inquired after Katina: "This my new girl, Inyna, (pointing at the desk) Katina gone now. She left hospital and stayed home. She not very good now. The attack has made her unwell and nervous. The company decided to pension her even though she is only young. It is kind of them. It is sad, she is not the same person any more. I suppose anyone would be like that after such an experience?" Contemplating this I thought wouldn't have happened if I had stayed home!

"So, what are you doing here today?"

"I need to hire another car, possibly a fire resistant one!" (Poor joke, but she chuckled.) For an indefinite period, nothing too fancy, but reliable like the last one. "The Gaz was OK." Natasha escorted me to the rear car parking compound and gave me a choice. I selected a humble Vauxhall two door, with an added roof rack. That made it look like a harmless family car. We returned to the office and observed Inya was have difficulties with the customer. Natasha interjected, heard the story from Inya and then put the customer firmly in his place. He had apparently just returned the vehicle. Earlier, after Natasha had passed her over to Inya he divulged the nature of an accident that had caused a severe scratch. After considering the accident, Natasha declared: "His fault, he loses the deposit. He stood no chance!"

I considered… don't mess with Natasha… had no intention of doing so!

The far end of the desk was selected and Natasha and I did the usual paperwork and without more a do… I was again escorted to the rear compound. We both looked around the vehicle for a visual inspection. It was "clean" Natasha gave me the keys in conjunction with a verbal "run down" about locking, petrol cap, alarm system, full tank of fuel, etc.

I thanked her. I thought for a minute she was going to kiss me on the cheek but thinking better of it shook my hand. Boldly, I loosely hugged her shoulder (I don't know why?) and soon I was off driving back to the hotel Marriott.

Nice lady, that nice lady Natasha!

The following day I breakfasted early and made my preparations to collect this man Black. I wish I had been given his first name. It all seems so impersonal. We are after all, on the same side. "Sods law," the road was congested most of the way to the airport due to an accident. A lorry had swerved and partially turned over. How it managed that is beyond comprehension. However, I did get through with thirty minutes to spare.

Having parked the car as close as I possibly could to the terminal, I made my way to the appointed outpouring of passengers. Finding the right position I stood by the barrier along with dozens of others waiting for their loved ones, business contacts, etc. and the occasional English moron in a funny beach hat who obviously thought Moscow was similar to the Costa Brava!

Straining my eyes, I watched the crowd pass through. Numerous greetings, hugging and kissing ensued. This would not be my method I'm pleased to say! Beyond the funny beach hat I saw a black trilby firmly seated on the head of a male figure, a man carrying a small suitcase. He searched the people fronting him, myself being one of them, and passed through. He stood motionless.

He was quite well dressed for a non-business traveller… although I suppose he was really on business but a most unusual one, compared to many.

I approached him. The distance of ten metres lessened as our eyes met, firmly fixed. I had that strange feeling that one gets… I know this person – yet I don't!

He was about my height, five foot nine but there the similarity finished. A very slim character, pale faced, even considered a gaunt face and expressionless. With our eyes still mutually attached I walked up to him. I smiled. He didn't.

"Cigarette. Would you like a cigarette?" His steely blue eyes seemed to speak in reply: "Ric Hartland."

"Yes. Pleased to meet you." I held out my hand to shake his. He transferred his suitcase from his left hand to his right hand. It appeared to be a way of avoiding the friendly handshake.

"I hope you had a good flight Any problems, turbulence or the like?"

"No turbulence."

He was probably tired. My introduction and gabbling was likely to be unwanted. I indicated to him where we had to take the lift and that he should follow. He did so without question. I was beginning to feel uneasy and wished he would question.

We walked in relative silence to the car after leaving the lift.

"This is mine. Shall I take your case… and hat?" He held up his case and simply said: "Case." I put it in the boot, by then he was seated in the car. I paid the car parking charge, similar to Heathrow… "robbery"… and drove along the road earlier traversed. Passing the lorry incident I could see the traffic congestion had improved on the other side. The lorry had been moved to the side of the grass verge.

"Chaos that was when I came past. Bloody nightmare. Nearly didn't make it." Silence.

It was obvious Black was not going to talk the "hind legs off a donkey" as the English saying goes, so, I turned on the radio, tuning in to some Russian folk music.

"Essential you have the radio on?"

"No, if it bothers you, I'll turn it off." I did. Silence.

"Suppose the old Russian folk music is not everyone's taste, eh?" Silence, no response.

What do I have to do to get this man into conversation? Some kind of rapport, anything!

"Traffic is quite good our way," I said casually glancing at him and then back to the road. "That is a bonus at least. I understand you are staying at The Moscow Star? You'll quite like it there. It's not the Hilton but the two sisters that run the place are really nice. One has reasonable English, the other doesn't really understand a solitary word, but I believe you speak good Russia, so that won't be a problem for you."

"No."

"When I drop you off I'll give you the keys to the car. I was informed you wanted a car so I organized this one from a local hire company. Not exactly a Rolls but it gets you from A to B, eh?"

"Apparently."

Bloody hell. What do I have to do to get this man to open up. All he seems to do is stare out front with his head rigidly fixed. The occasional words come from his mouth as if "taped!" I'm not used to chaffering a robot! I elected to remain silent unless he deemed it not to be below himself to speak. I let the noise of the engine, the highway traffic and the tyres be my only comfort. Arriving at The Moscow Star, I entered the rear car park and parked on the far side... just can't seem to park anywhere near the blacked fire stained surface from my previous car. I was about to relay the story of the car fire but changed my mind... pointless!

"Well. We're here." (a stupid and obvious statement) He then spoke... he actually spoke!

"Yes."

He still had that ridiculous trilby hat on? We exited the car. I opened the boot and took out the suitcase. By the time I did that, he was walking away? A bloody servant as well, am I?

I locked the car and caught him up as he was standing at the reception desk. Monika was on duty. Black gabbled away in Russian to Monika. Oh, you can speak then!

Monika rotated the day book his way. He filled in details. Looking over his shoulder I observed him write the words; "Black" for the name, and for the address... "London." I'm no wiser.

Monika continued gabbling away in Russian pointing sideways. I imagine she was showing him the direction of the dining room. I did follow her words when she gave him the hotel times for breakfast lunch and dinner. Dinner... do robots eat? I'm beginning to become automatically averse to this character and actually, he hasn't really done anything wrong... not really!

Monika gave him his room key and again pointed in the direction of the staircase. I handed him his case along with the car key. I gave him similar instructions that I had received about fuel, etc.

He took the two sets of keys and thanked Monika, but only one word... Spasibo! (thank you) Taking the car keys he said: "Thank you. Please let me have the address of this man Viktor Karasheno."

Blimey! Thirteen words all in one go! I explained to him, tomorrow I will be meeting his sister. She will have all information about Karashenko's whereabouts. Therefore, I will telephone him tomorrow afternoon if that is satisfactory.

"It is."

He went for the stairs and was gone. Although he seemed lifeless, his sudden absence was immediately felt. Not a bad feeling though! I was pleased to be alone again.

I smiled at Monika and asked if Irina was about today. She went into the back room. Out came Irina carrying a wad of papers and a ballpoint pen stuck through her hair. She was wearing a pony tail and bun today. Quite fetching!

I informed Irina I had just deposited a lifeless corpse into her charge named Black. She understood about the arrival of Black but not the bit about the lifeless corpse. She will soon understand!

We exchanged our usual greeting and confirmed our meeting tomorrow at Borodinos. With Irina, so often, she offers to collect me by car from the Marriott, but I will be happy to go by Marshrupta. I waved to Monika and was about to leave old homestead. That is what it seemed like.

I wonder if Black will form similar affections to The Moscow Star and its owners? I genuinely wondered whether the man could form attachments to anything or anybody?

"You can stay for coffee Ric, in the garden, I can bring it to you?"

I thanked Irina, kind gesture, but no. I will get on my way.

"Thank you... Spasibo... do svidaniya!"

A slow trot to the Marriot. Gave me time to slump on the bed and think about this man Black. It's funny how meeting someone who actually says almost nothing at all has such an impact upon one's self. I hardly know the man, and a change in that respect was unlikely, but I just didn't like him. He is not in Department Blue 24 for nothing. He is obviously a man who has a job to do and doesn't bother about the trivialities in life like friendly idle chatter.

Casting Black from my mind, not easy, I wandered down to have late light snack lunch.

The following morning, I chatted to a waitress during breakfasting.

"Any news on the man that fell from the window?" This waitress was from Ireland. Apart from a slight twang of an Irish Russian... quite fascinating accent, all was easily understood.

"Well sir, it's not for me to gossip 'bout this man, I don't really know anything, but I expect you be knowin' as much as oi do meself! No one seems to know who he is to be sure. He falls, he destroys the roof and dies, that be all oi know sir... more coffee?"

I nodded and said. "Please... is that all?"

"Well sir, the police have been talkin' to everyone, man and beast sir, and they take some away... but then they bring erm back again, to be sure, I don't for da loife of me know what is going' on. I don't know what me mammy would say if she knew I was working in a place like a circus sir! This is a noice place to work sir it really is, but dead people oh no... oi don't loik it one bit." I inquired if the state police are coming back to continue with their questioning?

"Well sir, oi don't really know that sir, but I think they might. More toast, sir?"

I had a feeling that this fascinating waitress that "didn't really know anything"... did know more than she was letting on. Probably, Hotel protocol not to hob-nob and gossip about this event.

I finished breakfast and took another look at the damaged roof light. Several men were working from platforms behind a barrier. It was imperative the hotel get this repaired PDQ.

After a short time spent in my room, I left for Borodinos. There was only two people waiting at the stop. The Marshrupta arrived ten minutes later and with a Russian grunt, the driver took my money. Leaving the bus I strolled along the road with thoughts as to what the photographs would reveal... not too much of Ivan I hoped!

Five minutes past the hour, I entered Borodinos and was beckoned by Irina who was seated with Galina and Kristina. Strangely, they all stood up... where's the royalty?

Kristina had resorted to her old and original non sartorial elegance. Boots with red laces were seen, her hair was no longer a civilised dark colour. This had been transformed to a mixture or reds, blues and greens. Her outfit was not something that one could associate with anything alive or dead. A polite description would be to say she appeared something like a cross between a cyclist and a circus clown. If you have ever been passed by a keen club pedal cyclist, then you know what I mean... and large black rings around the eyes, but the green lipstick... ouch!

It is amazing how quickly Kristina had transformed herself into a Hammer Horror film zombie. The dilemma for me was... why?

We all sat and offered our salutations. Galina ordered more coffee and an extra cup for myself. Kristina lifted her orange rucksack from the floor and took out a pouch. Numerous photographs were then strewn across the table top, some lodged between the saucers, there were so many. A beautiful display of Ivan the fleshpot could be clearly seen draped across the standing body of Captain James Macilroy. Never has he been seen in such a compromising position. There were about twenty to thirty photographs which Kristina had taken in a matter of seconds due to her motorized camera. She was an artisan. A pity she could not put her skills to professional use, but, looking like a dogs breakfast, who would in their right mind employ her?

After examining them, she placed them back into the pouch and returned them to her rucksack; "They good, da?" I replied: "They bloody good – da. They would have dropped Macilroy right in the custard."

"Custard?"

"Oh, no matter. Make sure you keep those safe Kristina, and out of sight. If we come to use them, the officials at the British Embassy would find it very difficult to excuse the private life of their diplomat, even though he is no more. So, Kristina... well done, a great job."

"Good, I like make trouble and photos make trouble." Her cousin Irina frowned at me and lifted her shoulders as if to say, that is her... take it or leave it!

We discussed the wrestling tournament that had taken place once again, between Macilroy and Igor. Galina informed me, apart from ripped clothing and some bruises, Igor got off unscathed.

Ivan had been belted by Macilroy and still bore the large blackened bruising to his eye. However, all agreed it was a job well done even though it caused a death… but it could so easily have been Igor's. Kristina stated: "Fun… I like."

I informed them about the current state of the roof light at Marriott's and mutterings that were going on about the State police investigations and their possible return.

"… but, they haven't caught up with me yet." Galina then advised;…

"Do not concern yourself about that, Ric."

That remark Galina made had some depth. I wonder?

The arrival of my "colleague"… Black was discussed in brief. It is not my duty to discuss those assigned to Department Blue 24, but I did make a comment about the man only talking in monosyllables. That word had to be translated to the others in Russian.

I obtained full details of Kristina's parents address. Galina soon located a map for me to pass on to Black. The house was identified by ball point pen in a red circle. Kristina advised, Viktor frequently stayed at his parents' house and occasionally at his girlfriend, Helena's house, but of course he no longer will, when he finds out.

"When he finds out… what. Finds out what?"

Galina provided a comprehensive account from the Pravda newspaper article about the demise of Helena Maitland. I was shocked to learn of that incident I had no idea she was dead.

"So, this lady, Pavvla Macilroy has not only lost her estranged husband but her housemaid as well?"

"That true," responded Kristina, "and he be next, Viktor, I hope!"

There certainly was no love lost there between Kristina and her brother, that is perfectly clear.

She has a justified grudge against her brother but… murder… uurrnn?

"When man go find Viktor?" asked Kristina.

"I don't know. I haven't asked him yet, but I will."

"Two weeks now… I sleep at friend house. Not my house," was the comment from her.

I advised that I will talk to our man "Black" and ensure he only contacts Viktor when he is alone in the house, if in fact he does visit the house at all. "I will request he ensures your parents are out when he makes his call. Is that OK for you, Kristina?"

"Da... he not hurt my parents... only Viktor he can."

I added the fact that I had been informed Viktor was also seeing a lady called Madielana but Kristina had never heard of her. Viktor seems to have a collection of ladies!

That well sorted, I moved on to another subject; Cafe Brodsky. Galina informed me the place is still boarded up. The water pipe leak has been fixed and it is now down to the insurance "boys" to sort out the liability and payment. The death and explosion did not help matters at all, and enquires about what happened to Svetlana are still ongoing. It will be quite some time before Cafe Brodsky is back on its feet, possibly a year or two. A great pity for Galina and the staff. The two waiters that had disappeared have never been seen since the explosion. That is suspicious in itself. Did they possibly have some hand in the deed? currently unknown to Galina and the investigating team. "The other factor now is the death of Macilroy and how the British Embassy will tackle the matter. His other accomplice in the heroin trade, that is Sir Grantham Hargreaves-Sykes, will now be left to deal with things on his own," Galina then added: "Not true. There is a third man Damian Boyle. We have been watching him for some time now. He in this too. We have not enough information on the Boyle man, but we know he is involved in the heroin smuggling business. I cannot give you any help as to if he involved in documents Ric. I do not know that. Sorry... and my department will not assist. That is your problem."

"I quite understand. I did not know about this man Damian Boyle... interesting!"

I paused for thought. My temporary appearance of melancholy must have passed across my face because Irina asked of me.

"Is there some trouble for you, Ric?"

"I was just thinking? I have a feeling, a sense of guilt. Since coming to Moscow on my assignment there has been one lady beaten, hospitalised and retired from her job, another drowned, the lady Svetlana blown to pieces in a bomb explosion and finally... well, I hope to say *"finally"* an Embassy diplomat killed in a fall from the Marriott hotel window."

"Why you worry?" was Kristina's unsympathetic remark.

"I worry because, if I had never been in Moscow at all, these people would probably still be alive! I'm not exactly king Midas, now am I?" That was an open invitation for Kristina to ask.

"You know a King?"

"This is the consequence of our trade, Ric. We all know what can happen when we get into this dirty business. Irina, Monika know too. They have had a lot of trouble over time. Many taken into police cells and prison and many die too. This what happens. This is what will still happen. I know Americans have a saying Ric. 'Don't beat yourself up about it'. Yes, da?"

"Yes... da!" I agreed, but I still have my thoughts!

After spending a pleasant few hours with "the siege team". I had a few words with Ivan and Igor. They were "Buzzing about" with their chores on the far side of the restaurant.

Neither had any regrets about taking part in the siege, although the death was dreadful, but mainly Macilroy's fault. Igor had in fact enjoyed the "bit of acting" he had to perform as a Mexican bandit even though it was only for ten minutes. Ivan was of the similar mind. He thoroughly enthused about his part despite the necessity of the strip, which did not faze him at all!

He said he had not removed all his clothes, only down to his brief swim trunks, so as to get the necessary photographs from the hip level up. He laughed saying, if he had gone any further, Kristina might have had a coronary! Igor by contrast laughed and slapped Ivan on his back saying, that if he *had* gone any further... who knows? Ivan might have had a friend for life!

We three then went into joint laughter. Galina came over and asked what the joke was about? "Oh, in England we would say it was a men's joke, nothing more," Igor then added, "In Russia we say that too!"

We said our farewells and made a date for a further review. Irina again volunteered to drive me back to the hotel but I said I would "save her the trouble". It's just that "thing" I have about not wishing her car to be seen at the hotel at present, so I took the Marshrupta.

Not lucky this time... the bus was very late and when one did arrive there was standing room only. I heard "snippets" of the conversation between the driver and a passenger. It was a hot day and the previous bus had become overheated and had to be taken out of service. I wasn't too concerned but regretted my refusal of the lift by Irina.

Arriving at the hotel there was a police presence. A uniformed official was standing at the door checking people as they attempted to enter. This it would seem, was going to be "my turn!" I was told in short abrupt Russian demands to go in and wait. This I did. Another official pointed towards a line of people waiting, leading to double doors to a side room. One by one we were shepherded into the room where a group of tables had been pushed together. After thirty minutes I was then at the front table. There sat two Russian officials, one uniformed, one in plain clothes. I assumed them to be State police. They sat alongside an immaculately dress male. This well-dressed gent sat with papers, pens and notes scattered amongst an assortment of items across the table. The plain clothes official (almost shouted) spoke to me and I naturally replied that I was English.

The English gentleman then took up the baton, so to speak.

"You are?"

I gave my name, my room number and the reason why I was staying at the hotel. A tourist.

This information was written down. He confided with the policeman adjacent, in Russian.

I asked who "he" was?

"Oh, yes, sorry, my name is Masters, Clive Masters, I am an official at the English Embassy. I am conducting an inquiry along with the State police into the death of an English diplomat." He then proceeded to ask the usual questions… Where was I on the blah blah at the time of blah blah and did I know the deceased man blah blah blah. The routine blah blah stopped in its tracks when he stated the man to be captain James Macilroy… and…

"I believe you have met him?"

I'm feeling uncomfortable and wriggled in my seat. The air con is doing its job fortunately.

"Not nervous are you Mr Hartland?"

"No, not at all Mr Masterson, just hot."

"Masters!"

"Yes, sorry… Mr Masters. How can I help you? I have met the man Mr Macilroy, he helped me with paperwork when I mislaid my passport, he was very helpful. Other than that, I know nothing more and I am surprised he was staying in the hotel. I never saw him at mealtimes? Is this definitely the unfortunate fellow who fell through the roof light?"

The Russian officer leaned into Masters left ear and spoke. Masters then said: "The officer is suggesting you know full well who the man was who fell. Is that correct?"

"No, not at all. There is no reason why I should know who the man was, only that it was *a man* and he fell from an upper window, and now you inform me it was Mr Macilroy. Tragic, absolutely tragic. Has the poor man left a family?"

The Russian plain clothes officer on the end shouts; "Liar!" I refused to be drawn...

"Tell me more about; the time he fell and your precise whereabouts during those moments?"

I gave all the details of my movements and reinstated I knew nothing more.

I then made a smart gesture of requesting assistance from the English Embassy, even though he was from the Embassy. I requested a secondary independent person is in attendance as I am a British citizen and seemingly being accused of something that I know nothing about.

He stared at me, not knowing how to react.

"That is not necessary, I am here to help you *and* the State police officers. I myself will assist you in any way possible. We are merely asking questions. We ask everyone similar questions."

"That is all well and good Mr Masters, but you know as well as I, that as a resident of the United Kingdom I have certain rights and it doesn't appear to me that those rights are being extended to me. I have told you all I know. You have made copious notes. I am staying in the hotel, so I am not going anywhere and can be easily reached, and I don't like being shouted at and called a liar... so may I go now, please?"

Masters chatted to the officer adjacent and then he, in turn, spoke to the officer beside him. They all whispered to each other in Russian and then Masters declared;

"Thank you so much for your assistance and patience, Mr Hartland. We might wish to examine your passport later. *I* believe the reception staff hold it? Certainly you may go, but don't change hotels or leave the country without informing us, will you?"

"Of course not. Thank you gentlemen. I'm glad to have been of assistance. Goodbye."

I smiled a half nervous smile, rose from the rather uncomfortable chair and departed.

"Phew, So, put that in your pipe and smoke it, comrades!"

I went up to my room, the one I should have been in an hour age! And I thought there would be just enough time to telephone "Blue". I did. He was still at his desk organizing people's lives!

"I thought I would just let you know I collected the man "Black" and he is now at the Moscow Star hotel. I organized a car and he has the keys. It's in the hotel car park. I will contact him tomorrow… I have a map showing the address of Viktor Karashenko… just thought I would update you."

"Excellent. Thanks. That all?"

"Well I'll be off now… one more thing though, this man Black, he's a bit of a strange type, can't get much of a rapport with him. 'spose its early days?"

"He's what I would call monosyllabalistic… if there is no such word, then I've just invented one. He talks in monosyllables… he doesn't say much more than yes… no… like a robot, and he doesn't take that ridiculous hat off, and it was twenty five degrees today!"

There was a long pause. I heard "Blue" taking a deep breath in… then out.

"He is a good man, not exactly a chatterer I know, but he does good job. It's not for you to question our operatives Hartland, but I will give you some basic details. Heard of the Triads?"

"Yes. The Chinese bunch of thugs."

"Yes, that's them. Ten years ago a Chinese thug hit him with a machete. It was obvious he was trying to decapitate Black. He luckily ducked, but the blade caught him on the top of his head. It took off the uppermost part of his skull and he was left for dead. The outcome, it was only… I shouldn't say only really… but it was only the skull top and not any of his brain.

"A long story short… the medics patched him up and he returned to work two years later. They said he was back to normal. He was always a quiet sort, not saying much, but he seemed much quieter than before. Those who knew him closely would have known a difference for sure.

"The hat… oh, as for the hat… the skull top was replaced with a stainless steel plate. Attempts were made by specialists to improve skin grafting and hair growth but it remained very patchy. So, Black always wears that trilby… you can't blame him, I expect he probably wears it in the shower! Shouldn't joke, it's far from humorous… anyhow… a good man and we are glad to have him back in Dept 24, and he is back in action performing just as he was before the accident all those years ago."

"Bloody hell. I feel awful asking about it now."

"Well, now you know, so, no hat jokes with him, eh?"

"Surely not, sir."

"Keep in touch Ric (ooo! – now its Ric again eh?) and carry on with the good work. Keep in touch. When Black has done his bit we will have to see about your return to the UK, eh? Bye."

The following morning I studied the map. The home of Kristina and family were easy to locate and only twenty or thirty minutes from here. It appeared to be a reasonably nice district, out of town, and likely to be a general mixture of semi and detached houses… that is at least my interpretation. After a good breakfast which was the "norm" these days, I telephoned Black. He was fairly easy to locate, sitting in the garden as I had often done myself. He was reading both English and Russian morning newspapers. Irina took my phone call and before fetc.hing Black to the telephone gave an observing opinion.

"He strange man, Ric, man with hat… he not say words to me, not many. I think he not like me?" I assured Irina – it was not just her he didn't like, if in fact he really didn't like her… but it was possible he didn't like talking too much. He is a quiet sort of person.

I did not wish to pass on my knowledge about Black's handicap, but even so, considering his "problem" I found it difficult to relate to the man… how do you get to know him?

Black came on the phone. I introduced myself with a jolly courteous greeting. He replied: "Yes?"

It takes one's breath away when a person is so abrupt.

"I have a map and the address of Viktor Karasheko's home. Perhaps we could meet up today, how about lunch time. We could then discuss matters and I could also introduce you to some of the Moscow sights that you might wish to see and visit, that is if you have the time?"

"A map, and the address?"

"Yes."

"Lunch is not necessary. I will drive over to your hotel and collect the map. Please have it ready for me to collect… how about… (he consults his watch) two hours from now, precisely?"

"Two hours from now, OK. I will wait in the foyer. When I see the car I will go to the car park."

"It is at the rear of the hotel. Will that suit?"

"Two hours from now." He replaced the receiver... bloody man... bloody rude!

Two hours later I hovered around the foyer frontage of the Marriott both inside and out. Precisely at the stroke of the agreed "two hours" Black arrived and turned into the hotel car park. It appears another of his foibles is precise timing... it is actually a virtue to be on time, so I mustn't hold that against him. I followed him into the car park and stood by the car door as he wound down the window... hat still firmly fixed to his head. I greeted him.

"Hello, Black, glad you found it OK. Do I have to call you Black... it sounds so formal?"

"You have the map?" I held the map and started to unfold it He stopped me saying it was not necessary to open the map in a public car park. I refolded the map.

I informed him, Karashenko is at his parents' house. His sister also lives there, but not for a couple of weeks, currently she is staying away. There will only be the three of them.

"I promised you would visit the house when Viktor himself is there and not his parents. So, it will be a good idea if you wait till they have gone shopping or something of that order, so you can tackle the man alone, is that all right with you?" Below the brim, his icy eyes glared directly at me; "Promises should not be made for other people, by other people." He took the map.

He wound up the window, started the engine and he was gone. Rude bugger!

This man Black does make it very easy to dislike him... what's wrong with having a lunch time chat... a get together... it's a friendly human thing to do... not to mention... his seemingly refusal to give a lesser formal name other than "Black!" It's no good... I just don't like him!

I returned to my room and made a phone call to "Blue" to update. To let him know I have passed the map and address of Viktor Karashenko to Black. I had no further information.

"This man Black does not tell me anything."

Blue's singular comment was; "Good, fine, thank you, bye." He must be taking monosyllable lessons from Black! The whole scenario leaves me puzzled. I know what is happening, yet paradoxically I don't know what is going on. We are on the same side, yet I feel, slightly out of the frame as the saying goes. However, I am now left some free time with little to do other than to please myself and wait for further developments. The only important issues now are the success or failure of whatever Black is going to do, and my return to the UK. Both matters are currently in the hands of others. So… time for myself. I flicked through the hotel guide and found a museum that was highly rated called The Armoury Chamber. A chance telephone call to Irina revealed it was worth a visit and "if you like," she could take a few hours off, accompany me, and drive me there. Irina's company is always worthwhile. She collected me and drove to the museum which was no great distance as it was at Tverskoy. The building was impressive, inside and out The layout and exhibits were like a palace. Originated in the sixteenth century but changed over the years. Containing the most fantastic armoury, art, military history, weapons… but as for the jewellery and glass display cabinets, so beautiful. Faberge and cloisonnes to make one's mouth water.

We had been there for two hours when I received a shock to the system!

Irina and I were viewing some spectacular items in an isle large glass cabinet; gems, chinaware and ornaments of exquisite grandeur when my eyes rose from the lower level of the display. I was then looking through the glass to the other side, meeting the eyes of Vladimir Petrov and another oik! I'm sure, neither were there to view the collection. Petrov was no longer in an arm sling but his wrist and hand were in a supportive strap. I nudged Irina. She recognized Petrov, last seen at the Night Flight club. We slowly moved away, as *they* did. Irina and I then moved rapidly walking, which developed into a run. Many people stared, annoyed. Petrov and oik crashed into a wheelchair and over he went including the occupant. We ran through a fire escape door to the side of the car park. Petrov appeared at the fire exit door some thirty seconds later.

Irina quickly fired the engine and drove at mac speed to the Moscow Star hotel.

"What he want Ric?" I replied: "Me I expect, no doubt! They must have followed us. It's odd. He knows where I am staying so why this?" I can't get into the mind of a moronic thug! (He wants to deal with me "personally"!)

Arriving at the "relative safety" of The Moscow Star, Irina parked the car. We both strolled into the reception area. We lingered whilst Monika dealt with a paying guest… very content with the stay and even a monetary tip! That put a big smile on Monika's face.

When the time was right, and no other guests were in "earshot" Irina launched into the full details of today's escapade and attempted assault by Petrov and co. Many words past back and forth in Russian, the majority of which were too fast for me but, the physical gesture by Monika drawing her open hand across her throat clearly indicated what she thought of Mr Petrov, and what she would like to do to him. I am rapidly coming around to her way of thinking!

It was still a pleasant afternoon, so Irina requested "sticky tape" waitress to bring two coffees into the garden. Two comfortable loungers were selected and we chatted. A mixture conversation about Petrov, but also the fabulous Armory museum along with a recent memory.

Whilst we were in there, an American tourist spoke to me when he heard my English, and gave his opinion.

"Great place eh buddy? Makes your limey crown jewels look like Meccano!" I knew what he meant but a rather harsh comment. Irina, quite angry, rose to the bait and replied on my behalf; "How you know? Pigs stay in sty's!"

"Blimey, Irina, let's move on!" I don't think she likes Americans very much!

Sitting on our loungers we went over that little scenario again and laughed;

"I think America man keep mouth to himself eh Ric?"

I could only but agree, but what about Irina's reply? ooo! Don't mess with Irina!

"Wait Ric. I not long, I telephone Galina."

The coffee arrived and the 'sticky tape' waitress wondered where Irina was. I gestured with my hands that she was on the telephone. She settled the coffee and biscuits on the table, did a nod, and left. Irina returned some ten minutes later to sample her cooling coffee.

"I ask Galina about Petrov. She find and phone back, da, OK?"

Thirty minutes later and into the second cappuccino, Monika came and spoke with Irina. A telephone call received; it was for me. Puzzled, I then left leaving *my* coffee to cool.

I collected the phone receiver placed on the desk of the back room. It was Galina.

Subject to Irina's initial call, Galina could not answer directly, but as the saying goes: "She knew a man who could." That is, an RIS man who knew a lot about Petrov. I could never quite understand the difference between the mob at Lubyanka and the RIS but Galina put me on the right track. The KGB Lubyanka were a bunch of mindless thugs (her words not mine) but her department were Intelligence officers who used their minds rather that their fists in the first instance. "Got it."

Galina's source had provided details of Mr P. Although Petrov was not elderly, far from it, he preferred the "old style" of KGB investigations and interrogations, (we know what that is!) Petrov and another man called Krull (I know him too!) have been personally responsible for numerous deaths and torture whilst under interrogation. Many never saw daylight again. Apparently, Petrov has a liking for taking matters into his own hands on a personal basis. Galina struggled for the word… but it eventually came… he has vendetta and likes to stalk. He will find you alone – and will then kill!

Oh, yes, he can bring the person in to Lubyanka and kick six bells out of the unfortunate, but he gets a great joy in stalking. What gives him the ultimate joy is getting someone down a "dark alley" and seeing to them personally, on a close face to face, one to one basis, on equal ground.

"He needs removing from planet earth," was Galina's comment; "We don't have room for this type of psychopath in a civilized society." I thanked Galina, I now understood more.

I returned to Irina and told her "all" Irina's view was then stated, and correctly.

"That why he watch you. Follow you Ric. He not take you to Lubyanka. He follow and watch."

I agreed with Irina… and I'm sure he has not forgotten the night at the club!

"You not go night dark back streets Ric, if Petrov there?"

"Irina… a truer word was never spoken!"

Chapter 13

The day after Viktor Karashenko arrived in Moscow, he needed to make three important telephone calls. Unknown to him at the time, two of those phone calls were to people who were deceased. The first call to Madielana. Tatiana answered: "She is not in. She is out buying stock today, clothes. Back at six. Sorry... any message?"

"Tell her Viktor Karashenko rang."

Receivers down.

Viktor then tried the home of Helena. Another lady (not Pavvla) answered in English, then in broken Russian, advising the caller (Viktor) Helena Maitland no longer work for Madam Pavvla, she dead, she drown in the river Moskva.

Somewhat "floored" understandably, even for Viktor, he rang off and sank into his soft sofa.

"Can't be true," he kept repeating. "Can't be true... drowned, and I never knew!"

Viktor made himself a calming large whiskey followed by a coffee. Feeling a little more relaxed he telephoned the British Embassy, asking for Mr James Macilroy.

"One moment please sir." Thirty seconds passed.

"Who are you, sir?" Viktor gave him name. "Just one moment sir. Bear with me."

Thirty more seconds passed.

"Mr Macilroy is not available sir and not so in the future. I'm sorry, I am not at liberty to give you any more information at this time. Can someone else help you?"

"Oh, speak please, Mr Grantham Harvey-Sykes?"

"One moment please sir. I'll try to connect." Thirty second elapsed.

"Mr Harvey-Sykes is on leave until the twenty fourth. I'm sorry sir, you are not having much luck today. I could forward a message to him, or is there a someone else?"

"I not know. Please give message him. Viktor Karashenko has envelope for him. Urgent please."

"Certainly, sir. I will pass a message to Mr Harvey-Sykes… tell him Mr Viktor Karashenko telephoned and he has an envelope for him, and it is urgent. Is that correct, sir?"

"Is correct. Thank you. I go and wait, da?"

"Yes sir. I'm sure Mr Harvey-Sykes or one of his colleagues will contact you. Does he have your telephone number or address?"

"Da, yes, he has number. I wait Goodbye."

Both receivers down.

Not a pleasing result for Viktor as far as the three telephone calls were concerned. He must simply wait for the Embassy to contact him… as for Helena, quite sad, he was fond of her… but there is always Madielana, she will fill the gap nicely and hopefully, she is very wealthy – a bonus!

Black was beginning to organise himself for the trip to see this man Karasheno. He plotted the route and easily located the district, then the house itself. A side road immediately opposite the house offered an ideal opportunity to watch and assess the situation. When is best to confront Karashenko? He was very resentful about Hartland taking it upon himself to agree to visit only when Karashenko was alone. This had an impact upon "his time". Who the hell does Hartland think he is anyway? However, Black did decide to comply… after all, he did not know who had requested this in the first instance… it might have been "Blue"?

Parked opposite he watched the house carefully. For two hours he observed. Not wishing to delay any longer he locked the car and walked half a kilometre to a small group of shops he had originally passed. Black had seen a telephone booth and soon he was dialling Karashenko's number.

An older male answered the phone. Black spoke in Russian. This male must have been Karashenko senior, his father. Karashenko junior came to the phone.

Black continued his dialogue in Russian.

"My name is Black. I am deputising for James Macilroy. I work with him. You have an envelope for us. I wish to collect it now."

Viktor mumbled on about it not being convenient at present... his parents were at home... and he did not want them to know anything about this so if he could wait, etc.?

"I am coming to collect now. Tell them to go shopping or for walk if you like, but I am coming now. The choice is yours. I will be there precisely in one hour." He replaced the receiver.

Black taking his usual impolite method of communication left Viktor is a "tight spot". However, he managed to persuade his parents to go out of the house for a shopping trip. This gave him a couple of hours for "the business in hand".

Exactly one hour later the door was answered by Karashenko. He held out his hand as the visitor said, "Black!" The handshake was not taken up!

Viktor led Black into the rear dining room and a seat was offered. A drink was also offered and refused.

"Can I take your hat?"

Black simply stated: "The envelope?"

Viktor was nervous. This man Black does not put one at one's ease. Viktor left the room to retrieve the hidden buff envelope and handed it to Black. Black's response;

"Have you opened this envelope?"

"No. I'm always told to deliver it but never to open it, so here you are. I'll see you out."

Black remained seated and commenced a laborious way of opening the envelope and removing its contents. He studied the map of the missile bases. Viktor, looking down at Black, was rather shocked at seeing this document not the document that Margarita had placed when he was in England. He could not stop himself when he stated: "Oh, what the... that's not the one... that's not the..." He finished abruptly.

"You tell me you don't open the envelope but you know it is the wrong document?"

Viktor begins to make a series of excuses and lies, written all over his face. Black continuous to study the map and grunts. He slowly replaces the map back into the buff envelope. Rolls it up and puts it into his inside pocket and takes out a piece of paper.

"You will sign this paper. It indicates you have given the document to me today."

Viktor studies the contents of the A4 paper. It is in English, so it was taking some time to fully digest its content.

Black takes out a fountain pen, unscrews the top and hands it to Viktor, "accidentally" stabbing his wrist very gently. Black apologises, (unusual for him!)

Whilst Viktor is rubbing his wrist and reading the English words, Black replaces the pen top, and to the other end removes that top... again, handing it to Viktor. He takes the fountain pen and declares; "This is some kind of confession. I'm not signing this. It is a..."

Looking from the paper to Black, he now can observe this is a "set up" Black is holding a Beretta straight at him. He pushes it hard under his chin.

"Come to the table now and sign, or lose your head. Which do you prefer?"

Viktor Karashenko sits down on the dining room chair aside the table and signs the A4 paper, clearly in ink, including date and time. Black carefully folds the paper when the ink is dry and places it in his pocket. He thanks Viktor in a condescending way and takes himself to the door. Black exits, saying nothing. He doesn't look back. After entering his car he calmly drives himself back to the Moscow Star. Listening to the Russian music on the car radio, totally unconcerned that the toxin from the fountain pen will be taking effect soon and by the time he reaches the hotel, Karashenko will be unconscious and will do no further business. Job done!

Two days pass and "things" were generally quiet. During lunchtime a message came over the hotel Tannoy for Mr Hartland to go to reception. Leaving my lightweight linen jacket to "keep my place" I answered the call. It was "Blue"

"Black has completed his work and is back in the UK."

Amazed at this news but not really surprised this odd fellow Black had not kept me informed.

"He's what? back in the UK already? So, where does that leave me sir? How come he gets a ticket home and I'm stuck here. Something not altogether fair about that, I think!"

I was reminded "once again" that the reason was, to let the dust settle. (I'm beginning to forget what the settling dust was!) but, as I had an open flight ticket, I was now free to travel, any time.

"Oh at last, thank you sir," (I could have kissed the bloody man)

It is now simply a question of settling the account at the hotel Marriott by signature only.

The fee will be paid direct. Just need to sign out and collect my passport.

"Get your plane seat organized, that's just a phone call to British Airways, and a cab to the airport. Say your farewells to the RIS girls (girls!) and that's all you need to do Hartland (oh its Hartland again is it!) You've done a good job. We will discuss a possible promo when you get back."

"Oh, not necessary sir (bloody hell, I don't want one!) but thanks all the same."

"Well done Ric. Bye." (Ah, its Ric again!)

I returned to my cooling lunch and ate heartily. My appetite was suddenly at its highest. Home, I'm going home at last. I will be sorry to say goodbye to Irina, Monika and Galina… not to mention the lads (lads!) Ivan and Igor. I might even miss Kristina and her Christmas tree appearance!

It's been an experience, and rightly, as "Blue" stated, it was a job well done.

The RIS team had to the best part, resolved a lot of the heroin difficulties, although it will never be totally finalized. For my part, the traitor Karashenko had been identified, as was the receivers of the Ministry documents from the UK. Macilroy was gone and Grantham Hargreaves-Sykes will be watched from now on.

Where the man Boyle comes in I don't know, but that is not my problem any more.

After my lunch I telephoned Galina and gave her the news. She was pleased for me.

I did however "drop a bombshell!" by stating I had some unfinished personal business to settle with Comrade Vladimir Petrov.

"I will never know whether it might be necessary to return to Moscow one day, so I want to make my peace with Petrov. I will therefore try to meet him on neutral territory." Galina blasted me! "Sorry to say this Ric, but, are you mad? This man is a psychopath and is not the type to accept an invite to one of your English cream teas for a chat. No Ric, don't consider it! Go home now." I did get her point, but I don't think she got mine?

"Cream tea was not what I had in mind… just an amicable chat to smooth things out. He surely must have a deep dark side where a human being is trying to get out eh, Galina?"

"Well I suppose if you believe a crocodile has a nice side, yes, but really Ric, is not a good idea. This man is KGB, a killer, he's not like the rest of us, he might kiss babies for photos but other than that he…"

I interrupted her.

"I would like to leave Moscow without any animosity as far as Petrov is concerned if at all possible. He is a man who bears malice... and that needs attention. I need to smooth matters with him."

"Ric, I think you mad, but have it your way. Come to Borodinos tomorrow, Thursday for noon. We will have a lunch date, yes? I will ask Irina to bring your car over as well."

"Oh, yes, I had forgotten the car, used by Black. I need to return it to the hire company."

"I'm sure Marcel, a senior in our division will come also for a friendly chat with you."

"Marcel, that's an unusual name for a Russian?"

"Marcel is of mixed origin, French mother and a Russian father.

"He is originally from French Interpol. With his experience, an ideal candidate for the RIS.

"He speaks French, very good English, obviously Russian, also German. He is quite a high flyer as English saying, but approachable man. He knows much about Petrov's movements and... well, I will let him tell you more when you meet... da, OK?"

In conclusion, we agreed to meet on Thursday. Noon at Borodinos.

I arrived at Borodinos at noon as arranged, Thursday. Galina and her colleague Marcel were already seated, chatting. Within a few seconds Irina followed me in. She handed me the car keys and informed me where the car was parked. Black had apparently not topped up the car with fuel. I was not surprised. A pig is always a pig! It was left to Irina to pay visit to the petrol station. She filled the car with fuel, I topped up her purse with Roubles to which she was grateful.

"My cousin Viktor in hospital, Ric. They not know what wrong with him. He unconscious when he Ma and Pa come from shopping, he on floor. He still unconscious. Doctors not know why?"

"Oh, I'm sorry to hear that Irina. (Black's doing!) Hopefully things will resolve themselves." We were then introduced to "Marcel" and the routine coffee was ordered all round.

Marcel was a pleasant type of man. Somehow he just looked French rather than Russian.

He stood up, both smiling, we shook hands and sat once again.

"Galina tells me... oh by the way, I assume you are happy for me to speak in English, Galina tells me you have some Russian?"

I informed him my Russian was: "School boy Russian, a bit like my school boy French." Marcel requested I define what I meant by 'school boy'.

"Well, it's what we English say when our knowledge of a language is rather pathetic!" Marcel wasn't convinced but fortunately continued in his excellent English.

"Galina informs me you want to meet this man Petrov on what you call, neutral territory?"

I explained my reasons to Marcel just as I had inferred to Galina previously;

"I realize you are aware this man is not a pleasant type and you have had personal experience of him. You left him injured after your last encounter, he won't like that. Be assured, he removes people for enjoyment, but if you insist on this, all I can do is give you some detail of one of Petrov's favourite haunts. The rest is up to you, but I advise you not to proceed."

I thanked Marcel and he then offered more advice along with details of a club of Petrov's "There is a club called *Comrades,* have you heard of it?"

"No."

"It is one of the last remaining occupied buildings down at the old part of the docks. This is where people and businesses are being moved out to make way for redevelopment. Almost all buildings are boarded up. The only reason why this club is still active, is because it is owned by a politician Toliakov. Have you heard of him?"

"No."

"This club is to be found in a dimly lit side street not far back from the river. Used in the old days as warehouses and also for other nefarious uses including ladies of the night. It was well known by sailors during earlier times. Apart from this club, it is a quiet dead place."

"Sounds inviting!" Galina added some information here.

"It's not, Ric. It a dreadful place. We watch it for drug dealing and prostitution but due to Toliakov there is not a lot we can do until it really is time for demolition."

I assured both Galina and Marcel that I would take care.

"Every Friday evening, we know this because we have a man who frequently visits the club ingor... incord. I forget the word?"

228

"Incognito?"

"Yes, that's it, he blends in and gets a lot of inside information," Marcel continued. "Every Friday, our man Petrov visits *Comrades* principally to drink to excess and meet women. He always leaves at midnight sharp. It's because his wife, who is a nurse at the hospital, does a late Friday afternoon duty and leaves the hospital at two o'clock in the morning. Vladimir Petrov is then always dutifully in bed asleep."

"It amazing," added Irina, "that even man like this need be home before wife, yes, da?"

"Yes, we can all remember the Nazi hunters who tracked down the German Gestapo murderers after second world war. Many of them had nice homes and families with children. They did not know, or believe their dear dad and husband could have been involved in such atrocities. Obviously, it can be paralleled that Petrov is one of those types. Nice wife, digs the garden and kisses babies eh?" Muted laughter from all. We needed some!

Marcel went into great detail about the club and the types that frequented there. From his vivid description I could not help but to think of Daphne du Maurier's book… Jamaica Inn. Hopefully they don't go quite that far and string people up from the rafters. Armed with all the information we settled down to a light lunch whereby the majority of subjects became more convivial.

However, in the midst of our chatting Galina asked: "Would you like to take my Berretta Ric. It may be a good idea to have it as a standby?" I thanked Galina and inwardly smiled as I knew where it was normally kept when out on assignments. It might still be warm!

"Many thanks Galina, but no thanks. I don't want to be tempted to use it."

Four o'clock and we had finished the business in hand. I advised them all I would see them again (possibly not Marcel?) after my assignment to visit Petrov, prior to departing to the UK. Once this matter was concluded I had no further reason to stay in Moscow. "Blue" had given me clearance. We said our temporary farewells and I drove Irina back to the Moscow Star. Here we had the routine coffee in the garden. I then said my thanks and goodbyes to Monika in the best Russian I could muster. kissing Irina on both cheeks, I then departed for the Marriott hotel.

After parking the car, I strolled into the restaurant. The roof light was now miraculously completely mended. No sign of the dreadful events were apparent and tables were once again, positioned beneath the sky. It all seemed an age away, but of course, it wasn't.

Returning to my room I slumped upon the bed. Starring at the ceiling, I thought about that pig Black. Leaving the car low on fuel... not even saying goodbye... and what precisely did he do to Viktor Karashenko? He is still out cold, and the medics don't know why. Surely, it must be poison?

A shower and change of clothes later, after a little more reading of "War and Peace". I was then down to evening dinner at eight. I avoided shaving. I need to look the part tomorrow.

I felt sociable that evening so I elected to join a table of eight people, all arriving virtually simultaneously. It's quite an education when one dines with people one knows, but when one doesn't know them... that is when the tall tales come out in exaggerated form.

The evening wore on and the drink began to take its toll on one of the diners.

One man could not stop informing us "bored to tears" guests how successful he was at work... and how much the "chaps" thought of him... and how the ladies thought he was such a "great guy" (his words) The bonuses were this, and that and his success was this, that, and the other and he might be running the company one day and his wife then interrupted him when in full flow.

"Do you think Douglas, we might move away, out of the semi and get a detached house one day?" This must have been the worst thing he wished to make public. A semi-detached... ooo!

The others enjoyed that rare moment when he ceased talking... stopped in his tracks at the public declaration that he lived in a semi! (People do) Playing Devil's advocate Mabel asked: "...and where do you live, Jean, you and Douglas, somewhere nice I bet... Hampstead, Mayfair?" Jean truthfully answered without the slightest delay or any sign of embarrassment: "'ackney!"

Friday arrived, soon enough. I didn't shave. I looked a little rough around the edges! That would be part of my image, even though I had no intention of entering the premises of *Comrades*, but one never knows, I might have to?

I spent the majority of the day relaxing. More reading, then a stroll to the shopping centre, just to aimlessly wander and view the goods on show for sale.

I snacked in a shopping mall and watched the shoppers as I munched my rolls and drank coffee served in the hateful polystyrene mug.

Wandering back to the hotel, the future events went through my mind like the rehearsal of lines for a part in a play. This reminded me of the last rehearsal with the Macilroy saga. I hoped this would go a little more smoothly than that scenario. Falling from a window was at least not on the agenda. Was I wise to refuse Galina's Berretta? Was I wise to not accept Marcel's advice… and not go at all? Possibly, but this is something I feel I have to do before leaving Moscow.

The afternoon came and went… as did the evening dinner. I expect some fellow dining guests might have thought I was in the early stages of a beard? Perhaps I will at that!

I did my usual slumping on the bed and spent more time reading.

I felt quite relaxed, reading helped.

At eleven o'clock I made my way to the car park and sitting in the car went over the possible outcomes of this meeting, both positive and negative. I kept thinking… "Berretta!"

I drove to the part of town where the old docks were, and easily located the road in question. Eleven thirty and a slight change in the weather. Light rain commenced – not useful!

I drove along the street and elected to park at the far end at the river side. It was a bumpy rattling ride down a very straight road, approximately one hundred metres long and as straight as an arrow. Parking at the riverside, I locked the car and strolled back. I lit a Gitanes. It was quite some time, since the earlier days that I sampled Russian "Sweet Dreams" cigarettes (without an "e") I did them a discredit – they were not really like cow dung, but actually very mild… that is why the girlies smoke them. Gitanes is my vice and will remain so!

The bumpy road was constructed of traditional granite setts. Beautiful but very uneven. Likewise, the narrow stone paved footpath was twisted and uneven and had the appearance of neglected teeth, that is, where I could see any paving.

It appeared to me the origins of this area was solely for warehousing goods. The narrowness of the road would have only permitted two horse drawn carriages to pass each other delivering goods. This area was constructed on a grid system with a series of straight roads leading to the river. There was only one street light column at each extreme end of the highway but the central part was exaggerated by the anomaly of *"Comrades"* itself. Right in the middle of the terraced run of the old warehouse buildings was the night club. Two units had been converted for the club and knocked together. No doubt Tottiakov's (or whatever his name is?) idea.

It appeared to be as if a lightning strike from "the gods" had hit the building. The whole of the night club was lit up like a Christmas tree from bottom to top, the sixth floor level. Every window aperture on the upper levels shone, advertising the likelihood of what was going on behind. The ground floor was obviously the drinking, gambling and dancing part of the club, as well as other illicit dealing. A sandwich board stood outside displaying the word *Comrades* and other small print which I could not easily read. Everywhere else up and down the street was blackness. All other buildings along the highway seemed to be boarded up. The club was virtually a rose among thorns, or was it the other way around?

I had originally thought of the story "Jamaica Inn" but this area displayed images conjured when reading a Kafka novel. This place was right out of "The Trial" with its sinister darkness.

I had no intentions of joining the revellers in the club. This fact I had not declared to Marcel, but my plan was to wait for Petrov to leave *Comrades* at the appointed hour. From what had been indicated Petrov would not linger too long beyond his scheduled midnight hour.

I had no intentions of entering the club with its selection of drunks and drug dealers!

I took a position diagonally opposite the club in a recessed doorway concealed within the shadows. The light from *Comrades* streamed across the narrow road, the dreadful raucous noise permeated everywhere.

The outside air and atmosphere was filled, totally monopolizing space with artificial light, the sound of dancing, music and raised voices.

One matter I hadn't considered was the possibility of "bouncers" patrolling outside, but being so late I imagined their duty was now to be predominantly inside the building and no longer the prevention of unwanted people entering as earlier on. That indeed was a bonus. I preferred my encounter with Comrade Vladimir Petrov to be on a one to one basis without others, who might "take sides" and leave me at a disadvantage.

Eleven fifty-five. I waited patiently for the witching hour. The loud noise of the club from within never abated. Two people came out which alarmed me, it's nearly twelve! They witnessed the light rain and ran along the highway. Quiet once again. (Quiet – what am I thinking!)

A few minutes after twelve the doors opened again and Petrov stood out front with a female. He fumbled in his wallet and gave her something, presumably money. She pushed the notes away furtively and pecked him lightly on the cheek. They spoke a few words and she re-entered the club. Petrov looked up at the sky.

Feeling the light rain he pulled his collar up and buttoned his jacket. He lit a cigarette, hunched his shoulders, putting his hands into his pockets crossed the highway and proceeded to walk along the middle of the road.

I stepped out of the shadows and partly blocked his way.

A very shocked and surprised Vladimir Petrov stood, rigidly poised. After a pause and an obvious struggle to make some recognition, due to the artificial light mixed with shadows.

I was partly in silhouette.

Petrov then, collecting his thoughts and recognition said: "Oh... chto ty zedes delayesh... you... Meester Hartland."

"I take it... from my rather poor Russian that you are asking, what am I doing here?"

Petrov removed his hands from his pockets and with arms folded replied positively: "Yes, you have followed me here. You have men nearby I am sure to cause me injury?"

I informed him I was alone and came here with no intention of harming him at all.

Petrov and I were then a few feet apart and the sneer on his face was apparent.

He smelt like a brewery. The thoughts of myself with "a gang of men" no longer being a threat, naturally gave him a degree of great comfort. With a sneer;...

"So, Meester Hartland, English spy, what you doing here?"

I reminded him somewhat pitifully that I was a tourist. He laughed out loud at that one!

"I will soon be returning to the UK. You and I have never seen eye to eye but I thought it would be better if I left Moscow, left Russia, without grievances. I would like to leave all trouble behind, if you follow me, and finish with all the hatred between ourselves. I quite like Moscow and would like to be a tourist again in the future without any encumbrances."

"You know, Meester Hartland, you very foolish man. You think you can attack me in a night club and walk away is easy thing to do da. Yes?"

I reminded him that, actually it was he was attacked me at the night club, not vice versa and he who locked me in a cell at Lubyanka prison when I first arrived, and he who injected me with a monitoring capsule, and he or his colleagues were no doubt the ones who set my car alight.

"I have a lot to complain about as far as you are concerned Petrov but I am prepared to let bygones be bygones, so I offer you my hand as a truce." I held out my hand... it was not taken.

"Ty mertzvets Meester Hartland... you are a dead man."

Petrov still had a leather wrist support. He unbuttoned his jacket and took a gun from his left side breast holster, previously concealed by his jacket, and repeated the words in English...

"You are a dead man."

He then slowly and carefully took a silencer from his right side pocket and slowly commenced the process of screwing it on to the barrel of the pistol. Why he thought a silencer was necessary with the noise of *Comrades* blasting away I'll never know? Logically, I imagine he had done this deed so many times it was simply an automatic thing he did.

This he surely did, but was to be his undoing, not mine!

I remember the words of Galina, or was it Irina?, about a crocodile not having a nice side! Clearly Petrov was all bad and there was no nice side to him. A mistake to have thought so. His sneering and slow turning of the silencer was enough time for me. I leaped forward and with a kick into his "vulnerables" – this not only disarmed him but temporarily disabled him.

I trust his "bits" will still be working when he next pays a visit to *Comrades* on Friday. His pistol and silencer were lost from his grasp. I knelt on the high part of his chest whilst he was rocking in agony. All I got from him were grunts in pain, swearing and a whole host of threats.

Pinioned to the floor by my knee, in a puddle (that being a bonus!) I spoke: "I wanted a truce Petrov and you chose otherwise. If you can't behave like a human being, so be it, but I did the best I could to form an amicable peace with you. You are scum I am afraid to say and I am not going to stand here and be gunned down by a moron like you. Don't cross me again Petrov, or if you do you may find I will be on the other side of the gun... got it?"

"Swine... English pig... bastard... you will die... etc., etc. you are no tourist!"

I said... "Got it?" Grunting... rolling... swearing.

"Da... yes... I got it, da... yes... get off!"

Lifting myself off I could see the ol' trick of nut cracking worked as well as ever. A regrettable attack but the best I could think of when seconds away from a bullet. I stood next to Petrov who was then flat on his back, still groaning. I collected the gun and silencer and said: *"Lzyinite… do svidaniya,"* (sorry… goodbye) and left, disappearing into the darkness to my car. Arriving at the riverside I tossed the gun and silencer into the river as far as I was able in different directions. Petrov will kill no more with that weapon, but will, needless to say, obtain another for his nefarious lifestyle. Driving back to the hotel I recalled his words… "you are a dead man." I am certainly a marked man as far as Petrov is concerned, but actually, I always was.

I slept well that night.

Expecting the possibility of an official visit from Petrov and his Lubyanka cronies, I organized my account after an early breakfast, signed all the parts on the dotted line where I was required, collected my passport and left the Marriott hotel for good.

I drove to the car hire shop and surrendered the vehicle. Natasha and I walked around the vehicle as before. No damage – nothing to pay. I thanked her and in turn she welcomed any return visit, should I require a car in the future. She had no more news about Katina.

I "hoofed" it to the bus stop with my luggage and caught a Marshrupta to Borodinos. Igor had volunteered to chauffeur me to the airport today. I was happy to accept his offer.

I had an early light lunch with Galina and happily paid the bill, thanking her for all her kindness and assistance during the past troubled times. We had a few laughs but then was particularly horrified at the event that took place outside *"Comrades"* last night.

"He will not forget that Ric any time soon, you know that don't you? Perhaps you should have taken my Berretta. If you had held him at gunpoint, perhaps he might have gone away peacefully?"

"The worry there is Galina, if I had it, I might have used it, and then I would be in a deeper mess than I am in already! I'm sure someone else will finish the man before too long?"

"He's virtually untouchable Ric. We at the RIS keep him at a distance. He not like us either, but you are right, there will be a time when someone will *take him out*… *a* good American term, eh Ric? The days of the Lubyanka torturers I am sure to feel their days are short."

After lunch and a farewell to all those I knew at Borodinos my two cases were placed in the car by Igor. I said a special goodbye to Galina and hoped we will meet again someday in happier times. "Goodbye Ric. I will always remember our adventures!"

"Adventures!" We both laughed out loud at this word!

Igor set off at a fair pace. He was possibly a contender for formula one racing! Cars in front of him appeared to not be permissible, any opportunity of passing, he was there. The chances of being late for the plane seemed unlikely! It was Just as well; I had left it a little late for my departure.

"How you fly back, Ric?"

"I originally came by Aeroflot and a lousy old Lada taxi, but I'm returning by British Airways.

"I re-arranged my flight by telephone. Originally, I had an open return ticket but I am pleased to say, due to the Aeroflot flights being well booked up, I was able to transfer to BA. In the UK that is almost impossible, however it was achieved."

"Yes. Aeroflot is not luxury, da?"

"No, true, but it got me here. The odds on the Lada taxi though were not good, but it did also get me here. Your car is much better Igor, and seemingly… faster!"

"Is my joy, Ric. It my baby. It drive fast, da?"

I knew what he meant. We do either hate or love our cars, if they serve one well.

We arrived at the airport in reasonable time. The four thirty flight should arrive at Heathrow at eight o'clock, if there are no hiccups. "Blue" has arranged for a taxi to collect me. After all I have been through, that is the least he could do!

Stopping at the main concourse entrance, we had two minutes. Igor removed my cases and rolled them on to the paving.

He slammed the boot shut. Hurriedly I said goodbye to Igor, who hugged me Russian style. He was so far down; it was similar to hugging one's young nephew. He certainly was a great chap.

I liked him. He jumped into his car and was off on to the "formula one" speed lane, leaving a sample of tyre rubber and a cloud of black smoke for all nearby foot passengers to enjoy!

Cabin bag over shoulder, I wheeled the larger of the two cases into the airport and seeing the BA check in area, I joined a short queue. Being a little 'brief' with my timing I think the majority of the passengers had already checked in.

Facing the petite British Airways check-in girl, I placed my large case on to the weighing machine as directed. Twenty-four kilos. She asked for my documents.

I explained as briefly as I could about the transfer arrangements and the reasons why I had no paperwork… not enough time for paperwork to arrive by post, etc.

The check-in girl studied her screen in some depth and simultaneously asked for my passport.

I handed my passport as she opened it with one hand, eyes still firmly fixed on to her screen. "Are, yes, here we are, Mr Hartland. Yes, you have a transferred ticket. Next flight. Seat number twenty four, isle seventeen… ah! there seems to be a … probleem here." Her words slowed as the details became clear on her screen, whatever they were?

She held the passport in front of her screen and seemed to be comparing with the monitor.

"Just one moment sir," she then looked over my shoulder, "Sorry madam, bear with me, there is a problem here, shouldn't take more than a few minutes. Mr Hartland, you have a block on your travel here. It says you must wait to be interviewed by the airport police before travelling."

"Eh? why… what is the reason?"

"I'm, sorry. I can only tell you what my instructions report here on the screen."

This previously happy smiling, friendly lady became more straight laced as the smiles evaporated. There are a lot of State Police here today.

She now thought me to be a criminal! "Blue" was right. They've blocked me!

"Sorry, sir, I now have to (whilst handing me my passport) ask you to leave the check-in desk and go to the passenger seating areas. You will be called over the Tannoy systems and will be given directions. It should be quite soon. If there are no difficulties, and the airport police give you clearance then, please come back immediately to me and I will hurry things through for you."

She looked over my shoulder, "Madam?"

Lifting my case from the weighing scales, I wandered away from the check-in desk. I had no intention of lingering a minute longer. I quickly found the exit, hailed the next waiting cab and was soon "winging" my way back to Borodinos. Up a ladder and down a snake!

I gave the driver an address two roads distant from Borodinos. The least known of my whereabouts, the better. He was keen to help me into the house… someone else's house! But, I gave him a tip, declined assistance and sent him on his way.

It wasn't late, but the noise from the plastic wheels of my case along the cracks of the pavement could have awakened the dead.

I nonchalantly strolled into Borodinos and was shown to a table by an unknown waitress.

I ordered coffee, the menu, and inquired after Galina. In Broken English I was informed that she was, "Out back, she come soon, you please wait, da?"

"Da, yes, I wait, spasibo, thank you."

I studied the menu and made my choice. The waitress returned and took my order. Galina wandered in carrying a large box from "out back". She quickly spotted me; "Moy bog… Ric… privet… hello Ric… what are you doing here?"

"Well, hello again Galina… seems I just love it here! You can't get rid of me that easily!" Galina sat with me whilst I informed her of the story of the airport scenario and my conclusion, that an interview with the airport police would not have been very wise.

"It Petrov, I expect, or it might be officials from the British Embassy. I remember you telling me some time ago your London department thought your travel might be blocked. What are you going to do now. You can't fly out of the country?"

"Can I stay here for a few days, I know you said you had a spare flat upstairs, or would you prefer it if I went to a hotel to get out of your hair? It will only be for a short time enabling me to get re-organized. Cash is no problem. My department head had already indicated that if I could not fly from Moscow, I would need to fly from Belarus, so that's my next port of call."

"Belarus!… that's hundreds of kilometres from here Ric!"

I explained my instructions from London were to fly home from Moscow, but should this not be possible, I was to hire a car and drive to Belarus. When there, a flight would have been pre-arranged, and that would be my "ticket home". These are my instructions… my orders. "Hire a car, Ric, and then what you do with it?"

"Abandon it. Leave it at the airport car park. It is not what I want to do but, so be it." She gave this matter some thought and informed me about the vehicle pound located adjacent RIS headquarters. Vehicles of all types were confiscated when part of criminal activities. After a short period of time when examinations are finalized, the vehicles are offered up for sale to the public. Occasionally, cars which are not desirable sit there for a long time and simply don't "shift".

"Ric, I will talk to the manager responsible for the vehicle park. If we can find a car that nobody claims to own, or wants to buy, it could be the one for you? This will be help to get rid of a car that just sits there. Space is always needed. It will be a favour to do this. They will thank you for it, even though car has not been sold for money, but there is no money if it sits there, da, eh, yes?"

"Well, I suppose that sounds a reasonable idea and a way to avoid dumping a hire car which I did not want to do, but there is the worry about breakdown and of course car insurance." Apparently, "getaway cars" are often in very good mechanical order, for obvious reasons.

Galina explained, if a good car can be found it would be checked mechanically and serviced. "Insurance cover for few days, Ric. This will not be difficult. We can do that. You will also need a Bill of Sale. Can you pass a few Rubles to the manager as a word of thanks?"

"Yes, of course, I will be happy to do that. Well… leave it to you then Galina, da, yes?" I was feeling a good deal happier than I was a few hours ago. Next, to plan the route. Time to depart, ETA etc., a place to stop for the night half way. There is a lot to organize yet.

I was settled into the spare upstairs flat. Very comfortable. I will visit a bank in town tomorrow, travel by Marshrupta to draw out a lot of cash. I needed to ensure Galina was not out of pocket, also the car fuel situation, hotel en-route, and any other sundry expenses… food, etc.

A telephone call to "Blue" gave me the opportunity of updating him with the latest plan. When I informed him about the escape and near encounter with the airport police, he replied.

"Ah!"

When I advised him of the new plan to travel to Belarus and all the potential difficulties it entailed, he said: "Good. Let me know when you want the plane ticket from Minsk? Good luck. Bye!" Thanks "Blue" as always about as helpful as a hippo in a public swimming pool! The following day "IT" arrived! Galina announced: "Ric. Your car is here. It's outside. You way home is assured!"

A driver came in to give me the keys. We went out front.

"Bloody hell, Its Barbara Cartland's taxi!"

The vision required not only sunglasses but breathing apparatus!

A long dark pink Buick assaulted my eyes! No wonder this was not wanted. Galina chuckled. "Don't think too badly, Ric. It's in excellent condition. Apart from the colour, it really is a great vehicle. It did not go well as far as the sale was concerned, the pink did not help, also the large five litre engine and the fact it is right hand drive, otherwise it is superb and reliable."

"It was owned by Rozzzetta... do you know of her?"

"No."

Galina then informed me "Rozzzetta" otherwise known as Rosa Kolo (Koloiskaya) was an English pop star. She left the UK five years ago to join her partially Russian family. She brought her pink limousine with her, imported by boat, and this is it!

"Are you sure you don't remember her?"

"Possibly. I have a vague memory. The fig tree song? Why have you got her car?"

The "pop star" had apparently got herself into trouble with drugs. She was pulled up one day when travelling in her pink limo at a very high speed through the town centre. She had in her car boot a considerable quantity of cocaine. After being arrested and charged her car was seized. Rozzzetta did a term in prison, but upon her release her vehicle was withheld. It mattered little to the "pop genius" because she had several other cars; Ferraris, Mercedes, a Maserati and a few Porsches not to mention seven large motorcycles that she never rode.

"It was unlikely she missed her pink Buick. It's alright for some people eh Ric? Who knows, you might get some adoring fans chase you along the road!"

"That possibility had not crossed my mind at that stage. I hope they don't!"

Upon close inspection, the car certainly seemed to be quite impressive. The interior was custom made and everything was in immaculate condition. The front two wings had dents which probably reflected the owners talent for driving. Apart from the awful colour it was a fabulous car.

Being pink, a huge V8 engine and right hand drive, only a mad enthusiast would buy this car, and up to that date, no one had shown interest even though it had belonged to the famous "Rozzzetta" and the number plate was a "giveaway": ROZZ1234. The car really was a "booby prize" for me but one cannot blame them for wanting it cleared from the pound. I'm not ungrateful!

"Sorry about the number Ric. There was not enough time to get that altered."

Chapter 14
Going Home!

The car was taken into the rear parking area of Borodinos. The quicker it was removed from the main highway and public view, the better I liked it.

A couple more days was wasted languishing at the Bistro whilst all the relevant paperwork was obtained. The day arrived for my departure so I telephoned "Blue" to let him know my movements. He needed to arrange for the plane flights from Minsk. I allowed a day to a half way point, stay overnight, then another day and a schedule for an evening flight appeared to be the right thing to do. "Blue" however had other ideas, which in hindsight were correct. To allow another day for contingencies… so that was set. Leave Moscow, head for Belarus and catch a plane on the third day. Galina handed me all documentation over the breakfast table. Insurance and Bill of sale along with immaculate pristine handbook detailing everything about the car. Naturally the previous owner had never turned a page. Registration documents were out of the question, that takes months to obtain but the Bill of Sale details my ownership.

I settled my account with Galina which she reluctantly accepted and added a fair "bung" for the vehicle pound manager.

"Wait. I will call Sofia." Galina left briefly and returned with Sofia her cook.

"This is Sofia, Ric. She speaks no English. She was the cook at Cafe Brodsky. She is so good at her work I transferred her to here. I was puzzled as they swiftly communicated in Russian.

"I think that is organized for you Ric. Sofia spoke to her Teten'ka and Dyadya yesterday. They live, in fact that is where Sofia comes from, they live in Smolensk. They have a small hotel, what you might call a B&B type of house and a room has been arranged for you for one night. That actually is tonight. You will have to pay them of course but it will not be expensive. It's good to have as a half way stopping place. Is that to be agreeable with you Ric?"

"Oh, yes, thank you… thank you Sofia… spasibo."

"Her Teten'ka and Dyadya; aunt and uncle to you Ric, are delightful people. Her uncle speaks English quite well, her aunt does not, but you can… what is the expression? You can get by."

"I'm so grateful to you both, thank you."

Sofia, smiled and nodded after translation and did a small bow. Then returned to the kitchen.

If her aunt and uncle are as nice as Sofia I will be happy to stay there.

"Cafe Brodsky, Ric. Good news there. It is now right for to commence works with builders. The investigation and Insurance matters, I am told will be complete in three months from now and I have a date for them to start. That is good news for us all here."

"Perhaps, one day I may be able to return and see the new Cafe Brodsky Galina?"

The journey ahead was outlined by Galina. She had assessed to be an eight to nine hour journey of approximately 750 kms.

I need to take the E30 highway and for most of the way stay on that route.

"South of Smolensk you must take some time to visit the Katyn monument. It is amazing."

"I will if I have the spare time. I expect it is a very sad place, high in atmosphere due to the horrors of what took place there all those years ago?"

"Oh you know about it, Ric? We decent Russians will not forget it, but I never certain if the world really know what happened there and our soldiers atrocities?"

"Oh, they do, and perhaps I am talking out of turn, but that lunatic Stalin must be in Hell now. The world, as you put it Galina, does not know enough about the dreadful behaviour of the Russian soldiers during both wars. So much of the events have faded as facts on paper. The treatment towards your own Russian people as well as the Polish race and the ordinary German citizens was beyond understanding or forgiveness. Sorry, I'm speaking too much!"

"That is all right, Ric. I am in agreement with you, but be careful what you say about the – 'lunatic'!"

"The other place you must visit Ric is the Turquoise Cathedral. It is truly beautiful building, and oh, yes, and the wonderful statue in the park to dedicate the defence against that other lunatic, Napoleon Bonaparte in 1812"

"Oh, I'm sorry Galina, I'm afraid I rather went off on one!"

"Off on one, Ric?"

"Yes, a rant, and going on far too long… you know, the Stalin thing."

"I quite understand. I agree with everything you said. It's just that you need to be careful who you say in front of. There are still idiots who think Stalin was a great man believe it or not, and some radicals can get quite nasty if they hear their hero insulted."

We wandered to the rear car park. I used a conventional key to open the door. I sat in the car and inserted the key into the ignition. The V8 leapt into life with a purr like a contented lion. I noticed the fuel gauge was showing full. Galina sat in the passenger seat as I drove to the front of the Bistro. She informed me that the vehicle pound manager had filled up the tanks with fuel. There were twin ten gallon tanks which should get me approximately half way to Belarus. (20 gals!) "I think the pound manager wanted to be certain you would not run out of fuel. He doesn't want to see that car again Ric!" Galina laughed. I think I know what she meant!

"Most generous!" was my reply.

I found my two cases had been brought out by Igor. For a second time he placed them in the boot. It was so huge they almost were lost in the cavernous space. Galina and I stood chatting about the journey when Monika and Irina arrived by car, just in time to say farewell… once again for a second time. All paper documents were placed on the rear seat, similar to the front, a long bench seat. In addition to those docs there was the name and address of Sofia's relatives and the telephone number of… as Galina put it – "our man in Belarus" all neatly written down. I was to telephone him and he would collect the car from the airport car park. It would not be diplomatic to simply abandon the car in the airport car par for the establishment to find it belonged to a man from the Ministry of Defence in the UK! The car would be collected and it would be left for "others" to determine what should be done with the Buick. I hope it will go to a good home. There must be some enthusiast out there who would want it? Yes, a V8, yes very thirsty and yes a right hand drive but a great vehicle.

I stood beside the car and said my goodbyes again. Entering the vehicle I started the throaty V8 and wound down the electric window, which responded smoothly with ease. I belted up, only one seat belt for the driver… unusual but true! Leaning out of the window I shook and grabbed hands with those who came to see me off. Ivan was there, as well as Sofia.

I blew kisses to the ladies. Irina and Galina did likewise in return. One cannot go through all we have been through without forming a genuine personal fondness for each other.

I slowly rolled off with the automatic gears taking control. With my right arm extended from the open window I executed a final wave combined with a thumbs up. I'm really going this time! Window up. It was a hot day so, on with the air-con. A gentle hum was noted. This was a big thirsty beast with an interior like someone's living room but it was luxury personified.

The springing suspension was amazing, the car body seemed to float along the road.

It wasn't long before I left the main part of the Moscow city and took the E30 highway which was a very good road, occasionally with numerous lanes. I hoped it would be like this all the way. I took careful note of the varying speed limits and abided by them. I would take no chances to invite the traffic police, not forgetting "my" car was like a pink floating Christmas tree!

I kept observing my rear view mirror. Many cars and lorries came and went, but I noted a black Moskvitch 400 on more than one occasion which frequently seemed to be a few hundred metres behind me. Doing the same speed as I... possibly? Using me as an innocent pacer... possibly, I do that sometimes myself... but it was so often there?

After another hour the signpost indicated Borodino. Well, that's spooky... I've just left. Borodino's... but of course, a very different one.

Eighty miles or so from Moscow I passed a sign with a slip turn showing the way to the Borodino monument. I was hesitant, I pulled over to a lay-by fronting the sign. Some parts were in English. I turned off the engine and read the sign. Did the Moskvitch pass me? No! Curious! I looked back but there was no sign of it. The phantom car must have left by the previous slip road. To myself I gave firm instructions: "Don't get paranoid, it's simply another vehicle, not a herd of assassins."

It is really too early in the journey to consider taking time away from my route. Rather a pity. This is obviously where the famous battle took place during the nineteenth century. From my poor school days memory I recall it was a win to the French, something to do with the number of casualties but never deemed to be a decisive victory. When one considers all the deaths and the eventual outcome, surely everyone loses?

So, on I cruised with my air-con doing its business and the radio offering various Russian folky and pop songs, some I liked, some I would have buried at birth. In my rear view mirror I could swear I could see a black car in the distance about 400 metres back. Was it the M400? I don't know.

Numerous towns and villages I passed. Feeling hungry and the yearn for a coffee I approached a place called "Chemoye" and an advertising board presented me with an advanced warning that the next right turn would see me into the front parking area of a Bistro Cafe. I arrived. It appeared quite wholesome. I turned into the vehicular concourse and parked away from other vehicles on the far boundary. No other cars were anything like mine! None on the planet were like mine!

I locked the car, as I turned I saw a black Moskvitch parked on the main highway, diagonally across from me, approximately two hundred metres distant. Coincidence? My Aunt Fanny it was!

I entered the cafe which… what a surprise, was called "le Borodino" Why "le" are they mad? A friendly lady waitress saw me in, and blurting away in fluent Russian took me to a table by the window, pleasingly on the shady cool side.

I could not see the black car from here. There were too many other vehicles obscuring the view.

I looked at the menu and coffee was first on the agenda. I selected my firm favourite Solvanka soup dish which is full of "things" Black Borodinsky rye bread and to finish with the terrific ice cream dish I had on two earlier occasions before called Morozhende.

The waitress appeared and I did my bit by saying "Privet" (hello) and then stumbled with my pronunciation over the remaining dishes. Abject failure!

"Ah… you American?"

She must have seen the floating bedroom arrive?

"No. English."

She took my selection in her fragmented English which so often I find is better than my disfigured Russian, and with a swish of her apron turned in the direction of the kitchen. My coffee came quickly which was a bonus. A large cappuccino which I slurped happily. Whilst slurping, I was looking out of the window at the passing vehicles when a figure appeared next to me.

"Hello. I heard you are English. I hope you don't mind me speaking to you?"

"No," I replied, puzzled at what was to come.

He was a casually but well-dressed young man, twenty-ish years of age and judging by his accent, either English or a very well educated Russian. He remained standing.

"Can I sit opposite. I won't take up much of your time?" He was holding an iced Coke in a glass.

I felt mildly irritated and compromised, but I gestured my hand to the seat opposite. He thanked me and proceed with the introduction. He did not seem to be a Moskvitch type of driver.

"I often come here by my bicycle. I have come here for the last five years, previously with my parents to visit my aunt and uncle, Dad's brother. He is Russian, she is English, they live here, not too far, about five kilometres along a country lane. There is not much to do around here. It might be my last visit, but I do it to please my parents. Sorry, you don't want to, hear all that clap trap?"

"It's ok. I expect not many English stop here and it's nice to hear someone who does things to please his parents. Quite unusual these days." I tittered!

"My wife came with me the first year but she hates the place. She says it is easy to 'love' the Russians but just as easy to hate them. A bit harsh, eh? My aunt and uncle don't have children so they are going to leave the farm to me. It sounds a bit mean, but that is why I keep up the visits... I'm not totally daft!"

"No, of course not."

"Your car. I saw you arrive. Are you Rozzzetta's husband by any chance?"

With some sense of relief I realised "I had been clocked," as the pop star's possible ol' man!

I laughed. My soup arrived. I commenced more slurping! "Hope you don't mind?"

"I was a fan in my younger years, and I have a poster, or at least I did have a poster on my bedroom wall when I was a teenage slob. Rozzzetta is pictured standing by her car. The pink one, so I knew it was the one, and that number plate. It is the same. It is hers, isn't it?"

In the briefest of terms I informed the Rozzzetta fan that I did not know his heroine very well, but I am a mere mortal who has purchased her car, number plate and all! This did not disappoint him. He continued with a lot about this young lady and what she was in her heyday, but particularly he was pleased to see the car that was in his very own picture poster. (It takes all sorts!) "Do you think... would you mind if I go outside and look at it. Stupid, I know for someone of my age but I would like to have a close look?"

"Yes… if it doesn't sound impolite, you seem a little old to still swoon over a faded pop star?"

"Oh yes, you are quite right, at my advanced years of twenty eight, it would be, it's just the old poster, and these days I am a mad car fan not a pop singer fan, it's the car that is fascinating."

"I don't mind in the slightest. It's probably like me, finding Marilyn Monroe's car. Can't touch *her,* but you could fondle her car eh?" We both did laugh at my stupid comment.

"Look, if you want to go out and have a gentle fondle, that's is quite agreeable to me. If you wish to wait and give me time to have my meal, I tell you what? You said you live not too far from here, we'll put your cycle in the car boot, its huge, I'm sure it will easily fit, and I'll take you for a short spin and drive you home to your uncle's farm How does that appeal to you – erm?"

"Sid."

"How does that sound, Sid. A ride in your pop heroines car. You can tell all your old teenage slob friends about it and you don't have to declare who the driver was, eh?" More laughter!

"That's great. I'll pay for my coke and go. I'll wait for you outside. Please don't rush your meal." He paid for his drink. Turned to smile as he left the cafe. I did as he expressed, and did not rush my meal. I had no intentions of doing so. I paid and left the Bistro forty-minutes later.

Two Lubyanka 'hit men' sat puffing their Sobranie cigarettes. Their second, since stopping to observe the "Meester Comrade Ric Hartland tourist and spy." Neither man had previously encountered Hartland, but from inside sources at the vehicle compound, they had been reliably informed Comrade Hartland would be travelling out of the city today in a long pink Buick. Their task was to "deal with him" or take him back to Moscow when they can find a suitable "transfer" place. Hartland was after all, an official of the United Kingdom's government and things such as this are often best done covertly so as not to be observed by witnesses.

Sid came out of "le Borodinos" and made his way to the Buick. Fedor still smoking but half asleep, nudged Andrei and pointed in the direction of the man they were after.

Sid approached the car and stood admiring it. He slowly walked around it. The attention of the Lubyanka thugs never wavered.

Sid brushed his hand lightly over the roof of the car as he strolled beside it, as if removing imaginary dust. Stopping at the wing mirror he rubbed his finger over the glass as if to give it a shine. He stood back to look at the dents in the front of the vehicle. The two thugs watched. "Look at the stupid bastard admiring his own trashy American car." The tyres were also rather special, soon noticed by Sid.

They had obviously been replaced numerous times over the years, but currently they were immaculate with bold clear white lettering all around the perimeter. Somewhat typical of an American Cadillac. Sid stood looking at them.

"Come on that's enough for me." Fedor and Andrei immediately left their Moskvitch 400, crossed the highway and approached Sid, who by that time was down on one knee reading the white lettering on the car tyre. Behind him Sid heard the words spoken in poor English.

"You check you tyre, da, for puncture, or, comrade, you have not enough air, eh?"

Slightly startled Sid replied that he was reading the lettering. He stood up. Fedor grabbed him and violently thrust him face down against the front wing whilst Andrei searched his pockets. Protesting as he may, Sid could offer little resistance. He wriggled. Fedor punched him in the kidneys, he began to sag. Sid was then lifted up by the scruff of his clothes, gasping for air.

"Nothing in his pockets at all Fedor. No identification at all. No wallet, nothing."

"Good. Take him."

They frog marched Sid over to the Moskvitch and threw him onto the rear seat with Andrei beside him. A revolver was then held at his head and he was told in broken English.

"You do as told and keep mouth shut, da, ok, you know what I say?"

Sid still in pain from the kidney punch protested, but that got him nowhere. The car was driven down a country lane. When all seemed quiet and remote, he was dragged out of the car.

Five days later the newspapers will report; an unknown male, aged about thirty, who had no documents on him was found in a field with a bullet hole in the back of his head. The local state police were conducting investigations and want to interview a man who possibly was the last to see the victim. They were seen talking at the "le Borodino" Bistro... etc....

If anyone has any information etc., etc., etc.

I paid my bill and gave the nice waitress decent tip. She was ecstatic. Don't they tip in this place? She held the front door for me and with some courteous remarks… left the Bistro. That was a delightful meal and also a splendid little Bistro cafe, almost in the middle of nowhere.

"Now where is, Sid?"

I wandered around the car park. No Sid. I returned to my car. Sids's cycle was fairly nearby, padlocked to the boundary fence, but no Sid. I imagine he became a little bored waiting and has gone for a stroll. I suppose three quarters of an hour was a tedious length time to wait. I unlocked the car and started the V8's gentle bubbling roar, a very satisfying sound that says…

"If you are chased… they won't catch you sunshine!"

I rolled out of the Bistro parking area on to the main highway. Looking to both sides, and in my mirror to the rear, there was still – no Sid, so I elected to get on my way. His loss, but no doubt, he will soon forget.

Back on to the E30, fed and watered, with 85 miles under my belt and soon up to ninety miles per hour once more, I'm feeling content with progress thus far. I've past the two hour mark and approximately three hours to Smolensk… and don't even think it but, providing no hiccups with the car or road conditions I should make Smolensk late afternoon/early evening.

That will then be 250 miles completed and time for a fuel top up. In overdrive, I expect to get 300 miles for my twenty gallons of free petrol. Thanks to the vehicle pound manager I have journeyed quite a long way gratis and for free!

What a kind Muscovite! He really didn't want to see me, or rather, the pink car, again!

No sign of that black Moskvitch 400 any more… pure imagination! What an idiot to think someone was following me all this way. If they had been, what would they have hoped to achieve? Nick me for doing twenty km per hour over the speed limit? Nahhh!

I felt a little apprehensive about the distance, so, at the next lay-by I pulled over to study the map. It certainly is a fair distance to Smolensk from here. It might be longer than originally anticipated? After a considerable time studying and calculating, I assessed it to be at least 180 miles from this spot, and that will take the best part of three to four hours.

Time now is just after two o'clock, so better get a move on and perhaps raise the mph a tad.

If I can average 70 mph it will only take two to three hours, but at that average speed it will actually necessitate me driving at eighty. That, of course is merely figures on paper. Reality is so much different. However, so be it. Get going PDQ!

Can I reach Smolensk by daylight? Yes, of course, no difficulty there, it is summer, but not forgetting the pit stop for fuel which knocks the average speed down. My personal bet is to reach Sofia's Aunt and Uncle at about five or six, even considering negotiating an unknown city and an address yet to be located?

Map away. I set off with keen interest on the speedo and the fuel gauge. The car uses petrol so fast one can almost see the needle move. The overdrive system however is a great benefit. That pushes up the mpg, but it all relates to actual speed.

Drive excessively fast and down goes the fuel needle. One simply cannot win!

Listening to the car radio, a news report came on identifying some air traffic control problems. (Oh no!) I could not comprehend everything but it appeared to only relate to one Russian air line.

I had previously telephoned "Blue" shortly before I left Borodinos to arrange for a flight on the third day at approximately three o'clock ish. I was to telephone "Blue" to confirm the arrangements had been successful, when in Smolensk. It is cutting things rather finely but being an important British Government department in the MOD, "Blue" can pull weight when it comes to getting his way. I felt reasonably confident that a British Airways seat would be allocated for me, Business class, anything, even if it is tourist class... as long as I get a flight home, that's all I care about now.

The journey continued to be faultless. Weather fine and sunny, the company of the radio music fair and the limo behaved perfectly.

The E30 took me right up to the north side of Smolensk at six o'clock. Traffic was busy. They have rush hours too! My instruction was to turn off the E30 and head south towards the main city and head for – The Tower of Veselukha... "Everyone knows it. You can't miss it!" How many times have I heard that one before?

However, the route was well sign posted and as stated The Tower was easily located with the use of numerous colourful corporate road signs.

Blimey! When I arrived I was not surprised. "You can't miss it." I expect it can be seen from outer space. It appears to be a huge fortress, part of the old walled city.

Finding a suitable place to stop I located the paper with Sofia's address details and held it under the nose of a smart lady pedestrian. Not always the best person to ask unless she is a driver herself. "Akh!" studying my paper she burst into Russian song, "blah blah blah blah etc. etc.…." but, she did point in a certain direction… and she did repeat the distance in kilometres several times. She also tore off a piece of paper, selected from her handbag and wrote something on it for me to show to the next person if I got lost. (I will) I couldn't interpret the words myself.

"Vozle etoy statui," she kept repeating *"Vozle etoy statui. Neer zis stitute."* (Hooray, English at last!) It's near a statue, I did get that bit. It is down that road, and not too many kilometres, yes, I got that part too! So off I go to find the road… "Neer zis stitute!"

En-route I saw a fire station. Filled up, I was ready for the next part of my journey. My car brought out several mechanics from their work to view the spectacle of the Buick. No autographs please! The route required was effectively demonstrated by the fuel cashier. I can't get lost now!

Without too many more negotiations and arm waving by pedestrians, I arrived at my destination.

The statue at the end of the highway defined the location as being the correct one. I was soon turning into the side access-way through a covered archway leading off road into the rear parking area, but to no avail! There were two cars already parked and would be no more space larger than for a pedal bicycle. This regrettably necessitated me having to slowly reverse my twenty footer out and back on to the main highway. I parked outside the main entrance, took my keys and quickly ascended the few steps into the main entrance hall.

I was greeted by a man who immediately became Sofia's uncle. His English was extremely competent and he shook hands with me like old friend. Sofia must have given me good credit!

I felt instantly at home and welcome.

We both hurried down to the car. The vision of it clearly "rocked" him and we took the two cases up to the reception desk. Ruffling through his table drawer he (Konstantin) offered me a parking permit which allows parking in the highway in an allocated position, which I easily found to the opposite side of the road. I appended the document to the front windscreen and returned to the hotel.

There waiting for me was Konstantin's (call me Kon) wife who speaking no English whatsoever, gave me a similar warm greeting.

I signed the day book at the desk and a young lad was assigned to show me to my room on the third floor. It was a delightful room where I had full view of the highway and most importantly, my Buick that stood proudly out front. I had… we *had*… made it. I was half way to the airport!

After the usual unpacking and showering etc. I made my way downstairs and spent a very pleasant evening, dining with Kon and Christine. They were very interested in myself and what I would be doing tomorrow.

I had been advised to see the Turquoise Cathedral and various monuments and also take a trip to Katyn, but how much free time I will have 'remains to be seen' was my natural response. I also added detail about Sofia and how highly she was regarded whilst working at Borodinos.

Kon and Christine were 'full' of information and advice which I absorbed with interest.

Quite weary at eleven thirty pm I pardoned myself from the very amiable Christine and Kon and bedded myself down to sleep like the proverbial log!

The following day, the second of the three days, I was awoken by a tap on the door at eight thirty. I let a very anxious Kon into the room who drew me to the window.

"They have much interest in your car, Ric?"

Surrounding my vehicle and sandwiched between two police cars were a bevy of policemen, making notes, standing with hands on hips, chatting and on their intercom phones.

"Oh deep joy. What is going on down there. Here I go again."

Kon and I ran down the staircase and out to the highway to confront the array of policemen.

Kon took the reins and babbled away in Russian for me. He interpreted numerous words for me. "Eto vasha mashina Comrade?"

"Yes, officer, da, it is *my* car. Is there a problem officer?"

"Akh… Angliyskiy."

"Yes. English."

"Zhadat." I knew that word to mean… Wait!

The officer called his other comrade over. They spoke in Russian but the second officer spoke in fragmented English to Kon and then to myself.

"Comrade Dimitri tell me you English and this your car?"

"That is correct officer. I am staying here (I pointed) for tonight and I have a parking permit."

"I see permit. It in order Comrade, but car not yours! We check, it is Rosa Koliskaiya car." Oh bugger. I can see where this is going! It is still under the registration of the pop singer.

"We talk now at station and you come. Bring passport and document if you have for car. Bring keys and Dimitri drive. You come in car with me. It not far. We not be long." I ventured to the hotel with Kon to collect all my documents. Kon advised me the police HQ was only one kilometre away and providing I have the correct documents it should not be a problem. I returned to the policemen.

I was "escorted" into the rear of a police car driven by one officer. My car followed, driven by Comrade officer Dimitri. The police HQ was only minutes away, something in my favour!

I was "escorted" from the police vehicle and shown into the police HQ and after negotiating several corridors and one upper floor level, the room eventually reached for the "interview".

A female officer (at least I think she was female) likely to be an ex shot putter, stood with her generous back to the door whilst I was "invited" to sit. On a serious note, it was very cordial, and no reason to complain about anything, other than being there at all in the first place!

A few minutes elapsed and in they came… would it be Laurel and Hardy or a Smolensk version of Petrov and Co? Actually it was neither! Both spoke fairly good English and shouting not on the Agenda… at least, not thus far, *it's early days,* I thought. They both sat opposite – it's customary. "Now you give all documents you have please and put on table."

I placed my passport, driving licence, car insurance certificate, A tourist visa document permitting me to drive in Russia, and the Bill of Sale for the hypnotic pink Buick.

All documents were examined by both officers and after close scrutiny;

"Your document Comrade Hartland, it say you buy car yesterday. Our information say that car is for Rosa Koliskaiya. You know this English lady with Russian name?"

"No, I don't know her."

1 explained the full details about the purchase arrangements from the Moscow RIS sales pound.

"I check."

One officer disturbed Hildegard the shot putter and went out for a few minutes. He returned stating he had made a telephone call to Moscow. The sale had been confirmed as genuine and it was clearly a vehicle legally in my ownership. So far so good!

"You here on holiday. It strange thing to buy a car when you soon go back to England?"

Blimey! He's got me there! Think, and be quick?

"I intend to return to Smolensk in the not too distant future so I will leave it at the hotel. They are nice people; I know them quite well and they don't mind at all."

I felt my nose growing longer, not for the first time.

"Akh, so you travel to Belarus for plane and friends collect nice car?"

"No, they drive me there and then they drive it back to the hotel." (It's going well!)

"Why you no fly from Smolensk. Why go Belarus?"

"I wanted to see Belarus as well. I have seen Smolensk but not Belarus, well, not yet."

The internal telephone rang. The officer spoke, frowned and looked simultaneously at me. He replaced the receiver gently and whispered a few words to his colleague.

"All your documents are in order Mr Hartland, (it's still going well!) but your car is no good." *(Oh, it's not going well!)*

"The luggage room in back says you have Cocaine. A drug test says it has drugs at some time, Comrade. Can you tell why it is?"

Oh, bugger. It is surely the remaining trace of Cocaine used by that bloody pop star. A blind sniffer dog would pick that up with a bag on his head!

The officer leaned forward with his hands on the table and asked: "Why is it drugs in car, Mr Hartland?"

I could do no more than give the full chapter and verse once, then twice, then again, and when they were satisfied my story was authentic they agreed I was genuine and could go. Was this true, has my luck changed? Can go!... Bloody hell. Zeus is with me at last!

"Can I ask you something officer… before I go?"

"Da?"

"If the car boot is contaminated with a trace of cocaine, surely that means my suitcases are also affected, and if so, I might get picked up at the airport?" He drew a short breath.

"It is true Mr Hartland. Your cases will be with the cocaine traces if it has been near it in car. I cannot say it is not to be found at airport. Testing machines detect Cocaine."

"I will give you writing on document to say what has happened today here. You give to airport people if it happens. This police document explain it for you and should be no trouble. If happens, you ask them to telephone this office here for me. It not right thing to stop you for this thing you have not done. You have no drugs; you tell them *no* drugs!"

The officer selected a piece of official note paper from the drawer, wrote a long paragraph, signed and stamped it. He folded it, placed in an envelope and handed it to me saying: "For you Mr Hartland. Tell your England friends we nice people and come for holidays, da?"

"Da. Spasibo," I replied… da bloody da indeed my new Russian chum!

He handed me all my docs and keys and took me to the rear pound where my car was sited. We shook hands and I was soon on my way back to my hotel. Things are not always as black as they seem, and in this particular instance, justice truly did prevail.

Arriving back at the hotel, both Christine and Kon were as amazed to see me, as I was to be there. "Too late for breakfast?" I calmly asked and all three of us laughed. Kon spoke to Christine…

she immediately disappeared into a side room. Kon informed me: "Breakfast late today but special for you Ric." It was a good one!

"Before that Kon, I must telephone London. I need information about my flight home." Kon led me into the front lounge and passing some late diners I was shown into a large office. "Here is phone you can call in quiet Ric."

I thanked Kon and promised to pay for the call on my bill. He shook his head. "Oh, no, no!" Seated at the desk I went through the usual channels in order to connect to London. After two minutes I was through to the correct office. A secretary answered and after another full minute the "famous Blue" materialised.

"Hello, Hartland. Ric. I understand it is you ringing from Smolensk. True?"

"Yes, good morning. Can you inform me of the arrangements for the flight back tomorrow?"

"I have the details here… Ah, just a second,"… a pause… My heart rate began to move up a notch. I don't want any disappointments of any kind now. My fingers began desk tapping!

"Ah, yes… British Airways, business class, front seat… you don't mind the front seat?"

"Any bloody seat… the toilet will do!"

"Yes, quite, steady down Hartland. Business Class. BA 222 from Minsk at two o'clock. You will need to be there at noon. That OK for you, Ric?"

"Yes, sorry, great, thank you, I suppose the BA check-in desk will have all the documentation even though I have nothing at all to support my flight?"

"It's arranged as a Government flight ticket. You won't have any difficulty Hartland. You are a Government official. Well, it's au revoir for now. Come to see me at the office the following day at… shall we say… eight am? don't be late. Good luck Ric. Bye."

Oh how generous! At the crack of day I'm on the carpet. Don't let me have a lie in will you? Still, I have a ticket, and Business class as a Government official. I did not dare say cocaine!

After breakfast I visited the Turquoise Cathedral by cab. I did not wish my car parking space to disappear to another… and the local police know it now!

The church, or cathedral as it is generally known is a place of extreme calm. A most stunning building inside and out. It is, I am informed, seventeenth century. Everything was left intact until "our friendly Germans." Stole a treasured Icon during the war. No surprise there!

Whilst walking around, the only bad comment I heard from an English speaking person was: "Nice building, but not much to do here." Stupid. What do you expect in a cathedral… Hang gliding! It was… it is… a fantastic structure and not to be missed if in Smolensk. I'm glad I visited. Very different for me from most of my recent adventures! Nothing quite like a bit of culture for the brain. There were so many things of great beauty and value but one particular item were the sandals of St. Mercury, the patron Saint of Smolensk. The Germans didn't take those… perhaps they were too small, the wrong size!

A few hours disappeared. The cab returned as arranged and I returned to the hotel.

I decided to miss a late lunch and wander into the centre of town and meander amongst the Smolensk shoppers to take in the ambience. It's just like all shops really, apart from the language. The city of Smolensk is a fine place and a re-visit is a necessity some future day.

The remaining time I spent relaxing and making some minor packing preparations for my departure tomorrow. It will be a very early breakfast if acceptable to Kon and Christine.

Evening dinner was once again spent with Konstatin and Christine within their own private area, leaving the meals and serving guests to their staff. A great amount of hearty discussion evaporated the hours and it was soon time to bed down. Early breakfast was agreeable to Kon and Christine and they insisted in packing a lunch for me to "scoff" en-route. How kind these people are.

To save any early morning "fluffing about" I settled up with them before departing to my room. I felt sure they had charged me far too little, but they insisted all was quite correct.

Up "with the lark" I had a shower, finished my packing and stood my two cases in the lobby. A huge cooked breakfast was easily demolished but avoiding too much coffee. I did not wish to find it necessary to find a tree en-route for relief purposes, although I'm sure that will happen despite the volume of liquid I consume!

The route was again established as the E30 and Kon helped me down the steps, over to my waiting pink dream! We warmly shook hands after placing the cases into the car boot and I caught site of the waving Christine on the steps out front. I was treated like family. I must write to Sofia.

I handed the parking permit back to Kon. He said it will be waiting for me should I come again.

The V8 engine fired with immediate enthusiasm. Window down, and with a final wave to them both, I headed back to the E30. I would stop at Katyn next. That should be in approximately in thirty minutes. The memorial, I was informed, "must not be missed".

Easily noting the roadside signposts, I followed along the side road slip to the Katyn gardens.

I easily parked and walked into the gardens. It had an atmosphere as if to demand quiet and sadness, and rightly so. The gardens and memorial were likewise most impressive and I was not embarrassed whilst standing there to shed several tears. I knew there are many memorials and statues in various parts of the world reminding all of this atrocity of the murder of thousands of Polish enlisted men, but to personally experience the atmosphere of the Katyn massacre in Katyn itself cannot be understated. Amazing. Will the world learn a lesson? I doubt it!

Soon back on to the E30 with Katyn firmly sealed in my thoughts I was currently thundering along comfortably within the speed limit at seventy mph. Three and a half hours to go, a full tank and a mileage of around 200 should easily get me to Minsk airport in plenty of time for the flight home.

After two hours I stopped at roadside lay-by in a rural area and had my wonderful lunch pack. More like elevenses, as prepared by the fair hands of Christine. It is great discovering all sorts of unusual foods when in a foreign country. Nothing was left… nothing ever is!

Back on to the highway, the Buick purring gently like a contented pussy cat, I carried on, the remaining time soon passed. I approached Belarus as planned. There is a boarder control when leaving Belarus to travel to Russia but not the other way, one simply passes through. It was mid-day, a little later than "Blue" had suggested but I considered two hours actually in the airport, excessive. Airport signage as in every country, was well prepared and I found my route into the airport without any difficulty. Like all others, car parks were everywhere denoting the amount of time one wishes to spend parked. English was shown in most places. I selected the long term car park.

My instructions were to park and leave the car keys stuffed up the exhaust pipe, but if difficult, not to be concerned as they have a spare key. (how come?) When in the airport I need to telephone "someone" to inform them where the vehicle is. They will then collect it at their leisure.

I locked the car, stuffed the keys up the exhaust pipe and pulled my large case over the bumpy concrete hard standing to the passenger lift. My other small case slung over my shoulder.

I was sad to say goodbye to the Buick. I had grown really fond. It had been a delight; providing it was viewed with sunglasses! I would have liked to have kept it, just to alarm the neighbours! The lift moved down to the main departure lounge. There I firstly found a telephone and conveyed all details to my contact – "someone" giving full details about the zone and adding the fact that the parking ticket I had locked in the car and placed on the rear seat. All done efficiently and the "someone" was satisfied with everything. I had effectively executed… all precisely as instructed. I observed the flight departure board and

BA222 was scheduled to be on time. I noticed there were many cancellations of a Russian air line. This must have been the one I heard on the radio news. It appeared not to affect any other air lines. So far, so good.

I found my way to the British Airways check-in desk queue and immediately had a feeling of déjà vu. My previous experience was not *a* successful one. This time it will be different.

Front of queue in twenty minutes, I was at the front and again "déjà vu"! "Good afternoon, sir. May I have your boarding card?"

I went into my rehearsed monologue of my travel plans. The nice BA lady looked at her screen; "Ah yes. Mr Hartland. Your ticket is fully paid. Here is your boarding card sir. You are in the first seat Business class. If there is anything you require the hostess will help you. Please keep your eyes peeled on the departure board and you will be called before the tourist class passengers." My case was placed on the weighing machine. Stickers appended and all was done. I was half waiting for the… "Ah sir… erm, just a moment… there appears to be a problem etc. etc." But it never came! Blimey! It's all going well! Clearly, "Blue" has performed admirably.

So, now it is the wait to be called, but first a visit to the Gents, then to a cafe for coffee and buns! Cafe soon located. I sat munching and slurping whilst hearing the slightly blurred frequent Tannoy announcements in Russian, often in English and occasionally in French and Spanish.

A pleasant looking lady stood and asked if she could join me as there had been a severe spillage "across the way" and mopping up was taking over. I must have looked English… she was English, well; Welsh to be precise and sitting with me was not a problem.

We had a long chat with all the usual; "Do you come here often" type cliche sayings… but she was a very pleasant lady with a fascinating Welsh countryside type of accent. We both agreed to have spent a happy time as tourists and would come again. (If she only knew!)

What would she have said if I had casually mentioned physical beatings, several deaths, a bomb blast, crooked diplomats, a burnt out Bistro, a car fire and close involvement with heroin mobsters? "Oh sir, you are a one for jesting!" So I didn't!!!

Time flashed by and she was called to her flight a few minutes before me. She was not travelling by British Airways so this was a final parting. It passed the time. It could have been worse!

The final section of the departure lounge was pleasant and comfortable and the few Business Class passengers, were called to the ultimate desk whereby my boarding card was inspected and passed.

I wandered down the tube to the plane and was greeted by the routine smiles and nodding by the hostesses at the plane door.

I was personally shown to my seat and informed that I should ask if there was anything I required; "Anything at all sir, just ask myself or my colleague."

I am really here at last. They can't stop me now. I'm really going home, leaving this nightmare. The plane arrived within minutes of the scheduled arrival time and in no time at all I was walking along the huge arrival concourse at Heathrow. It had been raining, how unusual! Fronting the concourse was a splayed chicane barrier. A lady with a dog was herding the passengers into a single line as they moved along. Large groups were being prevented from bunching together.

"Bags held low please or on wheels. For the dog. Thank you."

I only have my small cabin bag to wheel. My large case is in the hold. We walked casually. The Security lady ran along the line of people as the dog sniffed and wagged his tail frantically. Six people ahead of me, a lady was gently pulled out and asked to stand by the wall. The handler and sniffer dog then resumed their task, and of course, "Sods law" the dog sat in front of me cleaning the blasted floor with his tail whilst looking up at me, the master criminal.

Jack the Ripper reborn!

"Would you mind standing over by the wall please sir, just a formality." She pointed.

I moved to the side wall. I knew it was too good to last. I'm here, but I'm not here, not yet! Another officer who was standing by, arms folded addressed the lady and then myself. The sniffer search was still being conducted but we, being the first, were asked to follow the officer to a side room, separate side rooms. The customs control officer sat. We sat at a table opposite each other, always customary. I was asked for my passport It was thoroughly examined.

"Mr Hartland. Sorry for this inconvenience, but the dog stopped by you as an indication, detected that you may have a narcotic substance or may have been in contact with a substance of some kind. We will need to take your bag for a swab test, but meanwhile perhaps you would kindly answer some questions. It shouldn't take long, sir."

"That's ok, but before you go any further, I wish to inform you I am a government official with the MOD. Here is my ID." I took it from my wallet and handed it to him.

"You may telephone my office at Whitehall; the number is on the card for clarification." Next, I took the envelope from my inside pocket, removed the letter and handed it to him.

"I think it tells all about a cocaine issue. Please feel free to telephone the MOD and the Smolensk State Police office if you wish, but I have a car waiting for me, so I would be glad if this can be conducted quickly."

The officer made an internal phone call. Within a minute or two another officer, a lady, took the passport and documents away. Whilst waiting, the customs official talked in general terms about checking people for drugs etc.... all of which I confirmed, was perfectly correct and understandable. After ten minutes the lady customs control officer returned and whispered audibly;

"Everything is in order. The gentleman is free to go."

She handed my passport, letter and ID card to me with a smile and a... "Thank you sir." I was shown to the door and courteously, they both gave their apologies and farewells. "Thank you for your cooperation sir. Sorry to have detained you. I'm sure you understand?"

Mr Punch's phrase came to mind. "That's the way to do it!"

I was out of the room and back on to the concourse. There were some other "bods" standing against the wall. The black Labrador still frantically polishing the floor.

A long walk to the luggage collection and the famous carousel. I located my case fairly quickly, so no hold up there. Next, to pass the main customs control barrier exit, and soon, I was out! Entering the sight of the public, dozens of people were holding up cards; Mrs Blogs Eastbourne Cars, A. B. Cluckett Pretty Cars Ltd, Mr Blap Crappy Cars Plc, Mr Hartland – blank space. The car was parked out front where others could not stop. An official Government pass displayed on the windscreen. Cases into boot, door held open for me, people looked to see who the VIP was! I was on my way in a different kind of limo, sparkling shiny black, but not as long!

"Good trip, sir ... etc., etc., etc., blah, blah, blah?"

"Thank you, yes. Quite productive in many ways. Glad to be back though."

"I'll telephone the office to let them know."

The driver spoke on the mobile hands free phone and informed the office of my arrival. "Can I phone anyone sir. Would you like me to telephone anyone to let them know?" I gave him the telephone number, slowly dictated, as he contacted my dear lady at home. (Personal mobile phones not permitted – too much information stored.)

We of "Department Blue 17" are not permitted to personally contact anyone during assignments. The only way "loved ones" can gain information is by telephoning "the department" and they will be given basic details. It is not deemed appropriate to speak to anyone "Back Home" in case classified matters that should not be discussed are inadvertently disclosed, so this is the first contact with my good lady since leaving the UK.

The phone was connected.

"Just one moment madam… Mr Hartland, if you can shout your message please?"

I belted out a message from the back seat to her, I was at Heathrow, I was ok, and would be home in two to three hours from now.

The phone message was delivered and received with considerable satisfaction and joy!

The journey was plagued with troublesome slow jams. The M25 was up to its usual annoyance, but after a long journey in the chauffeur driven car I was delivered safely to my home.

Kisses and hugs all round, a cold drink and a sandwich across my lips without touching the sides, and I was soon in the land of dreams.

An early breakfast caused by "Blue" was consumed in great haste. My dear Jan drove me to the station for the seven five fast to Charing Cross. He wanted to meet at Whitehall, not Vauxhall my main office. A five minute walk to the MOD. Pleasingly the weather was kind, I was soon in the lift shooting up to "Blue's" annexe London office.

I sat outside the office of his highness – "Blue". It was seven fifty five. A message passed by Loretta; his secretary conveyed.

"He was sorry he will be a little late. Missed the train." Half an hour elapsed and in came Blue totally un-phased, "Morning Loretta, morning Ric. On time I see. That's good. Amazing the bloody trains seem to think we have to fit in with their timetable instead of the other way around." (What does he mean?) "Come through. Loretta, coffee, if you would be so good?"

We passed through the communicating door. He had an umbrella under his arm.

"Expecting bad weather sir?" (A light whimsical touch!)

"This has a solid lead core Hartland. It's not only for keeping off the natural elements!" We sat at his desk He opened a file already placed, and started, to read as he spoke.

"Now. Emnmm… Moscow. You have done an excellent job. Not only do we have those diplomat buggers by the short and curlies, one dead regrettably, but that bugger Karashenko is now residing in Hospital, permanently, he won't wake up, so no more documents to pass on, but, one of the best trophies is your involvement, although somewhat accidental, with the Russian Intelligence Service. With that, a real breakthrough there. We have glowing reports of your assisting them. We have never got on so well with those Russkies, so that is a remarkable plus Ric, and the way in which documents were passed. That heroin business is also a major breakthrough. You have done well Ric. Let's talk about promotion. I will put matters forward at the next Monday meeting and we'll go from there. How do you feel about a 20 percent increase and a move up to Department 18 or 19?" I'm thinking to myself; not bloody likely, no thanks… 17 is good enough for me or perhaps should I request a drop to Dept. 16? I'm not one for all this blood and thunder business!

"Good of you sir, but I don't think it necessary. I'll stay where I am if that's alright?"

There was then, an audible thump from the other room. A sort of "thrumbbbb" like a refrigerator door being slammed. The communication door was thrown aside and a male entered in a flurry of anguish holding a gun with silencer. I stood up. He fired and shot me through my right shoulder. I dropped to the floor. He shot me again in the leg. Blood everywhere. I heard the male say;

"I told you. I warned you. This is for you."

Looking at the ceiling in agony, I heard four more shots. Blue's chair fell back as did Blue himself. I passed out with the pain. Everything went dark!

THE END…
Or is it?